The DROPAS

BOOK I

BREAKING THROUGH THE WALLS

SCOTT R. ETTERS

PERIKLES PUBLISHING · NAPERVILLE, ILLINOIS

PERIKLES
PUBLISHING

Published by Perikles Publishing, Inc.
P.O. Box 5367
Naperville, Illinois 60567

First Edition 1999

First Printing 1999

Cover Art: Timm Etters

Etters, Scott R.
    The Dropas : Breaking through the walls / Scott R. Etters.
        p. cm.   (The Dropas; Book I)
        ISBN: 0-9672571-0-7
        1. Fantastic Fiction   I. Etters, Scott R.   II. Title   III. Series
813'.54 -- dc20
FIC

LC: 99-90583

Printed in the United States of America

For those people who still believe we can make this planet a better place to live, I challenge you to make believers out of those who don't, so we may venture forth in great numbers to make it a reality.

Acknowledgments

I want to thank all those people who have crossed my path, especially the ones who brought a positive and joyful influence to my life. This book is a result of those relationships (including the ones appearing short or insignificant), the events I partook in, and the experiences I lived through, all which helped form the person I am today.

I also want to thank the musicians who played alongside me as my story took shape. Their music filled the air for hundreds of hours as my story traveled from imagination to reality.

Thanks to Kris for being a part of the inspiration and to Pam, Deb, Jill and Catherine for all your help.

Finally, I want to thank my brother, Timm, whose art propelled my creativity to a level I had never before experienced.

Table of Contents

Author's Note

I have set many goals in my life, admittedly, one was not to write a novel. This is an example of the power and fulfillment of inspiration. In the Fall of 1993, the creation of the Dropas was just a form of stress release for Timm and myself as we joked about antics the Dropas might engage themselves in during certain situations. For the six months that followed, my imagination erupted with a journey for which these characters would embark. Passing it off as more creativity to fill up conversation was no longer satisfying. I began writing down my ideas for this story and could not avoid the inevitable; the creation of the Dropas, the development of the other characters' personalities, and finally, the completion of this book.

The walls that we, as nations and as individuals, have built around ourselves have grown higher and thicker over the years, even more so as our physical boundaries grow closer. They are walls built with blocks consisting of the need for power and money, hatred, destruction, cultural and religious differences, selfishness, and greed to name a few. My thoughts and concerns regarding the construction of these walls have grown as well. I have expressed them in many philosophical conversations with friends, family, and colleagues but not in the manner for which I have expressed them in this book. And now I want to share those thoughts with more than just a few and in a much lighter, although still meaningful sense.

My experiences, feelings, inspirations, and the constant pestering from the Dropas allowed me to express these thoughts in the pages that follow. I wrote this book because I had a story to tell. I created and wrote it in a way unique only to me. The story is an extension of myself; my experiences, my personal relationships, my education, and the moods and feelings I encountered during the story's creation. Most of all, it is a part of my mind, heart, and soul I have now set free.

Introduction

The story I am about to share with you has been created from the events that took place, the reflections and information I acquired from everyone involved, and from my own experiences. In places where information was unattainable, I called upon my imagination to formulate a realistic description of physical appearances or emotional feelings.

It goes without saying I am proud to be a survivor of the War. It has, and continues to be a remarkable experience, witnessing the entire human population unite in a global rebuilding never before conducted in the short history of the human race. I am leaving the story of the War, and the events leading up to it, for another time. It's the events which happened after the War I found to be most extraordinary. Below, I have provided you with a summary of key events prior to the War which will provide you with a foundation for my story.

It is in the not-so-distant future and nearly six and one-half years after the most devastating war in man's history ended. A world whose societies and governments had become consumed by capitalistic and materialistic beliefs finally collapsed and nearly eliminated the human race in the process. The near extinction of humanity was assisted by one man's – the Special Intelligence Agency simply nicknamed him the Human Virus – spread of detrimental government secrets through the newly developed but poorly secured World-Linked Information System (WLIS). This information leakage helped proliferate the greed and hatred toward the nations' governments, greed and hatred that had been mounting through the years. People around the world revolted against their governments in whatever way possible.

Initially, the armies defended their governments but soon realized they, too, were affected by the same corruption, even more so than the civilians. Before long, people were killing people everywhere. The global revolution escalated to the point where no one knew what side they were on, whom they were fighting, or for what cause they were fighting. Organized crime groups joined together and formed a third side of the destructive triangle. This group was known as the ForLords and led by a man named Lord Ozone.

The ForLords' primary weapon was the *Organic Destructor*, a biological weapon developed by the allied nations capable of emitting a deadly and extremely contagious virus. They also seized the few nuclear weapons which still remained as a result of the signing of the Global Nuclear Weapons Treaty five years earlier. The governments relinquished power to the "global revolutionaries" in a relatively short period of time. Attention was then directed toward eradicating the ForLords who had superseded the governments as the more threatening force to society. The revolutionaries eventually put an end to the holocaust and the estimated ten million ForLords.

The ForLords' fall was quick because they had lost their only two advantages – they had detonated every nuclear weapon and they had exhausted the supply of *Organic Destructors* – which were killing millions of people a day. Although the War had ended, people continued dying from the aftermath of the nuclear explosions and the effects of the *Organic Destructors*.

As it was later discovered, the virus emitted from the *Organic Destructors* was classified as an attenuating one. Consequently, its limited existence provided the only cure and, although the virus was responsible for a high percentage of the total fatalities, the resulting deaths eventually ceased. When the final tally was conducted, nearly two billion people had lost their lives. Several regions of the globe were declared nuclear wastelands, and inhabitation was forbidden, indefinitely.

Looking at what was before them, people didn't know who the fortunate ones were, themselves or the ones who had perished. Entire cities had been destroyed, and sickness, hunger, and homelessness were prominent. But one thing was clear – those who remained were more determined than ever to not only survive but make it so their children would survive, and their children after them. And not only would they survive but they would all survive in a harmonious world.

The rebuilding process commenced almost immediately after the War ended. Movement toward global harmony was progressing well, and many of the cities destroyed during the War had acquired new infrastructures. Like their ancestors of long ago, cultural activities had once again become a major part of everyday life as people reached out to enrich their minds and souls. Consequently, the art service provided by my brother, Timm, and I was flourishing. It was a service developed to help educate people and beautify the surroundings through art, and it fit well with the global revitalization. We brought Timm's art into all types of buildings, helping many to restore the image lost during the War or helping others to create new ones. Of the places we worked, we received the most enjoyment in schools, being with students and helping them enrich their lives.

And this is where my story begins . . .

The Vase

I was walking with the rest of our tour group through the middle of the Plaka, or open market of Athens. The other tourists, including my wife Lindsay, were busily picking out souvenirs to take home to their families. Having lost my interest in that activity, I strayed from the group and strolled into one of the local shops several blocks away from the center of the market. After all, I was accustomed to this, wandering off on my own and searching for the nontourist attractions. The shop itself contained everything imaginable, but it was evident the owners didn't have many visitors because of their distance from the main market traffic. It was exactly the type of shop I wanted to visit.

As I looked around inside, it appeared to be quite different from the normal "tourist" shops I was accustomed to seeing. I couldn't understand why, but I was about to find out. Sitting at a table to the left of the door, there was an old man who was preoccupied with mixing a solution in a clay bowl. He was so preoccupied with his activity he didn't realize I was standing in front of him. Spread out on his table were ancient crucibles sealed with small lids, but I noticed a few of the crucibles were left uncovered, so I took the opportunity to peek inside. From my view, each contained an unidentifiable, colored liquid which quickly dampened my curiosity. The rest of the table was cluttered with papers, broken pottery, and miscellaneous knickknacks.

The old man finally broke his concentration and peered up at me, his green eyes looking above his half lenses. I cocked my head back a bit, having noticed a strange glaze-like substance over his eyes. I had never seen anything like it before but figured it was due to his many years of hovering over those strange solutions. After several minutes of looking up at me and back down at his crucibles, he cleared his throat and spoke to me in heavily accented English.

"They told me you would be coming," he mumbled.

"Who told you I was coming?" I questioned with a sense of paranoia. I had never met this man nor any of his acquaintances.

"Who does not matter." The old man rose from his chair and motioned for me to follow him. "We don't have much time, so come with me."

My initial impression was correct. This shop was not like any of the others, and what made me follow this strange man, I'm not sure. I believe it was my curiosity overwhelming my desire to return to the tour group and continue shopping. Whatever the reason, I followed with surprisingly little hesitation.

We walked toward the back of the shop, being careful not to trip over the trinkets cluttering the floor. Once there, we stopped in front of an old wooden door that was barred shut with a large piece of lumber. The old man struggled to lift the board out of its iron holders, but with a few grunts and considerable determination, he dislodged the board and set it down behind us. The door hinges, which were definitely in need of lubrication, squeaked as he began to open the door. A cool breeze escaped from the other side, bringing with it a fair amount of dust which reflected the sunlight streaming from the window to our right. Its density, like that of a London fog, temporarily prevented me from seeing past the doorway of the now-revealed room. My guess was the door hadn't been opened in a few hundred years, maybe even a few thousand years. The room was unlit, but I was still able to determine that it had a dirt floor. The old man, who was quite a bit shorter than my six feet two inches, reached up for one of several lanterns sitting on a shelf to the left of the door.

He motioned for me to follow him into the room, lit the lantern, and turned the knob to increase the height of the flame. I accepted his invitation and followed him through the doorway. He had no trouble walking through it; however, I had to duck several inches to avoid hitting my head on the crossbeam. Unfortunately, I had to maintain this semierect posture throughout our little journey.

Cobwebs dangled from the ceiling and shelves located on both sides of us, and became entangled in my hair and ears as I followed the old man deeper into the partially lit room. The shelves contained hundreds of ancient vases with Greek writing and art inscribed on the outside of them. I also noticed the short distance between the shelves on each side, leading me to believe we were walking through a long hallway instead of a room.

I stood gazing at the endless shelves of vases, continuing to remove the cobwebs from my head. Suddenly, I felt his hand on my elbow and nearly jumped out of my shorts, hitting my head on the low ceiling in the process.

I turned to the old man. "You scared me half to death."

"We don't have much time," he replied, ignoring my pain.

I rubbed my head as I resumed walking. "What's the big hurry?"

"The planets will be aligned in a few minutes. We cannot waste anymore time."

Still not quite understanding what it was we were in such a hurry to see, I did not resist the old man's desire. We walked for some time, allowing me to become fairly proficient at brushing away cobwebs. My curiosity heightened as we made our way toward our destination.

We stopped abruptly and I nearly knocked the old man over as I walked into him. He hung the lantern from a hook secured to the ceiling. He then reached into his back pocket, removed a candle, and lit it using the flame from the burning lantern. It was only a matter of time until I saw the much awaited "attraction". As the flame on the candle grew, I was in absolute disbelief and wished I could have seen the expression on my face. We had entered some type of chamber or sacred tomb perhaps. I had been so busy removing cobwebs from my hair I hadn't realized we were no longer in the hallway. The chamber was free of dust and cobwebs, and the walls and floor were lined with etched stones. Struggling to focus on what was in front of me, I lit a match to improve the lighting. The old man instantly extinguished the match with his thumb and index finger, not even thinking twice about whether the flame would burn him. Amazingly, it didn't.

"More than one source of light will make her very unhappy," he explained.

"Make who unhappy?" I asked. "I don't see anyone in here but us."

At that point I was growing very impatient with a man I had known for such a short period of time. I consider myself to be a very patient person, but this adventure was getting a little out of hand as far as I was concerned. Regardless of my feelings, we stood in silence and waited inside the dim chamber for quite some time.

I again thought about rejoining Lindsay so she wouldn't worry about me. It was strange though, because I made no attempt to leave. Admittedly, I probably would have fallen on my face trying to get out of that darkened place, so I willingly stayed for whatever it was the old man and I were waiting to see. My wandering thoughts disappeared as my eyes suddenly zeroed in on a glowing object coming from the wall in front of us. From where I was standing, the object appeared to be in the shape of a star. I waited for my eyes to adjust to the brightness of the light, focusing on the object as they did.

It wasn't a star at all, but rather the helmet of Athena, the Greek Goddess of War and the Arts. Beneath her glimmering helmet, there was a table with a vase sitting on top of it. The vase was much larger than the ones I had seen earlier. Its lid had a handle in the shape of a half moon and the base had inscriptions of artists painting murals on walls; however, they were the most peculiar artists I had ever seen. They weren't men or women but rather creatures resembling water drops holding long paint brushes. Alongside the artists was a woman strumming the strings of her harp. Overseeing the artists and the musician was Athena herself, donned in her armor and holding a spear. She had an expression of complete complacency and fulfillment.

The old man reached over to the vase, gently lifted its lid and leaned it against the vase. From the glowing helmet, an intense beam of light slowly made its way downward into the vase. After reaching its contents, the single beam transformed into spectral arches of brilliant colors, and then shot out of the vase like a miniature fireworks show. It was difficult to determine how long the show lasted because Lindsay had my watch. I finally knelt on one knee as my back and shoulders were cramping from hunching over for such a long period of time. The light beam soon began to fade, taking the impression of the helmet with it. The old man quickly replaced the lid on the vase, handed me the candle, and put the vase under his arm.

We were obviously taking it with us. He motioned for me to follow him toward the entryway.

Upon our exit from the chamber, I grabbed the lantern, trying to determine the significance of what I had witnessed. The inscriptions of the figurines on the vase presented a small correlation to our art service back home. Timm was a mural artist, listened to music while he painted, and our logo included Athena, but I couldn't make anything more out of it. My thoughts were interrupted as I gagged on a mouthful of cobwebs and quickly removed them with my free hand.

"Owww!" I shouted as I hit my head on a crossbeam.

The old man ignored me. Stopping for a only a moment, I again caught up with him, still cleaning the remaining cobwebs from my mouth and rubbing my head until we finally reached the doorway. I squinted as I stepped into the old man's shop, my eyes reacting to the sunlit room. The old man quickly shut and sealed the door behind me, and walked away. I followed him over to a nearby table, still squinting as my eyes adjusted to the brightness.

On the table was a large bowl of fresh fruit a servant had brought out for us upon our return. It couldn't have come at a better time, because I was starving and cobwebs aren't very filling. Next to the bowl were two small plates, cloth napkins, and a sharp paring knife. The old man set the vase on the table, close to his side, and we both sat down to eat.

He meticulously spread the napkin in his lap and began picking through the fruit. I did the same but was not as picky with my selection. I was too hungry to bypass even the bruised fruit. The old man ate in silence. It was quite obvious he concentrated on the enjoyment of each of his meals and was not to be interrupted. I respected his way and ate my fruit in the same manner. The flavorful juices were tantalizing to the taste buds, and between the two of us, we finished all of the fruit except a few grapes approaching their "raisinhood". After we wiped our mouths of the leftover juices, the servant promptly cleared the table, and left us alone.

The old man moved the vase to the center of the table. I had a hundred questions to ask him, and as I started, he quickly placed his right index finger over his lips and extended his flattened left palm toward me. He then spoke to me in a serious tone.

"I know you have many questions to ask, but you are not here to ask questions.   You are here to listen, receive, and follow instructions. Do you understand?"

I nodded, although hesitantly.

"What I am about to give you is important to the existence of the human race," he continued.

Now, I don't know too many sentences capable of grabbing your attention like that one.

He continued, "Take this back with you and mix twelve drops with each liter of paint your brother uses on his murals."

The old man didn't waste any time telling me the story behind those drops. He went straight to the point and told me what I needed to do. *How did this guy know about my brother, let alone that he painted murals? What were these drops? Why us? Important to the human race?* As those questions tumbled around in my mind, the old man could sense my barrage of silent questions. I was about to begin my questioning when he extended his hands, signaling me to listen. I concluded the answers to my questions would present themselves when the time was right. My little adventure was becoming more interesting by the minute.

The old man held up his right index finger. "Again, twelve drops for every liter of paint. No more, no less. One drop in the protective finish. No more, no less. There are enough drops for a lifetime of painting. Take this now." He handed me the vase. "Protect it with your life and follow my instructions. I have done all I can. It is in your hands now."

That's it, I thought. *This is the excitement missing from my life. I would become a paint mixer.* I politely thanked the old man and placed the vase under my arm. I then extended my hand to shake his, but he had already turned and headed back toward the table where I first saw him. "Nice to meet you, too," I said to him, turning and exiting the shop.

I walked away dumbfounded, trying to figure out the recent events. As I moved further from the shop, it suddenly occurred to me it was dark. Only the sparse streetlights provided illumination, and without a watch, I had no idea what time it was or how much time I had spent with the old man. *Oh, God, Lindsay probably has the GGB officers looking for me*, I thought.

When I arrived at the nearest streetlight, I turned and noticed that what I had left behind was now dark and barren. The buildings and shops were gone, including the old man's. Looking back, I should have investigated the area, but I was more concerned with returning to the hotel and rejoining my wife. I reached into my back pocket and pulled out a folded street map of Athens. The street sign above me showed I was on the corner of Theorias and Dioskouron. *Not far from the hotel at all*, I thought. I was just north of the Acropolis and west of the Plaka. I could find my way back without the map so, I folded it and returned it to my pocket.

While I strolled down Theorias, the day's events played over and over in my mind; I had many questions and few answers. Before I could finish sorting through them, I was distracted by numerous voices in the distance. As I approached Dionissiou Areopagitou, the road which bordered the south side of the Acropolis, the voices grew louder, and I could see hundreds of people flowing into the streets.

The evening's theatrical performance at the Herod Atticus Odeum, the functional theater located at the base of the Acropolis, had recently ended. Although I didn't understand Greek, I perceived the performance satisfied this particular crowd. Some were smiling. Others appeared to be reenacting their favorite scenes.

Making my way through the crowd, I continued walking toward the hotel, heading south on Parthenonos. The hotel was only a block or two down the hill, but my day's adventure was not over yet. I knew that before heading to my room, I would have to answer a barrage of questions about my sudden disappearance.

One of the doormen greeted me as he held open the door. I kindly thanked him and entered the lobby. There was quite a gathering of people waiting for me, including some uniformed GGB officers. *Right on cue*, I thought. I figured Lindsay was nearby and headed toward the crowd of people. My thoughts of what I was going to say were suddenly interrupted.

"SCOTT!"

Only one person could yell my name like that. Lindsay had spotted me almost immediately, and the people in the lobby turned their heads to see who was causing the sudden commotion. Lindsay fought her way through the crowd and headed toward me. She embraced me like we hadn't seen each other in years and nearly knocked the vase out from under my arm in the process. I returned her hug as best I could, still holding the vase tightly under my arm. Admittedly, I wasn't as excited as she was; after all, I knew where I had been all along.

I didn't realize the disturbance my disappearance had caused, but it made me feel good to know so many people were concerned about my well-being. I gave Lindsay a kiss, before she pulled away, and repositioned the vase under my arm. The anticipated barrage of questions soon followed and, although I wanted to share my experience with Lindsay, I knew this wasn't the appropriate time, given the magnitude of what I witnessed. I also didn't think she would believe one bit of it, so I decided to save myself from the humiliation that might have ensued until I could grasp the events myself.

"Are you all right?" Lindsay asked.

"Yes, I'm fi–"

"Where were you?" she interrupted.

"I wand–" OK, I concluded those were rhetorical questions, and I should let her ask all of them before saying anything.

"You had me worried to death! How come it took you so long to get back? One minute you're standing right next to me at the jewelry shop, and the next minute you're gone."

"You know I don't like looking for souvenirs," I reminded her.

"We must have looked for you for an hour before leaving."

"Is that all I'm worth? An hour?" I joked, thinking my answers were still being ignored.

She grabbed my free hand. "Are you all right?" The questions were now being repeated, but this time I was supposed to answer them.

"I'm fine." I rested my head against hers. "I'm just a little tired."

"Where did you go, anyway?"

"I just wandered away from the tour group, and when I came back, I didn't find any of you. I looked for at least an hour and a half."

Lindsay let go of my arm and stepped back.

My sarcastic remark drew quite a stare, but I continued with my explanation. "I tried to catch up to you guys, but you had already left. So, I thought I would get a bite to eat before heading back to the hotel."

She hugged me again. "Well, I'm glad you're back."

While I was telling my story, about twenty people from the tour group had gathered around me. They quickly became uninterested and returned to their previous activities, although a few of them personally welcomed me back. I acknowledged those people with a few nods and waves before turning my attention back to Lindsay's questions.

"Where did you get that vase?" She reached out her hands. "Is it for me?"

It was only a matter of time before she asked that question, but I could tell by her tone she hoped my answer would be "no".

"No." I pulled it back. "It's for Timm."

"Timm?" she asked, crinkling her nose and brow. "What's he going do with a vase like that?"

I held it out for her to see and described the details of the artwork on the sides. "Here is Athena. And these little guys here are painting on the wall and listening to the music played by this harpist. It reminded me of Timm when he paints his murals."

She wrapped her hands around it to look closer. "Do they have others like this?" Now she was interested in them.

I reluctantly let her take the vase from my hands. "There are vases–" catching myself in mid sentence. The large number of vases I saw were behind the secured door. I doubted whether the old man would let me bring my wife into that same room for browsing, or even let me back in there. "Well, there are vases, but I don't know if they will have another one like this."

Unfortunately, my response didn't deter her pursuit of finding a similar vase.

"We have tomorrow to ourselves." Lindsay handed the vase back to me. "Will you take me there?"

I thought for a moment. "I can try."

"What do you mean, 'try'?"

"Well, remember I sort of just came upon this place. I don't know exactly where it is."

"If you don't want to take me, just say so."

Uh-oh, the guilt trip, I thought. "I'm not saying we can't go there, but don't be disappointed if we don't find it."

I had to give myself an escape just in case we didn't find a vase, or even the shop, for that matter. After witnessing what I had earlier, it was highly probable we wouldn't find either one.

"Well, we'll just search until we find it." Lindsay gave me another kiss. "I'm going to bed. Good night."

"Good night," I said.

I really wanted to go with her, but there were two GGB officers who wanted to ask me some questions.

That night, I dreamt about my unusual adventure with the old man. The vases. The cobwebs. The illuminating light show. The purpose. Everything. I never did ask the old man his name. I guess it really didn't matter. Besides, the old man would most likely have viewed it as another informality, and I obviously wasn't there to become friends with him. Instead, I was there to receive the vase and instructions on how to use its contents. I realized he was like me in that sense, not much for small talk, just get right to the point.

The next morning I awoke quite refreshed. Lindsay and I took our time getting cleaned up before we ventured out to savor our last day. We did some preliminary packing, limiting the amount we had to do when we returned. It was probably a good idea because we had to have our luggage sitting outside our door for the bellhops to take down to the lobby. That event was to take place at some ridiculous hour in the morning, and we didn't know how exhausted we would be after our last day of walking around the city and attending a farewell dinner that evening.

We zipped up our luggage and loaded our knapsacks with the daily necessities; food, water, and lotion. We then headed down to the hotel restaurant for a quick breakfast.

In the restaurant, Lindsay was quite inquisitive about my previous day's activities, and I had prepared myself for the question-and-answer session. I told her the truth, giving her as much information as I could remember. She was my wife and I could trust her, although, judging from some of her expressions, I don't think she believed everything. Would anyone? Even to me, it sounded like a fantasy story somebody would write in a book. I finished my story as breakfast arrived. Lindsay asked a few more questions while we ate, and I answered all of them, knowing she was more interested in the location of the shop and the souvenirs available.

Upon finishing our breakfast, we grabbed our knapsacks, and headed outside. It was another gorgeous day as we stepped into the bright sunshine.

"Clear skies and close to eighty degrees already," the doorman informed us while I checked my watch. It was ten-thirty.

"Beautiful, isn't it?" Lindsay replied. "It's going to be in the upper eighties today."

"But, it's a 'dry' heat," I joked. "So much better."

"It's a good thing we have our water," Lindsay assured me.

We had our typical attire on for the day: shorts, T-shirts, and walking shoes. At breakfast, we had decided to go to the top of Lycabettus Hill before searching for the old man's shop. Besides experiencing the wonderful view again, I would have the opportunity to look for the shop from high above the city. Having walked virtually everywhere when we went out on our own, we decided to bypass the funicular that went to the top – there was no reason to change our routine. Lycabettus Hill was about two miles northeast of the hotel. Unlike the last time we visited Athens, which was before the War, breathing the exhaust fumes from the automobiles wasn't a concern. One of the provisions of the Survival Treaty detailed the elimination of all pollution-emitting transportation.

* * * * *

As the survivors began picking up the pieces from the War's destruction, representatives from the world's nations developed, signed, and implemented the provisions of the Survival Treaty, the most substantial document humankind had created. It took six months to complete and was written by some of the most brilliant minds of our time. The elements of the Treaty implemented unselfish policies, something to which people were unaccustomed prior to the War, while moving toward global harmony. Those representatives formed the GGB, Global Governing Body, and located their world headquarters in Athens, Greece – one of the few historical cities left relatively unscathed from the War.

The world was long overdue for a Treaty of such magnitude, when near extinction of the human race was fresh in their mind. It was written for people to make an effort to understand each other's differences rather than turning against each other for those differences. The Treaty contained clauses guaranteeing future generations would always be taught about the events leading up to the War. It also included provisions to eliminate weapons, financial markets and the use of money, pollution, poverty, crime, drugs, hunger, sickness, overpopulation, etc. – all the problems that were supposed to be solved many years earlier.

People supported the Treaty and accepted their responsibilities. As long as they did, they were recognized and rewarded for their efforts by means of an unsophisticated credit system, which replaced the financial systems. This new system provided everyone with the essentials needed to live, as well as the opportunity to enjoy life. Law enforcement agencies consisting of GGB officers were established to aid in the apprehension of people who opposed/violated the Treaty and/or promoted the ForLord following. In all, the establishment of the Treaty was a move toward a global utopia so the human race, and all living things, could cherish their time on earth. The stride for newfound unity was a prelude to peace, indefinitely.

Once the Treaty was completed and signed, the representatives of the GGB returned to their respective countries and appointed regional liaisons. The provisions of the Treaty were made clear to the liaisons and to the people of their region. The stronger countries – strength was now determined by the number of survivors, remaining resources, and level of infrastructure – committed themselves to helping the weaker ones. The Global News Station was established in a matter of months to allow for global communication of activities and progression in each region. The people welcomed the Survival Treaty with open arms and were committed to making sure its provisions were carried out completely.

* * * * *

It was an exhilarating climb to the top of Licabettus Hill, but it was even more exhilarating, in a different sense, to see a view of the entire city of Athens. I began to wonder how many people, over the thousands of years, had climbed that same hill and experienced a similar view. It was absolutely breathtaking. What was even more breathtaking was realizing Athens was one of the few ancient cities to survive the War. There were absolutely no signs of the War anywhere.

We walked from one side to the other, absorbing the mystique before us. Being so caught up in it, I had almost forgotten to look for the old man's shop. From my pocket, I pulled out my map and unfolded it. Fortunately, I had poked a small hole in it, indicating the general area of the shop. I returned the map to my pocket and walked to the edge of the lookout. Locating and using the Acropolis as my reference point, I looked slightly northwest of it. The only things I could see were some ruins, even with the aid of my camera's zoom lens. At that point, I concluded the shop had to be in that general vicinity.

Although, neither Lindsay nor I wanted to leave the Hill, we knew we should if we were going to accomplish everything we wanted to do during our last day. I was starting to get hungry already and figured by the time we arrived near the Acropolis it would be time to eat lunch. We took an alternate route through the city streets to get a different view of the homes, shops, and buildings. We eventually passed by the hotel, dropping off one of the knapsacks as we did.

From the restaurant, it took us about twenty-five minutes to reach the corner of Theorias and Dioskouron, where I was convinced the shop was located before it "disappeared". I was sure this was the same place. Again pulling the map from my pocket, I located the small hole. To our left were some ruins covering the landscape. I walked down a dirt road, which I could have sworn was the road I took coming out from the area. There was only one problem. The road I took the previous day was made of cobblestone and not dirt. I was positive this was the right spot, but there was nothing there that even resembled what I had seen the previous day. It was all too weird as I started mimicking the theme music from *Twilight Zone*; however, Lindsay was not at all amused, and I could hardly blame her. Any amount of disbelief she covered up last night, and this morning, had resurfaced.

Lindsay stood with her arms folded. "Well, where is it?"

"I don't know. According to where I put my mark on the map, it should be right around this area.   I marked it at the nearest streetlight after I came out of the shop."

She looked around the area. "I don't see the old man, nor his shop, nor anything resembling a streetlight."

I couldn't see anything either. I was totally confused. How could a shop, let alone an entire street, just disappear? It was a mystery to me. Looking at the map, I certainly thought I had marked the spot correctly the previous night. It was dark, but I did make it home using the same map. I checked several times just to make sure.

Lindsay had enough of my little "adventure tale" and reminded me the Plaka was only a short distance from where we were standing. As we walked away, I reminded her of what I had said the night before, that I wasn't sure if I would find it again.   My justification went unnoticed.   I think she thought I was hiding something from her.   I wasn't.   I told her everything that morning. Without any proof to verify my unusual story, it would be hard to convince anyone.

As we walked in the direction of the Plaka, Lindsay gave me the silent treatment as if I had lied to her. I continued to look at the map, turning it from side to side, upside down, and front to back. At one point I walked backwards, looking up from the map and gazing into the emptiness, knowing the area was occupied the day before. *Thud!* My concentration was interrupted.

"Geeezz!" I had backed right into a streetlight.

"There's the streetlight you were looking for," Lindsay chuckled, breaking her silence.

Although she wouldn't admit it, she knew I was going to back into that light, and she purposely chose not to tell me.

Once we reached the Plaka, Lindsay began her browsing routine, trying to find a T-shirt she liked. She hardly said a word as we walked from store to store and, as she browsed, I sat every chance I could. I was still bewildered at the whole chain of events. Over and over, I tried to figure out the meaning of my adventure the previous day and how an entire city block could disappear.   I was dumbfounded.

My thoughts were interrupted as I saw Lindsay exit one of the shops. She had found her T-shirt, one with a map of Greece and the Greek Islands printed on it. She held it out for me.

"That's a nice shirt," I acknowledged.

"Thanks." She folded it and put it in the knapsack on my back. "Are you ready to head back?"

I rose from my chair. "Sure."

"Think you can find your way back to the hotel, Columbus?" Lindsay asked.

Now I don't think I really deserved that comment nor did Christopher, but I played along. "I thought we could stop at this little jewelry shop a local told me about. It's off the beaten path a bit, but we do have a map."

"I think I'll pass.   I want to make our flight tomorrow morning."

We both laughed as we continued to walk back to the hotel. It was a nice leisurely stroll, walking hand in hand and talking about our wonderful three weeks, with the exception of the most recent events. When we returned to the hotel, we took a short nap before getting ready for our farewell dinner.

Afterward, we freshened up and finished packing our luggage except for what we were wearing for dinner and the following morning. We acquired a box, to carry the vase, from one of the maids. Some of my shirts served nicely as padding around the vase. After carefully packing the vase and sealing the box, I changed into my casual dinner clothes, and we headed down to the lobby.

The dinner was held at a local restaurant, and it was a delightful evening for it. The dinner provided a good opportunity to exchange addresses and talk to everyone in our group. Some of us would be taking different flights in the morning, so it was the last chance for us to say good-bye.

The bus returned to the hotel around nine-thirty p.m. Everyone exited and headed to their rooms. Lindsay immediately went to bed. I decided to sit out on our room's balcony awhile and reflect on the last three weeks. A full moon lit up the cloudless sky as I stretched out on a lounge chair and breathed in the cool, night air. I began retracing our vacation in my mind while listening to the sounds of Athenian night life. I had a magnificent view of the illuminated Parthenon from where I was sitting and began thinking about Timm back home. I wished he could have seen it with me.

As I looked through the sliding glass door and stared at the box containing the vase, I knew it had a purpose, according to the old man anyway, but how it was to fulfill that purpose I didn't know. That was the last thought I remember until I was abruptly awakened by a taxi's horn sounding just below my balcony. I awoke in an awkward position and the right side of my neck was throbbing. I decided to sleep in my bed for the remainder of the night. The clock by the bed displayed 2:12 a.m.

I don't know what startled me more, the horn of the taxi I heard earlier or the telephone ringing in my ear at 4:30 a.m. That wake-up call came a little too quickly for me, but I dragged myself into the bathroom anyway for a quick shower. Afterward, I could hear Lindsay rummaging around outside the door as I brushed my teeth. She was packing the clothes we wore the previous night.

We exchanged a morning kiss as we passed each other in the bathroom doorway and, after her morning ritual, we made the customary checks for stray items. Confident we had everything, we placed the luggage outside our door. The vase, however, was staying with me.

With the box underneath my arm, Lindsay and I headed to the lobby, returned our room keys, and then met two couples for breakfast. We enjoyed our last foreign meal together and discussed what was waiting for us at home. Everyone had mixed feelings about returning home; however, I think each one of us was eager to resume our own lifestyles again.

"It's six-forty now." Lindsay looked up from her watch. "We should get going."

We all hesitated, as reality set in, and then rose from our seats. In the lobby, the bellhops were loading up the buses with everyone's luggage. One of them extended his arms to load the box I was carrying.

I quickly moved it out of his reach and politely shook my head with a smile. "That's all right, I'll be taking this one with me."

"No problem," he replied. "Have a safe trip."

"Thanks."

With every one aboard the bus, we were on our way home.

Just Another Day

A thens wasn't the only place where strange events were happening. There were also some peculiar things happening back home. It was around two-thirty in the morning, and Timm was sitting upright in his bed, having been awakened by another asthma attack. He was sweating profusely, and his hands and arms were trembling. The late-night asthma attacks were not uncommon, but Timm was becoming concerned over their frequency. It had been the fourth night in a row, and these recent attacks differed from his usual ones because he was coughing up tiny black particles. He noticed the particles two nights before when he coughed into his pillow. The particles left a dark, oval imprint of his mouth, where they came in contact with the pillowcase. He knew it couldn't have been from the paint particles emitted from his airbrush or spray gun because he wasn't using dark paints on his current mural, but they were similar to the particles he used to cough up when he played in the crawl space as a child.

* * * * *

From about the time Timm was in sixth or seventh grade, he made forts down in the crawl space of our house. Times were tough for him during that period and the crawl space provided an escape from reality for him. Our older brother and sister had moved out of the house, I was in high school, and our parents were on the verge of splitting up. Having a hard time understanding what was happening,

Timm sought out a more peaceful haven. The elaborate "apartments" he and his best friend, Bob, made underneath the house provided what he needed.   Eventually, they even slept there instead of in Timm's bedroom whenever Bob spent the night. As time passed, they finally outgrew the crawl space, literally, and had to seek another location for their escape.   Until that time came, they shared many secrets, solved each other's problems, and coped with the world before them, right under our noses.

* * * * *

The crawl space was probably the worst place for somebody with asthma, but that was Timm. He usually did what he wanted to do.   When he spent several days in a row down there, he usually coughed up dust particles or blew them out his nose.

Unable to recall being anyplace with as much dust, he reached over to the nightstand and fumbled around until he found his inhaler. He removed the cap and placed the open end into his mouth.   Two quick pumps accompanied by two deep breaths made up his usual routine. He sat back against his headboard waiting for the medicine to take effect. He could feel his heartbeat accelerate and his hands continue to shake as the medicine flowed through his lungs and into his bloodstream. The relief he desired was slow in coming, causing him to periodically inhale some more medicine.   Each time he repeated the process, he felt a little more comfort as his lungs began to clear, but an hour had passed before Timm finally fell back to sleep.

BEEP! BEEP! BEEP! BEEP! BEEP! BEEP! BEEP! BEEP! BEEP!   Timm mustered enough energy to reach over and hit the snooze button. It was seven-thirty, and he felt like he had been run over by a truck. Then again, he felt like that most every morning. Most artists I've run into will tell you they don't like getting up early in the morning, that is, anytime before lunch. Early to me is between five and six. "Sleeping in" for me is seven o'clock. I'll be the first to tell you I don't like waking up early everyday either, but I have more energy and creativity before lunchtime. Artists, well, they need to convalesce awhile before they rise and present themselves to the rest of the world. At least Timm does, anyway.

BEEP! BEEP! BEEP! BEEP! WHAM! Timm hit the snooze again, only this time with a little more energy. It was now seven-forty. He struggled to open his eyes, not even realizing he had lost ten minutes from his life. While looking around, he tried to determine if he was still alive.

Ring! Ring! WHAM! Before he realized he had hit the silent alarm clock, the phone rang again.

"Hello," Timm greeted the morning caller in his usual quiet and deathlike manner.

His morning greeting is best described as calling the morgue and having a corpse answer the phone. One should ask for drawer C-5 when they hear his meek little "hello" in the morning.

"Good morning," came a soft and bubbly voice from the other end of the phone.

It was Cherie, Timm's girlfriend. She was making her daily wake-up call to make sure Timm got himself out of bed.

"Good morning," he replied in his quiet and still raspy voice.

"How are you doing this morning?" She already knew by the strong wheeze she heard in the phone.

"Not very good. I had another attack last night."

"Are you feeling any better now?"

"A little bit."

"What time are you starting today?"

Timm cleared his throat. "I told Pockets to be here at eight-thirty."

Pockets was Timm's loyal assistant. *BEEP! BEEP!*   Timm was a little less violent this time when he hit the snooze before finally turning the alarm off completely.

"Are we still going to my parents' house for dinner tonight?"

Timm rolled onto his side. "I don't know yet. It depends on how the day goes. We want to finish the mural tonight, so it may be a late one."

"I haven't seen you in over a week."

"I know, but we're going to the musical this weekend," Timm reminded her.

"I know."

Timm looked at his calendar on the wall. "Are you going to stay here this weekend?"

"Yes," Cherie replied and then changed the subject. "Well, I have to get some papers graded before class starts. Call me later and let me know how it's going."

"I will."

"You better get in the shower. Pockets will be there soon."

"I love you."

"I love you, too."

They both said good-bye, and Timm hung up the phone. He flung the covers off and stepped out of bed. Before heading toward the bathroom, he grabbed a pair of underwear from his dresser, tripping over the piles of laundry as he went.

"I'm sick of this mess!" he howled as he kicked a pair of pants out of his way.

He then let out a short laugh, knowing those piles would stay there as long as he was working late nights and as long as he had the mini-washer and dryer in his apartment. The washer held about three or four pieces of clothing, excluding underwear and socks, before it was full.

He managed to find his way to the bathroom, avoiding as many of the other piles as he could in the process. Greeting him there was the mess on the bathroom sink: hair spray bottles, an electric razor, brushes, and dirty washcloths. A pile of dirty towels lay next to the bathtub, and the previous night's swim trunks were still hanging over the curtain rod. He pulled the trunks from the rod, throwing them to the floor in disgust, and turned on the shower. He then pulled his shirt over his head and flung it to the floor, followed next by his shorts. Checking the water with one hand and making the appropriate adjustments with his other one, he stepped into the tub and pulled the curtain shut.

"I don't believe it!" he screamed from behind the curtain.

He had forgotten to grab a clean towel from the linen closet before jumping into the shower. Knowing it was too late to do anything about it, he began his shower. The steam from the hot water began to loosen up the garbage in his lungs, and he started coughing again. This time he covered his mouth with his washcloth to try and trap some more black particles. His attempt was successful; however, the particles seemed to be disappearing. He hoped he was finally seeing the last of them. Waking up in the middle of the night and working long days were beginning to take their toll on him. He needed to get a good night's sleep and decided he would call Cherie later and tell her he wouldn't be going over to her parents' house for dinner.

He finished washing, rinsed himself, and turned off the water. As he pulled open the curtain, he thought momentarily about either running to the linen closet and hoping there was a clean towel remaining or just grabbing one of the towels from the pile next to the tub. Judging from the size of the pile, he decided on the latter, grabbing the top one and drying himself. *Who's going to notice, anyway?* he thought. He threw the towel down on the pile as if it was the first time he used it. *I really have to do some laundry.*

He walked over to the mirror, combed his hair and applied some deodorant. He then grabbed his electric razor and began shaving his two-day-old beard while thinking about what was left to paint on the mural. After finishing, he set the razor down and grabbed the bottle of aftershave. He poured some of the liquid into his hand, rubbed his hands together, and splashed his face, cringing as the liquid penetrated the pores of his newly shaven skin.

Back in the bedroom, he searched for his paint-covered jeans and one of his T-shirts with a recent mural replica printed on it. He miraculously found a pair of clean socks and sat down on the end of his bed. As he pulled them over his feet, he thought about the mess in the other half of the apartment waiting to greet him. There was a week's worth of dirty dishes overflowing from the sink and onto the countertops. In the living room, there were music disks and art books spread across the floor, some dishes on the coffee table, and colored pencils and paper strewn across the dining room table.

Arriving in the kitchen, he searched diligently for a clean bowl in which to pour his cereal. He found a small mixing bowl in the cupboard, poured himself the last bit of cereal, crumbs and all, and reached into the refrigerator for some milk.

"Geeezz!" he shouted.

He had forgotten to pick up some milk the previous night on his way home from work. There was enough for about a quarter of a bowl, and he knew he didn't have time to go out and get some because Pockets would be there soon. So, he poured the remainder of the milk slowly over his cereal, trying to make it fill the entire bowl. As expected, his method was unsuccessful. He then poured himself a larger than normal glass of juice to help wash down his dry cereal. Glancing at the clock, he knew Pockets would be sounding the door buzzer at any minute.

* * * * *

Pockets was an interesting person. He met Timm about three years earlier. One summer day he walked into Timm's studio and asked if Timm needed an assistant. Timm hadn't really thought about it, since he was so accustomed to working by himself. After a few hours of talking, Pockets convinced Timm that having an assistant would be good for our service. Timm and I discussed the idea, and we thought we'd give it a try.

Initially, Pockets didn't know much about painting, but said he had always followed Timm's work. He was a stock person at the local grocery store but lost his job when the family who owned the store retired. Pockets decided it was time to do something else, performing different jobs here and there, each less interesting than the previous. He finally approached Timm about being an assistant. He told Timm he was a fast learner, and that he was. He also was single and willing to work whenever, wherever, and for as long as Timm needed him. Timm informed Pockets the position wouldn't be very glorifying: he would be mixing paints, cleaning brushes, rigging airbrushes, base-coating walls, and performing other trivial tasks. Pockets didn't seem to mind. As we came to know Pockets better, we discovered he didn't have a problem with much of anything. He went along in life at his own pace, taking each day as it came.

Pockets also had a heart of gold, which worked out perfectly in the schools where Timm painted many of his murals. He acquainted himself with many of the children, as well as most everyone else, which came in handy when Timm couldn't afford to be distracted. Pockets would answer the children's questions and discuss what the mural meant to them. When they would ask questions, such as, 'When is it going to be finished?' and 'What's it going to be?', Pockets would simply respond to those who asked, 'Why? Are you in a hurry?' or 'What do you think it's going to be?'. He was also good at diverting the students' attention away from Timm, especially when Timm needed to finish a detailed part of the mural. Any other time, Timm would take time out to talk with the students.

Pockets always wanted to be a teacher, but he explained he didn't have the book smarts to make it through college. It's a shame because he would have made an excellent one. He occasionally described to the children how an airbrush worked, once he knew how it worked himself, and demonstrated how it worked by painting on their hands. They always thought it was cool to have a design on their hand when no one else did.

Pockets and Timm worked well together. They shared the same philosophy regarding children. Although it sometimes hindered our schedule when jobs needed to be completed, they knew it was important to spend extra time with them. Some of the children really needed someone to talk to during that time of their life. Besides being there for guidance and conversation, they taught the children there is more to art than just something to take up space on a wall.

Pockets was always punctual, too. As a result, he was good at keeping Timm on schedule, which was something I wasn't always able to do.

* * * * *

BZZZZZZ! Pockets rang the buzzer to Timm's apartment.

Timm looked at the clock. It was eight-thirty. He walked over and engaged the electronic lock to the outside door, so Pockets could enter the building, while opening his apartment door to meet him.

"Heeeyy!" Timm greeted Pockets, still chewing a mouthful of cereal.

"Good morning," Pockets returned the greeting, and then looked at Timm's shoeless feet. "You haven't eaten yet, have you?"

Timm stopped chewing. "No, as a matter of fact, I'm eating right now." He looked at Pockets suspiciously. "How do you always know when I've eaten?"

Pockets pointed at Timm's feet. "You always put your shoes on after you eat breakfast."

Timm gazed down at his white socks. "At least they're clean," he joked to himself.

"What did you say?" Pockets asked.

"Nothing. Come on in. I'm almost done."

Pockets followed Timm into the apartment. "Are we going to finish the mural today?"

"I hope so," Timm replied, picking up his bowl of cereal.

Pockets cleared off a chair and sat on it. "I think some of those kids are going to miss us after we leave."

"They usually do." Timm finished the last spoonful of cereal, proud of the fact he still had some milk to go with it.

"I think its different this time," Pockets added.

Timm raised his eyebrows as he drank the rest of his juice.

Pockets knew Timm didn't understand what he meant, so he elaborated. "I've noticed on the last two or three jobs that a number of students, and faculty for that matter, have developed a real negative attitude toward everything. Typically, most of the students and teachers will look at things a little differently after you come in and paint a mural. School spirit is heightened and people are affected by the symbolism in your murals. It seems more people, more than usual anyway, are not being affected in the same way."

"I guess I haven't really noticed it." Timm took his bowl and glass to the sink. Unable to rinse them out because of the overabundance of dishes, he placed them on the counter with the other dirty dishes.

Pockets rose from his chair. "I've noticed this negative attitude outside the schools as well."

"What do you mean?" Timm was putting his shoes on when he spoke before Pockets could answer the question. "Where are my keys?"

Pockets looked around the room for a second and spotted them on the dining room table. "Over there." He pointed to them and then answered Timm's question.

"Things have been going real smooth since the Treaty was put into effect. I realize it was a hard transition for a lot of people to make, but they were willing to make some of the sacrifices necessary for us to continue living on this planet. But, lately, it seems some people are reverting to the old selfish attitude that originally got us in trouble."

"I won't argue with you." Timm grabbed his briefcase, phone, and keys on his way to the door. "But, there are a lot of good things happening, too."

Pockets was already out the door and held it open for him. "I know. I'm not saying everyone is changing, but it seems to me the number of people with these negative attitudes is increasing."

Timm put his stuff in the back of the van, and they headed for the school.

"Just remember what Scott always says. There can always be something good found in something bad. Sometimes you have to look a little harder than other times. But what keeps us all going are the positive attitudes. Why do you think we survived the War? It's because there were enough people who wanted it to end and who also believed things could change. Ideally, you want to anticipate problems and prevent them before they happen, but it's not always possible, so you try to resolve them as soon as you can."

Pockets turned toward Timm. "Your brother's influence is apparent in what you're telling me, but I still don't like what I'm seeing. All I ask is you pay a little closer attention to people in the next few days and tell me if what I've been telling you is true or not."

"You got it." Timm quickly changed the subject. "Did you order the–"

"Did it," Pockets interrupted. "Two gallons of clearcoat were all we needed, right?"

"Yep."

Timm pulled into the school parking lot and parked the van on the sidewalk by the entrance closest to the mural. Waiting for them at the door was Joe, our supplier. He had the two gallons of clearcoat Pockets ordered.

"Hey, Joe," Timm greeted him.

"I wish you guys would place bigger orders in the future," Joe replied rudely. "It's hardly worth my effort."

Before Timm could respond to Joe's unexpected statements, Joe was back in his car driving to his next delivery sight. Timm was dumbfounded and looked over at Pockets.

"Man! What's up with him?"

"See what I mean?" Pockets asked.

"Yeah, I do now. Joe is one of the friendliest guys I know, even when he's had a terrible day."

Pockets grabbed the clearcoat and they entered the school. It was a passing period and some of the students were there to greet them.

"Man you guys missed a good one this morning," Lauren said. Lauren, a senior, was one of Timm's biggest fans at the school and couldn't wait to tell him and Pockets what happened. "A huge, nasty fight broke out in the commons. They had the GGB officers here and everything. About twenty kids were hauled off."

"How did it start?" Timm asked.

"Some guys started to spray paint the walls in the commons and some of the baseball players tried to stop them. Then before you knew it, there were bodies flying all over the place. It was really scary. Luckily the teachers and some of the other students were able to break it up."

"Was anyone seriously hurt?" Pockets asked.

"No, but we have a big play-off game tonight, and some of our best players may not be able to play."

Pockets and Timm again looked at each other. Timm didn't like hearing or seeing what was developing.

"Come on. I want to show you the damage caused from the paint," Lauren insisted. She grabbed Timm's arm and led him to the commons. Pockets followed, still carrying the two cans of clearcoat.

"How come you aren't in class?" Timm asked.

"I have Study Hall this period, remember?" Lauren softly hit his arm.

"That's right. How many times have I asked you that?"

"Only about twenty since you started working at our school."

When they arrived at the wall, Timm and Pockets were stunned. Pockets almost dropped the two cans of clearcoat. He set them on the ground and walked over to the wall to get a closer look. The paint had partially eaten away sections of the brick wall, exposing the block wall behind them.

"Are you sure it was paint they were using?" Pockets inquired as he was about to touch the exposed area.

"Don't touch it!" Timm pulled Pockets' arm away from the wall. "It may still be wet and it could eat right through your hand."

"Thanks." Pockets stepped back and turned toward Timm. "Even after working with you for this long, I still have a hard time determining if breaks in walls are real or if you painted them."

"I had nothing to do with this," Timm assured him.

"In answer to your question, Pockets, what they used sure looked like paint to me," Lauren replied. "It was in a normal spray can."

"Did the staff confiscate any of the cans?" Timm asked.

"No, they disintegrated during the fight."

"The cans disintegrated?" Timm was amazed. "Holy cow!"

"No one really noticed it until after the fight was broken up." Lauren pointed to an area on the floor. "When everyone began leaving, one of the teachers discovered only the bases of the spray cans were left on the ground. Then smaller skirmishes started breaking out again, and Mr. Barnaby thought about calling off school for the rest of the day because everyone was too riled up from the fight."

"Why didn't he?" Pockets asked, still examining the wall.

"It's too late in the school year to make up any days. Graduation is tomorrow." Lauren patted Timm on the shoulder. "I have to get ready for my next class, but I wanted to make sure I told you guys the details. I'm sure Mr. Barnaby will tell you his story, but he'll leave out stuff. Principals always filter the news."

"I'm glad you told us. Thanks," Pockets replied.

"Well, I'm outta here, dudes. Catcha later." Lauren scurried off to her locker.

"Bye," Timm and Pockets said in unison.

"Pockets, let's go find Mike." Timm turned and headed for the main office.

Pockets grabbed the two cans of clearcoat and walked beside him. "That was some pretty destructive paint, or whatever it was."

"You're telling me. The scary thing about it is–" Timm paused for a minute.

"The scary thing about it is, what?" Pockets tried coaxing Timm into finishing his sentence. They made a right turn down the main hallway toward the office.

Timm stopped, looking off into the distance. "The scary thing is, I've seen that before."

"Seen what before?"

Timm furrowed his brow. "I remember seeing or hearing about somebody using that type of paint, but I can't remember where."

"You know, I think you're right."

Timm scratched his temple. "Where did I see it?"

"Maybe your brother knows," Pockets suggested. "We can ask him when he gets back."

They continued toward the main office again.

"Good idea. Speaking of my brother, what is today?"

Pockets looked at his watch. "It's Friday, June 6th."

"Scott gets home tomorrow." Timm paused a second. "No, he gets home today."

"Right you are," Pockets agreed.

"I can't wait either. I hate taking care of all of the paperwork. I hope I didn't mess up the credit book."

"I'm sure you did all right."

"I hope so. One good thing about it though–"

"What's that?" Pockets interrupted.

"I do understand a little bit more of what he does."

"That's good. Who's picking him up?"

"I am." Timm checked his pockets. "That reminds me, I have to find the piece of paper with the flight information."

"Not again."

"Whaaat?!" Timm exclaimed defensively.

"It amazes me the number of things you misplace. It's probably in the van. Practically everything you own ends up in the van."

"You're probably right."

They both laughed.

Pockets lifted one of the cans to his chest and pulled on his pocket. "You need to get yourself one of these."

Timm laughed and then changed the subject. "You're going to have to stay behind to clearcoat and pack up the supply box."

"No problem. Just take me home at lunchtime so I can get my car."

"Remind me again at lunchtime to look for that piece of paper."

Pockets nodded.

"What are you doing tomorrow?" Timm asked.

"Nothing in the morning," Pockets replied.

"Do you want to meet me hear about nine o'clock to get the supply box ready for Monday and then load it into the van?" Timm looked at Pockets in a quizzical manner.

"Sure." Pockets returned the same look. "What's wrong?"

"Where's the clearcoat?"

"I put it in my pocket; I got tired of carrying the cans."

"To this day, I still don't understand how you can fit all that stuff in there."

Pockets just smiled and kept walking. They reached the main office door at the same time the bell rang through the hallways, quickly ducking inside to avoid getting trampled by the students scurrying to their next class.

"Hi, guys," came a soft voice from behind the counter. It was Mr. Barnaby's secretary.

"Hi, Judy," Timm and Pockets chimed simultaneously.

"Is Mike in?" Timm asked.

"Yes, he is. Do you want to see him?"

"Just for a minute."

"Mr. Barnaby, Timm and Pockets are here to see you." Judy released the button on the intercom and waited for his reply.

"Send them down. I'm just finishing up here."

"There you go, guys."

"Thanks," Timm said.

Timm and Pockets walked around the counter and headed toward Mike's office, passing a couple of GGB officers on the way. Mike was standing in the doorway and waved Timm and Pockets into his office.

"Good morning, Mike," Timm spoke first.

"Good morning, Mr. Barnaby," Pockets followed, never calling a principal by their first name.

"It's far from a good morning." Mike pointed to the two empty chairs and then sat at his desk. "Did you hear what happened this morning?"

"Bits and pieces," Timm replied.

"In the twenty-four years I have worked in school systems, I have never seen anything like what happened here this morning." Mike leaned back in his chair and shook his head. "Some of those kids could have been seriously hurt. The thing most puzzling is it was started by three of our best students. I know exams are a stressful time, but these kids have never acted like this in the past."

"I don't think it was the exams, Mr. Barnaby." Pockets couldn't hold back his concern any longer.

"Huh, what did you say?" Mike really didn't expect anyone to interrupt his story.

Timm wasn't sure whether he should stop Pockets or let him continue. He decided to let Pockets continue since it had obviously been on his mind for some time now.

"I said, I don't think it was the exams, Mr. Barnaby."

Mike leaned forward and put his arms on the desk. "What do you mean?"

Pockets explained to Mike what he had told Timm earlier about people's attitudes changing. He also included Joe's earlier incident as another example. Surprisingly, Mike didn't think Pockets' observation was so bizarre.

Mike put his hand on his chin. "Come to think of it, there has been a handful of students, and teachers for that matter, who have been acting somewhat strangely over the last two weeks or so. What do you think it might be?"

Pockets thought for a moment. "I'm not sure, but I'm going to pay a little closer attention to people."

"I will, too," Mike agreed.

"If you hear or see anything peculiar, let us know," Timm said.

"I certainly will."

"Well, we need to get back to work," Timm said to Pockets and then turned to Mike. "We plan on finishing today."

"Really?" Mike asked surprisingly.

Timm nodded.

"That's great." Mike paused for a moment. "And I suppose you need a contribution credit today?"

"That would be nice," Timm replied.

"I'll have it ready for you by the end of the day."

"Great. Oh, could you give it to Pockets since I won't be here?"

"Sure thing. Pockets, stop by before you leave. I'm sure I'll be here late today." Mike's frustration level was rising again.

"I will do that, Mr. Barnaby."

They all stood and walked to the door.

Mike paused for a moment. "I really want to thank you guys for what you've done for the school. It's been a great uplift for the school's spirit and, as always Timm, your artwork is magnificent. We really appreciate it here." He extended his hand to Timm.

"Thanks, Mike." Timm shook Mike's hand.

"Thanks, Mr. Barnaby." Pockets also shook Mike's hand. He then reached into his shirt pocket and pulled out a large set of reference photos, books, and other school paraphernalia Mike had given them to use for the mural.

Mike gave Pockets a puzzled look and then looked at Timm.

Timm shrugged his shoulders, "Don't even ask."

Mike shook his head, opened the door for them, and patted Pockets on the shoulder as they left. "I really meant what I said."

Timm stopped, turning to face Mike for a moment. "I know you did. Thanks again. We'll see you later."

"See you guys." Mike paused for a second, "I'm going to try and get you guys back here."

"Great. We'd love to come back," Timm replied.

Timm and Pockets then headed toward the main office door, saying good-bye to Judy as they passed by her.

Timm had finished all the detail work and touch-ups. The only step remaining was the clearcoating and Pockets was going to take care of that. It was about one-thirty when they packed up the box and headed back to Timm's for lunch. Timm finished a little later than he wanted, but he spent about an hour saying good-bye to a number of the students who stopped by during their lunch hour. He also wrote down addresses of those students who wanted to keep in touch. Jermaine and Roberto wanted to know if they could get together with Timm over the summer so he could show them some of the dance moves he performed years earlier. Lauren also stopped by again to ask if Timm and Pockets would come to the graduation ceremonies. Most of all, the kids just came by to tell Timm what a great job he did on the mural. It was a typical last day for Timm and Pockets.

While Pockets was in Timm's kitchen fixing sandwiches and cleaning up the minimum number of dishes needed for lunch, Timm was nervously looking for the paper with the flight information on it because neither one of them were able to find it in the van. Before turning the place upside down looking for it, he decided to call Cherie. He picked up the phone and dialed her work number.

The voice from the school's answering machine came on line. "Thank you for calling Highland South High School. If you know your party's extension, you may enter–"

Timm entered Cherie's extension and waited for someone to answer.

"Foreign language department," a woman's voice said.

"Is Cherie there?"

"Just a minute." After a brief pause Cherie came to the phone.

"Hello, this is Cherie."

"Hi, it's me."

"Hello," Cherie said, somewhat surprised it was Timm. "What's up?"

"I can't find Scott's flight information. Do you know what I did with it?"

"Yep." Cherie cradled the phone between her head and shoulder while pulling her purse from one of her desk drawers. "You gave it to me so you wouldn't lose it." She started searching the inside pockets.

"That's a relief," Timm sighed.

"I thought you'd be gone already."

"Me, too."

"Sandwiches are ready!" Pockets shouted from the kitchen.

"OK, I'll be there in a second," Timm shouted back.

"Be where in a second?" Cherie asked, somewhat confused.

"No, I was talking to Pockets. He's making lunch."

"Here it is," she giggled.

"What's so funny?" Timm asked.

"Nothing. I can't believe–, yes, I can." She giggled again.

"Whaaat?" Timm was getting impatient.

"I can't believe you gave it to me so you wouldn't lose it, and then you forgot you gave it to me." She giggled again.

"You're getting a real kick out of this, aren't you?"

"Yep. Do you have a paper and pen?"

"Ready."

"OK, the flight is BA flight 417." She paused. "And, let's see, it gets in at three twenty-five this afternoon."

"Great, gotta go."

"Good-bye."

Timm hung up the phone before Cherie could say her farewell. He stuffed the piece of paper into his front pocket and walked toward the dining room table. Pockets had soup, sandwiches, chips, and fruit punch waiting for him, while half of Pockets' sandwich was already gone. Timm sat down and began eating.

"Did she have it?" Pockets inquired.

"Yep. I need to leave in about ten minutes."

They devoured their lunches without saying a word, which was very unusual for Timm. He typically ate slowly and liked to talk during his meal. After finishing, Timm ran to the bathroom, and Pockets brought the dishes to the kitchen.

Timm ran out of the bathroom and stumbled over one of the piles of dirty laundry. "Aaarrrrggh!"

Pockets couldn't help but laugh. "Are you all right?"

"I'm fine," Timm scowled.

"Sorry, I don't do laundry, only cooking," Pockets joked.

They both laughed and headed outside. Timm locked the glass door and walked to his van, while Pockets climbed into his car.

Pockets stuck his head out the window. "Are we still meeting at nine tomorrow?!"

Timm popped his head above the roof of his van. "How about ten?!"

"No problem! See you at ten!"

Timm laughed to himself wondering if he would be there at ten; he knew Pockets would. Funny thing is, Pockets had the same thought. Timm stepped into the van and checked his electric charge level. He figured he had enough charge to get to the airport and back. It would have to be; he didn't have time to recharge it even if he wanted to. He started the engine, followed Pockets out of the parking lot, and headed to the airport.

Back Home

*L*indsay and I left Athens on time and were scheduled to arrive in London about forty-five minutes before our connection flight's departure, and an exciting one it would be. We were about to partake in a major historical event; being aboard one of the last planes flown out of Europe. Implemented as part of the Survival Treaty, the transcontinental and transoceanic rail systems were replacing all forms of high-speed, pollution-emitting modes of transportation as the new way to travel and move cargo. Development of these massive systems had begun before the War, so the infrastructure was already in place. The transcontinental rail systems started operating several years ago and the final connections of the transoceanic rail system were near completion. Both systems were comprised of magnetic-levitation trains which utilized superconducting magnets. They were now capable of safely moving people and cargo at speeds of 350-400 miles per hour.

The London airport was crowded as usual, and planes were lined up waiting to depart. As a result, the pilot informed the passengers we would be circling the airport until given the clearance to land. After the initial pass, I rang for one of the flight attendants. It took him longer than usual because he was already strapped into his seat. I explained our situation; we only had about thirty minutes until our connecting flight left, and I asked if we could grab our carry-on luggage and move closer to the exit door. In our present seats, it would be impossible for us to deplane in time. The flight attendant was quite courteous, considering the situation, and immediately surveyed the front portion of the plane. He spotted two seats, about twelve rows from the door, and motioned for us to hurry along.

At that moment, the captain announced the plane had clearance to land. Lindsay and I grabbed our carry-ons from the overhead compartment and from underneath our seats, including the box containing the vase. We then moved forward to the unoccupied seats. Luckily, one of them was an aisle seat. We decided Lindsay would sit there so she could quickly deplane with the lighter luggage, the two small knapsacks and the camera case. I would carry the heavy duffel bag and, of course, the vase. She was to exit the plane and run to our next gate as fast as possible because my heavy load would not allow me to get to the gate on time. If necessary, she would make up some lame excuse as to why she couldn't board if I hadn't shown up yet. I was to catch up to her as quickly as possible and hope for the best.

The plane came to a full stop and the seat belt bell sounded, signaling it was clear to get out of our seat to deplane. Lindsay darted into the aisle and headed to the exit door. She did real well, leaving only ten people in front of her and twenty or more between us. *Runners take your mark*, I thought to myself. The door opened and she soon disappeared from my sight. I had less than fifteen minutes to get to the gate.

I patiently waited for the "cattle drive" to move along. Now only five people from the door, I carefully scanned the people in front of me to identify whom I would pass once I was in the walkway. They were all adults, with the exception of two little girls standing by their mother. I had to make sure I didn't trample them as I scurried off the plane and down the walkway. Upon arriving at the door, I could see that a small opening was my only restraint.

"Buh-bye," one of the flight attendants said in her British accent.

"Good-bye," I said.

"I hope you make your flight," said the flight attendant who assisted us.

"Me, too, and thanks for your help."

I threw the heavy duffel bag over my left shoulder and tucked the box containing the vase under my right arm. It was quite awkward at first, so I repositioned the box to ensure it would not slip out from under my arm. Off I went, walking as fast as my lean legs would allow. I quickly came upon the woman with the two children, now with one on each side of her. The right side had the widest gap and I headed for it. At that moment, the small girl on the right side broke the grip of her mother's hand and wandered aimlessly toward the walkway wall. I immediately pushed on the back of the duffel bag with my left hand, sending it forward enough to clear the head of the girl as I passed her. *That was too close*, I thought. I was now at the end of the walkway and about to enter the main terminal. My attention was immediately directed to the overhead signs to help guide me to my destination, and I relied on my peripheral vision to spot slow-walking people and small children.

This was only my second time in London, the other being three weeks earlier. So, I really had to rely on the signs to get to my gate. Fortunately, we acquired the gate number while on board the plane, so I didn't lose precious seconds asking someone what it was. Lindsay, as expected, was nowhere in sight. I could only hope she found the gate and was able to stall them long enough for me to get there. I scurried along, weaving in and out and sometimes walking between people, while constantly excusing myself to get around others. Fortunately, I hadn't knocked anyone over yet.

As I glanced down from the overhead signs, I saw a single file line just ahead of me. Avoiding the line wasn't an option; it was the entrance to my terminal. As I waited in the line, seemingly forever, I dropped the duffel bag off my shoulder and carried it like a suitcase. My shoulder was throbbing, and the rest was well needed. I approached the belt on the X-ray machine, set the duffel bag and box onto it, and continued to the metal detector arc. *BEEEEEP!*

Just what I needed, I thought. The person in front of me set off the alarm. I wasn't about to stick around to find out what he had in his pockets. Before his second pass through, I cut in front of him, brushing against his right elbow as he was pulling his hand from his pocket. I didn't look back to see what happened next, but the sound I heard was that of keys hitting the tile floor. Under normal circumstances, I would have apologized and even helped him pick up his keys, which had broken away from the chain and scattered all over the floor, but the circumstances weren't normal as far as I was concerned. I pulled the box from the belt, once again tucking it under my arm, and slung the duffel bag over my shoulder, while letting out a grimacing moan.

I scooted along for about a minute before a thought concerning the vase darted into my mind. *Was I supposed to avoid putting the box in the X-ray machine?* The momentary distraction caused me to take a wrong turn.

I looked up at the sign. *This isn't right*, I thought. *This isn't the right intersection.* Turning around, I headed back to the previous intersection until I again saw signs with my gate number on them. I was back on track, but was I too late? I picked up the pace, walking as fast as I could without breaking into a run. The beads of sweat rolled down the sides of my face, and I momentarily forgot about my throbbing shoulder.

"Over here!" Lindsay yelled, having noticed me first. She was four gates away, and as promised, she hadn't boarded. We handed the gate attendant our boarding passes and stepped onto the walkway, thanking her as we passed.   Lindsay and the gate attendant quietly laughed.

"What was that about?" I asked as we headed down the walkway toward the plane.

"They were holding the plane for us this whole time regardless of me arriving ahead of you," Lindsay laughed.

"You're kidding me?"   Initially, I was somewhat irritated, having to almost run through the airport with heavy, awkward luggage, but then I had to laugh, too.

Lindsay stepped onto the plane, while continuing her story. "As I was waiting for you, the attendant explained to me they were notified of our flight's late arrival from Athens, and we were the only ones on that flight making this connection."

I stepped onto the plane, acknowledging the flight attendant's greeting with a smile. "Well, I'm glad they held it for us. It was nice of them to go out of their way."

"To be honest, they didn't go out of their way," Lindsay reminded me. "Remember, we're one of the last scheduled flights back to Chicago, so they had no intention of leaving until all passengers were aboard."

"The important thing is that we're on the plane and on our way home."

Our seats were nice, but not because we were in First Class. They were located right next to the kitchen, which meant we would get served quickly, and we could also store some of our luggage behind the seats, giving us more leg room. We were still perspiring from our dash through the airport, and the body heat of the other passengers didn't help. Lindsay had a little time to cool off while she waited for me, but we both cooled off completely once the pilot turned on the air conditioning. We buckled ourselves in as the plane backed away from the gate. The flight itself was relatively uneventful, primarily because we slept most of the way home, awakening only to eat and to use the bathroom.

It was so good to be back in Chicago. The view of Lake Michigan and the rebuilt city skyline was a welcome sight. It was a beautiful, sunny day with the reported temperature at seventy-six degrees.

Lindsay and I departed the plane in a more relaxed manner than in London. Having all of our luggage with us, we made our way to Customs. The lines were small, requiring very little time to get our things checked. As we headed for the main terminal, I wondered if Timm was going to be at the airport on time.

We made our way through the walkway toward the terminal exit, seeing only friends and family of the other travelers. Timm was nowhere in sight.

"I knew we should have asked somebody else to pick us up," Lindsay griped. She obviously didn't see him either.

"I can't wait to shed this luggage for good," I replied, purposely changing the subject as my shoulder began to throb again.

"Me, too."

"Heeeey!"   A familiar voice came from behind us as we entered the terminal.

It was Timm. He was standing in front of the wall next to the drinking fountain so we wouldn't see him as we walked into the terminal. It was quite a pleasant feeling to see a familiar face again.

"It's been a long time. I'm glad you made it back safely," Timm said with a huge smile on his face.

"We are, too," Lindsay and I sighed in unison.

"I bet you guys didn't think I would be here, did you?"

"I did, but someone else didn't."   Turning toward Lindsay, I received a sharp glare from her, but continued my ribbing.   "You should be ashamed of yourself."

"Can I take one of those?"   Timm asked as he pointed to my luggage.

I looked at Timm, then back at Lindsay with a smile.

"Don't you dare," she said.

"Don't what?" Timm asked innocently.

I couldn't resist. Off came the heavy, black duffel bag. I handed it to Timm, doing my best to pretend it wasn't very heavy. He took it from me and nearly dropped it to the floor.

"Oh, thanks a lot," Timm moaned.

We all started laughing as Lindsay extended the two knapsacks in exchange. Timm willingly accepted and handed the duffel bag to me. Somehow I didn't think that was right, but I wasn't about to let anyone carry the vase, either.

"I came in those doors over there."   Timm pointed and headed to the exit doors across from the second luggage carousel.   We followed.   "Sooo, how was the trip?"

"Awesome!" I exclaimed.

"Fantastic!" Lindsay added.

"I took over seven hundred pictures," I informed him as I readjusted the duffel bag.

"You're kidding me?"

"I took pictures of everything I could."

"And in every position," Lindsay added.

"What do you mean by that?" Timm asked.

Lindsay explained. "We were in one of the small Duomos in, I think, Florence. As I moved along with the rest of the crowd, I turned to say something to Scott. Well, he was no longer next to me. So, I started to look around for him and noticed a number of people looking at a section of the ceiling, while others were looking at the floor underneath it. I looked up first and noticed a mural painted inside the cupola. Well, someone else noticed the mural, as well. I proceeded to look down at the floor and there was Scott, lying flat on his back, taking a picture of the mural."

"I wanted to make sure I took the picture at the best angle; besides, my neck was beginning to ache from constantly looking up," I said, defending myself. "I don't know how Michelangelo did it."

"I'm not sure how long I could do it," Timm added.

We made our way out of the airport and headed toward the parking lot. The familiar scenery was so nice to see, even if it was the airport – soon to be Chicago's transcontinental rail system terminal. While in the parking lot elevator, Timm's curiosity finally overcame him.

"What's in the box?" he asked.

"It's for you," I replied.

Timm's eyebrows raised and a big smile lit up his face. "Cool. What is it?"

I gave him a look letting him know I wasn't going to tell him. The elevator doors opened on our floor and we exited. Lindsay and I followed Timm toward his van.

"You'll find out later," I assured him.

"Let him open it in the van," Lindsay offered.

"No, he can open it later tonight at his place."

Lindsay looked at me with a furrowed brow. "Geez, we're not even out of the airport yet and you guys are already having a meeting."

I readjusted the position of the vase. "Vacation's over."

"Aren't you even the slightest bit tired?" Lindsay asked.

"Not really. There's a lot of stuff we need to catch up on." I was getting excited about being home and revealing the contents of the vase, although I was sure this latest rush wouldn't last long. It had been a long, eventful trip. "Besides, I need to see if Timm was able to keep everything in order."

"Oh, thanks a lot," Timm replied. "I think I did pretty well."

"We'll have to wait and see, won't we, my little business wizard?" I couldn't resist giving him a hard time. I knew how much he hated handling the company's paperwork.

We finally reached the van, and Timm unlocked the hatch so we could place the luggage inside the back end.

"What a relief," I said, throwing the duffel bag into the van.

"You can say that again," Lindsay replied.

I did, however, hold onto the box. Lindsay made a motion to take it from me and put it with the rest of the luggage, but I pulled it even closer to me.

"What is it with you and that box? You've been holding it like a baby holds its blanket."

"It is my blanket," I replied as we walked to the side door.

Timm unlocked the doors and we all climbed inside the van. Lindsay rode in the back so she could sleep and I rode shotgun with the box on my lap. We were less than an hour away from home.

"Thanks for picking us up," Lindsay said.

"Yeah, thanks, Timm," I added. I would have thanked him eventually, but I had so many things on my mind about the vacation and, of course, what was in the vase.

"No problem."

I just smiled, knowing it wasn't as simple as Timm made it out to be.

Talking about the vacation made the ride seem shorter than it was. As I expected, Lindsay fell asleep before we left the airport. I knew she was exhausted, and she's the type of person who could fall asleep anywhere and at anytime.

During our conversation, Timm brought up his earlier discussion with Pockets, about people's attitudes. He also told me about Joe and what happened at the school that day. Timm was extremely distraught about it and admittedly, I couldn't blame him. Up to that point, I really hadn't thought much about it either, but I recalled a few instances in Europe when I encountered the same types of behavior.

We concluded it was on a global scale rather than just local. Merely coincidence? I didn't think so. The commonalities were too similar. It was not a good sign. People's attitudes had to remain strong and positive as they continued rebuilding their world. The lack of a positive attitude was what led to the War in the first place. I thought we were moving forward and were learning from our mistakes. It appeared the cycle was beginning to repeat itself. But what was the cause? Was the Survival Treaty not working? I told Timm we really needed to pay more attention to our surroundings, in hopes more clues would be revealed.

Our conversation changed flavor as Timm pulled into the driveway. Home sweet home. How true it was. I reached back and tapped Lindsay on the shoulder to awaken her. It was a little past five. The neighbors were tending to their yard work or playing with their children. Our yard looked nice, too. Ted, across the street from us, cut it while we were away so it wouldn't look like a prairie when we returned. While we unloaded our luggage and carried it into the house, a few of the louder neighbors welcomed us back. Lindsay and I replied to their greetings.

Timm and Lindsay took the luggage upstairs, while I went into the kitchen, set the box on top of the counter, and checked phone messages. As I was finishing, they walked into the kitchen.

"Isn't that amazing?" Lindsay quipped. "I didn't think you would ever put that thing down."

I looked at Timm and shook my head. "Well, bro, I hate to desert you, but we have to pick up Zeus. I'll come over after we get back."

Zeus was our hundred-pound Alaskan Malamute, and he was staying with Lindsay's mom. Lindsay and I both wondered how that went. He was only about fifteen months old and had never been away from us for more than half a day.

"All right, I guess I'll see you in a few hours." Timm checked his pockets. "When you come over, I want you to take a look at my new canvas painting. I've been struggling with it lately, and you may have a few ideas for me."

"Will do." I noticed Timm looking around the room. "What's wrong?"

"Keys?" Timm directed the question to himself. "Where are my keys?"

I looked at Lindsay, shaking my head. "Some things never change."

"Oh, I think I know where they are," he replied, ignoring my comment.

Timm ran upstairs to the bedroom, where he was certain he left them, while I gathered up the mail to take with on the ride up to the in-laws. I went out the front door while Lindsay, with our car keys in hand, headed to the garage.

"I found 'em!" Timm ran down the stairs and caught up with me outside.

"Thanks again for picking us up today," I said.

"No problem." Timm stepped into his van and started the engine. He noticed he had just enough charge to get home. "I'll see you in a few hours."

"OK. See you later." I waved good-bye to him as he pulled out of the driveway.

Lindsay unplugged the car and pulled it out of the garage. While I walked around to the passenger side, Ted strolled over to harass us some more. He was good at it.

"You guys just got home and you're leaving again," he joked.

"We have to pick up Zeus," Lindsay explained.

"How was the trip?"

"Fantastic," we both replied.

"How many times did you mow the lawn?" I asked. I wasn't really interested in the answer, but I knew Ted liked to talk lawn maintenance; after all, it was his profession.

"Only twice. The last time I brought one of my mowers home from the job. That baby had a fifty-four-inch cutting path. I think it only took me twenty minutes to cut your lawn and fifteen to cut mine."

Lindsay and I both laughed. I could picture him doing it, too. He's always bringing some piece of equipment home to do yard work. I don't blame him; I would probably do the same.

"I'll let you guys go get the pooch," he continued.

"See ya, Ted, and thanks for taking care of the place," I said.

"Yeah, thanks a lot," Lindsay added.

"Anytime." He strolled back toward his yard. "Later, guys."

Lindsay backed the car up and pushed the button to close the garage door. Just what we both wanted to do, drive for two more hours. Admittedly though, we were both excited to see our "baby".

Only Lindsay's excitement kept her awake for the one-hour trip to her mother's. It was a good thing, too, because she was driving. We didn't say much on the ride up, both of us being extremely exhausted, mentally and physically. Occasionally, I made a comment as I sifted through the mail, taking about half the ride to read all of it. When I finished, I put the seat back, closed my eyes, and quickly fell asleep. I knew I had to be extremely tired because I normally can't sleep in a car.

"Scott! We're here," Lindsay said before kissing me on the cheek.

I brought the seat forward again as Lindsay pulled into the driveway. Her mom's car was missing; however, Don, her stepfather, was sitting in a lawn chair on the patio. We both stepped out of the car, looking for Zeus.

Don stood up from his chair and yelled through the screen door, "Zeus! You have some visitors!"

I had to laugh. It sounded like Zeus was in an institution or something, and we were coming to visit him.

"Hello," Lindsay and I greeted Don.

"Hi, Lindsay. Hi, Scott," he replied. "How was the trip?"

How many times would we hear this? I wondered.

"It was great," Lindsay replied.

"Fantastic!" I added. "How was Zeus?"

"Oh, I have lots of stories about Zeus."

His response didn't surprise me. Don had stories about everything. The hard part about listening to his stories was determining which parts were real.

As we approached the screen door, we could hear Zeus's nails clicking on the linoleum floor as his excitement grew. I put my face up to the screen, and he immediately began to acknowledge my presence in his usual manner.

"Wooooo wooooo wooooo!"

I opened the door and walked inside, Lindsay right behind me. "Hi, Zeus. Remember us?" Yeah, like he was going to answer, right? I knelt on both knees so he could give me one of his hugs.

"Wooooo wooooo wooooo!" With his tail wagging, he jumped up on his hind legs, put his front paws on my shoulders, and licked my face like I was an ice cream cone. After a few seconds of his slobber, I put his paws back on the floor. He was too excited to even begin to calm down. Back up on my shoulders he went, with his tongue darting and his tail wagging. I put his paws back on the floor and rose to my feet. It was Lindsay's turn. Thank God, I was beginning to drown in dog mucous.

"Woooo woooo woooo!"

Lindsay received her tongue lashing, in both senses of the word. Zeus continued his greeting as I went to the washroom to wash my face. I could hear Lindsay giggling in the kitchen as Zeus washed her face the same way he did mine. Although there was a small price to pay, it was worth it.

We dismantled Zeus's cage and gathered up his toys and dishes. With everything loaded in the car, including Zeus, it was time to go. We had only been there for about twenty or thirty minutes, but I wanted to get back so I could meet with Timm.   Don bid us a farewell and apologized for Lindsay's mom not being home. We asked him to pass along our thanks and stepped into the car ourselves. Keeping my end of the bargain, I drove home.

We arrived home around seven-thirty, and I quickly began unloading the car. Lindsay took Zeus and his chain around to the back of the house. There she screwed the stake into the ground, let Zeus do his thing, and then circled back to the front to help me unload the rest of his possessions. It only took us a few trips to get everything into the house. Lindsay finished bringing in the smaller stuff while I set up Zeus's cage in the basement. When I came up the stairs, Lindsay was putting our fast-food dinner on the table, which we had picked up on the way home. I let Zeus in from the backyard. He had already eaten, so we didn't have to bother with feeding him.

Lindsay and I sat down at the table and began unwrapping our burgers. After taking our first bite, we both looked at each other with the same expression. We knew we were back home.

Uncovering The Secret

I t was almost eight-thirty when I arrived at Timm's apartment. I parked my car in the closest spot and walked toward his partially-opened sliding screen door.

I let myself in and announced my entrance. "Timm!"

"I'll be there in a minute," Timm yelled from his bedroom.

I set the box on the only empty spot I could find atop the dining room table. His place was a mess, which for all practical purposes was normal – Timm never did have a clean room, even when we were kids. He came out of the bedroom and walked over the laundry piles like they weren't even there.

"Hey, dude!" he greeted me.

"Nice place. I see you haven't done any major redecorating while I was away."

"You don't waste anytime, do you?"

We both laughed.

"Do you want to open your present?" I slid the box closer to him.

"Surrre," he replied, reaching out for the box.

I pulled it back. "It's not as much a present for you as it is for us." I moved the box toward him again.

Timm picked up the box and looked at it. "What d'ya mean?"

"There's a long story behind this, so hurry and open it."

"Are you going to tell me?"

"Eventually," I replied, knowing Timm hated whenever I didn't tell him everything at once.

Timm set the box back on the table. "Great. How long do I have to wait this time?"

"Not long." I pushed some of the stuff on the table to one side, making a little more room to put the vase.

Timm grabbed a dirty knife from the kitchen sink and slit the tape holding the flaps down, forcing them open. "Shirts? This is what's so secret."

"The shirts are mine." I held out my hand.

He handed me the shirts encasing the vase and then pulled the vase out of the box. "Cooool! Ha ha, look at those little guys on the front." He pointed at the inscriptions on the vase, laughing again in his unique, but familiar, way.

* * * * *

I think laughter, along with being someone Timm looked up to, is one of the reasons why we're now able to get along and work together so well, but it wasn't always the case. There was a period in our lives when I was in college and Timm was just experiencing early manhood. We all go through this period, speaking from a male perspective only, when we become self-centered and nothing else matters. I guess it's the hormonal change, the one we can't control and the one mothers fear, when we grow hair in places we didn't have it before, and our voices become deeper. Timm was becoming a man, and I was, let me say, continuing my maturation and searching for my purpose in life. Having a five-and-one-half-year age difference, as well as being 175 miles apart, didn't help improve our sibling relationship either. I think Timm felt I abandoned him. He looked up to me when we were growing up, and now I was away at college during some of his most challenging times. When we did see or talk to each other, my enthusiasm was not the same as his, but I could always make him laugh.

In the beginning, we were definitely on different paths, but as we later discovered when our paths converged, those paths were laid that way for a reason. I could talk about anything, and the only thing he talked about was his art. It was difficult for both of us, or at least for me, because his art was all I heard about whenever we spoke. I guess the most irritating part about it was him telling me about all the customers he had, yet he had no money to show for it. We were very different and certainly didn't share the same values, especially about money. He spent every penny he had and then some. I saved as much as I could and bought things only when I had the money.

Not accepting our differences was our mistake. As a result, we built a wall between us, and one much stronger than the one separating our childhood bedrooms. At the time, we didn't respect each others' differences. Our differences, however, were what made us unique and what made us who we are today. It stands true for all people. People's differences should be accepted and people should not be undermined because they are different.

Even when I came home to visit, Timm was off doing his own thing. Our wall grew thicker, but deep in my heart I knew one day we would walk on the same path. If it was going to happen, we had to break through the wall we created. The only way I knew how, during that period of our life, was by making him laugh. The laughter provided a small crack in the wall, but it would be the only crack we needed to eventually break through it. My dry and sometimes crude sense of humor was always enough to get him started. Laughter is a wholesome and cleansing emotional response. I think it is a wonderful stress release, and with all Timm and I had experienced, laughter turned out to be the only chisel we needed.

* * * * *

"Why is this thing so heavy?" Timm asked.

"Because it's full."

"Full?" Timm looked up from the vase. "With what?"

"Let's see if I can remember exactly what he told me."

"What who told you?" Timm was confused.

"I'll get to that. Ah, yes. Now I remember. It's filled with something 'important to the existence of the human race.'"

Timm laughed and looked at me like I was crazy. I knew I wasn't convincing when I quoted the old man's words. Still mystified myself, especially with the observable progress humanity was making as a result of the Survival Treaty, I remained confident I would solve the mystery.

Timm set the vase on the table. "What in the heck are you talking about?" He then removed the lid from the vase and peered inside it, adjusting the angle of the vase to allow more light to shine in it. Swirling the liquid, he still didn't see anything he thought would save the human race, so he placed the lid back on the vase.

I pulled a chair out from under the dining room table. "Sit down, it's story time."

We both sat down, and I proceeded to tell him the whole story. The old man. The passageway. The light beam. The disappearing building. Everything. People get locked away for telling similar stories, but Timm just sat there in amazement and said nothing until I was finished.

Timm put his hands around the vase. "How is putting this liquid in paint going to help save the world?"

I returned his quizzical look and replied, "I haven't figured it out yet, but I will."

"I'm sure you will."

We talked about the mysterious liquid for more than an hour without resolution. I was tiring but not quite ready to go home. The effects of the time change and the actual vacation itself were finally taking their toll on me; however, my curiosity about how this liquid was important to human survival kept me temporarily energized.

Timm motioned me into his studio to show me his latest canvas painting. At first glance, it was obvious he was struggling. After all, he had started it well before I left on my vacation. The canvas had a gradient blue sky with clouds and a rainbow. I admit he was further along than when I left, but not much; the only addition to the canvas was the clouds. He didn't know what he wanted to do next, and he quickly balked at my suggestion of adding his familiar broken wall effect, saying he wanted to try something a little different. Timm was extremely frustrated, so I suggested it might be a good canvas to experiment with the liquid from the vase. Timm agreed.

"I'll clean out an airbrush," Timm said. He walked to the bathroom sink and began cleaning out the dried paint in the airbrush's cup.

"While you're doing that, I'll concoct the *magic* potion." I looked around the studio. "Do you have a container that holds at least one liter of liquid?"

"No, I don't think so. Why?"

I walked toward the bathroom and lifted the lid from the vase. "I need something to mix the paint and this liquid."

Timm turned off the water, drying the brush with his shirt. "I have some small flower pots from when I transplanted my plants last month. They might be big enough."

"That should work perfectly. Do they have holes in them?"

"Not all of them."

"Good. Now the million dollar question. Where are they?"

Timm started laughing because he knew I was indirectly criticizing his pathetic housekeeping. He had finished drying the airbrush and headed back to his studio, still laughing. "They might be in my bedroom."

"That's a good place to repot plants," I said sarcastically.

"I didn't repot there, I just didn't have anywhere else to put the pots when I was done."

I knelt and looked under the bed. "That was easy," I said to myself.

"Did you find them?" Timm asked.

"Yep, they were under your bed." I took one of the pots into the bathroom and washed it out in the bathtub with soap and water.

"See, I know right where everything is," Timm said confidently, connecting the air hose to the airbrush.

I looked around for a clean towel before settling for one from the dirty pile. I didn't think a dirty towel would pose any problems, besides the old man didn't mention anything about the container having to be sterile. I brought the pot into the studio and poured out exactly one liter of white paint, while Timm was busy organizing his work area. Using an eyedropper I found in Timm's medicine cabinet,

I filled the dropper about a quarter of the way with the liquid and squeezed out precisely twelve drops into the pot. I momentarily thought about what the old man had said about using the correct number of drops, but the thought quickly vanished with my excitement over the potential results. I then carefully stirred the paint with a paint stick, making sure the paint didn't spill over the edge of the pot. Confident it was thoroughly mixed, Timm filled the airbrush cup with paint and gave me an inquisitive look. Neither one of us knew what was going to happen next. *Was the bright light going to appear again? How would it affect the paint?* I wondered, still clueless about the liquid's importance to the human race.

Timm held the airbrush to the wall which already had a multitude of colored doodles on it. He usually sprayed there first to make sure the paint flowed smoothly out of the airbrush. Initially, the paint did flow smoothly but it quickly changed into a wide splatter containing traces of different colors. For whatever reason, the airbrush had clogged, splattering the paint all over the wall, the nearby table, and on a section of the canvas.

"NOOOOO!" Timm raised his arms in the air.

I quickly grabbed a rag from the drawing table and headed for the kitchen sink. Leaning over the counter, I wet the rag with warm water, and rang out the excess. "Timm!" I wheeled around and threw the rag to him.

He furiously tried to get the paint off the canvas with little luck, but did manage to get the spatters off the table. We also noticed a number of weird-shaped drops on the wall; however, we didn't think much of it at the time.

"What's going on? I just put a new needle and tip in this airbrush yesterday. I don't understand why it did this."

Timm sprayed the airbrush again on another area of the wall. This time, the paint flowed smoothly, covering the area evenly. Timm proceeded to paint another cloud over the spatters on the canvas. He then leaned back and looked at it. I looked at it. We both looked at it for several minutes in anticipation, but in anticipation of what, we didn't know.

"Is that it?" I asked, now even more baffled.

"Maybe it needs to sit overnight," Timm suggested.

Timm sprayed the remaining paint onto the wall and went into the bathroom to clean the airbrush. I stood in front of the canvas for a few moments and looked at it from different angles. I didn't see any noticeable effects, but maybe Timm was right about the paint needing to sit overnight. I could wait. I had all I could take for my first night back. Timm rinsed the airbrush and, this time, went into the kitchen for some paper towels.

I put the lid back on the vase. "Do you have a cover to put over this container so the paint doesn't dry out?" I placed the vase in its box.

"Cover it with this." Timm tossed a box of plastic wrap over the counter.

I pulled out a sheet and tore it off. Of course, the wrap tore off from the roll and stuck to itself. I crumpled the first sheet and threw it on the floor. More cautious the second time, I pulled another sheet from the roll and successfully tore it away from the box. I then covered the container, making sure the plastic clung to the entire surface of it and didn't leave any air pockets. I reached into the desk drawer and pulled out a rubber band to stretch across the top of the container and then placed the container on top of the desk where it wouldn't get knocked over. Exiting the studio, I turned off the light behind me.

"Are we going to have our meeting now?" Timm asked.

I looked down at my watch. It was after ten. "What the heck, but I don't know how much longer I can last," I said as I felt like I was getting my second, or even third wind.

"Do you want something to drink?"

I leaned on the countertop. "What d'ya have?"

Timm opened the refrigerator door and peered inside it. "I have fruit punch or ice water."

"Punch, please. Do you have any clean glasses, or do we have to drink it out of the pitcher?"

"Geeezz, Scott! I haven't had time."

He knew I was still giving him a hard time about the mess in his apartment and eventually chuckled as he brought the pitcher to the table with two freshly-washed glasses.

"I see you haven't lost your touch since you've been gone," Timm said.

"No, it's only accumulated for the last three weeks." I joined him at the table. "It's very difficult to joke with people when most of them don't speak the same language, and if they did, they didn't understand my dry sense of humor. I did, however, enjoy the challenge of trying to communicate with people who didn't speak English. It's difficult, but it's possible. We should all work as hard to communicate with each other, even when we speak the same language. I think it would help people understand each other better."

Timm nodded in agreement and handed me a glass of punch. "Welcome back!" He held up his glass, and I pushed mine toward his until they chimed.

"It's good to be home, but I'd go back there in a second."

"Well, maybe I can go with you next time."

We both took a drink from our glasses.

"That would be cool." I took another drink. "You would go nuts over there, with all of the history, architecture, and especially the artwork. It was truly phenomenal."

"I definitely want to go."

I could see the disappointment on Timm's face because he wasn't able to be there. I quickly changed the subject. "What do you want me to do with this stuff on the table?"

Timm pointed at the floor. "Put it down there."

"I figured as much, but I wanted to make sure you didn't have some hidden order to this chaos." I couldn't help but laugh.

Timm laughed with me. I cleared off the table, putting the papers, pencils, and mail on the floor. Timm took the cereal boxes and set them on the crowded kitchen counter. I went outside to my truck to retrieve my briefcase. Timm retrieved his briefcase from the coffee table, brought it to the table, and pulled out what he thought was necessary for our meeting. I did the same. The first order of business was to take care of our credit accumulation register. As I expected, it wasn't current.

"Just like the old checkbook, isn't it?" I asked.

"Oh, no." Timm knew it wasn't current. "You know I hate that stuff."

"Well, it will be a whole lot easier once they get the network up and all of this is done electronically. All we'll have to do is ask our clients to transmit the credit for our work, and it will be verified based on our job submittal we put in prior to starting. It will be a piece of cake."

"Easy for you to say," he argued.

I looked up at him. "Timm, it will be so easy, even you can do it."

"Thanks a lot. Thanks a whole lot."

I put the register aside. "OK, what's next?" I checked my calendar. "Job status."

"Pockets and I finished the Warrior mural at the high school. We're going to meet tomorrow morning to get the box ready for the next job." Timm paused. "What is the next job?"

"I came back just in time, didn't I?"

"Just tell me where I need to be and when."

"Let's see." I checked the schedule. "It looks like a community center." As I started writing down the directions to the center for Timm, I heard a soft rustling sound.

"Cool. I have some great ideas for that one."

I lifted my pen, looked up at Timm, and whispered, "Did you hear that?"

"No." Timm replied softly. "What was it?"

I put my index finger to my lips. "There it is again," I whispered.

We both listened for a few seconds.

"Now I do." Timm tilted his head. "Where's it coming from?"

We quietly pushed our chairs away from the table, dropping to our hands and knees. Timm dimmed the dining room light, and we started crawling around trying to figure out from where the sound originated. There was another soft rustling sound.

"Scott, did you hea–?"

"Yeah, it sounds like it's coming from your studio."

"I agree." Timm looked at me. "What do you think it is?"

"It wouldn't surprise me if it was a laundry mouse," I joked.

"Yeah, right," Timm replied and then thought for a moment. "A laundry mouse?"

We both laughed, covering our mouths as we headed for the studio doorway. When we reached the doorway, we paused to listen again. It was quiet for a couple of minutes. The next sound we heard confused both of us. It sounded like a faint giggling sound. Timm and I looked at each other with dumbfounded expressions.

"What the heck was that?" Timm whispered.

"I have no idea. It sounds like people giggling. Those must be some really happy mice."

"I don't think those are mice." Timm felt pretty good he was able to come to that conclusion.

"You're right."

"That laugh sounded like a cockroach." Timm laughed, amusing only himself.

I raised my hand. "Shhhh!"

We listened again, trying to pinpoint the location of the giggling. I was having problems detecting the location because I was also hearing a whistling sound, a familiar sound I had heard a million times.

"Will you stop wheezing for a minute?" I joked in a whisper.

Timm started laughing again.

"Shhhh!"

Timm covered his mouth. "Then stop making me laugh."

"I think the sound is coming from your easel." I reached for the switch. "I'm going to turn the lights on, so keep your eyes in that direction."

"Wait!" Timm pulled my arm down to the floor. "Don't you think we should have a weapon?"

Before I could say anything, Timm quickly crawled into the kitchen. I raised my hand to the light switch and waited for him to return, wondering what weapon he would choose. He returned with a wooden spoon.

I covered my mouth to muffle my laugh. "Mom taught you well." I was alluding to our childhood, when we were occasionally spanked with a wooden spoon.

"What?" Timm looked at what he was holding and understood my comment. We buried our mouths in our hands, again muffling our laughter. Timm finally regained his composure and crawled to his ready position. We waited until we heard the giggling again.

"Ready?" I asked.

"Ready."

I flicked the switch, sending a rush of light into the studio. We heard several rustling noises which resembled those of little creatures scurrying for a hiding place.

"Do cockroaches run that fast?" Timm asked.

"Never timed one before."

We both stood up, Timm still clenching the spoon in his right hand, and looked around for several minutes without finding a trace of the intruders. We didn't see or hear anything even after moving everything on the floor.

"I don't see anything, do you?" Timm asked.

"Nothing, not even droppings. This is really weird."

"Not as weird as this." Timm was pointing at the airbrush spatters on the wall. "Do you see anything up there?"

I looked closely at the spatters. "I don't see anything except your doodles."

"That's just it. The spatters are gone!"

We moved closer to the wall.

I raised my brow. "You didn't wash them off?"

"No, I only washed the canvas and the table." Timm thought for a moment. "What's going on here?"

"I don't know, but you better do some cleaning. Maybe dirty apartments are these creatures' feeding ground," I joked.

"I'll be more than happy to clean my apartment. Looks like I have the easy part."

"What are you talking about?" I asked, wondering what could be harder than cleaning his apartment.

"Well, if the liquid had anything to do with the noises we just heard and the paint falling off the wall, you better figure out what this all means."

"Believe me, I'm trying."

"Are you sure you mixed the paint right?" Timm set the spoon on the table. "That's all we need is to have paint fall off the walls. I don't want to be repainting murals."

"Of course I mixed it right," I said, giving him a glare. "Check the carpet under your doodles." I was reaching for answers. "Maybe the spatters fell to the floor."

Timm knelt and checked the floor for paint. He rubbed his hand near the baseboard but could only feel the carpet. "This is where the paint would have fallen. There's nothing here."

Timm showed me his hand. I burst out laughing. Timm looked at his hand, and he started laughing, too. It was covered with dust.

"I'll clean tomorrow," he said.

"Shhhh!" I turned quickly, seeing something out of the corner of my eye. "I think I just saw something move on your desk."

"What?" Timm jerked his head up and hit it on the bottom of the easel. "Owww!"

We heard the giggling sounds again, only this time it was more prominent. It was obvious whatever was in the studio had a sense of humor. Our persistence to capture these creatures overwhelmed any sense of danger we were facing. I moved over to the desk to where I thought I heard the sound. A faint sound, resembling an "Uh-oh" came from behind the books on the desk. I started moving papers and picking up everything on the desk. Timm jumped up from the floor, rubbing his head with one hand and assisting me with the other. We still couldn't find anything, but we didn't know what we were looking for, either.

"These are not mice, and they're not cockroaches," I said, stating the obvious.

"Then what are they?"

"I don't know, but they're sly little devils with a weird sense of humor."

Timm looked at me and smiled. "Kinda like you, huh?"

"You could say that," I said proudly.

We cleared the desk and still found nothing. As for myself, my patience had finally run out for the night. I was now totally spent and not in the mood to play hide-and-seek.

I threw my hands in the air. "I'm outta here."

"What d'ya mean? You can't leave now."

"I can hardly think straight, and I still have to drive home."

"Are we finished with our meeting?" Timm already knew the answer and began putting the stuff back on his desk.

"We'll finish tomorrow, when I can see and think again." I helped him put the rest of the stuff back on the desk.

He followed me out of the studio and turned off the light.

"What about those bugs or whatever they are?" Timm asked pointing behind him.

"Did you sleep OK last night?"

"Yeah."

I started putting my papers together. "Well, they were probably here last night, and you slept fine."

Timm put one hand on his hip and pointed into his studio with the other. "Yeah, but I didn't know they were here last night."

I looked at him. "For someone who used to sleep down in the crawl space as a kid, you sure have become squeamish in your old age." I loaded the folders and papers back into my briefcase, trying to fight the fatigue.

Timm was standing in the studio doorway listening for more sounds. He finally closed the door, thinking it would keep the creatures from visiting the rest of the apartment.

"What time are you coming over tomorrow?" Timm asked.

"No idea." I closed my briefcase and finished my glass of punch. "I'll call you before I do."

"How about if I call you. I don't know when Pockets and I will be finished loading the art supply box."

"Fine." I grabbed the pile of T-shirts and my briefcase. Walking toward the door, I was careful not to step on anything. "See you tomorrow."

"See you tomorrow, dude."

I slid the screen door open and stepped outside. "Sleep tight and don't let the bedbugs bite," I joked.

"Oh, thanks." Timm slid the door closed. "Later."

"Later."

After the little fiasco in his studio, Timm was actually motivated to do some cleaning, beginning with the kitchen. He started the dishwasher with a full load and washed the remaining dishes by hand in the sink. After finishing, he wiped off the countertops and the dining room table. Every so often, he looked at the closed studio doors and paused to listen, knowing he couldn't hear anything because the dishwasher was running. He rinsed the rag again, laid it over the faucet, and pulled the sink plug. Next came the dining room and living room. When he finished, he decided it was enough cleaning for one night. His apartment was looking livable again.

Walking toward his bedroom, he stopped for a moment to listen at his studio door. The dishwasher had finished running so he thought he might, although he hoped he didn't, hear sounds again. He placed his ear next to the door and heard the same rustling sounds as before. *Great! Why did I do that? I should sleep real well tonight*, Timm thought.

Timm turned the lights off in the kitchen, dining room, and living room and then flipped the hall light on so he wouldn't trip over his laundry piles. In the bathroom, he conducted his usual nighttime ritual. He then headed toward his bedroom, turning off the light behind him, and reaching around the corner to turn on the bedroom light. He sat down on the edge of his bed and buried his head in his hands. Pulling his head up along his hands, he stared at the laundry piles.

"Tomorrow is definitely laundry day," he said to himself.

He took off his jeans and dropped them on the floor, knowing the darks were in the hallway. He removed his T-shirt, located the appropriate pile, and threw the shirt onto it. Next came his socks and underwear. He then reached for his nighttime sweat pants and T-shirt. Into bed he crawled, hitting the light switch on the way. He laid there for some time listening for the noises from his studio, but he heard nothing. His mind began cluttering, as it usually did when he went to bed. He thought of the creatures, my vacation, the current mural, the next mural, and the ideas he had for his next five or six paintings. His imagination ran wild as he fell into a deep, deep sleep.

Setting The Trap

The next morning Timm awoke around eight-fifteen to a phone call from Cherie. She called to tell him she was leaving for Germany in a few hours. One of the teachers, chosen to go, went into the hospital for an emergency appendectomy. Cherie explained to Timm if she couldn't go, the students' trip would be canceled. She was apologetic for not spending time with Timm the last couple of nights and about being unable to visit him before she left. Having such short notice, she had to make sure everything was in order for her trip. It was imperative she be ready; after all, it would only be her and one other teacher chaperoning sixteen German students for three weeks.

Timm described the events of the previous night, but Cherie was preoccupied with the trip. They talked for only a short time, but during that time, Timm asked Cherie if she would pay attention to the people she encountered, particularly their attitudes and actions toward others. Cherie said she would. They then said their good-byes, expressing their love for each other and how much they would miss each other.

Timm hung up the phone and stared at the ceiling. He thought about Cherie for a short time before he finally mustered enough energy to roll himself out of bed, yawning as he headed toward the bathroom to take a shower. Looking down the hall, he noticed the door to the studio was still closed. A slight chill ran down his spine as he thought of a million bugs crawling over his paintings and art supplies. He decided to shower before his encounter with the creatures, whatever they might be. As he did, he started feeling guilty about not spending time with Cherie, and now she was going to be away for three weeks. Those thoughts continued throughout his shower until he turned the water off and realized, once again, he had no clean towels.

Timm stepped out of the shower and dried himself with the same towel he used the day before and returned it to its pile.

"That's sick," Timm said aloud as he put on his bathrobe. "That is the first load of wash."

He moved over to the sink and ran a comb through his hair. Looking at his face in the mirror, he decided not to shave. He put the load of towels under his left arm and opened the door with his right one. He shivered a little as the cool air swept in from the hallway. As he walked to the washer, which was located in his bedroom's walk-in closet, he wondered if he had any clean underwear left.

Once inside the closet, he opened the lid to the washer, selected the appropriate water temperature, and hit the switch to start the water flowing. He pushed the load of towels into the machine and reached for the soap.

"I know it's here somewhere."

He searched around until he found it underneath a pair of pants. Unscrewing the top and flipping it over, he measured out the correct amount of soap, poured it into the washer, and closed the lid.

He turned toward his underwear drawer, praying a clean pair was in there. Closing his eyes as he opened up the drawer, he peeked inside and was fortunate to find one pair remaining.

Oh, great! These are Scott's from the last time he changed to use the pool, Timm realized and then began to laugh as he held them in front of him. *It figures. His waist is only about three or four inches bigger than mine.   This should be real comfortable.*   Timm shrugged his shoulders. *He'll never notice.*

He put the underwear on and started laughing at the large gap around his waist.   He then put on a clean T-shirt and a pair of his tightest shorts.   Back in the bedroom he sorted the loose clothes and stripped the sheets off the bed.

By the time he was finished, his stomach was growling in anticipation of breakfast. He headed for the kitchen, making sure he was as far away from the studio door as he could get when he passed by it.   The light on his recorder was flashing and he figured somebody called while he was in the shower.   It was actually a message from the previous day.   He hit the "play" button and walked into the kitchen.

"Timm, it's Pockets.   I just wanted to tell you I finished clearcoating and we'll be able to load the supply box tomorrow.   I'll meet you at ten, but call me if you can't make it.   Oh, were you late getting to the airport?   I know how your brother is about being on time.   Later."

Timm checked his watch.   It was 9:10.   He needed to hurry if he was going to meet Pockets at ten.

"NOOOO!" he said as he opened the refrigerator door, forgetting to pick up milk again.

Timm called Pockets to tell him to meet at the apartment instead.   He grabbed his wallet from the counter and then felt his front pockets.   "Keys.   Where are my keys?   Geez, why can't I ever find my keys?"

He looked around the three adjoining rooms and finally saw them on the coffee table.   As he slipped his feet into his sandals, he heard a loud, muffled sound come from his studio, like something had fallen off a shelf.

"That's it! You bugs are dead!"

Already upset about not having breakfast, Timm wasn't in the mood for his new residents. Throwing his keys on the dining room table, he went into the kitchen, grabbed the wooden spoon he had used the previous night, and ran to the studio door. With one quick motion, he thrust open both doors to the studio.

"All right you little–" His mouth dropped at what he saw before him. "What the heck?"

His painting had been altered. At first he was angry at what he saw, thinking someone was playing a joke on him. *Who could have come in after Scott left, and why would they break into the apartment to alter my painting?* he thought. Then he started looking at the painting a little closer. The right corner of the canvas had been detached and was now drooping, and there was a long rip through the middle of the canvas. Through the hole and the rip, Timm saw outer space with nebulas and a moon. The outer space was actually painted on the wall behind the canvas, but from his angle, it looked as if it was part of the painting. There also was a border around the canvas painted to look like granite.

"I've been invaded by an art burglar," he mumbled as his anger subsided. Inspired by what he saw, his mind filled with new ideas and he instantly decided he was going to incorporate them in his future murals. Timm also noticed most of his paint brushes were missing from the brush can, and sections of the brush handles had been partially cut off and scattered across the carpet. He concluded the creatures had trimmed the brushes to a more manageable size. Everything else appeared to be in its place and the windows were still locked. *I wonder what made that noise,* he thought. He ran to the kitchen phone to call me, making sure to leave the studio doors open.

"Hello," Lindsay answered.

"Hi, Lindsay. Is Scott around?"

"Yeah, are you all right?" Lindsay asked, noticing the concern in Timm's voice.

"Yeah, I'm fine."

"Are you sure?"

"Positive. Is he around?"

"Just a minute."

Timm waited a few seconds while he stared into the studio, looking for clues as to what was in there.

"Hello," I answered.

"Hey, you have to get over here right away."

"Now? I thought you were meeting Pockets at ten."

"I don't think this can wait." Timm looked for something to move. "Some even stranger things went on last night after you left."

"Like what?"

"I'll explain it when you get here. Just come over as fast as you can."

"All right. I'll be there shortly."

Timm hung up without saying good-bye.

Was the mystery of the vase about to be solved, I thought. I had already showered, so I was ready to go.

"Lindsay!" I called, as I walked into the next room.

"What?"

"I'm going to Timm's."

She looked up from the book she was reading. "I thought you weren't going there until later." She was a little confused. "What's so important that it can't wait until this afternoon?"

"I don't know; he wouldn't tell me, but something's up."

I didn't wait for a reply. I ran up the stairs to the bedroom and grabbed my keys from the dresser. Back down the stairs I ran, stopping only briefly to give Lindsay a kiss, and then into the garage. "Good-bye," I said as I shut the door behind me.

I hit the garage door opener switch and stepped into the truck. I started the engine and shifted into reverse, barely giving the door enough time to completely open, and off I drove. A thousand thoughts passed through my mind about what might have happened. I didn't know if he was in trouble or what. I again started thinking about meeting the old man, the importance of the vase, and the missing drops from the wall. As before, the answers still eluded me.

Pockets and I arrived at the same time. It was obvious he didn't know what was going on either, because he was very deliberate getting out of his car. As I rushed out of the car, Pockets looked at me quizzically.

"Hi, Scott. Where's the fire?"

"It's in Timm's apartment."

"Oh, no!" Pockets ran toward the screen door before I realized he had taken me literally.

"Wait!" I grabbed the back of his shirt. "Pockets! There's no fire!"

He stopped and turned. "What?"

I released his shirt. "You don't know what this is about, do you?"

"No, not at all. I got a call from Timm this morning saying I should meet him here instead of at the school."

"Well, that makes two of us."

"Hurry up!" Timm said, standing at the screen door waiting for us. He slid the door open for us so we could enter through the living room. "Come on."

"Relax," I said, trying to calm him down.

Pockets and I followed Timm to the studio. Standing in the doorway, we looked at Timm with the same reaction. "You finished your painting," we both complimented him.

"That's cool, Timm," Pockets added.

"I didn't do it."

"Who did?" I asked.

"That's it." Timm approached the painting and pointed at it. "I don't know who did it, but it was like this when I walked in here, right after I called Pockets."

I bent over to look at the painting. "I don't think it is a matter of who, but rather what."

"Time out! Will someone tell me what's going on here?" Pockets insisted.

Pockets was thoroughly confused, and he had a right to be. I briefly explained to Pockets what had been going on the last few days. He still wasn't sure what was happening, but neither were Timm or I. We all turned to leave the room. Pockets didn't see the baseball lying on the floor in front of him.

"Pockets! Look out!" I reached out to grab him but it was too late.

"Whoooa!"

Up in the air he went. Timm and I instinctively moved to brace his fall, but we were met by a ladder falling out of Pockets' shirt. He came crashing to the floor with a big thud, which jolted more stuff out of his pocket. In all, there was the ladder, six airbrushes, a twenty-foot air hose, a fifty-foot extension cord, a bucket of rags, and a six-pack of pop. Fortunately, those were the only items. Timm and I knelt beside Pockets.

"Are you all right?" Timm asked.

"I think so," Pockets replied, still in a daze.

"Pockets, why is all of this stuff in your shirt?" I inquired.

"I just want to make sure I have everything when Timm asks for it."

"How do you–" I caught Timm's look and stopped myself. "Forget it. I don't want to know."

Pockets didn't like talking about his uncanny ability of storing things in his shirt pocket, and Timm and I had promised him we wouldn't pursue it. But, for as many times as we saw him pull things from his pocket, we were still amazed.

"Well, this is what fell to the floor earlier, my baseball," Timm said as he held it up in the air.

Still kneeling, we heard a chorus of giggles come from around the studio. It was the type of giggling heard from little kids when they're trying to be quiet.

"Oh, was it that funny?" Pockets asked, somewhat annoyed. He was sensitive about people laughing at him.

Timm and I both looked at each other, then at Pockets. "We weren't laughing," we replied.

For a moment, Pockets thought he recognized those giggles but could not recall where he heard them. "Oh, and who was it, then?" He was still dazed from the fall.

"I don't know who's laughing, but it shouldn't be hard to find them," Timm replied. "They took my paintbrushes out of the can and cut off the ends, so all we need to do is look for the missing brushes."

I pointed to the paintbrush can. "If that's true, then the creatures are in there," I replied. The paintbrushes were all standing upright in the can.

"No way! They must have put them back when I was meeting you guys at the door. That was the only time I took my eyes off the studio."

More giggles came from the hidden areas of the studio. It was becoming clear these little creatures could not only see us but also hear and understand us. Their sense of humor was also becoming more and more like my own; my kind of creatures.

"It looks like we're dealing with some pretty smart little buggers. We need to beat them at their own game and I've got the thing to do it," I concluded.

"Which is what?" Timm asked.

"That's what they want to hear." I motioned for Timm and Pockets to follow me to the dining room. "Come on."

Timm closed the studio doors behind us and gave me some paper and a pencil. We sat at the dining room table, and I began writing, word for word, the steps necessary to capture the little creatures. Upon completion, I tore off a corner of the paper and handed it to Pockets. His job was to pick up the one supply we needed to set our little trap. He stuffed the paper in his pocket – *where else* ? – and walked to the screen door.

"Pockets, destroy the paper when you're done with it!" I said, as Pockets walked outside. "For now, we'll assume they can read, too."

"Will do. I'll be back in a flash," he replied as he headed to his car.

I then reviewed the instructions with Timm. He quickly understood his role, knowing it was up to him to ultimately set the trap.

Timm attended to his laundry while I lay on the couch, waiting for Pockets to return. I must have dozed, still adjusting to the time difference, because I nearly hit the ceiling when Pockets came running into the living room.

"It was the last one," Pockets said.

I looked at him, still half-dazed and half-puzzled. "Where is it?" I quickly realized I had just asked a stupid question.

"Right here." Pockets reached into his shirt pocket and pulled out a can of extra-sticky spray adhesive. Timm joined us in the living room. It was time for him to execute the plan, while Pockets and I went back home.

"I take it we're going to pick up the supply box tomorrow," Pockets said.

"Yep," Timm replied, taking the adhesive from me.

"What time do you want me here?" Pockets asked.

"Let's try for nine," Timm replied, randomly selecting a time.

"No problem. See you guys later." He was out the door.

"Bye, Pockets." I turned to Timm. "Let me know tomorrow what happens, or even tonight if you catch them."

"Even if it's in the middle of the night?"

"Even if it's in the middle of the night." I stood up and walked out the door. "Good luck."

"Thanks. See you later."

"Later."

Timm turned on some of his favorite painting music and then headed into the studio with the can of spray adhesive, setting the can on his art supply cart next to the easel. He removed the painted canvas from the easel and laid it on his drawing table. From under the table, he pulled out a new canvas to replace the painted one. It was a smaller canvas, shortening the time needed to paint it. The design was simple, a broken wall with a blue sky and clouds; a painting fit for a trap, not an auction. He mixed the necessary colors and began airbrushing the blue sky. As he painted, he heard faint noises coming from behind him, little "oooohhhhhs" and "aaaahhhhhs" similar to sounds heard from people at a fireworks show. Timm thought about looking behind him, but he figured it would be better if he ignored them. He just smiled and kept painting.

About an hour had passed before Timm stepped back from the canvas. He was quite pleased with what he had painted. *Now for the final touches*, he thought. He grabbed the adhesive can and removed the cap. Simple as it was, he really liked this painting, his hesitation demonstrating the fact. But, remembering the mission, he shook the can and sprayed the canvas, knowing he could paint another one like it and add his ideas then.

With the canvas completely saturated, Timm started laughing quietly when he heard little coughing sounds coming from around the studio. The creatures were obviously not used to the odor and/or the over-spray. *They must not like this stuff, and they'll like it even less later,* he thought.

Timm replaced the cap on the can and set it on his art supply cart. Remembering what I had said earlier, he took his airbrush with the black paint and painted over the outside of the can, so the creatures couldn't read it. His part was complete and all he could do was wait. He left the studio, closing the doors behind him and headed to the bedroom to change another load of laundry. His hunger reminded him that he needed to eat lunch and do some grocery shopping. That would help pass the time instead of just sitting around waiting for the creatures' capture. He grabbed his keys and wallet from the dining room table and headed to his van.

Timm would have been home sooner, but he stopped after lunch at a nearby park, shot a few pictures, and talked with some children. Most of the children knew him because he had painted a mural in their school during the spring of the previous year. He wanted to stay longer, but he was curious to see if anything happened in his studio, and he still had to pick up groceries.

It was almost five o'clock when he returned. After parking the van, he unloaded it, brought the bags into the kitchen, and set them on the counter. *It's a good thing I cleaned this place last night,* he thought proudly.

Timm turned on some classical music, and walked toward the studio doors, anxious to see if the trap had worked. He quietly opened the door enough to see the canvas. It was as he left it. He then closed the doors and headed into the kitchen.

He put away the groceries, except what he needed for dinner. He went back to the bedroom and took care of some more laundry, happy to see there were only four loads left. *I might be able to finish this tonight,* he thought. Since he had eaten a late lunch, he decided to clean the last two rooms in the apartment.   The bathroom and bedroom took less time than he thought and he finished cleaning the bedroom by putting a fresh set of sheets on the bed. Before leaving the room, he straightened the remaining laundry piles and turned to look at his accomplishments for the day. He was finished.

He still wasn't hungry for dinner, and he had noticed earlier his plants needed some serious attention.   In the kitchen, he grabbed the watering can from underneath the sink and filled it. He attended only to those plants desperately needing it, watering them and removing their dead leaves and branches. Taking care of his plants was one of the few things he found relaxing.   In fact, it was therapeutic at times, especially when he listened to music. He was definitely in his own world when he "tended to his garden", much like when he painted. After watering the last plant, he emptied the excess water into the kitchen sink and placed the can underneath it. He was hungry again, but decided he would swap another load of laundry before starting dinner.

As he returned from his gardening world to reality, the thought of the little creatures once again entered his mind. Knowing curiosity would once again overcome his domestic activities, Timm fought the urge to look inside his studio as he passed by it countless times. He didn't want to look in there too often, thinking it might ruin the trap. His urge was soon overcome by a sense of accomplishment. The laundry piles had virtually disappeared, and every room in the apartment was clean once again.

It was finally time for dinner, and Timm prepared a steak, seasoned noodles, and some vegetables. While eating, he listened to his music and thumbed through an old art journal, shaking his head at a piece of art he didn't like or quietly expressing his appreciation for another. Periodically, he would look over at the studio doors and wonder if the catch had been made.

After dinner, he took his dishes into the kitchen, rinsed them, and set them into the sink. He decided to do the dishes in the morning with the breakfast dishes prior to leaving for work. As one might imagine, that was how his apartment began to reach its previous state. He'd put things off and then be in a hurry the next day, or get distracted, and the piles would spontaneously take over the apartment; a characteristic I believe is in his genes.

Although it was still early, about half past eight, Timm was becoming quite tired. He actually thought about going to bed but decided he would finish the rest of the laundry. He swapped another couple of loads before returning to the living room where he selected a movie from his collection and turned off the music. For a brief moment, the apartment was silent, long enough for him to hear those familiar giggling sounds. This time, however, the giggling sounds were different, sounding more like panicking gestures. Thoughts of a successful capture entered his mind.

He approached the studio doors, not knowing what to do next. His palms began to sweat as a hundred thoughts raced through his mind. *What if we did catch them? What are we going to do with them? What if they are big hairy things? Should I call Scott? Pockets? No, they might escape by then. Quit being a wuss; they're probably no bigger than a spider...* By the time he had reached the studio door, he sensed an overwhelming panic in the creatures' voices. He convinced himself they were stuck to the canvas but he needed to confirm it. Deciding not to open the doors, thinking it would scare them away if they weren't stuck to the canvas, he knelt and peeked through the keyhole. He moved his right eye near the hole while closing his left one. Peering through the hole, he only saw darkness.

"Shoot!" he whispered.

He had forgotten he put the key in the hole from inside the studio and he knew if he tried to push it through, it would possibly ruin his chance to see the creatures. He quickly thought of the crack between the two doors, hoping it would be wide enough to see the canvas.

"Geez!" he muttered.

There was no gap. The doors were closed tightly together. *Now what?* He thought for a moment. *The windows!*

He quietly jumped to his feet and headed toward the sliding screen door. With the utmost care, he slowly slid the screen door open, making sure it didn't make any loud, startling noises. Once outside, he lowered himself to his belly, avoiding any chance of being seen, and began slithering like a snake toward the studio windows. His heart was pounding, and he could hear and feel himself begin to wheeze. Upon reaching the window, he slowly raised his head up to the window sill.

"Timm?" A voice came from behind him.

"Ahhhh!" Timm nearly wet his pants as he collapsed on the ground. His heart was now pounding faster, and he could feel the adrenaline race through his body.

"Timm, is that you?" the voice asked again.

"Yeah, it's me," Timm replied as he tried to calm himself. Timm lifted himself back to his feet and turned toward the voice. As he did, he quickly recognized the short, silhouetted figure as his neighbor. "Hey, Paul."

"Why are you crawling around that window?" Paul asked, not realizing Timm was standing in front of his own window.

Timm quickly thought of an explanation, knowing he couldn't tell Paul the truth. "I stepped out for a bit of fresh air and appeared to have locked myself out of my apartment. I was checking to see if I had left a window open."

It was a good thing Paul wasn't real perceptive. Had he been, he would have noticed Timm's screen door was wide open.

"Come on. I'll let you in through the building door."

"Thanks, Paul."

Timm positioned himself between Paul and the screen door, hoping to block Paul's view. They both walked in silence around the corner toward the main door to the complex, and Paul unlocked it with his key. Paul wasn't real good at idle conversation, or any conversation for that matter, and Timm was preoccupied with the creatures.

Inside, Paul stopped to get his mail, and they both entered through the hallway door leading to their apartments, Paul living directly across the hall from Timm. Timm arrived at his door first and prayed it was unlocked as he inconspicuously turned the knob. It wasn't. He quickly turned to face Paul as if he hadn't tried opening it yet and waited for Paul to go into his apartment.

"Well?" Paul asked.

"Well, what?" Timm looked at Paul.

"Aren't you going inside?"

"Not yet." Timm folded his arms and looked toward the ceiling. "I think I'm getting an inspiration, and I don't want to lose it."

"Really? Can I watch?"

Timm looked at Paul. "Paul, you can't watch inspirations."

"You can't? Why not?"

"Paul, if you keep talking, I'm going to lose this one."

"Oh, yeah, uh, sorry, Timm." Paul unlocked his door and turned the knob. "Well, good night."

"Good night, Paul, and thanks for letting me in."

Paul walked into his apartment. "You're welcome."

The door to Paul's apartment closed. Timm waited a few seconds before making a move because Paul always looked out his peep hole after entering his apartment. Timm stared at the walls and ceiling until he thought Paul was gone; then he bolted for the door.

Seconds later, he was back at the spot where Paul discovered him. He again lowered himself on his hands and knees, crawled to the window, and raised his head to the window sill, his eyes in the general direction of the easel. He hoped the creatures were still entrapped and the moonlight was bright enough to see inside the studio. As he started scanning the room through the glass, he could feel his heart pounding again, and his wheezing was getting stronger after running back to the window. Sweat was forming on his forehead and palms, while his eyes located the easel and began to focus. He could only imagine what he would see through the window.

"Timm?"

"AHHHHH!" Timm nearly jumped out of his shorts.

"Is that you again?"

Timm knelt, calming himself again. "Yes, Paul, it's me, and will you stop sneaking up on me?"

"Sorry. Did you lock yourself out again?"

"No, I didn't lock myself out again. I think I lost something from the first time I was out here." Timm figured it would be better if he asked the questions before Paul became too nosy. "Why are you out here again, Paul?"

"Oh, uh, I had picked up a few things from the store and forgot to bring them into my apartment."

"Is that all?"

"Yeah." Paul approached Timm. "Do you want some help, Timm?"

"No, I found it. Thanks anyway."

Timm's heart rate was returning to normal again. He quickly walked toward his apartment and went back inside before Paul could start any new conversations. Peeking from behind the blinds, he could see Paul backing out from the passenger side of his car with his arms full of bags.

"You know, Timm, you should really–" Paul said before realizing Timm was no longer there. "Boy, I can never keep up with him."

Timm waited for the building door to slam shut and used the sound as his cue to go back outside. He wondered if the creatures were still there, because he didn't hear any noises coming from the studio while he watched Paul carry in his bags. Back on his hands and knees, he crawled over to the window, looking over his shoulder to make sure Paul wasn't behind him. He peered into the glass but was getting a reflection from the moonlight. Raising himself a little higher, he cupped his hands around his eyes, and peered inside. The moonlight was providing more than adequate illumination as Timm moved his eyes across the room toward the location of the canvas. Fortunately, the side of the canvas was facing the window, allowing him to see if the creatures had been caught. As his eyes located the canvas, he noticed some movement in the upper right-hand corner and focused in on it.

"Ohhhhh my GOD!"

The Dropas

Timm could not believe his eyes. They were creatures, indeed, but he couldn't identify what kind of creatures. He remained motionless as he continued peering through the window. From his position, he could only see one of them. *There must be more than one*, Timm thought. Although the moon was full, the moonlight was still too dim to get a clear view of the creature's features, but he could see it was stuck to the canvas and could not pry itself loose.

As he stared at the "little guy", Timm began to feel sorry for it as it struggled to free itself. He continued his search for the other creatures before noticing movement on top of the canvas. "Bingo!" he whispered to himself, now convinced there were others.

Timm wanted to see more than their silhouettes. He needed to get closer, which meant going inside his studio and viewing the creatures in the light. After only laying eyes on the creatures for a few moments, Timm's feeling of attachment was already overwhelming. It was a bizarre feeling, one he couldn't explain. He wanted to do more than look at them. He decided to free the little one stuck to the canvas, if it would allow him to get close enough.

Timm jumped up and away from the window, obviously forgetting where he was. His body was immediately redirected from its original path as his legs hit the bushes bordering the apartments and flew out from underneath him. He found himself falling head first over the bushes. Instinctively, his arms and hands reached toward the ground to brace his fall. The adrenaline was once again rushing through his body and flashbacks of his dancing days filled his mind. He had been in that position a thousand times, although purposely before, and it was evident from his reactions. His dancing experience was the only thing saving his face from reconstructive surgery, because on the other side of the bushes was the concrete sidewalk, waiting to greet his head with open arms. His hands hit the sidewalk first, absorbing most of the initial impact; still his arms bent, but only far enough that his thin, straight hair was the only part of his head to come in contact with the concrete. With his face only inches away from kissing the sidewalk, his arms pushed up in a spring-like action and thrust the rest of his body upward into a familiar handstand. His hands and arms moved along the sidewalk, helping him to gain his balance. He couldn't believe what just happened, and a huge grin lit up his face. One second he was kneeling along side his window, and the next he was walking on his hands ten feet away.

"Timm? Is that you again?" a man called from the darkness.

The unexpected, but familiar voice nearly caused Timm's arms to buckle. Fortunately, he was able to maintain his balance. The man with the voice walked closer, and Timm recognized the distinctive red sneakers.

"Yes, Paul, it's me."

"Why are you standing on your hands?" Paul knelt to bring his face near Timm's. "You aren't still looking for your keys, are you?"

"No, I was–"

"No, don't tell me," Paul interrupted, "You got another inspiration and figured you needed all the blood in your head so you could remember it, right?"

Timm let his feet fall to the ground and pushed his torso up with his arms. His head was pounding, and he could feel the blood flow out of it as he stood upright. The lightheadedness which followed quickly subsided.

"You are quite perceptive, Paul." Timm played along. "How did you figure that out?"

Paul stood up and looked at Timm. "You're an artist, and I know artists are strange people."

"Oh, really?" Timm scraped away the small stones embedded in his hands as he and Paul walked toward his apartment once again. He had to get rid of Paul and assist the creatures.

"Yes, really." Paul shook his finger at Timm. "Did you know Vincent Van Goff cut off one of his fingers?"

"It was Van Gogh, and he cut off his ear."

"Van Goff, Van Gogh, it doesn't matter. What matters is, cutting off your foot isn't normal."

Timm wasn't about to correct Paul again; he had to help the creatures. Timm slid the screen door open, being careful not to open it too wide, and entered his apartment. Paul was right at his heels.

"I'd like to chat about artists all night with you, Paul, but I really need to get some work done." Timm slid the door closed, causing Paul's face to press up against the screen.

"Oh, that's OK. I know after living next to you all this time that when you get an inspiration, you like to paint it right away."

"I'll see you later, Paul."

"Right." Paul finally realized where his face was and pulled it back from the screen. "Good night, Timm."

Timm felt bad getting rid of Paul. He really was a nice guy, even though he didn't make sense most of the time, but Timm had to tend to more important things at the moment. He slid the glass door shut and locked it, preventing Paul from disturbing him again. The last time he left the sliding door unlocked, Paul came into the apartment and stood behind Timm while he was cutting some frisket film. When he finally commented on Timm's work, Timm cut a six-inch slit in the canvas. From then on, Timm kept his doors locked.

Timm knew he had to enter his studio with the utmost caution. He turned off all the lights and waited for his eyes to adjust to the darkness before he opened the studio doors. Slowly he turned the doorknob on the left door, being ever so careful not to startle the creatures. He could still hear the panic in their voices and started feeling remorse about being involved in my plan, wondering if he had hurt the little guys. He gingerly pushed the door open and began to walk inside. The little silhouettes scurrying across the canvas caught his attention first, but the creatures were oblivious to his entrance. The moonlight, now blocked by cloud cover, no longer provided sufficient light for him to see a clear path. While bracing his left hand on the wall underneath the light switch, he lifted his right foot and set it down in front of him, unaware that the baseball was still on the floor. His foot met the ball and up in the air he went. His left hand flew upward, hitting the light switch and allowing the light to completely engulf the room, while he came crashing to the floor.

"Arrrrrgggggh!"

Timm lay motionless for a few seconds before he was able to restore his senses. When he did, he found himself staring at the ceiling, momentarily forgetting why he was in the studio. Even with the noise and the lights being on, the creatures were still oblivious to Timm being in the room. He pulled himself to his knees and stared at the canvas with an open mouth, now able to see the creatures clearly.

Five of them were stuck to the canvas, a red one, a black one, a blue one, a white one, and a yellow one. Each creature's head and torso were shaped like two water drops connected at their points, but the torso was proportionately larger than the head. Their remarkably smooth and shiny bodies were approximately one and one-quarter inch tall, had arms and legs about the width of a toothpick, and consisted of only one color. Their hands and feet were shaped similar to humans but without distinguishable fingers or toes; however, when open, their hands resembled mittens and were capable of grasping, since two of the five were holding paintbrushes. Their faces lacked noticeable eyes, ears, noses, and mouths, yet they appeared to have similar human senses as speculated earlier.

Timm was not only in a state of shock but still a little dazed from the fall. As he stared at the creatures on the canvas, his attention soon shifted to four more jumping up and down on the top edge of the canvas. There was an orange one, a green one, an indigo one, and a violet one. As he looked at the nine creatures, he realized they made up the colors of the spectrum plus black and white. Was it by chance? After the events which took place to bring those creatures to life, he didn't think so.

Timm walked gingerly toward the canvas, holding his throbbing back with his right hand. Still the creatures were unaware of his presence. *Maybe they can't see after all*, Timm thought.

The creatures on top of the canvas were lined up in a peculiar fashion. The green and orange ones were standing side by side, but the violet and indigo ones were a greater distance away from the other two. Timm moved closer to the canvas where he noticed another creature's body, but it appeared to be suspended in the air without arms or legs. Putting his face to within a foot of the suspended body, he found out why. The light was now reflecting off a tenth creature, but it was virtually transparent. Timm also noticed the transparent one seemed to be calmer than the others, possibly the leader of the group.

The transparent one waved its arms, motioning for others to hurry and confirming Timm's original assumption. Timm looked to his left and noticed two more creatures, a silver one and a gold one, running on his desk and carrying paintbrushes. They were approaching from the can of mineral spirits. He concluded they were attempting to wash away the adhesive from the feet of the ones stuck to the canvas. *I have to call Scott, but if I leave, I may miss this,* he thought.

Timm quickly decided to stay as he watched the gold and silver ones swiftly scurry to the edge of the table. Without slowing down, they leaped from the desk and attached themselves to the left side of the canvas. They attended to the blue one first, one of the two others holding a paintbrush. It was quite an escape plan they were executing, and all the while they didn't know Timm was watching. Or did they? They were very deliberate in their actions and knew exactly what they wanted to do. The blue creature raised its brush to the top of the canvas and extended it to the green, orange, indigo, and violet creatures. They in turn proceeded to grab hold of the other end of the brush while the transparent one continued monitoring the rescue.   Simultaneously, the silver and gold creatures, with mineral spirits loaded on their brush tips, carefully brushed around the feet of the blue creature, whereby it was immediately pulled to the top of the canvas by the others. Next came the white one, and it was lifted to the top in the same manner. The creatures at the top then lowered their brushes down to the yellow and black ones, and waited as the silver and gold creatures once again returned from loading up their brushes.

Timm noticed the paint, where the mineral spirits had been brushed, was beginning to bleed and run down the canvas. Knowing he couldn't do anything about it, he quickly directed his attention back to the creatures as the silver and gold ones returned rather swiftly. This time they appeared on the drawing table just to the right of the canvas. Executing their quick, yet meticulous brush strokes, the black and yellow creatures were freed and now stood at the top of the canvas with the others. There was only the red one remaining.

Again the silver and gold creatures ran for their final load of mineral spirits while the others began to perform an incredible feat. The creatures at the top began lowering each other close to the red one which was attached to the middle of the canvas, each holding onto the other's feet, while the bottom one extended a brush. The black one, holding yet another brush, climbed down the other four until it was holding on to the other end of the first brush with one hand while extending the second brush with its other hand. Meanwhile, the yellow, green, and white creatures had run to the bottom of the canvas and were climbing on each other's shoulders toward the red one still attached. The silver and gold creatures returned one last time and were soon climbing atop the bottom three creatures where they would perform their brushing assignment. Unfortunately, they were still short of reaching their friend.

Timm decided it was time for him to assist the little guys. He took a brush from the can and dipped it into the mineral spirits behind him. He then brushed around the feet of the red one. Being oblivious to Timm's presence, the ones at the top weren't expecting the red creature to be freed as they continued to pull vigorously on the brush handle. Consequently, the black and red creatures were catapulted through the air over the top of the canvas. Losing their grip in the process, and letting out high-pitched screams, they flew over the others until finally splattering against the wall behind the canvas. The creatures on the top and bottom of the canvas all began giggling at their companions' misfortune. But as quickly as they splattered, they reformed into their original shapes. In a matter of seconds, all the creatures were reunited at the top of the canvas around the transparent one and were dancing and flailing their arms in the air with joy. All of them were caught up in the celebration, except for the transparent one, now looking directly at Timm.

Their celebration came to an abrupt halt as one of the colored ones noticed Timm next. "Uh-oh," a high-pitched sound came from the violet one.

The colored creatures scattered themselves throughout the studio. It was as if they had come out of their trance, and were now coherent to everything around them again. The transparent one just stood there for a few seconds and extended its right arm as if it was either greeting Timm or thanking him for his assistance. Timm quickly obliged, extending his forefinger to the transparent one. For some odd reason, he was able to understand the creature. He could barely feel the creature's hand; it was similar to touching the head of a straight pin. The transparent one was definitely the leader, and it was apparent it had brought its band of "drops" to help. Help do what? We didn't know at that point. The transparent one signaled for the others to come out of hiding and greet their new friend. They did so, although hesitantly. As the transparent one had done with his companions, Timm told it he had some friends for them to meet, as well. They all bowed their heads, gesturing they would be honored.

Timm glanced at his watch as he walked out toward the kitchen. It was almost nine-thirty. As he looked up, the last sound he heard resembled a warning cry of "Look Out!". Timm was airborne a second time and parallel to the floor. He had stepped on the baseball again and was not as fortunate as the first time. He crashed to the floor, landing more on his head than his back. Everything went dark. Seeing this, the creatures scurried from the top of the canvas down to the floor where Timm was lying motionless. They ran up his arms and met again on his face. Joining hands in a circle, they chanted and danced around for sometime in what appeared to be a healing ritual.

After completing their dance and before Timm awoke, their curiosity took over as they began investigating his face, darting in and out of his nose and ears and jumping on his lips. Whatever they did worked, although at the time, Timm was unaware of what it was they had done. He began to regain consciousness, but as he did, he felt weird, tickling sensations in his nose. The creatures were too enthralled in their little game of facial hide-and-seek to notice what was happening. Suddenly, Timm sneezed, ejecting the indigo creature hiding in his nose across his chest, causing it to do somersaults over his T-shirt while sending the yellow and orange creatures jumping on his lips straight into the air. The force of the sneeze was so great the two creatures splattered against the ceiling. As before, their drops quickly reformed, and they scurried down the walls to rejoin their friends. The others were all on their backs, legs kicking in the air and arms wrapped around their bellies, giggling uncontrollably.

Timm found enough energy to sit up, bracing himself with his arms behind him, while all of the creatures ran to the tops of his knees. Timm thanked each of them for their help and reached his flattened hand out for them to climb aboard. They did so, and he slowly rose to his feet, still a little dazed from his fall. He noticed the ball in the middle of the floor and finally returned it to its place on the shelf. The creatures danced around on his hand or ran up his arm as he walked into the dining room to call me on the phone.

Timm grabbed the phone, dialed my number, and leaned against the wall. As he waited for me to answer, he set the creatures down on the table. Still intrigued with Timm's features, they scurried back up his arm and spread out on his head and shoulders. Some swung from his hair while others played in his nose and ears. He didn't seem to mind one bit, occasionally giggling himself as the little creatures played their silly games.

"Hello!"

"Scott! Mission accomplished."

"We caught them?" I asked.

"Yes, but it's not what you think."

"Do you hear that noise in the phone?"

Timm played coy. "No, not at my end."

The creatures were sliding down the phone and yelling as they went.

"Yeah, it sounds like the noises are coming from your– Hey, what's going on over there?"

"I can't explain it." Timm giggled as the creatures played on his face and shoulders. "You have to see it to believe it."

"Now?"

"You told me to call you anytime, right?"

"Yeah, I remember. I guess I'll see you in a bit."

"See ya."

Timm hung up the phone, somewhat proud he was withholding information from me for a change. He barely waited for the dial tone, before dialing Pockets' number, inviting him over as well.

Pockets arrived before I did, eagerly awaiting the introduction of the creatures. Timm had taken them back into the studio so he could introduce them in his own special way. Pockets and I sat at the dining room table and patiently waited while Timm retrieved the creatures. I really didn't know what to expect.

The studio doors swung open and out came Timm carrying a cake plate with the top covering his little friends. I could already sense Timm's attachment to the creatures just by the way he was making a big deal out of their introduction. He set the plate on the middle of the table with his right hand on the handle.

"Scott and Pockets, I present to you the, uh, well, the creatures," he stumbled, not knowing what to call them.

"Whooa!" Pockets gasped and leaned back in his chair.

"H-h-holy cow!" I said, leaning forward to get a closer look. As I did, the creatures shyly huddled together around the transparent one. They were the coolest looking things. Timm motioned for them to form a single line, side by side, with half of them facing me and the other half facing Pockets. They did and then extended their skinny little arms to greet us. Pockets and I returned the greeting, feeling awkward at first, but enjoying every bit of the introduction – although Pockets seemed to feel more comfortable. As we finished shaking the hands of the ones facing us, Timm rotated the plate so we could shake the hands of the others.

"No offense, Pockets, but, Timm, they seem friendlier to me than Pockets."

Pockets just smiled.

"While I was waiting for you guys to get here, I told them you were the one who brought them here," Timm said.

"Did they seem happy about it?" I asked.

"Oh, they were ecstatic." Timm tapped the yellow one on the head with his finger. "I also taught them this greeting."

"They are amazing little creatures," Pockets commented, half smiling as if he knew something we didn't.

"We need to name them," I said. "We can't just keep calling them 'the creatures'." I extended my forefinger to the blue one and gently pushed it in its belly. It let out a small giggle. I did it again, receiving the same result.

"You know what that sounds like, Scott?" Timm asked.

"Yep. However, they're not made of dough but more like wet paint." I examined my forefinger. "Although when I touched the blue one, I didn't get any on my finger."

"They certainly feel like they're made of paint, and they look like paint drips or drops," Timm added.

"That they do, but calling them drips has a negative connotation. I do like drops, but we need a fancier derivation of the word, something classier."

Pockets and Timm agreed. By now, the creatures realized their introduction was finished, and it was time to play again. Several of them walked up Pockets' arm, while I twirled two of them around my forefingers. My two little circus performers were absolutely loving it.

"Timm, watch this," I said.

Timm knew exactly what I was up to. I twirled them faster and faster, being careful not to send them airborne. Then I set them down on the table, and we all watched them as they struggled to keep their balance. No matter how hard they tried, they couldn't. The other creatures momentarily stopped what they were doing and giggled at their companions. We also joined in the laughter. The others turned away and continued to scale Pockets' arm, while our two dizzy friends, now knowing they couldn't stand without falling, just sat and stared at each other until the dizziness subsided.

"I think you should name them the Dropas, with a long 'o'," Pockets suggested, making sure he was included in naming the creatures.

Timm and I looked at each other with raised eyebrows.

"I like it." I looked at Pockets and then back at Timm. "How about you?"

"I like it, too." Timm flipped the red one off his forefinger. "That's a cool name. The Dropas."

"From now on, we'll call them the Dropas," I said.

"What about their individual names?" Timm asked.

Pockets leaned forward in his chair, but before he could say anything, I made a suggestion. "I think we should call them by their colors."

Pockets leaned back with a grin. "I think that's a good idea."

"Me, too," Timm agreed, as he motioned for the Dropas to form a line. He pointed to each of them and called out their names. As he did, they each stepped forward and bowed. "Blue – Orange – Red – Yellow – Green – Gold – Black – Silver – White – Indigo – Violet – and, uh–"

"Clearcoat," Pockets interjected.

Timm finished his roll call. "Yeah. And finally, Clearcoat."

The three of us gave the Dropas a round of applause and they acknowledged us by bowing simultaneously. Timm motioned for the Dropas to continue playing and they promptly returned to their activities.

I noticed Violet lifting the pocket flap of Pockets' shirt, trying to get a peek inside it. "I'd cover that pocket of yours. Our little friends might fall in and never get out."

Pockets agreed and buttoned the pocket flap, before flicking Violet onto the table with his index finger.

"Can people go in that thing?" I asked jokingly.

"No one has yet, but I don't see why not," Pockets replied. "Would you like to try?"

"Someday I might take you up on that," I replied.

Most of the Dropas were now heading for Pockets' face. Timm told us how he encountered the little guys and said they had an overwhelming fascination with his face and hair. It was now being demonstrated for us.

Meanwhile, Red and Yellow were using Timm's forefinger as a springboard; each crawling up his hand and taking turns jumping off his finger, doing flips, twists, and other acrobatic moves. Timm cheered for each and everyone of them.

It was Red's turn next, and Yellow quietly approached Red from behind, making a loud noise as Red was jumping off Timm's finger. Red ended up performing a cock-eyed jump and fell head first onto the table, although not hard enough to splatter. Once again, the other creatures erupted into laughter. Red stood up and shook its head, making sure all of its "marbles" were still intact. We once again joined in the laughter.

Six months had passed since our introduction to the Dropas. Only a couple of weeks remained until Christmas, and it would be the first for the Dropas. Like every other aspect of their time with us, they were having a ball with the Christmas activities. They loved to swing from ornament to ornament on the decorated trees, yet they were very careful not to knock them off the branches. They also loved running around and playing inside the little Christmas villages. In fact, they loved the Christmas festivities so much, that one night, Timm and I decided to take them with us to experience the mall festivities.

The malls after the War were much different than what they were before it. The ones before typically consisted of fifty or more stores and a food court. They were always packed with people who were overspending their hard-earned money as they frantically searched for Christmas presents. The malls after the War were set up as places for people to socialize, much like the forums of Ancient Rome, only it was all under one roof. Here, people would talk about the current events or whatever was on their mind. They were especially nice to visit during the holidays when they were decorated for the season, and they usually had private rooms designated for different musicians, bands, and choirs performing holiday music. Food was seasonal and abundant, but it was served from small kiosks spread throughout instead of one food court.

Timm and I walked around with the Dropas on our shoulders. We were quickly immersed into the crowd and the numerous Christmas activities, momentarily losing track of the Dropas, which was not a good thing to do. We never knew what kind of mischief they would get into or, more often than not, create themselves, but we always found out. Passing by the middle of the mall, we stopped to watch the kids while they waited for their turn to visit Santa Claus. As we stepped closer, we both noticed the Dropas playing around Santa's face, once again displaying their fascination with the human face and hair.

"Do you see what I see?" I asked.

"Y-yup, I sure do," Timm replied as he took a step toward them. "Should we go after them?"

"Not just yet." I pulled his arm back. "Let's see exactly what they're up to with ol' St. Nick."

Timm and I leaned up against one of the brick planter boxes, anxiously awaiting the new episode of "The Dropa Show".

Now, the Dropas don't weigh very much, and they are quite good at concealing themselves, usually by blending in with the colors around them. A mother had placed her little girl on Santa's lap so the girl could get her picture taken while talking with Santa. Fortunately, Timm and I were the only ones to notice what happened next, only because we were expecting something mischievous to occur. A fraction of a second before the photographer snapped the picture, the Dropas pulled down Santa's beard, exposing his face to the camera. They were able to do it so quickly and so gently, not even Santa Claus knew what happened. At first, Timm and I couldn't help but laugh; however, we knew we had to put a stop to it before too many parents became upset when they saw the developed pictures.

"Timm, I have to cut in line and get them out of his beard," I said.

Timm looked at me. "How are you going to get in front of all those people? Most of them have been standing here for hours."

"I've got an idea." I motioned to Timm. "Follow me."

We both hopped over the little picket fence and headed to the photographer's booth. We had to hurry because one of the mall attendants, who had caught sight of us, was now in pursuit.

"Hey, you guys can't cut through the line!" the attendant yelled.

We were now the center of attention as the crowd looked our way toward the commotion. The attendant was only twenty feet behind us when we reached the photographer.

"Timm, stall this guy."

"Stall him?" Timm stopped in his tracks and turned toward the attendant. "How?"

"Any way you can."

Noticing what was happening, Black and Silver scurried down from Santa's belt, positioned themselves between Timm and the attendant, and painted a 10-foot high iron fence on the floor. Timm immediately reached down, grabbed hold of the fence, and stood it upright while the Dropas fastened it to the floor just before the attendant reached them. They quickly painted three adjacent sides, trapping the attendant in a small cage.

"What the heck's going on here?" the attendant asked in disbelief as he peered helplessly through the iron bars.

"You just sit tight for a few minutes while we tend to some business," Timm replied, giving a thumbs up to Black and Silver.

The attendant was trying to grab at Timm through the bars with little success. Meanwhile, I started talking to the photographer.

"You're not supposed to be here," the photographer quibbled.

"I know, but I need to get in and see Santa."

"Yeah, well, so do a million little kids. Don't you think you're a little old to be sitting on Santa's lap?"

"Yes, I am, but I need to see him."

"Well, if you really need to see him, the end of the line is over there," he said as he pointed directly behind me.

"Look, if I told you that you shot a picture of Santa with his face exposed, would you let me in to see him?"

"You're a nut, aren't you?"

"Will you?"

"Sure." The photographer peeled off the paper from his photograph and stood there in silence with his mouth open wide. Still looking at it, he reached down and unlatched the gate to Santa's house.

I ran over to Santa, ignoring the jeers from the now irritated crowd. "It will only take a second, folks." I called out, trying to calm them. "Sorry for the interruption." I ran over to where Santa Claus was sitting.

He didn't know what to expect, and I could hear the Dropas giggling inside his beard.

I looked at Santa and then at his beard. "Ignore everything I'm about to say, because I'm not saying it to you."

"Who will you be talking to then?" Santa asked.

"You'll see in a minute, but I need to grab your beard." I reached out my hand toward Santa's beard.

"Hey, wait a minute!" Santa backed away from me. "Why do you need to grab my beard?"

"Because you have something in it."

"What d'ya mean?" Santa ran his fingers through his beard. "I don't feel anything."

"Do you think I would have gone to all this trouble to grab your beard just for the sake of grabbing it?"   I took a quick look over my shoulder to see if the attendant was still detained.

"I don't know what to think."

I looked back at Santa.   "Trust me.   It will be quick and painless."

"Yeah, sure, whatever you need to do."

The giggling stopped, and I heard several of the Dropas cry out, "Uh-oh."   I grabbed the long, white beard and shook it like a dust rag.   The Dropas went flying in the air, some doing somersaults and others doing twists.   Santa's eyes, as well as those of the people who were watching, popped wide open as they caught a glimpse of the Dropas for the first time.   I caught a couple of them in my hand, but most of them landed on the floor or on Santa's suit.

"You guys get up here right now," I told them.

They gathered themselves and swiftly ran up the outside of my pants, up my shirt, and onto my shoulders.   I turned and motioned to Timm I had all of them, and he let go of his thought making the cage real.   The cage transformed into paint, covering the attendant's face, hands, and clothes.   You could hear the laughter from the crowd as the attendant stood there looking at himself wondering what had happened.

Timm and I made our way through the cheering crowd, each with several Dropas on our shoulders.   The people thought it was all part of some magic act.   The Dropas were loving it, too, waving their arms and hands in the air as if they were riding in a parade.   People were reaching out to touch them and showing their children the Dropas.

"I think we've had enough excitement for one day.   Let's get out of here," I said.

"I'm with you," Timm replied.

We headed to the mall exit closest to the van.

* * * * *

Timm was the one who discovered the painting talent of the Dropas. It was soon after we were introduced to them. He was working on a mural, and Pockets was out getting lunch. Some of the Dropas were playing on the mural box while others were actually playing inside it. Timm was concentrating so hard on laying out the perspective of the wall he forgot Pockets had left. He extended his arm and asked Pockets to hand him the level so he could draw his lines. When he didn't receive it, he asked again. The level was placed in his hand, and he began marking his lines.

Moments later, Pockets had returned with their lunch and asked Timm who lent him the level. Timm explained he thought Pockets had given it to him, but Pockets pulled the original one out of his shirt pocket.   Timm became confused and because his concentration had been interrupted, the level turned to paint and splashed to the ground, splattering everywhere. Timm had a feeling he knew the level's origin. He turned to the Dropas and asked for another level. Before his and Pockets' eyes, Black and White had painted another level and all the Dropas handed it to him. Timm then forced himself to believe it wasn't real, producing the same result. He figured the Dropas were able to paint whatever they wanted, whenever they wanted, and as fast as they wanted. And whatever they painted became real if the person using it completely believed it was real. The Dropas also demonstrated their ability to clean up paint spills, soaking up the splattered paint like sponges.

* * * * *

As we exited the mall, we noticed it had started to snow. Timm and I looked at each other and nodded. "Snowriding" was the Dropas' favorite winter activity. They would climb to a high place, a roof or a tree, and "catch" a snowflake much like a surfer would catch a wave. Some of them liked to ride a single snowflake all the way to the ground. Others preferred a good slalom on the flakes, either jumping or swinging from flake to flake. No matter their preference, they had a blast, and we had just as much fun watching them, although we were jealous we couldn't participate.

We told the Dropas they could ride for a few minutes before we had to leave. It could only be for a few minutes, because similar to normal paint, the Dropas couldn't be exposed to cold temperatures for very long. Although the time was short, they welcomed the opportunity to get in a little snowriding whenever they could. Timm and I headed for the nearest light post, the tallest structure in the parking lot, which they used as their snowflake lift. It also gave us enough light to watch their performances.

Off our shoulders they sprang and up the post they ran. They'd get about halfway up the post and then catch a flake. Luckily, it wasn't very windy which kept them close to their take-off point. After about five minutes, we informed them it would be their last ride. As each of them landed, they quickly ran up our clothes and sat on our shoulders underneath our heavy coats.

While we waited for Blue to finish its descent, we noticed a car whose driver was looking for a parking spot. Blue was in no danger until a small gust of wind carried it into the car's path. Timm and I knew we couldn't jump in front of the car and we heard the other Dropas blurt out their familiar "uh-oh" followed by a chorus of giggles. We thought the Dropas would save their companion by painting something, a road barrier perhaps, but they remained on our shoulders giggling.   All we could do was watch and hope the car would find a parking spot and quickly turn into it before hitting Blue. Unfortunately, the row was full, putting Blue and the car on a collision course. The other Dropas, who were now on the outside of our coats, put their hands over their faces as Blue hit the ground. Just as it did, the left, front tire rolled over the top of Blue, followed by the rear one.

Our hearts sank as we ran over to the flattened Blue, thinking the worst. When we reached it, Timm and I knelt to get a closer look at the poor guy. As we did, Blue popped up, causing us to fall backwards and causing the Dropas to fly off our backs and onto the wet pavement. Once again, they were laughing hysterically at their companion's mishap, lying on their backs and waving their arms and legs in the air. It didn't matter how many times this happened to one of the Dropas, the others would find it hysterical. We sat up and laughed with them. Blue was about three times its normal width and height, as thin as a piece of paper, and had tread marks running up it.

While we were busy laughing, Blue quickly began reshaping itself. People probably thought Timm and I were crazy, sitting there on the wet, snowy pavement of the mall parking lot laughing our heads off, but we didn't care. Blue was finally able to pop its head and body back to its original shape. It then shook its body like a wet dog to get all of the moisture off itself. Timm and I extended our arms so Blue and the other Dropas could crawl back up to the warmth of our shoulders, and we headed to the van. We could tell the Dropas were getting cold because they huddled together inside our coats to absorb our body heat.

Timm and I sat in the van as we waited for it to warm. We were shivering a little ourselves, so we knew the Dropas had to be cold as well. While we sat there, we talked, as so often we did, about the memorable Christmases we had when we were kids.

* * * * *

We knew Mom and Dad struggled throughout the years to try and make ends meet. Dad was working seven days a week trying to bring in enough income to pay the bills and provide the family with the necessities of life. Meanwhile, Mom made sure everything was in order at the house, especially us kids. But as they struggled, they always made sure our Christmases were special. The house was beautifully decorated, many times taking several weekends to complete – I never saw a house decorated like ours. And Christmas music always played in the background, usually starting as soon as the decorations came down from the attic, shortly after Thanksgiving.

On Christmas morning, we would wake up early, discovering Santa had arrived while we had been asleep. The cookies and milk were gone, and in their place were many of the gifts we wished for during the year. After quietly sorting the presents into appropriate piles, snacking on the goodies left in our stockings, and running out of patience, we would wake up Mom and Dad so we could open our gifts. Our present-opening activity was typically followed by a large, homemade breakfast, usually eggs, bacon, sausage, muffins, and the like, while the topic of conversation always revolved around the gifts we received. After breakfast, we would put on one of our new outfits before riding to our grandparents, where the same events would happen all over again. And for us, it happened to be "over the river and through the woods".

As I grew older, the true sense of giving was always embedded in my mind. I really didn't care if I received any gifts, knowing the real joy for me was celebrating Christmas with family and friends. What brought a smile to my face was seeing everyone open the gifts I gave them, whether it was something they wanted or something they needed.

Over the years, the true sense of giving disappeared. Christmas became more commercialized and started, in many stores, right after Halloween. Seldom were kids taught the meaning of giving, but rather that of receiving, asking for everything and throwing tantrums when they didn't get what they wanted. Until after the War, the true meaning of giving had been lost.

* * * * *

Timm was about to put the van in reverse when I grabbed his arm. "Wait! We can't leave yet."

"What d'ya mean?" Timm replied as he took his hand off the gearshift.

"We were so caught up in de-Droping Santa Claus we forgot to pick up the homemade cider," I reminded him.

"You're right."

We turned to each other with concerned looks. We knew going back into the mall would most likely create another adventure with our little friends.

"Do you want me to stay in the van with them?" I asked.

"No. I think they learned their lesson from earlier," Timm replied. "Maybe they'll be too cold from snowriding to get into any trouble."

"Well, let's go then before they warm up." I jumped out of the van.

Timm turned off the engine, and we headed back toward the mall. Inside, we quickly made our way toward the cider kiosk. I took a peek under my coat to see if the Dropas were still cold.

"Uh, Timm?" I said in a troubled voice.

Timm rolled his eyes. "I don't think I want to hear this."

"Learned their lesson, eh?"

Timm looked under his coat. "Geez, where did they disappear to now?"

"Let's hurry up and get the cider. I don't want to come in here a third time with those guys."

We each picked up two gallons of cider and then retraced our path from the mall entrance.

"Where do you think they may have gone this time?" Timm asked.

"I have a pretty good idea." I headed for a small group of food kiosks. "Follow me."

"Where?"

"Think about it." I picked up the pace. "They were cold when we came back in here, right?"

"Right," Timm agreed.

"Remember passing anything which might have warmed them up in a hurry?"

Timm thought for a moment. "No, not rea– Wait a minute." He lifted his nose in the air as he caught the scent of freshly popped popcorn.

"Bingo, let's get going," I said.

Timm and I ran to the popcorn kiosk. We knew how much the Dropas loved sitting on the edge of my popcorn maker, waiting for the kernels to pop. As they did, they would catch a freshly popped kernel in mid-flight and fly through the air on it. However, there was one major difference: mine was an air popper. The one we passed had kernels falling out of a hot pan and was encased with plastic sides. The heat in that particular popper would be too much for the Dropas to handle if they stayed in it too long. We finally reached the popcorn kiosk but saw no signs of the Dropas inside the popper.

"Can I help you, sir?" the popcorn server asked.

"Unfortunately, I don't think so," Timm replied.

Suddenly, Timm and I heard a high-pitched scream come from two kiosks away and turned in time to see a ball of cotton candy flying through the air. We darted toward the falling candy, almost knocking a few people over in the process. I reached down and picked up the candy before anyone else could, while Timm tried to calm down the woman who had discovered our friends. As I spun the stick holding the cotton candy, I found the cause of the woman's scream. Red and Orange were tangled up in the candy like flies caught in a spider's web.

"Come on, we have to get the rest of them!" I yelled to Timm.

"Right behind you."

"Hey, my candy!" the woman yelled.

"Follow us, and we'll get you another one," Timm promised.

We reached the cotton candy kiosk where I grabbed a paper stick and twirled it inside the candy maker, while Timm explained to the cart attendant what we were doing. This was by far the worst of their antics. Even Clearcoat was involved in this escapade. It took three sticks to retrieve all of the Dropas and, as promised, we also had a candy stick made up for the woman.

"Well, this is one way to keep them out of trouble," I said as we headed to the van for the last time.

The Dropas were so intertwined in the sugar strings they couldn't move. It took the four of us – Lindsay and Cherie were waiting for us at my house – a few hours to get them cleaned up after their little adventure in the mall, but as each one became clean, they assisted us in cleaning the others. They apologized repeatedly for the trouble they had caused and promised to stay away from cotton candy. After we finished, we decided to let the Dropas do what they had originally intended to do when they left us the second time. I pulled out the air popper, loaded it up with seeds and turned it on. The Dropas lined the side and anxiously waited to board their kernels. We all watched the air show, drinking hot apple cider and listening to Christmas music. The evening was filled with Christmas spirit.

Darkened Skies

Winter and spring had come and gone, and the warm days of summer were upon us once again. The Dropas had adjusted quite well to our world while forming a strong bond with Timm, Pockets, and myself. Being with Timm almost everyday, their bond with him was the strongest. Sharing the same unequivocal love of art, without a doubt, played a major role. It was incredible to watch them create together. Timm's artwork had progressed to an even more magnificent blend of color, creativity, beauty, and realism – bringing out his inner soul. His art also reflected the influence of the Dropas, their time period, and their place of origin.

Strangely enough, the Dropas also had a unique attachment to Pockets. It's hard to explain and I couldn't substantiate my intuition, but I sensed Pockets and the Dropas already knew each other. I never approached Pockets regarding the matter, but I kept my senses alert. The thought of the Dropas being time travelers had occurred to me on several occasions, but I really had nothing to base it on other than my intuition. Timm and I wanted to know more about the Dropas – where they came from and most importantly, why they were here. Unable to completely understand their gibberish left many questions unanswered.

In addition to his friendship with the Dropas, Timm had also acquired quite a following over the past year. People were now traveling from all over the world to view his murals. As countries continued rebuilding, Timm was being asked to bring his art to them, helping to put the finishing touches in, and around, their new buildings. Once our summer schedule was complete, we would embark on our first international trip.

During the first half of that year, Timm's art seemed to be one of the few things keeping people happy. The return of the gloom and negativity surrounding people began about the time I arrived home from Greece, although it probably started before then. The concerns Timm and Pockets had about people's attitudes changing back to the way they were prior to the War was what focused my attention toward the issue. It was reconfirmed when Cherie returned from her trip to Germany, and over the last year the situation had only worsened. A large number of people's attitudes had turned negative, including some of our closest friends. Word leaked out about the ForLords regaining strength in numbers, a real concern for the GGB and everyone else. Frequent, unexplained deaths were occurring everywhere and, coincidentally, many of them happened near people whose attitudes had changed for the worse.

It was hard to understand why, because all of the provisions defined in the Survival Treaty, with the exception of one, were being successfully carried out as planned, far better than anyone could have envisioned.

Over the previous twelve months, there had been a growing concern about the amount of pollutants entering the atmosphere. It was only in recent weeks a cloud blanket formed around the planet, only a few miles above the ground. This cloud covering obstructed everyone's view of the sun and diminished the amount of its warmth, brightness, and energy which normally reached the surface. The cloud blanket was an abnormal phenomenon of an unidentifiable pollutant and of unknown origin. Fortunately, life-supporting rays were still able to penetrate the cloud blanket, although at a reduced level. The gloominess, however, was constant.

A number of scientists believed it was a delayed effect from the nuclear fallout of the War. Others, like myself, believed it was caused by something else. On the surface, there was little relationship between the recent attitude change and the environmental concerns. I wasn't convinced of the scientists' findings and decided to investigate the matter after a good friend of mine, William "Willie" Johnson, our GGB regional liaison, told me about an incident which happened a month earlier along Barrow's Ridge, which is located in the Rocky Mountain Range.

According to Willie, a tremendous amount of activity, involving numerous ForLords, was occurring on the West side of the ridge. Everyone knew ForLords still existed, avoiding capture during the War, but no one knew how many or where they were hiding. News spread stating the remaining ForLords had initiated a movement to retrieve what they believed originally belonged to them before the War and before the Survival Treaty was implemented. Based on intelligence information and a fair amount of speculation, the ForLords were growing in masses and organizing somewhere in the States. The increase in ForLord strength and the timing of people's attitude changes led me to believe the ForLords had a weapon capable of causing this "brainwashing" effect. I also believed the weapon was only available in small quantities and the effects could be resisted; otherwise, everyone would have fallen victim.

The GGB became aware of a possible central location when several ForLords were caught stealing large amounts of toxic and ozone-damaging chemicals from a disposal facility near Barrow's Ridge. During the War, those chemicals were used to manufacture highly destructive, chemical bombs. The bombs would explode on impact, delivering chemical spray in all directions and eventually disintegrating everything it touched. Although the bombs were effective, they weren't considered viable weapons during the War because they took too long to destroy what was in their path. Instead, they were used more frequently in hit-and-run, terrorist attacks.

After intense interrogation, a ForLord named, Carl, finally surrendered vital information pertaining to the final destination of those chemicals. Carl described the destination as a facility located at the foot of the mountain range. Not aware of any active facility in the area, the GGB immediately ordered a team to investigate the site. Fifty investigators were driven to a position about ten miles from the facility.

Anticipating a trap, the team members were equipped with immobilizers, the only weapon allowed after the War. Its primary use was to aid in the capture of Survival Obstructers, mostly ForLords. Immobilizers shot an energy beam which paralyzed any organic substance it hit. A mobilizer was the only instrument capable of reversing the paralysis. It was usually carried on a different part of the user's clothing in the event the immobilizers had been confiscated by Obstructers.

Arriving at the site, the investigators encountered a wide canyon, two hundred feet across and one hundred feet deep, with a shallow stream of chemicals flowing along the bottom. It was exactly as Carl had told them. The canyon was not intended to be crossed; however, the GGB investigators, knowing conventional methods were impossible, were equipped with special equipment to cross it.

From their position, the investigators saw a large wall about two miles away which they presumed was the front of the facility. Using binoculars, they couldn't see any pollutants entering the atmosphere from behind the walls; however, their heat sensors detected gases being emitted into the air. It appeared the pollutants were invisible at normal temperatures, making their origin virtually undetectable.

The seemingly well-prepared investigators immediately broke up into four groups of twelve. Two investigators remained on the west, or near side of the canyon and set up a communication base. They were ordered to observe the events taking place, assist the other investigators, and report details of the mission to the GGB in the event something went wrong.

One of the lead investigators retrieved a launching gun from his vehicle. The gun was loaded with a carbide stake containing an eyelet near the blunt end of it. The top of the barrel was slotted, allowing the eyelet to be exposed. With one end of a long rope attached to the eyelet, the stake was then fired into the far canyon wall. The other end of the rope was anchored to the ground on the near side. This procedure was repeated three times, each rope spaced about twenty feet apart.

Ten members from each team had crossed the canyon when one of the investigators noticed several airborne objects approaching them. Carl failed to warn them of any such objects, and it became clear why he was so eager to reveal the location of the facility. The eight investigators still crossing, hurried to make it to the far side, while the others scrambled for cover behind some large rocks. The objects were approaching rapidly, and the two investigators standing guard had a clear view of them. They described the objects as being autonomous and shaped in a long, narrow, cylindrical fashion. They ranged in length from approximately four to twelve feet and were no more than two feet in diameter. Their propulsion systems were located on top of the cylinders. They each had one rear wing and a wing on each side. The nose of each aircraft had the appearance of an airbrush nozzle, and the underside carried a minimum of four bombs. The six aircraft flew in a distinct formation: three four-footers in the front, a six-footer in the middle, and two twelve-footers in the back.

Flying swiftly toward their targets, the aircraft were within range of the immobilizers. Forty immobilizer beams fired simultaneously. Composed of inorganic materials, the aircraft were unaffected. The investigators, now completely defenseless, were only witnesses to their demise. The front four aircraft headed directly for the investigators still crossing the canyon. In unison, each aircraft fired a chemical stream toward the ends of the ropes and then released from formation. They did so before crossing the canyon, ignoring the two investigators on the near side. The ropes split, sending the eight investigators slamming into the near wall. Upon impact, six of the investigators immediately lost grip of their ropes, and they painfully slid down the sides of the wall, eventually splashing into the chemical stream. The two investigators who survived the impact, shattered every bone in their legs. The excruciating pain eventually drained the strength from their hands, sending both to perish with the others. Momentary screams echoed throughout the canyon as their disintegrating bodies quickly vanished into the relentless stream of chemicals. The two helpless men on the near side could only stand and watch in astonishment.

On the far side of the canyon, the two twelve-foot aircraft continued the assault, releasing four bombs from underneath their fuselages. The bombs exploded on impact, emitting a chemical spray which disintegrated everything in its path.   These bombs were different than those originally designed for the War, disintegrating targets almost instantly. Unlike the eight who perished in the canyon, the other investigators died a painless death as the chemical paralyzed them before vaporization. Those who escaped the first onslaught were met by the six-foot aircraft. It released six bombs on its initial pass, wiping out the remaining investigators who hid behind the rocks. Several investigators fled from cover, only to be overtaken by the three four-foot aircraft. The pursuing aircraft zeroed in on their targets and unleashed another shower of chemical streams, quickly wiping out the fleeing investigators. The six-foot aircraft made another pass, releasing another barrage of chemical bombs. Within sixty seconds, the forty-eight investigators had been eliminated. The aircraft regrouped into their original formation and headed back toward the facility, completely ignoring the surviving investigators on the near side of the canyon.

The two survivors stood motionless in shock, their minds running wild over the events they had just witnessed. Forty-eight of their colleagues had been gruesomely murdered. It took them a short while to regain their composure before quickly heading back with their report.   What they couldn't understand was why they were left unharmed. They could only conclude the aircraft were limited to the boundary of the canyon.   Not anticipating an assault of such magnitude, the GGB was stunned when they heard the horrifying details reported by the investigators. The ForLords had given the GGB an indication of their strength and capabilities.

After hearing Willie's account of the story, I recalled my conversation with Timm after returning home from Greece. He had asked me if I remembered a newspaper article printed several years before the War. It was about an artist who was intentionally and ruthlessly sabotaged by a group protesting his work. At the time, I didn't think it had any significance, but after hearing Willie's story, I attempted to locate it again. Since most of my possessions had been destroyed during the War, I visited the library to see if I could find the information I was seeking. Fortunately, I did.

* * * * *

Leonard Ozoney was one of the most controversial artists of our time. His work was either loved or hated. Ozoney's last showing, which was held in New York City about five years before the War, depicted life in the underworld as a glorified place for people to exist after death. Arriving in large numbers on that fateful day, Ozoney's opposers wanted to personally discredit him and his newest exhibit.

The streets outside the Art Center swarmed with people and additional security measures had been taken in the event of a riot. Surprisingly, the opposers did nothing more than shout obscenities at the Ozoney supporters. The opposers had made many threats prior to the show, yet none were realized. Something was brewing; however, few knew what it was.

The doors to the Art Center opened, and the people forced their way inside, knowing only a limited number of them would witness the exhibit. They headed toward Exhibit Hall A, the largest exhibit room in the Center. Inside, Leonard Ozoney was standing on stage surrounded by a hundred domestic and international reporters who were allowed in an hour earlier for Ozoney's press conference; however, they were not allowed to preview his work. Ozoney's art remained covered by curtains and was protected from any previews by chains and guards. Ozoney wanted everyone to see his art simultaneously. He showed no favoritism, not even to his closest friends who had begged to see his work before the public unveiling. As people rushed in from the street, the room quickly filled to capacity, still leaving hundreds outside waiting.   Occasional obscenities could be heard from Ozoney opposers, but they were quickly drowned out by the cheers of his supporters.

The curator of the Art Center stepped to the podium, waving her arms to silence the crowd. She gave a short welcome speech to the guests and then introduced Leonard.

He was an imposing figure, tall and well-built. His hooked nose was his prominent facial feature on his otherwise average-looking, yet pale face. He wore his hair long and combed back, not caring that his receding hairline was quite noticeable. As he stepped to the podium, it was obvious by the cheers that significantly more supporters made it inside the hall than did opposers. He told the people he wasn't going to give a lengthy speech, because they had waited long enough to see his latest pieces. He welcomed his fans and encouraged his opposers to open their minds to his work. Turning to the curator, he then gave the signal for the curtains to be raised.

"And now I unveil my latest art to the world," he said.

The curtains raised to the ceiling, and the crowd gasped. It was a gasp like no other. What went wrong? Ozoney's smile was erased from his face, and his expression was clearly replaced with one of rage. His supporters stood silent in disbelief while his opposers began laughing loudly in mockery.

"May you rot with the devil, Ozoney!" one of them shouted.

"What have they done to my work?!" Ozoney shouted in anger.

Every one of his paintings had been sabotaged by a destructive chemical. Some of the paintings had holes where the chemical had disintegrated the canvas while others had paint eaten away, making them unidentifiable. Ozoney jumped from the stage toward the closest painting and began rubbing his hands over it. Knowing it was hopeless to save them, he turned his back to the wall, slid down it, and buried his head in his hands. His supporters wanted to stay and console him but knew their words would do little to help.

The people and the media were quickly escorted to the nearest exit of the Art Center by the security guards. Outside, the opposers were chanting loudly. The catastrophic news spread through the crowd like wildfire. Soon the anticipated riot started between Ozoney's supporters and his opposers. Even the large number of security officers were not enough to prevent it.

Moments later, the fighting abruptly halted as Ozoney himself burst out of the Art Center, holding his head in his hands and screaming in agony. The skin on his hands had been consumed, and as he pulled them away, it was obvious the same was happening to his face. It was a gruesome sight: exposed facial muscle tissue and even bone. Any additional amount of chemical would have completely eaten him away. The crowd was silent as he staggered in agony from the doors to the top step. He wanted to speak in spite of the tormenting pain.

His voice shook in agony but still roared with rage. "You all thought my paintings depicted Hell. None of you have witnessed Hell yet, but you will. It will be worse than you could possibly imagine; that is, if you live to tell about it. Remember my name, because you can no longer recognize my face. I will return with a vengeance and make all of you suffer for this day."

Leonard Ozoney collapsed and rolled down the first tier of steps. Some of his supporters ran to his side, but most of them, along with everyone else, dispersed into the streets. A few small scuffles developed amidst the crowd, but the majority of the people left the area. Leonard Ozoney was rushed to the nearest chemical burn facility . . .

* * * * *

"The Human Virus, of course," I whispered. It was the first thing entering my mind as I sat back in my chair. I printed out a copy of the article and placed it with the others already on the table. I then tried to piece the puzzle together to prove my initial thought. *No one listened to Ozoney that day because of the circumstances bringing on his statements. And then, no one ever hears of him again. Along comes the Human Virus, a man with no identity, who gets access to top secret information and releases it to the public, knowing the public is already hostile by the current state of the world for which they blame their own governments. The people of the world become outraged. The governments try to calm their people by broadcasting around the world the Human Virus has been eliminated, but it's too late, because the people have already crossed the point of no return. They take things into their own hands which leads to the War. Ozoney's conception of Hell.*

"Unbelievable," I whispered as I leaned back in my chair with an open mouth. Ozoney's statements "None of you have witnessed Hell, but you will" and "It will be worse than you could possibly imagine" rang in my head. *He masterminded and started the War, but I bet he didn't think it would end like this, a utopian-type world.* I was still a bit puzzled. *But what did this have to do with the chemical facility near Barrow's Ridge?*

I looked down at the printed article again. I had subconsciously scribbled on the paper as those thoughts echoed in my head, inadvertently crossing the 'na' out of the last 'Leonard'. I examined it for a few seconds and then crossed out the 'e'. My heart raced as I crossed out the 'y' in Ozoney. It spelled 'Lord Ozone'. *Oh my God. He's still alive, and I will bet my life he's operating that facility,* I thought. I snatched up the article and shoved it in my pocket. I ran out of the library as fast as I could, leaving behind the remaining articles. Outside, I hopped into my truck and sped to Timm's, needing to tell him what I discovered. As I neared his apartment, Ozoney's last words rang in my head again, *'I will return with a vengeance and make all of you suffer for this day'.*

I turned into Timm's complex and parked my truck. As I ran to the sliding glass door, I pulled the article from my pocket. Seeing me pull in, Timm was standing in the doorway.

"Hey," Timm said.

I held the article in the air. "Boy, do I have something to tell you."

"Let me finish my phone—"

"Call 'em back," I interrupted. "This is more important."

I plopped down on the sofa and started to read the article again as I waited for Timm, noticing another article underneath the one I took. It was an excerpt from Ozoney's biography.

* * * * *

. . . was killed in a car accident on the way to the hospital. Leonard never saw his father. His mother, Josephine, devastated by her husband's death, attempted a homicide-suicide. Apparently, Josephine had tried to smother Leonard with a pillow but only managed to force him into unconsciousness before taking her own life. When Leonard regained consciousness, he started crying. The Ozoneys' neighbor and good friend, Jennifer Smithson, was working in her garden when she noticed Leonard's continuous crying.

Jennifer knew it wasn't like Josephine to let Leonard cry for an extended length of time. She put down her garden tool and rushed to the Ozoney house to see if there was anything wrong. No one answered when she knocked and called Josephine's name. She let herself in through the screen door and followed the sounds of Leonard's cry while calling out Josephine's name. When she reached Josephine's bedroom, she saw Leonard on the bed, crying and kicking his legs in the air. She rushed to the side of the bed and picked up Leonard, holding him close to her bosom. Aside from being frightened by the attempted suffocation, Leonard was perfectly fine. Jennifer's recollection of the following events is captured as follows:

"Where's your mother, Leonard?" she asked, knowing Leonard couldn't reply. "Josephine! Where are you?"

As she turned to exit the bedroom, she noticed condensation on the dresser mirror. She knew it was a humid summer day, but not enough to do that to a mirror. The bathroom door was slightly open, and steam was flowing out from behind it.

"Josephine? Are you all right?" There was still no answer. Holding Leonard in her left arm, she walked toward the bathroom. She grabbed the door knob and pushed the door open. A cloud of steam billowed outward into her face. She momentarily turned away, protecting Leonard's face with her right hand, to allow most of the steam to leave the room. When Jennifer turned toward the bathroom again, she saw Josephine lying face down in the bathtub. The faucet was running, and water was overflowing onto the floor. Jennifer nearly dropped Leonard from her arms as she screamed in horror. "Josephine!!!!"

Startled by Jennifer's scream, Leonard began to cry again. Jennifer laid Leonard on the bed and ran into the bathroom, nearly slipping on the wet floor. She reached over and turned off the water with her left hand while frantically searching underneath Josephine's face for the chain attached to the rubber stopper. Water was pouring over the side of the tub as Josephine's body bobbed against Jennifer's arm. The front of Jennifer's clothes were now soaking wet. Successfully turning off the faucet, she raised Josephine's head out of the water as she continued to search for the chain. Suddenly, she realized the chain was missing, and she tried several times before successfully pulling the stopper by its metal eyelet. As the water drained, Jennifer attempted to pull Josephine from the tub, but Josephine was too heavy.

Jennifer gently shook Josephine. "Wake up, Josephine, wake up! Come on, Josephine, you can't die on me! Please! Oh God, please wake her up!"

Jennifer felt helpless. She didn't know how to administer CPR and just sat on the floor trying to think of what to do next. She scrambled to her feet and headed for the bedroom phone, nearly slipping again. She caught herself on the vanity, but knocked over an empty prescription bottle in the process.

After regaining her balance, Jennifer ran into the bed where Leonard continued to cry. She picked up the phone on the nightstand and dialed the operator.

Hearing a voice, Jennifer screamed, "This is an emergency! My best friend has tried to commit suicide! I need a doctor here immediately!"

"Try to calm down, ma'am. I need to get some information first."

"Please hurry! I can't do anything to help her!"

"What's the address?"

Jennifer hesitated while she attempted to clear her mind long enough to figure out where she was. "Uhh. I'm at 24, ummm, no, 240 West Maple Street."

"240 West Maple Street. Got it. Is your friend conscious?"

"NO, she's not conscious, she's not moving, and she's not breathing! Will you get somebody here immediately?"

"I'll get someone there as soon as possible, but first–"

Jennifer dropped the phone and ran into the bathroom. She leaned over the side of the tub and brought Josephine's hand to her face. Tears flowed down Jennifer's cheeks as she wept over her friend while Leonard continued to cry in the bedroom. She could only wait for the ambulance to arrive . . .

* * * * *

"What are you reading?" Timm interrupted.

"Geez!" I sat up on the sofa. "You scared the heck out of me."

"Sorry." Timm sat at the other end of the sofa. "So, what are you reading?"

"An excerpt from the biography of Leonard Ozoney."

"Why?"

"Remember the conversation we had last summer about a newspaper article featuring an artist named Leonard Ozoney."

Timm looked at me, deep in thought. "Yeah, vaguely."

"With all these strange things happening, I decided to do some research on our boy, Leonard."

"Our boy?" Timm paused and looked at me strangely. "What has 'our boy' done?"

"I think he is the man responsible for, not only this cloud over our heads, but also starting the War."

Timm looked at me in disbelief. "Are you serious?"

I told Timm everything I knew or had concluded up to that point. He was just as amazed as I was that one person could have the hatred and vengeance to try and wipe out the entire human population. The fact of the matter was, Ozone fed off the hatred and negativity already possessed by hundreds of millions of people. He knew he couldn't carry out his terrifying plan alone, but he knew hundreds of millions of people could. Fortunately, his first effort fell short of total human annihilation, and if we had anything to do about it, so would his next one.

I stood up from the sofa and walked to the kitchen. "I have to make a phone call."

"Go ahead," Timm said as he began reading the articles.

I dialed Willie's number at his GGB office and waited for his secretary to answer.

"Willie Johnson's office, may I help you?"

"Hi, Sarah."

"Oh, is that you, Scott?"

"It sure is. How are you these days?"

"I've been a little down lately. This overcast weather is really taking its toll on me."

"I know what you mean. Is Willie in today?"

"He sure is, but he's on the phone."

"Would it be possible to interrupt him? It's really important."

"For you, no problem. Hang on a second." She put me on hold.

My mind wandered as I listened to the music playing on the phone. While I waited for Willie to pick up, I noticed something peculiar and covered the phone. "Timm, where are the Dropas?"

Timm looked up from the article. "They went out again last night and haven't returned yet."

"Any idea where they've been going these last few weeks?"

"Not a clue, but I was thinking of joining them one of these nights to see what they've been up to."

"I think that would be a good idea. Who knows what kind of entertainment they've been creating for themselves."

"If they were getting in any trouble, we probably would have heard about it by now, don't you think?"

"You're probably ri–" I interrupted myself and removed my hand from the phone to talk to Willie. "Hey, Willie."

"I'll have you know I cut my conversation short with the Western Region Liaison to talk with you," Willie said.

He was feeding me a line, because I knew he wouldn't put me ahead of another GGB officer.

"What were you talking about, you're next tee time?"

"Actually, I was discussing dinner plans with May."

"I knew you weren't talking to the GGB."

"What's so important?"

"I need you to look up a Jennifer Smithson for me."

"Never heard of her."

"Nor did I, until today."

Willie opened the appropriate database. "What do you need to know?"

"First, I need to know if she's still alive. If she is, I need to know where she's presently living."

"Sure. Let me call up the right screen."

"Thanks." I pulled out a pen from my pocket and took a napkin to write on from the dining room table.

"This might take a few minutes."

"That's all right," I said as I pulled out a chair and sat down.

"Why is this Jennifer character so important?" Willie asked.

As I waited for Willie to find the information about Jennifer Smithson, I told him what I had discovered about Lord Ozone, my theory about Ozone's involvement in the War, and that it might all be related to the incident near Barrow's Ridge. He couldn't come up with any information to prove me wrong, not even about my theory linking The Human Virus to Leonard Ozoney, now masquerading as Lord Ozone.

"Here it is."

I rose from my chair. "Tell me she's still alive."

"Better than that, ol' buddy. She is still alive and living with her sister about an hour from you."

"Can you break away from the office and drive out there with us?"

"I think so. Let me check my schedule." There was a pause. "No problem."

"Meet me at Timm's place." I returned the pen to my pocket. "It shouldn't take long to get here."

I gave Willie directions to Timm's apartment before hanging up the phone. He arrived about ten minutes later. Timm and I hopped into Willie's car and we headed for Jennifer Smithson's sister's house. During the drive, our conversation consisted of two issues; Lord Ozone and the events leading up to the current darkened skies. I was hoping Jennifer could give us some information about Lord Ozone, although I wasn't sure what it was we needed.

Willie also informed us the GGB sent another fifty investigators to the suspected Ozone facility, but sent them through the forest on the south side rather than across the canyon. The investigators made their way through the dense forest, making it right up to the walls of the facility. This is where the investigators encountered resistance, but this time from the towers on the walls of the facility. Only one investigator survived this time, and he described the facility as an impenetrable fortress with large nozzle-type guns located at the top of each tower. The walls were forty feet high and made of stone. Between the towers, ForLords lining the top of the walls fired their chemical-spraying weapons. With assistance from the tower guns, the ForLords totally annihilated the GGB investigators. Willie said that without any formidable weapons, the

GGB could do nothing to penetrate the facility or even stop Lord Ozone. Even if they had been properly armed, it would not have helped, because the facility was built to withstand more than any assault the GGB could mount.

We pulled up to the house where Jennifer was staying. I suggested to Willie it would be better if he introduced himself as a GGB liaison and then introduced Timm and me. Most people in each region know who their liaison is, and it wouldn't look like some strangers were barging in on them, which is what we were doing. We walked up to the door and Willie rang the doorbell. After a brief moment, an elderly lady approached the door and peered at us through the screen.

"Ms. Davidson?" Willie asked the woman.

"Yes," the woman replied, trying to identify Willie.

"I'm Willie Johnson, your GGB liaison." Willie proceeded to show his identification.

"Oh, yes. I thought I recognized you. Hello, Mr. Johnson."

"Please, call me Willie."

"OK, Willie, how may I help you?"

Willie turned and pointed to the two of us. "These are friends of mine, Scott and Timm."

"Hello, Ms. Davidson," I said.

"Hello." Timm followed.

"Oh, this is so formal. Please call me Jane."

"We were wondering if your sister Jennifer was still living with you. We would like to ask her a few questions about a Mr. Leonard Ozoney," Willie said.

"Oh, yes she is, but she hasn't talked about the Ozoney family since the death of Leonard following his art show."

Jane's last comment struck me as a little peculiar, and I could tell Willie was puzzled as well. I didn't remember hearing or reading anything about Leonard dying from the art show incident. It was getting more interesting by the moment. Willie's curiosity wasn't as peaked as mine. In fact, he turned around to leave, thinking we were on a wild goose chase.

"Could we please try?" I grabbed Willie's arm and pulled him toward me. "It's really important."

Jane looked at the three of us for a moment. "I guess it wouldn't hurt any. Come on in." She opened the door and let us in.

Inside, Jane offered us a glass of lemonade, and we accepted without hesitation. She then led us outside through the back door and pointed us in the direction of her garden, about a hundred feet from the house. Jennifer was there, pulling weeds from around the tomato plants. We followed Jane toward the garden.

"Jennifer! Jennifer!" Jane called to her sister. "These young men are here to see you."

Jennifer slowly rose from her knees, dirt still clinging to her slacks where her knees rested in the soil. She, too, was an elderly lady and looked much like her sister Jane. She was still clutching a hand shovel as she walked toward us, partially hunched over.

"Good afternoon," she said in a soft voice.

"Good afternoon," we all replied.

"These gentlemen want to ask you some questions about the Ozoney family. I'm going to leave you fellows here so I can get back to work," Jane said.

We thanked her for the lemonade and directed our attention back to Jennifer, who was now sitting in a lawn chair by the garden.

"Didn't Jane tell you I don't talk about the Ozoney family anymore?"

"Yes, she did, but we wanted to ask you some questions regarding the matter," I insisted.

"Did you believe her when she said it?" she scowled.

"Well, yes, ma'am, but I thou–"

"If my sister told you I don't talk about them anymore, then it's true. End of conversation."

Jennifer rose from her chair and headed back toward the garden. Willie grabbed my elbow and pulled me toward the house, but I wasn't through yet. I pulled my arm away and followed her.

Willie turned to Timm. "Tell me he's not going to te–" It was too late.

"But, we think he may still be alive," I told Jennifer.

Jennifer stopped in her tracks, and Willie walked toward me from behind. She turned and faced me, raised her shovel to my face, and proceeded to give me a good tongue lashing.

"How dare you! How dare you come here and tell someone you don't even know that a dear friend of hers, who was murdered years ago by ruthless people, is still alive! Have you no respect for the dead or even the relatives of the dead? Don't you ever show your face around here again!"

Jennifer turned and walked toward the garden again. I still wasn't finished, at least I didn't think I was, until I felt Willie's big, black hand cover my mouth as I was about to speak again.

"I think you've said quite enough for one day," Willie said angrily as he held his hand over my mouth from behind and wheeled me around in the direction of the house. I wasn't about to try and break free because he was much stronger than me. I could hear Timm snickering, knowing I couldn't break loose. We walked around the house in the direction of the car before Willie finally uncovered my mouth.

"Nothing like getting right to the point. Why did you do that?" Willie asked.

"I wanted her to think about it," I replied.

Willie finally let me free and turned me so I was facing him. "What do you mean you 'wanted her to think about it'?"

"We know, and she knows, he didn't die at the art show. Something tells me she'll be to talking to us again very soon."

"What makes you so sure?" Willie asked.

"I've just got a feeling."

"Oh, I hate it when you get those feelings."

"Yeah, well, they're usually right," I reminded him.

"That's what scares me."

The ride back to Timm's apartment was quiet. Willie's anger had finally subsided and he was back to his usual self. He dropped us off in front of Timm's complex.

"What time do you want Lindsay and me over for dinner?" I asked, leaning on Willie's door.

"Tell Lindsay to be there at seven o'clock," Willie joked.

"Seven it is," I replied, ignoring his remark. "What time do you want to leave for the Bubble Festival tonight?"

"It doesn't start until around nine-thirty, so I figure we'll head over around eight-thirty or nine."

"Sounds good." I stepped away from the car.

Willie looked over at Timm. "Are you going?"

"I wouldn't miss it for the world, but I have some things I need to do first," Timm replied. "I'll meet you guys down there a little later. I should be there before the bubble show starts."

"Then I'll see you gentlemen later this evening," Willie said as he rolled up his window.

"Later, Willie," we said, waving to Willie as he headed home.

Timm and I walked toward my truck.

I stopped momentarily to gaze into Timm's apartment. "Looks like the Dropas are back."

Timm looked toward his apartment. "How can you tell?"

"I can see the chandelier swinging back and forth," I replied.

"Oh, great! I better get in there and put an end to that."

"Take the wooden spoon to them."

Timm started laughing and ran to his apartment. I stepped into my truck and hurried home so Lindsay and I wouldn't be late for our dinner engagement with Willie and his wife, May.

* * * * *

The Bubble Festival was an annual event everyone greatly anticipated. It was a celebration reminding people of the hard work they had contributed to make the world a wonderful place to live in again and for generations to come. The bubbles serve to bring people back to their childhood – the innocence, yet the fragility. The synchronous bubble show around the world was created by several scientists who watched their children play with simple, bubble-making devices during a Sunday afternoon picnic. From those devices, the scientists then created numerous large, bubble-making machines and demonstrated them to the GGB council. The council members were completely overwhelmed by the machines that one of the GGB members recommended a Bubble Festival be conducted on an annual basis in celebration of the Survival Treaty accomplishments. The council unanimously voted to hold the annual event. Each subsequent festival is greeted with more anticipation than the previous because the scientists modify their machines each year to produce many variations of bubbles: variations in shape, size, color, and clarity. It is truly a magnificent spectacle to watch, not only the bubbles but the people as well.

* * * * *

The Sky Is Falling

Timm decided to enter his apartment from inside the building rather than through the sliding door. He wanted to sneak up on the Dropas and catch them in the act of their newest game. With one swift motion, he unlocked his door, turned the knob, and opened the door.

"Hey, what are you guys doing?" Timm yelled, making sure they heard him over the loud, Greek music playing on his stereo.

Yellow was swinging hard on the dining room chandelier when Timm exploded through the door, forcing Yellow to release prematurely. Consequently, it missed its intended target, which was the kitchen sink, and splattered against the side of the counter. The other Dropas were bent over in laughter. Timm joined in as Yellow dripped down the side of the counter onto the carpet. The Dropas regained their composure and swiftly ran to the aid of their comrade, throwing Yellow's spatters back into its body.

Timm continued watching as he fumbled with the remote to turn down the music. He then walked into the kitchen where he realized what game the Dropas had been playing. They had filled both kitchen sinks full of paint and were diving from atop the swinging chandelier. Paint covered the kitchen counters and floor.

Timm pointed to the Dropas and then to the kitchen. Knowing exactly what he wanted done, they swiftly ran into the kitchen to begin their clean-up duties. The Dropas on the floor painted a large shop vacuum and began sucking up the paint from the linoleum. The others painted squeegees and pushed the paint covering the counters over the edge and into the two sinks. After they finished, Timm picked up the shop vacuum and washed it down the drain along with the squeegees.

Once the kitchen was cleaned, Timm motioned for the Dropas to sit on the counter while he fixed something to eat. As he did, he told the Dropas he wanted to go out with them that night. Clearcoat immediately rose to its feet and objected to Timm's request, reminding him of the danger. Timm told Clearcoat he was going with them regardless of Clearcoat's objection. He knew the Dropas were probably right, especially after what transpired that afternoon. Nonetheless, Timm was determined to see what the Dropas had been up to the past few weeks.

Timm turned off the music and turned on the news station as he sat down to eat his dinner.

". . . at least three dozen more people have died from undetermined causes. Presently, there are no explanations for what people believe now to be an epidemic. The total number of these mysterious deaths has now surpassed twelve hundred in the United States alone. Experts still have no clues as to the cause . . ."

Seeking something more pleasant, Timm returned to his music. The Dropas had gathered around Timm's plate, some sitting on the edge, while others lay on the table with their legs crossed and hands behind their heads. This had become a ritual for them – sitting around and watching Timm eat his meals. They were so intrigued by the concept of eating because they never ate. But it didn't really matter what Timm did, they just liked being with him. The only time the Dropas weren't with him was when they were on their excursions. I don't know what Timm would do if they decided to return to their home. He became so emotionally attached to certain things, it was scary in a way. Breaking their bond would be the same as ripping out his heart. I've witnessed it only a couple of times and hope to never see it again. The feeling of helplessness overwhelmed me, and there was nothing I could say or do to make him feel better.

Timm carried his dishes into the kitchen, with the Dropas now sitting on his shoulders. The dishwasher was full again, and he was out of soap, so he rinsed them off and put them in the sink. He walked back to the bathroom and prepared for bed. It was only seven o'clock, but he was going out with the Dropas and needed some rest before their nighttime adventure. He told the Dropas to wake him about a half hour before they were ready to leave. They agreed, and he went to bed while they ran off to the studio to play, for they didn't require sleep either.

Timm almost immediately fell into a deep sleep and began dreaming intensely as he normally did. He dreamt of a faraway place where three suns illuminated the blue sky. Inside his small, rubber raft, he drifted down a river, enjoying the sounds of the water swirling around him. The calmness and serenity were hypnotic, and the heat from the suns beating down on his bare chest was soothing. Occasionally he dipped his hand into the cool water and splashed it on his body. The feeling of goose bumps on his skin sent shivers through his whole body; it was refreshing nonetheless. As he drifted along, he leaned his head back and listened to the wind rustling through the leaves and the birds singing in the air as they searched for food to bring to their young. It was so peaceful, so euphoric.

He was quickly brought out of his calmness by the sound of rushing water. He had heard that sound many times before on other rivers he dreamt about, but not on this particular one. His raft was closing in on a rapid, one he never knew existed. As he floated around the bend in the river, the rapid ahead revealed its swirling face. The speed of his raft heightened as the water underneath began to carry him swiftly toward the white water. He had no oar with which to row himself ashore, for he never needed one on this river. Using his hands, he tried to paddle to safety but the current was too strong. He could only clutch the sides of the raft with his hands and ride it out, hoping he would survive the unforgiving rapid awaiting him.

It was hard to tell the direction at which the water was hitting the rocks ahead. Timm could only see the white foam surging over them and calm water appeared nonexistent. He tightened his grip and balanced himself in the raft as he hit the white water. The unmerciful rapid tossed him around like a raging bull tossing its rider, and the ice cold water splashed against his half-naked body.

Another dip in the rapid and his body jerked backwards nearly flipping him out. The water splashed against his face, and he painfully tried to open his eyes, knowing if he let go to wipe them, he would certainly be thrown into the foamy water. Again the water splashed up against his face, this time catching him with his mouth open wide. Coughing to expel the water from his lungs, he vanished into the raging rapid, virtually blindfolded and hanging on for his life. For a split second, the water disappeared from underneath him as the rapid hurled the raft over a small waterfall. His flight was short-lived when it crashed on top of the river below, sending another jolt through his entire body. Again and again, the water splashed against his body and into his face . . .

While Timm was dreaming, the Dropas were standing on top of the headboard watching. His hands clutched both sides of the bed and his body was jerking uncontrollably. Red, Black, and Blue were giggling so hard they lost their balance and rolled off the edge of the headboard and onto Timm's pillow. White, Yellow, Indigo, and Orange continued throwing water onto Timm's face as he flopped around in his sleep. The Dropas had no idea what he was dreaming about, but the water splashing against his face was what sent Timm down the rapids in the first place. In his dream he was fighting for his life, while in reality he was just a victim of another practical joke by our little friends.

Timm awoke abruptly as he saw himself about to crash into a large rock jutting out from the rapids. Simultaneously, Black and Blue had climbed onto his nose and woke him. His body jerked in an upward motion, and his eyes opened wide. Still incoherent, he saw the "creatures" on his nose and swatted them away with his right hand, sending them sailing through the air until they splattered against the wall. The rest of the Dropas, already laughing as they watched Timm dream, fell onto the bed in hysterics. He remained motionless for a few seconds before he recognized the giggling sounds, his face and hair dripping wet from the water the Dropas had splashed on him.

Timm sat up in his bed and looked at the wall where Black and Blue had splattered. They were busily popping themselves off the wall and gathering up their spattered remnants. He glanced at the clock; it was eight-thirty. He finally realized the Dropas were waking him so he could go out with them. Leaning over the side of the bed, he held out his hand. Black and Blue happily climbed aboard. He brought them over to the remaining Dropas who were now sitting on his pillow.

"You guys are always coming up with something new, aren't you?" Timm asked as he wiped the remaining water from his face.

Timm reached for his pants at the end of the mattress, but they were no longer there. He had kicked them off during his "ride down the rapids". Eventually finding them on the carpet near the foot of the bed, he snatched them up, and put them on over his underwear, followed by his T-shirt, socks, and shoes. He stood up from the bed and walked toward the bathroom, letting out a big yawn as he tried to wake himself. Once there, he dried and combed his hair, still yawning, still half asleep.

Meanwhile, the Dropas retrieved their paintbrushes from the studio. Timm could hear them rummaging around as if they were looking for something. After brushing his teeth, he went to see if he could help. As he walked into the studio, he noticed the Dropas gathering his airbrush needles.

"So, you're the ones taking my needles. I've been ordering large quantities of those, and they keep disappearing. Now I know why."

The Dropas all hung their heads in shame. They knew they should have told Timm they were taking them, but they didn't think it mattered. Clearcoat explained to him they needed them to shoot the bubbles. Timm, still half asleep, shook his head in agreement, thinking this was just another one of their games they were going to play during the Bubble Festival. Some of the Dropas had painted themselves bows and quivers to carry the needles. Timm didn't bother asking anymore questions because he knew the Dropas were eager to start their day, or night as it was.

Timm felt his pockets as he walked to the dining room. "Now, where are my keys?" he asked himself. He checked the kitchen counter and the dining room table.

His search was unsuccessful and he motioned for the Dropas to help him look for them. They immediately dispersed throughout the apartment and within minutes, Orange and Yellow returned carrying the keys.

"It's a good thing I have you guys here to help me," Timm said as he patted them each on the head with his finger, making sure he didn't mash them like the first time he performed that gesture.

They both stepped back and bowed. The Dropas then ran up Timm's arm and took their usual position on his shoulders. Realizing he didn't need to take anything else, Timm turned off the lights, and slipped out through the sliding glass door.

"Hey, Timm," Paul's voice came from behind him.

"Uh-oh," Timm whispered to the Dropas as he turned to face Paul. "Hey, Paul. What are you doing out this late?"

"I'm heading down to the Bubble Festival."

"You know the GGB has requested people stay in their houses at night, or at least travel in groups, until they find out what is causing those mysterious deaths."

"Ahhh. That stuff doesn't scare me." Paul posed himself in a goofy-looking karate position. "After all, I've got a black ribbon in karate."

Timm and the Dropas started laughing. "Well, then you have nothing to worry about, Paul."

Paul came out of his stance. "Hey, what are those lumps on your shoulders?"

Fortunately the outside lights by Timm's apartment were not working properly so it was hard to make out the Dropas sitting on his shoulders. He didn't have time to tell Paul the real story regarding the Dropas, for Paul still knew nothing about them; so he improvised.

"Well, it's a bad case of acne breaking out on my shoulders. That's why I'm not going to the festival. I'm sort of embarrassed about it, you know what I mean?"

"Oh, sure, Timm. No problem. I understand completely and I won't ask any more questions."

"Thanks, Paul." Timm turned toward his van. "Well, I have some errands to run."

"All right. Nice seeing you again."

"Same to you. Good night, Paul."

"Good night, Timm."

Timm hopped into the van and headed north. As he drove, he couldn't help but laugh at the goofy story he had just told Paul.

Based on the instructions given to him by Clearcoat, they were traveling to one of Timm's first murals. He wasn't sure why they were going there, but at that point, he really didn't care. He was happy to be going out at night with the Dropas. The ride went relatively quickly as he and the Dropas listened to the music and talked. Although they didn't speak our language, Timm, Pockets, and I became proficient at basic communication with them. But Timm was by far the most adept at it, after all, he spent the most time with them.

Timm pulled into the empty parking lot of a junior high school he painted murals in years ago. The parking lot lights provided the only source of illumination since the cloud cover was blocking the moonlight. Timm walked up to the gym door and realized he had no way of getting into the school. The Dropas also realized this and painted him a key to unlock the gym door. Timm picked up the key, turned the lock, and opened the door. They didn't have to worry about being spotted because there was no one in the school, not even a night custodian.

As Timm walked into the empty gym, he could feel the Dropas running down his arms. In a matter of seconds, the vapor lights above began to illuminate the gym, making their infamous humming sound. Although they weren't refinishing the gym floor, Timm knew something else was being painted. On the floor under the mural there were gallons of paint, some roller pans, and a pan of mineral spirits with several paint brushes soaking in it. As the lights became brighter, the mural became more visible.

Timm was eager to see all the murals he had painted there. It had been quite some time, and he wanted to see how much his style had changed over the years. The school's mascot was a Dragon, and these were the only murals he had painted depicting that particular mascot.

"Ugh! My work has really changed," Timm said as he laughed out loud and turned to the Dropas who were no longer beside him.

The Dropas wasted no time getting to work. All of them, with the exception of two, climbed the wall and began repainting the mural. Silver and Gold stayed behind to keep Timm company.

"Hey!" Timm yelled to the Dropas. "What are you guys doing?"

Silver and Gold assured him everything was all right; the Dropas were repainting the mural the way it currently appeared on the wall. They had been doing the same thing for the last few weeks, repainting Timm's murals with the liquid I had brought back from Greece. They knew he wouldn't be able to repaint all of them in time.

"In time for what?" Timm asked.

Silver and Gold ignored his question and ran over to where the gallons of paint were located. They pushed a quart can of paint from behind the roller pans and slid it right next to one of the gallon cans. Silver took its paint brush, laid it across the top of the quart can, and balanced itself on the hairs of the brush. Gold climbed to the top of the gallon can and positioned itself at the edge. In one motion, Gold jumped off the can and landed on the other end of the brush, sending Silver flying in the air. They did this several times, each taking turns flying through the air before Timm decided he wanted to be a part of their game.

Timm stood up from the free throw line and walked toward Silver and Gold. The Dropas above were oblivious to the activities below as they continued to repaint the mural. Timm sat down next to the quart of paint and pushed the gallon can away. Silver positioned itself on the brush. But this time, Timm hit the end of the brush instead of Gold, sending Silver about three feet straight in the air. He used one hand to catch the flying Dropa, and then replaced both the Dropa and the brush on the can. Silver and Gold started getting creative, doing somersaults and unusual twists while they flew through the air. As they became comfortable with each new height, Timm would hit the brush a little harder sending the Dropas higher into the air.

It was Silver's turn again, but this time Timm had placed the brush on the can so the hair was on top of the can rather than dangling off it. He was too caught up in the game to realize what was about to happen when he hit the end of the brush in his usual manner. Silver, instead of flying straight up in the air, flew at an angle over the can. Timm leaned over toward the other cans attempting to catch the misguided Silver, but it was too far out of his reach. He fell over on his side, hitting his elbow on the gym floor. Silver was now on its downward flight right over the top of the roller pan containing mineral spirits. *Splllassssh!*

"Ahhhhhhhhh!" Silver let out a high-pitched scream, one Timm had never heard from any of the Dropas.

The Dropas on the wall heard Silver's cry, immediately stopped painting, and ran down the wall to aid their companion. Timm looked into the pan and could see Silver's body dispersing in the mineral spirits. He spread out one of the rags sitting in a pile next to the cans. Meanwhile, the other Dropas had gathered around their friend. Silver was dissipating so rapidly it couldn't even grab an end of a brush Gold was extending to it. Timm reached into the pan with his hands and scooped Silver's drops out of the destructive liquid and laid them on the rag. The rag began soaking up the mineral spirits with parts of Silver as well. The Dropas then formed a circle around the helpless Silver, their heads hanging. Timm could no longer hold his tears back. *If only I had paid closer attention to the position of the brush, it wouldn't have happened*, Timm thought, sitting helpless as the Dropas joined hands. They tightened their circle on the rag around Silver, making sure they didn't step in the mineral spirits themselves.

Timm motioned for one of the Dropas to paint a strainer. They ignored him. Again he motioned, but they were deeply involved in reviving Silver. Similar to their procedure they performed in Timm's studio when he was unconscious, they were oblivious to anything around them when one of the Dropas was in danger. Timm decided to run out to his van. He had a fine mesh strainer he could use to scoop out any remaining parts of Silver from the pan of spirits. As he ran to the door, the tears rolled down his cheeks. He was truly saddened by the loss of his little friend and felt badly for the other Dropas as well. *I should have just stayed home and let them do their thing*, he thought.

In his van, Timm searched diligently for the strainer, knowing it was in there somewhere. He threw aside old sweatshirts, paper bags, and other items that had no reason being in the van.

"Got it!" Timm stepped out of the van, slammed the hatch closed, and ran swiftly to the gym door. With his heart pounding and breath shortening, he could feel his lungs tighten as he began to wheeze. "Oh no! I left the key inside."

He banged on the door, hoping one of the Dropas would let him inside the gym. Again he pounded on the door with his fist, and again it went unnoticed. He turned around and leaned his back against the door, sliding down until his rear end hit the cement. He threw the strainer to the ground and buried his head in his hands.

Pulling his face away from his hands, Timm noticed the clouds brightening up above the gym. He quickly rose to his feet and turned toward the door. Putting his face next to the small window, he peered through the glass toward the Dropas.

Inside the gym, a magnificent spectacle was taking place. The Dropas, hands joined and in a circle around Silver, were chanting as only they could chant. As they did, an opening in the gym ceiling formed, then another one formed through the pollution cover. And finally, the hidden clouds parted, allowing a brilliant beam of light to make its way to Silver. It was similar to the beam of light I witnessed with the old man just a year earlier. The light streamed down, causing Silver to glow, while the Dropas continued their circling and chanting. What was left of Silver's body and its spattered segments began to rise up off the rag where Silver lay. Its remnants rose about a foot off the ground before stopping to hover in that position.

From the light source above came Athena, her image about three times as tall as the Dropas. She continued down until she was floating right along side Silver. Raising her arms from her sides, she flattened her palms and passed them several times over the top of Silver's dissipated body, causing the spattered segments to slowly rejoin with the larger, remaining portion of its body. Down on the floor, the other Dropas continued their ritual, still oblivious to anything outside their circle. Athena continued to pass her hands over Silver's body until the final segments were rejoined. Then with her right hand, she slowly passed it over Silver's entire body, starting at its forehead. Upon completion, she raised both arms toward the sky and lifted herself toward the light source while lowering Silver's body to the gym floor. As she passed through the ceiling of the gym, the hole closed and the light disappeared. The holes also closed below her as she ascended through the pollution cover and eventually disappeared into the night sky. The Dropas' chanting immediately ceased as they gathered around their friend. Silver sat up and kneaded its body as if to put the once spattered segments back in their rightful positions. Then, as if working as one, they began to look around the gym for Timm.

Timm backed away from the gym door and looked toward the sky, following the light beam into the clouds. As the cloud cover closed and the light dimmed, he noticed a strange object coming straight for him. It was floating in the air, and he could barely make out the object's features in the parking lot's dim light. From what he could tell, it looked like a huge bubble. *The bubble show must have started already*, he thought. He also had trouble distinguishing the object's outline but clearly saw the reflection of the school, although it appeared discolored. Jumping to his feet and forgetting momentarily why he was outside in the first place, he stared at the bubble.

"That's so cool," he said as he examined the details of the reflection.

Before the words completely left Timm's mouth, the thought of people's changing attitudes and the recent, mysterious deaths flashed before his eyes. He took two steps before the greenish-brown bubble completely engulfed his body. Struggling to free himself, he yelled for help but knew no one could hear him. Beautiful thoughts began to flow through his mind: childhood memories, first-love memories, painting memories, sunshine, blue skies, swimming. He was reliving everything that made him feel good. However, the memories were not flowing through his mind but rather flowing out of it. After the last beautiful thought, he began seeing images of gunfire, poverty, hunger, fighting, rioting, and war. People were maliciously being killed in those horrible thoughts. He tried to fight them and release them from his mind, but as he did, he could feel the bubble closing in on him. With each effort to rid himself of the terrible thoughts, the bubble collapsed further around him, exhausting more of the air inside. He continued to fight the horrible feelings, while his life was being suffocated. As he gasped for air, he tried desperately to cry for help. His heart rate, slowing down with the loss of oxygen, was about to cease as he took his last breath. With the bubble adhering to him like a piece of cellophane, he fell onto the asphalt pavement.

Suddenly, the air once again swept through his lungs. His heart rate began to approach its normal beating pattern and he now saw himself in Heaven. The whiteness was so bright, but the feeling of eternal life brought a smile to his face. While walking toward Heaven's Gates, a pair of Angels approached him. As he drew closer to the Angels, his eyes still closed, he felt a beautiful butterfly land on the tip of his nose, bringing another smile to his face as he lay there motionless. He opened his eyes to see the beautiful creature.

"Ahhhh!" Timm screamed. Blue and Red were standing next to his face brushing his nose with their paintbrushes. "Where did you guys come from, and what happened to me?   I thought I was in Heaven."

Silver jumped out from behind Blue and Red, holding its bow high above its head. Silver had shot the bubble with one of its airbrush needles and not a second too late.

"I'm so glad you're alive," Timm said as he reached his finger out to Silver.

Silver bowed in front of Timm and then started dancing on the pavement with its arms up in the air. The other Dropas soon joined the small, abbreviated celebration.

"You guys are incredible," Timm told them. "How did you know I was in trouble?"

Clearcoat came to the front and explained to Timm that when they finished reviving Silver, he was nowhere to be seen. Yellow found the door key on the gym floor and the Dropas decided to look for him outside, knowing he couldn't get back in the gym without their help. Once outside, they found him trapped in the collapsing bubble. Silver drew a paint-coated needle from its quiver and immediately shot the bubble, popping it on impact.

Timm patted Silver on the head and thanked the rest of the Dropas for saving his life. As he continued to recover from his encounter with the bubble, he looked up into the darkened sky. He could see the outlines of more bubbles floating far off in the distance. He told the Dropas they needed to pop those bubbles as they did the one around him. They explained to him it was more important to go inside the school and finish their job.   Timm couldn't understand why, now knowing the effects the bubbles had on people. However, after a short discussion with Clearcoat, he finally agreed. It was only then he realized why the Dropas required the needles.

Inside the gym again, Timm thought about the bubbles. He became terrified picturing himself as a ForLord, had he not fought off the negative thoughts or if the Dropas had not popped the bubble in time. While waiting for the Dropas to finish painting, thoughts of the victims who would become ForLords or die in the process cluttered his mind. He desperately wanted to help save the people outside from the bubbles, but his personal encounter had robbed him of his energy and he eventually drifted off to sleep.

It was nearly ten-thirty when the Dropas finished the last mural located in the cafeteria. Returning to the gym, they found Timm in the exact position they had left him. This time they woke him up in a friendlier manner, knowing it wasn't the right time for any pranks. Although their work at the school was completed, their work for the night was still unfinished.

Timm and the Dropas restored the gym to its original state, putting back the paint cans and the rag they had moved during their short stay. There was a number of areas on the gym floor where the mineral spirits had removed the finish. After Timm wiped up the standing spirits, Clearcoat re-coated the damaged areas. They took one last look at the gym and agreed everything was in order. Before turning out the lights, Timm glanced up at the mural and didn't notice anything different about it. He turned to Clearcoat.

"What have you guys been doing all this time?"

Clearcoat replied that Timm would know soon enough. He sensed by the tone in Clearcoat's gibber the issue wasn't open for discussion. Although he wasn't satisfied with Clearcoat's answer, he didn't pursue it any further.

Timm and the Dropas exited the gym and headed toward the van. Once inside, the Dropas quickly positioned themselves throughout the van as Timm put the key in the ignition. He thought their behavior was quite odd, considering they normally sit on his shoulders or even on the steering wheel when he drives. They had positioned themselves at the windows on all sides of the van, opening them so they could aim their bows outside. Clearcoat stood up on the dashboard and directed Timm to take an alternate route. He complied and, as he looked into the night sky, quickly realized they were going on a bubble hunt.

Timm headed toward the historic section of the city, the location of the Festival. Thousands of people were expected to attend at this location alone and with other celebrations going on across the globe, the gatherings provided prime locations for the dangerous bubbles to appear. As they neared the Festival, the sounds of a large party could be heard.

It was ten forty-five when Timm's van pulled to within viewing distance of the crowd. Although most people were requested to stay in their houses during the night hours, this was an exception. Because of the recent restriction, more people showed up than expected. The streets and alleys were overflowing with people and the featured band was playing music on the main stage – everyone seemed to be having a wonderful time. Timm started feeling the music as well, tapping his fingers on the steering wheel as he searched for a parking spot. His effort was interrupted as his van was soon overtaken by the people in the streets.

While the music echoed through the city, the Dropas drew their bows. Timm turned and looked at each of the Dropas whose bows were loaded with needles and ready to fire into the sky. He then turned to the people in the streets who noticed the bubbles drifting over the building rooftops and down upon them. Pointing in the air, the celebrating people began to cheer the arrival of the main attraction. Timm jumped out of the van, pushed his way to the stage, and grabbed the microphone out of the lead singer's hand. The music stopped abruptly, and his voice shrieked through the air.

"Take cover! Take cover! Those aren't from the Festival! Take cover!"

Most of the crowd was confused by the abrupt announcement. Timm repeated it a few more times. The majority of the people finally realized the danger and started running for cover, throwing their food and drinks to the ground. They pushed and shoved each other in an attempt to return to their vehicles or find other means of protection. Those who fell were being trampled by the mass exodus from the streets and those who stayed, stood and watched the bubbles continue their descent upon them.

The Dropas, realizing their position inside the van was inadequate, climbed out the windows and positioned themselves on the van's rooftop. The first barrage of needles flew from their bows. Each needle hit a different bubble with the accuracy of a master archer, causing the targeted bubble to pop and sending a large amount of polluted residue onto the crowd. Another onslaught of bubbles descended from the sky, and another flurry of arrows pierced through the air, providing the same results. The streets were clearing except for those people who chose to ignore the earlier warnings. Still more bubbles floated over the buildings, more than the Dropas had needles. Again, the Dropas hit their targets; however, four bubbles escaped untouched and engulfed their prey. Those standing next to them tried desperately, but with no success, to free the victims from the impenetrable bubbles.

Clearcoat directed four of the Dropas to leave their current positions and assist the bubble victims. The remaining Dropas reloaded their bows with their last set of needles and readied themselves for another round of bubbles. Even the Dropas didn't expect this many bubbles to appear.

Back inside the van and feeling helpless, Timm remembered the power of the bubbles and knew he couldn't go back outside to assist. He knew only the Dropas' needles could destroy the evil bubbles. As he sat in the driver's seat, thinking of a way to help the Dropas, he remembered he had picked up another shipment of airbrush needles the previous day. He jumped to the back of the van, and searched for the box. Finding it wedged under the passenger's seat, he reached in the box and grabbed a handful of needles. He then crawled to the open window and extended his hand to the rooftop of the van. Opening his hand, he could hear the needles drop and roll across the metal roof. Upon Clearcoat's direction, Silver and Gold ran over and began coating the new needles. They passed them to the other Dropas who quickly reloaded their bows for another strike against the bubbles.

On the pavement, Yellow, Red, Orange, and Green had reached the first two victims. The victims' were suffocating as they fought diligently to fend off the evil power of the bubbles. Green and Red drew their bows and drove the needles into the bubbles, sending particles spraying into the air.   Yellow and Orange, meanwhile, ran off to find the other two victims.   Another stream of needles were seen flying through the air, again hitting their targets, but leaving two more bubbles free to prey on the defenseless people below.   After witnessing the power of the bubbles, the majority of the crowd had now sought shelter.

The two descending bubbles homed in on their targets and headed toward them. Seeing this, Green and Red followed their path and intercepted them before the bubbles engulfed their victims. Meanwhile, Yellow and Orange discovered two other victims, but they had arrived too late.   One of the victims had succumbed to the forces of the bubble, allowing it to pop as his negative thoughts prevailed while the other victim, his wife, lay dead on the sidewalk, having fought the bubble to the end.   The man, however, having been successfully drained of his positive thoughts, ignored his wife laying on the ground and fled the scene, disappearing into the darkness.

Yellow and Orange stood next to the woman with their heads hung. Knowing they did their best to save the woman, they were still saddened by her death. After finishing off the remaining bubbles, the other Dropas joined their saddened companions. Timm was close behind, constantly looking over his shoulder and above his head for any stray bubbles. The Dropas had eliminated all but two of them.

It was at this point I spotted Timm again. "Timm!"

Timm turned around and saw Willie, May, Lindsay, and I running toward him. Fighting the crowd, which was rapidly filling the streets again, we finally met.

"When did you get here?   Did you go out with the Dropas tonight," I said.

"Right before I jumped on stage," Timm replied as he pointed to the Dropas, who were on his shoulders. "I told you I was going out with them and would be here before the bubble show started. Only, I didn't expect it to be this one."

"What do you mean, this one?" Willie asked, somewhat distracted by the Dropas.

Lindsay looked at Willie and May. "You guys remember the Dropas?"

Lindsay knelt on one knee and extended her hand. Green and Red, who had returned from their ground mission, stepped onto it. She stood up and held her hand out so Willie and May could see them. The Dropas extended their hands.

"They're the cutest little things," May said as she held out her finger to touch Green.

"Green and Red, you remember Willie and May?"

Green and Red nodded as I pulled Willie and Timm over to the side.

"What the heck is going on here?" I asked.

Willie turned his attention toward Timm. He, too, was more than curious.

"I'm not sure, but I believe those bubbles are the cause of the attitude changes and the mysterious deaths. One of them swallowed me over at a school I was at tonight."

"School? What were you doing at a school at this time of the night?" Willie interrupted.

"Taking night classes," I quipped.

"Very funny," Willie chirped back.

"That's what the Dropas have been doing for the past few weeks," Timm continued.

"The Dropas go to school now?" Willie asked with a confused look on his face.

"The Dropas don't go to school to learn, they go there to repaint my murals," Timm replied.

"Why are the Dropas repainting your murals?" Willie asked, scratching his head.

"I don't know yet, but Clearcoat said we would know soon enough," Timm replied.

Still a little paranoid, Timm looked around for more bubbles. He then proceeded to tell us about his night's activities with the Dropas and especially what he could recall about his encounter with the bubble. He explained how the bubbles try to remove all positive thoughts from their victim's mind, leaving them left with only negative thoughts and motives. He also explained how the bubble collapses and eventually suffocates its victim the more they resist its negative forces and influences. We concluded the woman lying dead on the sidewalk fought it until the end while her husband obviously gave in to its effects. We knew he would soon become a member of the ForLords.

"And hence, the mysterious deaths," Willie added.

I turned to Willie. "As Timm said earlier, we also have an explanation as to how so many people's attitudes have been changing. I would venture to say many of those people have retained bad thoughts about the condition of our society before and during the War.

Willie rubbed his chin. "That certainly makes sense."

"I also suspect many of those people are not completely in agreement with the provisions set forth in the Survival Treaty," I continued.

Timm held out a coated airbrush needle. "It only gets worse. The only way to destroy the bubbles is with specially-coated needles."

I took the needle and looked at it. "That explains our increased demand for needles over the last few weeks," I said.

"Exactly," Timm agreed.

"That's not a problem. We'll just step up production of those needles and make sure they are distributed across the globe," Willie said.

I turned to Willie. "Is it going to be a problem explaining to the GGB council throughout the world they need these special needles to counterattack the bubbles?"

"After what happened here tonight, I don't think so," Willie confirmed. "We just need more needles."

"The needles aren't the problem." I held the needle in front of Willie and ran my opposite index finger along the tip. "The problem is coating them all with the Dropas' paint," I responded.

Willie started to speak and I knew exactly what he was thinking, so I took the liberty of interrupting him. "You are not putting the Dropas on an assembly line. With what Timm has told us, they are preparing for something much bigger. You're just going to have to make it mandatory that people are not allowed in the streets after dusk until this crisis is over."

As Willie and I were discussing the need to inform the people of what was happening, we didn't realize Timm had stepped away from us. Off in the distance, he had noticed a silhouetted figure wearing a beret and a rancher's trench coat. Timm thought it was very odd for someone to be dressed that way on such a warm summer night. He approached the figure, but the figure noticed him, too, and walked away, occasionally looking over his shoulder to see if Timm was behind him. Timm continued to follow, decreasing the distance between himself and the figure. The figure began to walk faster and so did Timm. *Why is this person running away?* Timm thought.

Timm broke into a sprint after the figure as the figure darted into an alley. Timm knew the alley led to a dead end, and he would soon find out the identity of the stranger. Timm continued his pursuit. Turning into the alley, he saw the figure standing in front of the brick wall which marked the dead end. The figure turned to face Timm. Without seeing the figure's face, Timm sensed he already knew who it was.   As the figure approached, the alley light lit up the figure's head which was covered by a ski mask, hiding the identity. Timm took one step and then felt a sharp pain in the back of his neck. Within seconds he became lightheaded and could barely stand. Looking at the figure, Timm saw two, then four, then too many to count. He felt his legs wobble before they finally buckled, collapsing him to the ground. Everything went black as he lay motionless on the pavement of the alley.

Ozone Alert

illie and I decided on a plan for informing the public. We would simply tell them the truth. Because Willie was associated with the GGB, he would make sure the message was clear and accurate regarding what had happened at the Festival and inform everyone what to do next. We rejoined May and Lindsay who were playing with the Dropas. Clearcoat was in his usual observatory position, sitting on Lindsay's shoulders and watching over the others.

The GGB officers had worked quickly to clear the streets of people, except for a few they were questioning, and the deceased woman had been removed by medical officials. Other GGB officers were surveying the area, keeping their eyes open for ForLords. Willie strayed away from us to talk to the officers, while I stayed with May and Lindsay. Only then did I realize Timm was gone.

"Lindsay, why are all the Dropas with you?" I asked.

"Timm asked me to watch them while he checked something out." She saw the concerned look on my face. "Is something wrong?"

"I don't know." I scanned the area again. *Why would he leave the Dropas, especially after what happened tonight?* I thought.

I caught a glimpse of Timm's van down the street and walked toward it, thinking he may be looking for something inside it. I looked in and around the van before I noticed a limousine-type vehicle driving toward me. The limousine had a distinct sound to it, one I hadn't heard for some time, and it was moving faster than what current electric cars were capable of. I really didn't give it much thought since many of the GGB transportation services had those types of vehicles, but as it sped by, I also recognized a distinct odor. It was exhaust from a fuel-burning car. *Those types of vehicles were supposed to have been eliminated because of the pollution they emitted into the atmosphere,* I thought. *Only one person would be daring enough to drive a fuel-burning car.*

"Ozone!" I turned toward Willie. "He has Timm!" I waved my hands and shouted louder. "WILLIE! WILLIE!"

Willie, who had finished talking with the officers and was standing with May and Lindsay again, finally looked toward me.

"WILLIE! OZONE HAS TIMM!" I shouted again.

"You two, come with me!" Willie ordered.

"Who in the heck is Ozone?" May asked.

"Lindsay will tell you," Willie replied as he and the two officers ran toward the van.

Lindsay proceeded to tell May the story I told her after reading the articles. Like everyone else, they weren't sure what Ozone's motive would be for kidnapping Timm.

Willie and I opened the van doors and jumped in the front seats, while the two officers hopped in the back. I reached for the keys to turn the ignition.

"I don't believe it!" I shouted as I leaned back in the driver's seat.

"What's wrong?" Willie asked.

"Timm's always forgetting where he puts his keys or he leaves them in the van, and the one time I need them, he has 'em."

The four of us stepped out of the van and slammed the doors shut.

"Now what?" Willie asked.

"I don't know. You and I walked here tonight." I looked at the two officers. "How about you guys? Do either one of you have a car here?"

"No, we're on foot patrol tonight," one of the officers explained.

"By the way, how do you know Ozone has Timm?" Willie inquired.

"Just call it a gut feeling," I replied as I looked around for a vehicle. "Doesn't anyone have a vehicle we can use?!" I was becoming aggravated as I scoped the area for anything drivable.

"Another gut feeling?" Willie shook his head. "We need facts, my friend."

"I know, but I don't have any right now." I snapped. "I'm just trying to put the clues that we have together. So far, I've been right." I changed the subject. "Willie, the questions can wait. We need a vehicle!"

Willie turned to the officers with his brow raised and dropped his jaw. "Why are you two still standing here? Find us a vehicle."

The officers ran off in search of a vehicle.

Willie continued his questioning. "Maybe you've just been lucky so far, but how do you know that was Ozone's car?"

"It was a fuel-burning car."

"Are you crazy? Those haven't been around in–"

"In years," I interrupted. "I know they haven't, but there's only one person who would be daring enough to drive one – knowing it could easily outrun any electric-powered car."

Willie thought for a moment. "What the heck would he be doing here? I thought he was at his facility in Barrow's Ridge."

"He must have decided to pay a personal visit to Timm."

Willie thought for a moment.   "What would he want with Timm?"

"I don't know!"   I was frustrated and irritated Ozone was getting away and we were still standing around waiting for someone to find a vehicle.   "When I do, you'll be the second to know!"

Willie stepped back.   "All right. Take it easy."

"Willie!   While we're standing here twiddling our thumbs, Ozone is driving off with my brother!"   At that moment, I saw headlights approaching from around the corner.   "It's about time!"

The car's tires squealed as it made the turn and headed straight for us.   The two officers, who had returned without a vehicle, drew their immobilizers and aimed it at the oncoming car just in case it was Ozone returning.   The car sped toward the van and then came to a screeching halt.

"Don't shoot!"   I shouted as I recognized the car.   "He's a friend of mine."

"Yeah, well your friend drives like a maniac," one of the officers snapped as he lowered his weapon.

"Well, at least he has something to drive," I responded.

Pockets stuck his head out the car window.

I ran up to meet him.   "I thought you'd be down here earlier."

"I would have been, but Timm's apartment was ransacked," Pockets answered, "and they've taken everything from his studio."

"Tell us about it in the car," I replied as I gave Willie a look of confidence about my gut feeling.

Willie motioned Pockets to move over to the middle of the seat so he could drive while the rest of us jumped in the car.   Willie turned the car around in the direction Ozone was headed, and we took off after him, knowing he already had a significant head start.

"Why were you at Timm's when he wasn't even home?" I asked.

"He told me I could stay there since he was going to be out tonight. He wanted me to get an early start on the next mural tomorrow. I mean today," Pockets corrected himself as he looked at his watch and then continued. "So, I decided to clean some airbrushes before heading down here tonight."

I motioned to Willie. "Take a left at the next corner."

"You think he's headed for the transportation depot?" Willie asked.

"Most likely. I'm sure he didn't drive all the way out here," I replied and then turned back to Pockets. "What happened in the apartment?"

"I was in the bathroom, luckily with the door open, when I heard someone cutting the glass on the sliding glass door," Pockets started to explain. "I walked down to the end of the hallway and peeked around the corner. That's when I saw three men standing outside the window about to push it through. I wasn't about to take all three of them on, so I ran back into the bathroom and hid behind the shower curtain. I could hear them walk past the bathroom and into the bedroom. Once they were convinced Timm wasn't there, they went into the studio. I could hear all kinds of noise but couldn't figure out what they were doing until after they left. When it was safe to come out, I went into the studio where I found most of his supplies missing. Just about everything was gone, even the box we need for tomorrow's, I mean today's job."

"Why would somebody want to steal art supplies?" Willie asked.

"Ozone was a famous artist," I reminded Willie. "I just wonder if he's going to make Timm paint for him. Remember, Ozone's hands were severely damaged at his last showing."

"That seems pretty far-fetched to me. I thought the man was trying to eliminate the human race," Willie replied.

I braced myself as Willie took a wide turn. "I know it does, but do you have any other explanations?"

"Not really, but it seems like it has to be more than just wanting Timm to paint for him."

"I agree," I said as I nodded.

"Over there!" One of the officers shouted from the back seat as he pointed at some lights in a distant field.

We looked over and saw taillights from a car disappearing into some unusual type of aircraft. Willie took the first opening into the field and headed straight for the aircraft. It had to be Ozone's, because that airstrip hadn't been used in over a year. The car was driving up into an aircraft similar to the ones described by the GGB investigators during their encounter at the canyon near Barrow's Ridge. The only difference between the one we saw and the ones at the fortress was this one was large enough to carry a car.

"Stop the car!" I shouted.

"What?!" Willie shouted back in utter surprise.

"Stop the car now and turn off the lights!"

Willie hit the light switch and slammed on the breaks while everyone braced themselves for the sudden stop. The wheels locked, causing the car to skid across the grass field some fifty feet or more.

"You better have a good reason for stopping this car!" Willie said.

I could tell Willie was upset, but I had just the thing to calm him down. "Take a look over there," I said, pointing at a position slightly above the loaded aircraft.

"Good enough for me," Willie said.

Over the tree line came three cylindrical aircraft, again similar to the ones the investigators at the canyon encountered. There were two four-footers and one six-footer. Under normal circumstances, three small aircraft would be insufficient protection to fend off any threat to the large transport vehicle, but considering the GGB had no substantial fire power to strike back, it was more than adequate.

"He's too smart to bring a large aircraft in here without protection," I said as I hit my fist on the inside of the car door.

I was frustrated not only because Ozone and his ForLord hoodlums had kidnapped Timm but because Ozone was gaining momentum in his effort to carry out his devious plot. He was getting stronger as more and more people joined the ForLords. Those who weren't changing were in more danger than ever. He had to be stopped, but how?

We could only sit there and watch the aircraft leave. As long as we didn't pose a threat to Ozone, the three aircraft would ignore us. The transportation aircraft took off and headed west. The three armed aircraft flew into formation around the larger aircraft, the six-foot one in front and the smaller ones flanked on the sides. When Willie figured we were out of danger, he turned the lights on, and we headed back to pick up May and Lindsay.

"What's our next move, Willie?" I asked.

"That's a good question, and I wish I had the answer," Willie replied.

Pockets squirmed in his seat to get comfortable. "We need to do something before Ozone carries out the rest of his evil plot. Thousands of people have already lost their lives, and the ones that don't die are increasing the size of his ForLord army."

Willie glanced at me. "On my way home, I'll stop at the office and call an emergency meeting of the GGB, if one hasn't been called already. I want you there with me."

"You think they're really going to let me in their meeting?" I asked uncertainly.

"Oh, yeah! I'll make sure they will."

"Good."

Willie turned his wrist to look at his watch. "My guess is, it won't be until shortly after lunch when all the members are gathered." Willie made a right turn and drove up to where we had left Lindsay and May. "When they do, we will hook up via satellite with the other members of the GGB around the world."

"Perfect." I thought for a moment while I rubbed my chin. "That will give me some time to visit our friend again."

"Our friend?" Willie asked hesitantly.

"Jennifer Smithson."

Willie stopped the car, sighing as he looked out his window. "I knew it would only be a matter of time before her name arose again," he said turning toward me, "but I think you may be right."

"I know I am. She's hiding something, and I'm going to find out what it is."

"Just go easy on her ol' buddy."

It was eight o'clock in the morning when I headed out to see Jennifer again. I was still tired from the previous night's activities, having slept only a few hours, but I had to give myself enough time to question Jennifer and make it to that afternoon's meeting. I didn't want to walk in late on a GGB meeting, especially since I was the guest of honor, so to speak.

The news of the morning's events was featured throughout the local media. One picture showed a victim trapped inside a bubble. I had to chuckle for a second because if one was to look close enough, they would have noticed two of the Dropas in the picture about to pop it. The scary thing about it was the Global News Station was also reporting how upset the people were getting, especially since nothing was being done to stop the repeated occurrences. I could only imagine the number of people showing up outside the GGB regional office for our meeting later that day. It was bringing back bad memories of the events prior to the War and the way past politicians failed to handle critical issues.

I pulled into the driveway of Jane's house. Jennifer was sitting on the porch swing sipping tea. Surprisingly, she didn't run into the house when she saw me get out of the car. It appeared as if she was expecting me. As I stepped up onto the porch, she pointed to the empty seat next to her.

"Please sit down," she said. "I'm sorry. What was your name again?"

"Scott," I replied, taking the seat next to her.

"I would have called, but I figured you would come here on your own time."

"You did? Why is that?"

"Please don't play innocent with me; I'm much smarter than you think."

"I'm sor–"

"Let me say what I need to say," Jennifer interrupted rather rudely. "When I'm finished, you can ask questions. Agreed?"

"Agreed." I sat back in my chair, and Jennifer set her tea on a small table next to her. Characterizing her forwardness, I had to admit she reminded me of the old man in the shop I encountered back in Greece, but she obviously had some things to say and wasn't about to waste any time with small talk, which was all right with me.

"I heard on the news what happened to your brother and I am deeply sorry."

I leaned forward in my chair and was about to reply to her sympathetic words but quickly sat back as Jennifer delivered a glare, reminding me to remain silent. She was a very strong-willed woman and intelligent as she alluded to earlier. I just hoped what she had to say would be worthwhile.

She continued. "You and the GGB are dealing with a very vengeful and dangerous individual.   What makes Leonard so dangerous is the fact he is a very emotionally disturbed individual but extremely intelligent. For some reason, as much as I didn't want to, I believed you yesterday when you told me he was still alive. After hearing this morning's news, I was convinced the recent chain of events, especially last night's kidnapping of your brother, could only be done by Leonard. Only Leonard would kidnap an artist, and especially one who touches so many hearts and brings out the goodness in people. Until this morning, your brother was the biggest threat to Ozone's plan for human annihilation. I'm sure Leonard is very jealous of your brother's work but admires it as much as he would his own. I assure you he didn't kidnap him to kill him."

As sincere as Jennifer's words may have been, I really didn't feel much assurance from them. But it did make sense. After all, here was a guy whose life consisted only of painting, much like Timm's, but he no longer had the ability to continue doing what he loved to do.

"If you haven't figured it out yet, Leonard is still carrying out his promise he made on those steps of the Art Center, the promise the War did not fulfill. You see, I knew of everything he planned to do, and eventually did, before and during the War. I didn't care what happened to other people, because at the time, I felt sorry for Leonard and I became enraged at what those terrible people did to his art and to him. If only you could have seen him experience the pain like I did while he was in the emergency burn unit, and the weeks that followed. No one deserved to go through that, no one. To make things worse, Leonard couldn't pay for the reconstruction of his hands and face. I couldn't help him because I, too, had no money. Even his friends, his best friends, turned their backs on Leonard. I had nothing in my life worth living for, either. And you know, as well as I do, the time leading up to the War was a terrible time to be alive. All of humanity was in a frenzy. So, I made a promise to Leonard I would help him carry out his vengeful plot as much as I could." Jennifer paused for a moment. "You see, Scott, I was the one who provided him with the access to all the government files. I was the one who helped him create the Johnny Appleseed program, the program which spread the information across the globe."

Her eyes began to tear as she turned her head and stared into the morning sky. My mouth dropped open when Jennifer admitted being an accomplice to the death of nearly two billion people. I was stunned but I could also tell she regretted her actions because she couldn't look at me after her confession.

Jennifer's voice trembled as she continued, "I understand by saying all of this, I have basically convicted myself of a heinous crime, one which is replayed day after day, over and over in my mind. When you visited yesterday, it intensified those memories and my guilt. But, because I enjoy the renewed life the Survival Treaty has brought to people, including myself, I can't live with what Leonard is doing anymore." She paused again as her throat knotted. When she spoke again, I could barely hear her words. "And as much as I love Leonard, I realize what he has done is unforgivable, and he must be stopped from doing it again."

She looked up at me, tears flowing from her eyes. I scooted forward in my chair and reached out my hands. She grabbed them with both of hers, squeezing them tightly, and stared into my eyes with a glare of rage.

"You must find a way to stop him, or he will wipe out human civilization as we know it. And remember, he doesn't care if he dies in the process, as long as everyone dies with him. He will do everything in his power to make sure it happens. Your firsthand accounts should tell you that."

I looked straight into her eyes. "We'll do everything we can, but the Treaty did not account for someone of Leonard's capacity and willfulness to destroy."

"Well, I guarantee you, it won't be with any conventional means. You have to find another way."

I didn't have an immediate solution to stopping him, but given time – I didn't know how much I had – I knew I would think of something. "Do you know anything about his fortress near Barrow's Ridge?"

"Not a whole lot," Jennifer replied, wiping the tears from her face with a handkerchief. "Leonard and I stopped communicating when he started renovating that facility shortly after the War. All I can remember him saying is no one would be able to penetrate his walls."

"In more ways than one," I added.

Jennifer gave me a puzzled look. "How do you mean?"

"Are you familiar with my brother's work, particularly the broken walls he uses in them?"

"Oh, yes, very much so," she replied and then thought for a moment. "I think I understand you now. No one will break through the walls of his fortress nor through the walls he has built around himself – the ones preventing goodness from penetrating and evil from leaving."

"Exactly," I confirmed. "His walls are so thick from the tragedy he suffered at his final exhibit, he is unwilling to forgive and reach out to anyone. He is a remnant of what people were like before the War. Everyone was so caught up in their own accomplishments, acquisitions, and sole-survival they tended to forget why they were really given the opportunity to live on earth. Most of the problems people encountered were related to money. You could only survive if you had money, and everyone was so caught up in it you forgot about the other aspects of your existence: your mind, your soul, your spirit, and an inner ability to make life enjoyable for humanity. We totally forgot about the immaterial things in life and how much joy we can bring to others, as well as ourselves."

"I couldn't have said it better." Jennifer smiled. "My walls have been broken through, and I credit the people who created the Survival Treaty and our new way of life for making it happen."

I smiled back. "You're not alone."

She patted my hand. "As much as I would like to sit and talk with you some more, I am really tired, and I must take my medication."

"I understand, Jennifer, and I thank you for spending some time with me. You have been most helpful."

We both rose from our seats and walked to the end of the porch. Jennifer turned to me.

"Should I be expecting a visit from the GGB for my arrest?"

"I don't think so. Although what you have admitted is truly a terrible thing, I want you to put it behind you for good. We don't need to rekindle the bad experiences of the War, experiences people are trying to put behind them. Having to wake up each and every day, knowing you were a part of a plot to potentially eliminate the human race, is, in itself, the worst punishment you could experience."

Jennifer extended her arms toward me. We hugged for a brief moment before I pulled away from her. She looked up at me as I held her hands in front of me. I could see the guilt in her eyes and, at the same time, her concern.

"Please stop him," she said.

"We will," I promised.

Jennifer released her grip, turned and walked inside, the screen door closing behind her. She turned again and waved.

"Good-bye, Scott."

"Good-bye, Jennifer."

I hopped into the car and drove to Willie's office. I thought about the things Jennifer had told me, feeling extreme emotions of anger, fear, sadness, and helplessness. We had to stop Ozone, and I had to find Timm.

Timm awoke to a knock on the door. He could feel a sharp pain where the needle had penetrated his neck and began rubbing the area with his hand. At first he didn't know where he had been sleeping for the last several hours, but as his eyes focused, he realized he was in an unfamiliar, but lavish, suite. The ceilings were high and precisely trimmed in the corners and on the surface with beautiful wood molding. The walls were trimmed with molding, as well, but also covered with floral wallpaper revealing a most elegant pattern. The furniture accented the Victorian era bedroom as if it was a bedroom of royalty: its floral designs carved in the wood, velvet cloth covering the cushions, and marble tops on the tables, dressers, and vanities. Fresh flowers filled the room with an incredible aroma one might only find in a floral garden. The bed in which Timm slept had a high, hand-carved headboard and was piled with plenty of blankets and fluffy pillows.

He heard a second knock on the door. The memories of the previous night and that morning began to spring in his head. Only now did he realize he was in the hands of Lord Ozone.

"Come in," he responded, his mouth and eyes dried out from the substance injected in his body.

The door opened and in walked a petite woman. She was plainly dressed and wore her deep-black hair in a bun which complemented her medium-dark skin. She was carrying a large, white bowl with a matching pitcher of hot water and had some clean towels draped across her arms.

"Good morning, Master Timm," she greeted him, walking toward the vanity.

"Good morning, ummm–" Timm replied, rubbing his eyes.

"Sharlene, with an 'S', but you can call me Shar, like everyone else does."

"Good morning, Shar."

"Lord Ozone has requested your presence at breakfast in the courtyard." She set the bowl and towels on the vanity. "I have brought you some clean towels and washcloths, along with some hot water for you to freshen up."

Timm remained motionless. "Thanks, but what if I don't want to have breakfast with Ozone."

"That would not be wise," Shar admonished, turning to face Timm. "Lord Ozone would not take kindly to that."

"Yeah, right, Lord Ozone." Timm moved his head and felt the sharp pain in his neck again. He rubbed the area and continued. "Just thought I'd ask."

"Unfortunately, you'll have to wear the same clothes you were wearing when you were brought here." Shar pointed to his clothes draped over the back of a chair. "The seamstresses have not finished your new clothes as of yet. I will bring them to you when they are ready."

"There are seamstresses here making me clothes?" Timm was impressed.

Shar faced Timm and put her hands on the footboard. "Yes, Master Timm."

Timm raised his brow. "And how did these seamstresses get my measurements?"

"I gave the measurements to them this morning."

Timm paused for a moment before replying. "And how did you get those measurements?"

"I took them while you were in bed," she replied innocently.

Timm was feeling a little awkward and somewhat embarrassed as he looked under the sheets and saw he was completely naked. "Let me get this straight." He looked back at her. "You took my measurements while I was in bed?"

"Yes, Master Timm. I have only done as Lord Ozone has asked. Did I cause you some embarrassment?"

"No," he replied, blushing. "No, not at all." Timm looked under the sheets again before pulling them up to his chin. "Did anyone else see me?"

Shar put her hand over her mouth as she let out a soft giggle. "Oh, you thought I took the measurements from your body?" she asked, pointing at Timm.

Timm nodded.

She turned and pointed at the chair. "I took them from your clothes. You put yourself to bed. I assure you, no one saw you naked, Master Timm."

"Oh." Timm felt foolish for the assumption he had made.

"I must be going now." "Is there anything else you request of me, Master Timm?"

"Just two things."

"And what would those two things be?"

"First, just call me Timm."

"All right, Timm. And the second one?"

"How do I get to the courtyard once I'm finished getting dressed?"

Shar nodded. "Ohhh, I'm sorry. I almost left without telling you." She paused to organize her thoughts. "When you walk out the door, take a right and walk down the hall until you come to the stairs. Go down the stairs and take a left at the bottom. Walk behind the staircase and head straight out the double-glass doors. Lord Ozone will be waiting for you."

"I can handle that," Timm confirmed.

"Oh, one more thing." Shar said, putting up a finger. "Breakfast is at nine, and Lord Ozone doesn't like to be kept waiting."

"What time is it now?"

"It's a quarter of." Without another word, Shar turned and exited the room.

Timm only had fifteen minutes to get ready. He threw off the covers and walked toward the vanity where Shar had set the water and towels. He marveled at the softness of the cashmere rug underneath his feet. *This guy's probably just like Scott, he gets very cranky when he doesn't eat on time,* he thought. At the vanity, Timm picked up the vase with hot water and poured it into the bowl. The steam rose from the water and fogged up the lower half of the mirror. He then dropped the washcloth in the water and made sure it was completely wet.

"Oww! That's hot!" he exclaimed, carefully poking the cloth.

He pulled the washcloth out of the water by one of its corners and held it in the air to help cool it. The excess water ran off the washcloth and back into the bowl. After a few moments, he washed his face. He repeated the process several times until he had washed his entire body. By the time he finished, the water in the bowl had cooled enough for him to dip his entire head into the bowl so he could rinse his hair. He then dried his hair with the towel and combed it with the brush sitting on the vanity. Cringing at the thought of having to put on his dirty, smelly clothes from the previous day, he carefully slid his legs into his jeans and his arms through his T-shirt which were both heavily soiled from his falls in the school parking lot and the alley. And then there were his socks, which he hesitated to even wear, but did anyway. Finally, he put on his shoes, laced them up, and walked into the hall.

Timm took a right down the long, wood-trimmed hallway. The two walls were lined with many of Ozone's paintings, each having its own light shining on top of it. Timm wanted to stop and look at all of them but knew he would have to do it another time. He followed Shar's directions exactly, noticing the parts of the house he saw were decorated in a style similar to the bedroom where he slept. As he approached the glass doors, he could see the courtyard was full of trees and flowers, accented nicely with an occasional statue placed in its own, perfect location. The ground was covered with cobblestone arranged in a circular manner. In the center of the courtyard, there was a large, magnificent fountain spurting water from its numerous openings. Sitting at a table next to the fountain was Lord Ozone. Timm felt a chill run through his veins and down his back. He looked closer. There Ozone sat, dressed in a black robe with a hood over his head.

Timm opened the doors, feeling the fresh air move across his face. The courtyard was filled with a medley of sounds from singing birds and a variety of refreshing scents coming from the garden flowers. The only thing missing from that beautiful setting was the warm sunlight and the bright, blue sky. Timm walked toward the table where Ozone was sitting. The pain in his neck grew stronger as he approached Ozone, stirring the anger Timm had toward the man he hadn't officially met. He pulled out the chair across from Ozone and sat down.

"You're two minutes late," Ozone greeted Timm, slurring slightly and refusing to look up from his plate.

"Excuse me, but you didn't give me much time to get ready," Timm snapped.

"I apologize. Next time I will give you more." Ozone pointed at Timm's plate. "Please eat, the food is wonderful."

Timm sat down and immediately removed the cover from his plate. Underneath, there were three eggs, three strips of bacon, and two slices of buttered toast. Next to the plate were glasses of orange juice, milk, and ice water, and in the middle of the table was a large bowl of fresh fruit and a pitcher of hot tea.

"This looks great." Timm smiled at his feast. His hunger had momentarily suppressed his anger, and he began to eat as if he hadn't eaten for days. Periodically, he looked up from his plate at Ozone. He couldn't see Ozone's face, but Timm could hear soft blowing and pumping noises emanating from underneath the hood, similar to those he heard from his compressor and airbrush, but at a much lower volume. After several minutes of eating without conversation, Timm finally broke the silence.

"Pull back your hood," Timm said boldly.

"Why?" Ozone replied, keeping his head down.

"Because I like to look at people when I talk to them."

"I assure you that you don't want to look at me."

"Look, Leonard–" Timm began.

Ozone slammed his fist on the table in response to Timm's disrespect. Several pieces of silverware jumped off the table, and Ozone's glass of water spilled onto the table. He pointed his gloved finger at Timm, who was now sitting back in his chair trying to keep from choking on his last bite of toast.

"Don't you ever call me Leonard again!" His words became less distinctive the louder he talked. "You will address me as Lord Ozone!"

"All right, all right. Geez. What do you want from me anyway?!" Timm was now just as angry. "You have your hoodlums shoot me up with some sleeping potion, drag me off to your fortress, away from my family and friends, and then you're not even man enough to show me your face when you talk to me! I don't care what you look like! There's much more to a person than their appearance! You have to look beyond the surface to see what truly makes up an individual!"

"Don't bore me with your philosophical beliefs. You want to see my face so badly, then here it is." Ozone pulled the hood back over his head, allowing it to rest on the back of his neck.

Beneath the hood was a hideous-looking face. His nose and eyelids had been completely consumed by the chemicals. His cheek bones, near his nose, were partially exposed where the scar tissue failed to cover them. He had no lips which allowed food and liquid to occasionally drip out of his mouth and explained his strange speech pattern. Sparse areas of facial hair covered his face where it wasn't covered by scar tissue.

The critical areas of his face were covered by a partial mask, held on by straps going over the top and around the back of his bald head. The mask consisted of a frontal, air-intake filter covering his nasal cavity. The covering was screwed directly to his facial bones, securing it to his face and preventing unwanted particles to enter his nasal passages under the seal. A thin, clear visor covered his eyes, which looked as if they were ready to roll out of their sockets at any time. Four tubes, two on each side, protruded from holes near, but under the ends of the visor. The tubes were connected to two oblong compressors, one screwed to each side of his head, slightly above the ears. Two more tubes protruded from holes above the visor and were connected to the top of the compressors. As horrible as it was, Timm didn't look away once. He wanted to reach out to this man not because of what he looked like but because of how and why this happened to him.

"Thank you," Timm simply said. He knew there was nothing he could say that would make the situation any better, but he was curious about the facial apparatus itself.

"Are those airbrush parts on the side of your head?" Timm asked.

"Yes, they are." Ozone was surprised at Timm's nonreaction to his appearance. "I designed this system myself."

"I'm quite impressed. Tell me more about it."

Ozone was silent for a second and then proceeded. "Well, I couldn't afford reconstructive surgery on my face, and I was tired of wearing the facial mask given to me to assist my breathing and to keep the particles out of my eyes and nose. You see, it didn't keep my eyes moist, and they would periodically stick unless I kept my eyes continuously moving. I also had problems with mucous running out of my nasal cavity."

Timm inwardly cringed as he clearly pictured Ozone's descriptions but made sure he hid his reaction from Ozone.

Ozone continued. "So, I began designing the Inverted Transfer System or I-T-S. That, in turn, is made up of the Air Transfer Apparatus or A-T-A, and the M-R-T-A or Mucous Recycling Transfer Apparatus." Ozone paused for a moment as Timm became lost in the acronyms. "You look confused, so let me show you how it works."

Timm sipped his juice. "A little bit."

Ozone used his index fingers to trace the path of the system as he explained its functionality. "A portion of the air I breathe in and out funnels its way through the top tubes under my eyes and into the small compressor up here, the ATA. This air is then filtered, regenerated, and sent through these tubes to the Particle Deflector, up here above my eyes."

Timm leaned forward to acquire a better look through Ozone's visor.

Ozone gave Timm a little time to look at it before continuing. "The Particle Deflector then expels a constant stream of air in front of my eyes which keeps any minute, foreign particles from reaching them. The air is then pulled out through these vents here." He returned his fingers to the tubes under his visor which originate from his nose piece and began tracing the next path. "These tubes funnel mucous to the MRTA which recycles it and sends it to the moisturizing outlets in the Particle Deflector. This keeps my eyes moist and prevents them from sticking in my sockets. The nose piece, well, that's obvious what it does. So, that is pretty much it."

Timm studied Ozone's face and his mask a little longer. "How is your vision at night?"

"Ah, yes. I almost forgot that part." He pointed to a small slot on the mask, slightly above the visor. "See this here?"

Timm nodded.

"This is a light sensor. When it becomes too dark to see through this visor, it automatically gives me infrared vision."

Timm raised his brow and dropped his mouth. "That is quite impressive. How long did it take you to design and build it?"

Ozone sipped his tea, keeping the liquid inside his mouth, and set his cup on the saucer. "A couple of weeks, at most."

"Wow! Do you have any problems with it?"

"Not now," Ozone replied proudly.

"The batteries must be tiny," Timm assumed, thinking it had to be operated by an external source.

"It doesn't use batteries," Ozone responded smugly.

"How is it powered then?"

"I have it feeding directly off neural impulses from my brain."

"No way!" Timm was amazed and completely absorbed in Ozone's contraption.

"That was one of the kinks I worked out. It became a real pain when the batteries kept dying, so I figured out a way to connect the system directly to my brain." He pointed to the compressors with his index fingers. "When the mask is put on, these compressors are snapped onto the outlets coming out of my head."

"That is so cool. Do you ever take it off?"

Ozone paused and took several sips of his orange juice, being very careful not to drink too much at a time. "No, it is very dang–" Ozone caught himself, looked at Timm again, and changed the subject. "You're the only person who has been able to look at me without becoming sick. Why is that?"

Forgetting what he asked, he instead responded to Ozone's question. "I told you, I don't care what you look like. I don't care if you're black, white, red, or yellow. I don't care if you walked around with your face smashed into the back of your head. Don't you understand? It doesn't matter."

"I told you not to bore me."

"Then don't ask me questions which will cause my answers to bore you." Timm paused briefly as he sipped his juice. "OK, I won't bore you anymore, but answer me this. Why did you start the War and kill all those people?"

"I didn't kill all those people; they killed themselves," Ozone replied emotionless.

"You were responsible for starting the 'fire'."

"I may have started the fire, but the fuel was already in place. Back then, people had so much hatred toward their governments and each other," Ozone flicked a piece of fruit off the table, "I just gave them a small nudge over the edge."

"They had so much hatred toward each other because, rather than taking time to understand each other's culture, heritage, and the characteristics which made everyone different, each tried to force others to become more like one's self."

"Exactly! Humans are naturally selfish and greedy people, having been born with that trait."

"No, they are not born with it," Timm argued. They are taught to be that way. People are taught to hate and taught to be selfish."

Ozone didn't respond but continued sipping his tea.

"You have no guilt about being responsible for the death of almost two billion people, do you?"

Ozone set his cup on its saucer. "Why should I after the pain and disgrace they put me through? Just look at me."

"I am looking at you. And I hate to tell you, but two billion people were not responsible for the destruction of your art and the harm brought to you."

Ozone thought for a moment. "It was more than that."

"Was it?" Timm challenged.

Ozone evaded the question.   "It doesn't matter, they all deserved to die, every last one of them."

"Why didn't you kill me?"

"Because you're the one person who can bring back to me the passion I once possessed and released through my hands."

"Why did you bring me here instead of admiring my work outside your fortress?"

"Two reasons. First, you and your art are the only things keeping people from turning against each other again. I had to eliminate that aspect of their life. And second, I dearly miss the emotions I felt when I painted. I want to get as close as possible to the feeling of painting again; watching the art come alive in front of me. I want you to paint for me. I want you to paint my fortress."

"Let me start by saying this. There are more things in the world than my art that are making people happy again. With the new ways of life implemented by the Treaty, people are discovering who they really are and why they're here. They're learning the ways of other people and sharing with them experiences, beliefs, and history previously covered up with bloodshed. In the past, our governments didn't believe it was in the interest of 'their' people to figure out what the problems really were and then solve them. How many times did you see the leaders who declared war actually fight those wars? Very few. In fact, it was always the soldiers, innocent people fighting for their governments. The people sacrificed their lives because of the selfish, greedy principles of our governments. Then, over the course of centuries and even eons, the hatred our governments had toward one another eventually permeated society resulting in people hating and discriminating against other people – people they didn't even know. They were hating each other because they lived in a different country, their skin was a different color, they worshipped a different God, or they just did things differently." Timm raised his finger. "We are here one time, and one time only. Why should we go through life hating each other? There is so much more to learn from people, and life itself, if we try to learn, share, and laugh with each other."

Ozone sat in silence as if Timm might have made some sense. Then he spoke again, "I used to laugh. I used to laugh all the time, but no more. I figure the people who took the laughter and dignity away from me no longer deserve to live. It is exactly why I brought you here. The laughter and happiness need to be removed from society for my plan to succeed."

Timm leaned forward on the table and glared through Ozone's visor. "I feel sorry for you."

"I don't need, or want your sympathy for what I look like," Ozone shot back.

"You misunderstand. I don't feel sorry because of the way you look. I feel sorry for what you've become, because of your looks. You've become worse than those who did this horrible thing to you. And now you sit here with plans to revive the War."

"They destroyed my art and my life!" Ozone slurred.

"You just don't get it, do you? You can have more than one dream, more than one passion in your life. Sometimes it may take a little more effort to search inside, find, and even accomplish them."

Ozone put his gloved hands on the table and pushed himself away from it. "Believe me, I will accomplish my other dream." He then stood up from his chair and replaced his hood over his head.

As he turned and walked away, Timm stood up from his chair and called to Ozone. "Ozone! You better find someone else to paint your fortress! I have no intention of putting one drop on this place!"

Ozone stopped and turned toward Timm. "Maybe not today, but eventually, eventually you will paint my fortress." He turned away and disappeared into the house.

Timm sat back in his chair and stared into the gray sky, having no idea how he was going to get out of his current situation. He leaned his head on the back of the chair, still exhausted from the events which happened the previous night and early that morning. Closing his eyes, he listened to the birds sing in the trees as he drifted off to sleep.

That afternoon, Ozone sat in his communications room, sipping a glass of lemonade Shar had just poured for him.

"Will you need anything else, Lord Ozone?" Shar asked.

"No. That will be all for now. You may leave."

Shar bowed slightly in front of Ozone. She turned toward the door and left. Ozone flipped some switches on a large panel in front of him. The panel was covered with various types of switches, dials, and meters. It controlled the small monitors lining the walls and the large one straight across from where he sat. The small screens showed various views from security cameras positioned near the canyon and around the fortress. The large screen was still a bit fuzzy as Ozone continued adjusting his own satellites until he finally zeroed in on the correct position and frequency to intercept the GGB's broadcast signal. Willie could be seen finishing his address to the GGB and was about to introduce me to the Board. Fortunately, Ozone's patience was short, and he didn't see me or hear what I had to say. Ozone interrupted the meeting, broadcasting himself to each and every one of the GGB members.

"Good afternoon, ladies and gentlemen. For those of you who don't know me, I am Lord Ozone, but some of you may remember me as the Human Virus."

The members were absolutely stunned at the image they saw on their screens and began grumbling amongst themselves trying to figure out how Ozone had become a part of their meeting and who knew how many other meetings.

"Please don't be alarmed. I only need a brief moment of your time. You might as well go back to your families and spend some time with them because your time here on earth is running out. My plan is right on schedule, and it will only be a short time now before I eliminate the human race. You have to face reality now. Your utopian system has left you defenseless. You can't stop me. No one can. Enjoy your remaining time here on earth and spend it wisely. Good-bye and good riddance."

Ozone stopped transmitting and returned control over to the GGB signal. The members sat silent for a moment. They knew they couldn't continue the meeting via satellite, even though Ozone had no interest in it. They agreed to meet in person at another, more secure location. Realizing the urgency, they left immediately.

Waiting for the GGB to meet and then implement their procedures was not in my plans. Even the GGB had flaws and they were definitely not prepared for something of this magnitude. Ozone was already moving forward with his vengeful activities. It was time I took the situation into my own hands. Although I didn't know what to do next, especially since my army consisted of Pockets, the Dropas, and anyone else who wanted to join me.

I left the GGB meeting before Willie could catch me. In the lobby, I found the nearest phone and called Pockets, asking him to organize a meeting for later that evening in the school gym where he and Timm had just finished painting a mural. It had to be held at night, so no one would know what we were plotting, even though I knew it was highly probable we would encounter the bubbles again. Pockets agreed and said he would take care of everything.

The Dropas were sitting on my dashboard, patiently waiting for me to return from the GGB meeting. I knew they were still saddened by the kidnapping of Timm because they weren't up to their usual antics, although they were happy to see me when I hopped into the truck. I told them about Ozone's speech, and that I had decided to take the matter into my own hands. They assured me everything was ready, and they would be with me all the way. I wasn't sure what they meant but I didn't give it a second thought at the time. I also informed them they needed to have plenty of paint-coated needles ready for the meeting. Again they assured me they would. Everything was set.

"Now, I just need a plan guys," I said to the Dropas.

Welcome To Our World

*L*ater that night I arrived at the school where the meeting was being held. I was astonished by the number of cars and bicycles filling the parking lot but more by what I saw inside. Pockets had done a wonderful job rounding up people for the meeting. It was only when I walked inside and saw who occupied most of the gym that I realized the majority of people Pockets actually knew were students. The remainder of the crowd consisted of teachers, administrators, parents, and a fair number of townspeople.

The crowd turned silent as I walked toward the far wall of the gym. I could feel their compassion for me and their own feeling of loss after hearing Timm had been kidnapped. Having reached the front of my captive audience, I still didn't know what to say.

"We're behind you all the way, Scott!" a young voice shouted from the bleachers as Pockets handed me the microphone.

The Dropas, who had been standing on my shoulders, ran down my arm and sat on the edge of a chair next to me.

"Whatever you want us to do, we'll do it!" another voice shouted.

At that moment, the students started pounding their feet twice on the bleachers followed by three hand claps. As they continued this, they chanted, "No more G - G - B! No more G - G - B! No more G - G - B!"

Standing there in disbelief, I raised my hands to quiet the rambunctious crowd. Thinking for a moment, the words finally started flowing from my mouth. "Many of you have heard that my brother was kidnapped by a man who calls himself Lord Ozone."

Well, that opening statement ignited the crowd into a chorus of boos.

Again, I quickly quieted them, but now I knew I had their attention. "Up to this point, we have not heard any demands, or even any reports about whether Timm is alive or dead. Until I hear otherwise, I am assuming he is alive." I paused momentarily, thinking about Timm. "I'm not here to speculate about the disappearance of my brother. Instead, I'm here to address a much larger issue. Before I do, I must admit I am bewildered by your angry attack of the GGB."

"All these recent deaths are their fault. They can no longer protect us!" an angry voice shouted from the crowd as others voiced agreement.

"People are changing attitudes and becoming violent again and the GGB can't prevent it!" another shouted.

Again the pounding and the chants echoed throughout the gym, "No more G - G - B! No more G - G - B! No more G - G - B!"

I finally quieted the crowd with the assistance of Pockets, who sounded a fog horn which he pulled from his pocket. The crowd quieted, but now I wondered if they wanted to listen to me.

"I want you people to understand this is not the fault of the GGB. Since the provisions of the Survival Treaty have been implemented, have you not seen a dramatic change in our world?"

"Yes," the crowd hesitantly echoed back.

"But, what about this Ozone?" a woman shouted.

"Yeah!" the crowd bellowed in unison.

I raised my hands again to keep them under control. "Since the Treaty, has your life become more fulfilling? More fulfilling because everything you do is no longer driven by a monetary system. You no longer need money to buy clothes, to eat, to travel, to simply enjoy life. Has your life become more fulfilling in that respect?"

"Yes," the crowd echoed back, only a little louder this time.

"Since the Treaty, have you been able to not only experience and understand the values and cultures of the people around you, but also of those people abroad?"

"Yes," the crowd echoed back with still more volume.

"At what price are you able to do this? Almost nothing. As long as each of you is working to keep our society and our species alive, for everyone and not just for yourself, you are provided with the necessities of life and the opportunity to enjoy all the wonderful things in the world – traveling, music, art, athletics, literature, and most importantly, each other. Poverty, hunger, overpopulation, pollution, crime, and drugs have virtually been eliminated from our world and will be very soon. This is what the GGB has done for you, and this is what you have done for yourselves."

The cheering crowd rose to its feet as the decibel level approached that of a rock concert. The gym was moving, but I knew the vibrations were caused by the noise of the crowd who had quickly realized it was not the fault of the GGB. Once again, Pockets quieted the crowd with his horn.

"Some of you are too young to remember the War and what led up to it. Those of you who do remember it, do not forget it. Do not forget what our society had been; one of corruption, greed, and undeniable selfishness. It was no longer the exception, but the rule. It eventually led to the death of nearly two billion people. Those of you who don't know much more than what you have been taught or have read in class, I urge you to talk with the survivors. I will personally sit down with you and tell you how it was before and during the War. Many wanted to die so they wouldn't have to see the bloodshed and the senseless, malicious killing happening day after day after day. As horrible as the War was and for as many lives it took, our lifestyle today is a result of that tragedy. It is unfortunate it took a war of such magnitude to finally wake people up, but we cannot change the past. We can only move forward and make sure it doesn't happen again. Over the last few days, I have uncovered some information about the man responsible for igniting the War."

The crowd gasped, because up to that point, no one had ever been singled out.

I continued. "It is the same man who has kidnapped my brother and a very dear friend to you all.

The crowd grumbled in disbelief.

"Lord Ozone is responsible for starting the last War. He is responsible for the death of so many innocent people, yet he remains alive. We have concluded the events occurring over the last year are part of Ozone's malicious plot to finish what the War did not. Once again, he has sufficiently assembled his forces of destruction, and will carry out his horrifying mission. I've invited you here tonight because of what Ozone is about to do. We, as a group, must act to bring down the evil Lord Ozone for good and–"

Before I could continue, the stamping, clapping, and chanting started once again. Only this time they were chanting something different.

"Bring down Ozone! Bring down Ozone! Bring down Ozone!"

The noise grew louder and louder. I could feel the energy travel right through my body. Pockets sounded his horn, but they wouldn't stop. The noise heightened as the crowd was determined not to let Lord Ozone bring death upon them and their families again. The ground trembled as did the walls and steel girders above, moving the lights back and forth, faster and faster. Like a small earthquake, the gymnasium shook, making it hard to maintain one's balance. Suddenly, the crowd stopped their clapping and chanting, but the shaking continued.

"Look, up there!" a girl shouted from the crowd as she pointed above the mural located behind me.

She was pointing at the ceiling where a hole began to appear. The lights went out and the crowd gasped, too frozen in their seats to head for the exits. The hole grew bigger as the gym continued to shake. I looked down at the chair next to me and noticed the Dropas had joined hands and were dancing in a circle, similar to when they revived Silver. A beam of light, the same beam of light I had seen with the old man, appeared through the hole and was now shining on the mural behind us. Pockets and I turned around to face the mural of the metallic Hawk, or "Robohawk" as the kids had named it. The light continued to shine upon the Hawk for some time before anything happened. The gym finally stopped shaking, and the crowd was dead silent as they watched in anticipation.

Once again, the image of Athena descended the light beam, stopping when she reached Robohawk. But, unlike the time she saved Silver, she was now carrying her spear and shield. She floated five feet in front of Robohawk and raised her weapons. The crowd was completely silent as they watched Athena radiate the gym. After holding that pose for several minutes, she pulled back her spear and, with one powerful motion, thrust the spear into and through the heart of Robohawk. We could hear the Dropas' gibbering chants grow louder and louder through the gym as Athena ascended through the ceiling and out of sight. After she disappeared, the Dropas ceased their dancing, faced Robohawk, and bowed before him.

The crowd became even more stunned as Robohawk started to come to life. First, its eyelid began blinking, and its eye moved around as if it was searching for prey. Next, its head moved from side to side, peering down at the paralyzed crowd. Several people became frightened and ran to the doors on the opposite side of the gym but continued to watch from the open doorway. With its head now completely free to move, the Hawk let out an ear-piercing screech. It was coming alive right before our eyes, and you could see the life traveling down its body, from its head to its talons and out across its massive steel wings. As Robohawk came to life completely, the wall began to shake again when Robohawk began emerging from it without resistance, demonstrating it was not afraid of entering our world.

The crowd on the floor began to retreat, giving the Hawk room to land when it flew out from the wall. It would need every inch of space, too. It was twenty feet high from head to talon, and no one knew how long its wingspan was when fully extended. As it initiated its first flight, its armored feathers reflected the emergency lights illuminating the gym. Amazingly, the wall stayed intact as the mighty Hawk freed itself and finally entered our world. With it's wings completely spread, some fifty feet or so, it flew from the wall and landed on the darkened floor, shaking the entire gym as it did. The wooden floor panels could not withstand the tremendous weight of the Creature and buckled underneath it. Sounds of the popping boards releasing from the floor echoed throughout the gym. Robohawk's talons pierced the boards underneath, as it scanned the crowd until it finally found what it was looking for, which happened to be me. It again let out one of its high-pitched screeches.

I looked down at the chair again where the Dropas were now engaged in a private celebration. They were quite excited with the results of their hard work.

"Of course! The paint!" I exclaimed as I looked over at Pockets who was smiling from ear to ear.

The crowd gasped again as three more Hawks unexpectedly flew out from the blue sky of the mural and landed on the gym floor, causing even more boards to pop off the floor. They weren't as big as Robohawk, nor were they metallic, but nonetheless, I still wondered where they had come from since Timm had only painted the one. There must be more to their world than what we can see. How true it is with so many things.

The light beam, following Athena's departure, retreated into the sky, sealing the hole in the ceiling as it did and restoring power to the lights. The Dropas stopped their dancing and swiftly ran up onto my shoulders. Clearcoat whispered instructions into my ear. I raised the microphone to my mouth and relayed them to the bewildered audience.

"May I have your attention, please?" I said, holding my free hand in the air. "Please, may I have your attention? We need to exit the gym so the Hawks can leave the building without harming anyone."

Pockets took the liberty of shouting the same instructions into his foghorn, nearly deafening me and scaring the Dropas half to death. The crowd began to leave the gym, but slowly, so they could get a better glimpse of the Hawks as they walked by them. The Hawks just continued to scan the premises, having a look in their eyes like they were definitely here for a reason. As the crowd exited, I felt a tap on my shoulder. It was the school's principal, Mr. Babcock.

"Excuse me, Scott, but exactly how are the Hawks going to leave the gym?"

I turned to look at him as if the answer was quite obvious, which it was. "Well, since they can't fit through those small doors, I would imagine they're going to fly through the walls leading to the parking lot."

"I was hoping you wouldn't say that. We just finished rebuilding this gym."

I could see the grief come upon his face as he pictured what his gym would look like after the Hawks' departure.

"I can't bear to watch this," he continued as he turned and went into the hallway just outside the gym. Pockets and I looked at each other and started laughing.

"Poor guy," Pockets said.

The crowd, now completely vacated, had scattered throughout the parking lot, standing well clear of the outside walls. One by one, the Hawks crashed through the wall, sending blocks and concrete flying out and onto the nearest parked cars. Windshields were broken and the metal bodies were dented from the impact of the flying debris. Robohawk was the last to leave the gym, and the people outside distanced themselves even more for his departure. As it took flight and blasted through the wall, it sent debris a hundred feet from the gym. The steel girders supporting the ceiling collapsed and fell to the floor as the wall they rested on had disappeared.

Fortunately, Pockets and I had joined Mr. Babcock in the hallway. After Robohawk's exit, Pockets and I peered into the gym. It was a total disaster. Rubble and debris were scattered across the gym floor and all over the bleachers. There was so much dust we could barely see across the gym.

We decided to exit through a side door and walked around the school to the parking lot where we met up with the Hawks. As we did, we could see beams of light piercing through the cloud cover all across the sky. I turned to Clearcoat.

"Is this happening to all of Timm's murals?" I asked.

Clearcoat nodded.

"You mean the Tigers, Panthers, Knights, Chargers, Eagles, Dragons – every one of them?"

Clearcoat nodded again.

"So you little guys are what the old man meant when he said the contents of the vase would save the human race."

Clearcoat explained to me the old man knew nothing of their existence, but it was the power of the paint, the art, and the positive energy of the people, coupled with Timm's ability to paint realistic figures, that brought these Creatures alive. The Dropas were modest, too. Clearcoat emphasized it was now my responsibility to formulate a plan which would best utilize the Creatures in an effort to bring down Lord Ozone.

After getting a glimpse of Robohawk and thinking of all the different Creatures coming alive, I knew we could rid the world of Ozone and destroy his fortress, but not without some assistance. From the stories Willie had told me, it was clear Ozone had built an almost impenetrable fortress around his facility, but it didn't take me long to figure out how the fortress walls could be weakened, penetrated, and eventually brought down to the ground.

I turned to Clearcoat again and asked if it was possible for some of the Dropas to go on a small, but dangerous mission.

Clearcoat informed me it would be possible, but the Dropas were not accustomed to being apart, and it didn't know if any problems would arise. I then asked Clearcoat how long it would take them to get to Ozone's fortress, and it informed me it would take them about half a day with the help of the GGB. The GGB would have to get them over the canyon. From there, the Dropas would have to make their way to the fortress, get inside, and then locate Timm. After contemplating Clearcoat's information, I decided I would send a message to Timm with Clearcoat and the other Dropas. I told Clearcoat I needed Silver and Gold to stay behind with me and assist with organizing the mural Creatures and preparing any people I chose to go on this mission. Those selected would need protection against the chemicals Ozone used. Clearcoat agreed. My next step was to contact Willie.

The next morning, Timm awoke early to the singing birds in the courtyard. Waking up early was very unusual for him, but he couldn't resist the peaceful sounds coming from outside his window. He took his time washing and putting on the new clothes Shar had brought him the previous night. The clothes were much like a sweatsuit, but lighter and more comfortable. He then grabbed a banana from the fruit bowl and headed for the courtyard.

Outside, the sounds of the birds were even more spectacular than from his room. The refreshing songs they sang were almost enough for Timm to forget where he was. Almost, until he looked up at the blanket of gray blocking out the sun and the blue sky. Rather than letting himself get dejected, Timm allowed himself to get absorbed in the mystique of the courtyard, walking on the cobblestone path and admiring the marble statues standing tall amongst the trees.

He was so caught up in admiring the art he failed to hear footsteps approaching from behind.

"You like it?" Ozone asked.

"Geeez, don't do that," Timm said as he turned to face Ozone, his heart racing. "You scared the heck out of me!"

"I apologize. I thought you heard me coming."

"No, I didn't hear you." Timm looked at the statue in front of him. "I was admiring the statues. Who's the artist? I've never seen these before."

Ozone turned toward the figures. "I am. I did these about thirty years ago and liked them so much I decided not to sell them."

"They're beautiful," Timm admired.

"Thank you." Ozone looked at Timm. "You know, whether you want to believe it or not, we have a lot of similarities."

"We do?" Timm walked to the next statue. "Like what?"

"For instance, you didn't hear me walk up behind you because you were so enthralled by the art. I, too, can become the art as I admire it."

"Well, we have a lot of differences, too," Timm quickly reminded him. "I can't believe you have chosen to take the view of the bright blue sky and the sunshine away from us. Sometimes, it's the only thing people look forward to, being able to walk outside, look at the sky and feel the sun's energy flow through their bodies."

"That's exactly why I did it. It's part of the plan, you see." Ozone held his hands behind his back as he walked to the next statue. "Besides, people don't appreciate what nature has given them. You know that as well as I do."

"You know, if you would just walk around and talk to people, you will see that things have changed." Timm stopped for a moment and looked at Ozone. "Get out of your little cocoon, put aside what humanity has done in the past, and enjoy the rest of your life."

Ozone continued to remain unmoved. "Even if their attitudes have changed, it took the deaths of almost two billion people to finally convince them this planet is the only place they have to live. And as a result, they won't even get to enjoy part of it because it was destroyed in the War."

"We have you to thank for that," Timm countered.

"All this doesn't matter. It doesn't matter how people think or how they get along with each other or even if they do appreciate nature. It won't erase what they did to me."

Timm shook his head. "You really are pathetic. Why don't you get off it already and quit feeling sorry for yourself. As I've told you before, people finally woke up and are beginning to enjoy life and the people around them, that is, until you started messing things up again." Timm walked away in disgust.

Ozone followed him, still unmoved by Timm's statements. "Now, you're the one who's not seeing the picture here. People will never change. They will always remain the same greedy, selfish people they've always been and find a way to screw things up. People haven't been able to get along since they were put on this planet. They're the only animal species possessing the intelligence to make things work, yet they continue to screw it up, time and time again."

"You are so very wrong." Timm turned and pointed a finger at Ozone. "People can and have changed." Timm turned and walked toward the next statue.

Ozone hesitated and then followed.

As soon as Ozone was close enough behind him, Timm spun around to face him. "I've reconsidered your earlier demand, but only under my conditions."

"I knew you would." Ozone nodded emphatically. "What are your conditions?"

"I want my supplies, and–"

"Already here," Ozone interrupted.

"What?" Timm was caught off guard by Ozone's response. "What do you mean they're 'already here'?"

"We brought your supplies when we brought you."

"You broke into my apartment and took my supplies?" Timm was furious.

Ozone shrugged. "Didn't want to make two trips."

"You just don't care about anything, do you?" Timm's eyes flashed with anger as he approached Ozone.

"At this point, not really," Ozone replied holding his hand out to keep Timm from getting any closer. "But, just relax, they only took your supplies."

"How do you know that?"

"Because they wouldn't dare go against my orders."

"But you said people will always be selfish and greedy," Timm argued. "I would be careful with these ForLords, as you call them. Don't turn your back on them."

Ozone paused for a moment. He knew Timm was trying to throw his own words back into his face. He also knew his ForLords wouldn't dare betray him, for the consequences would be fatal.

"Enough of this babble," he said as he quickly changed the subject. "What is your second condition?"

"I paint wherever and whatever I want."

Ozone thought for a minute. He was quite familiar with Timm's work and decided whatever he painted would help brighten the dingy walls around his fortress.

"Fine. I will take you to your supplies."

They began walking toward the entrance to the house. Timm stopped for a moment to look at the last statue and then turned to Ozone. "You will not win, Ozone."

"Don't you ever stop?" Ozone was becoming quite annoyed at Timm's persistence. "Face it. Your life, my life, and everyone else's is nearing its end."

"Don't count on it. Don't underestimate the people on the other side of your walls, Ozone, the ones you have so easily blocked out."

Ozone raised his finger. "Funny you should mention the people on the other side of my walls. My little spies tell me your brother and your assistant are up to something."

Timm put his face right up to Ozone's and pointed his finger at him, shaking it in the air as he spoke. "Don't you touch my brother or Pockets, or I swear you won't see another day."

Ozone calmly stepped back and pushed away Timm's hand. "My, my, we are feisty today. But don't worry. I haven't decided what to do with them yet; however, they are no match for Lord Ozone."

"Don't even think about laying a hand on them!" Timm stepped forward again.

"Enough of your petty threats. Remember one thing: I can eliminate you anytime I want. I don't necessarily like you, but I like your art, so I have decided to keep you around until the end. Just don't cross me, or I'll get rid of you like that." He tried diligently to snap his fingers, but only a soft, muffled sound came from his deteriorated, gloved hand. He immediately turned and walked toward the house with Timm close behind him.

Once inside, Ozone directed Timm down a long hallway on the first floor. At the end of the hall was a door leading to Ozone's studio. Ozone opened the door, and they both entered. The studio was filled with dust-covered statues and paintings, finished and unfinished. Ozone had more supplies and equipment than an artist could ever dream of possessing. The supplies and equipment were completely covered with dust and cobwebs, but everything appeared to have escaped damage from the War. Over in the corner, Timm saw his supply box and the rest of his equipment. Not having dust on them, they clearly stood out from the rest.

"I haven't been in this room since they moved this stuff here," Ozone said as he waved his hand from one side of the room to the other.

Timm could hear the anger in Ozone's voice. He really wasn't in the mood to hear Ozone's story again, so he walked over to his box of supplies.

"Looks like everything is here and undamaged," Timm observed.

"Just like I told you," Ozone responded. "You should start believing me."

"I have no problem believing you, Ozone. I just don't believe what you stand for."

"Silence already! I will have some of my men take this stuff out to where you want to begin. Where would you like to start?"

Timm considered several locations for a moment. "Have them take it to the west entrance of that hideous-looking fortress wall. I'm also going to need scaffolding set up before I begin."

"We have it here, too," Ozone quickly replied.

"I'm sure you do," Timm said unsurprisingly. He then put his hands in his pockets and started laughing.

"What's so funny?" Ozone asked, rather defensively.

Timm continued to chuckle. "Well, I'm always looking for my keys or forgetting to bring them somewhere and now, when I really didn't think I'd need them, here they are." He laughed again as he pulled his keys out of his pocket and showed them to Ozone.

Ozone was hardly amused. "You have a strange sense of humor."

Timm nodded. "I didn't think you'd understand."

I took the Dropas over to Willie's office so we could discuss how the GGB would get the Dropas to the canyon near Ozone's fortress. Getting them there wasn't the problem, since Ozone's defenses didn't care what was happening on the other side of the canyon. The problem was how to get them across the canyon without any detection, since they couldn't travel through the chemical stream running along the bottom. Willie pulled in one of the surviving investigators, Jim, to ponder the problem with us.

After several minutes of silence, Jim finally spoke. "I think I've got it."

"What?" Willie and I asked.

"Let me ask this first." Jim leaned over and looked closely at the Dropas who were sitting on the edge of Willie's desk. They looked back at him, just as curious. "How durable are these guys?"

"It depends. What do you have in mind?" I asked.

Jim stood erect again and faced me. "We could load them into our stake-shooting guns and fire them across the canyon."

The Dropas heard this and became immensely excited. They were up for being fired out of a gun so they could fly through the air. I turned to Clearcoat and asked if they would be able to withstand being shot out of a gun. Clearcoat let me know it wouldn't be a problem as long as they were encased in a tube.

"Can the guns be loaded with their brushes and needles?" I asked.

"Better yet, we can stuff everything in a small knapsack and fire it across," Jim replied.

"What about the patrolling aircraft?" Willie asked, voicing his concern for the Dropas well-being.

"They're small enough they should go undetected."

"I don't think I like the 'should' part of your answer," I responded.

"I can't guarantee anything, but they should be all right."

I looked at Clearcoat and the other Dropas. They all looked at me and gave me the thumbs up sign. I knew how badly they wanted to see Timm again and also how badly we needed them inside the fortress walls.

"OK, let's do it," I said, "but we need to finish up a few things before they're ready to go."

"I'll get going on the logistics of this mission and will have everything in place when you've finished," Jim assured me.

"Sounds good," I replied.

Jim left the room, and I was right behind him with the Dropas back on my shoulders. I closed the door to Willie's office and stood outside it for about half a minute. I partially opened the door again, slipping my head between it and the door frame. Peering in at Willie, who had not moved from where he was standing, I could see the smirk on his face which told the whole story.

"You're going to make me ask you, aren't you?" I asked him.

"You got that right," he replied as he folded his arms, "and you better do it soon before I change my mind."

I walked into the room. "You sure you want to be a part of this?"

Willie walked up to me. "You know I want Ozone as much as you do. Whatever you're planning, I want to be a part of it."

"Willie, you know there isn't another man I'd want by my side."

"The same goes for me." Willie gave me a big, bear hug.

He was my best friend and we had been through quite a bit together. We both knew it was going to be a dangerous mission, but we also knew if we waited for the GGB to act, it might be too late.

I stepped back. "OK, how are you going to explain this to May and your two kids?"

"I'll take care of it; besides, didn't you say Lindsay was going to be involved in something at this end?"

I nodded. "Yes, I've asked her to take charge of eliminating Ozone's bubbles when we leave for the fortress, which brings me to one of the things we need to take care of before the Dropas can leave. We have to coat a huge supply of needles."

"I'm sure May would be willing to help out in any way she can," Willie assured me.

I pointed to the phone on his desk. "Give her a call and tell her to meet us at my house. You, Pockets, and I can discuss how we're going to get these Creatures together without Ozone's ForLords knowing. We also need to review my plan of attack." I used a second line to call Pockets.

Willie hung up the phone. "I'm ready."

"Let's do it then."

"You realize I could lose my job, going against the GGB like this," Willie said, half jokingly as he walked out from behind his desk and turned off the light.

"That you can replace." I put my hand on his shoulder as we strolled out of his office. "You can't replace your life."

The Assembly

While Willie and I were driving to my house, I could feel the Dropas' anxiousness as they sat on my shoulders. Timm had only been gone a short time, but I knew the Dropas missed him dearly. They would soon be reunited, but before they were, we needed to get the mural Creatures assembled in one location. We needed to do it fast, and we needed to do it as inconspicuously as possible so the ForLords were unaware of our intentions. Knowing it was unlikely that the Hawks' exit from the gym went completely unnoticed, there was a good chance Ozone already knew something was cooking. In any event, the sooner we acted, the better chance we had of maintaining the element of surprise.

Now, it's one thing to transport a normal-sized bird or cat, but it's another trying to transport a twenty-foot Tiger or thirty-foot Astro without anyone noticing. To complicate matters, we had to move over 200 of these large Creatures. Willie reminded me of the underground drainage system connecting most of the northern counties. He also suggested the Creatures be directed toward an old abandoned warehouse about twenty miles from my house. Both of us were familiar with the tunnel network, and we knew it eventually led to the warehouse, the only place large enough to accommodate our friends until we were ready to move them to Barrow's Ridge.

I put Clearcoat in charge of gathering the Creatures, with the exception of the Astros. Being located near a train depot, they would temporarily stay put. I had a special mission for them and they needed the rail system to transport them to the designated location.

Timing was one of the critical elements of my plan, and the Dropas were well aware they needed to complete the assembly before they could journey to Ozone's fortress. Once assembled, I would explain to the Creatures our plan of attack on the fortress.

At the next traffic light, I let the Dropas out of my truck, with the exception of Silver and Gold. I wished them good luck before they quickly disappeared. Silver and Gold rode on the steering wheel for the remainder of the trip home. I think they saw it as a form of exercise, trying to stay at the top of the wheel, especially during turns. Willie and I finished discussing how the Dropas were going to be transported to the canyon outside of Ozone's fortress. Jim would escort them to the GGB office via the rail system and then drive them to the canyon. Once there, the Dropas and their supplies would be shot across the canyon, we hoped undetected. From there, they were on their own as far as getting my instructions to Timm.

I pulled the truck into the garage and closed the door. The four of us went into the house where we found May, Lindsay, and Pockets sitting at the kitchen table. Cherie would have been there as well, but she was attending an international conference in Europe. She was now stranded there because the GGB had banned intercontinental travel after Ozone lit up their meeting. Willie arranged for the GGB liaison in that location to take care of her since Timm was now in Ozone's hands, while Lindsay and Cherie's family kept in touch with her on a regular basis. She would return as soon as they lifted the ban.

"Good, you're finally here," Lindsay greeted us with a voice of concern.

"Why, what's up?" I asked.

"This phone has been ringing off the hook," she replied.

"Who's been calling?" Willie asked.

"Principals from the schools. They're all telling me their murals have been vandalized. As one woman said, 'Their mascot had been taken right off the wall.'"

I walked into the kitchen and poured Willie and I each a glass of lemonade. "What did you tell them?" I inquired, handing Willie his glass.

"I just told them you would get back to them as soon as possible. Pockets took some of the calls after he arrived and told them you guys would look into it."

I drank the entire glass and put it in the dishwasher. "I'm afraid to ask, but how many have called?"

Lindsay turned to May. "May, what was our last count?"

"I think it was forty-seven," she replied.

"Geez, I don't have time to return all those calls. We have a lot of things to take care of and it's going to require everyone's help." I moved to the next issue of importance. "Lindsay, did you pick up the shipment of needles?"

"Yeah, they're in the living room," she replied.

"Great. Silver and Gold will help you coat the needles."

"All of them?" she asked surprisingly.

"All of them," I confirmed. "We need to be prepared for Ozone's bubble attacks, and not just here." I handed Lindsay a list of countries reporting the highest bubble activity. "We're sending shipments to these places in the morning."

She assured me they would have the most critical shipments ready. Silver and Gold would fill their quivers and eliminate the bubbles in our area that night. Lindsay, May, and whoever else they could recruit, would handle that job while we were gone.

Willie, Pockets, and I went downstairs to my office to figure out how to best utilize the mural Creatures. I cleared off my desk, and Willie laid out a schematic of Ozone's fortress he had produced from the most recent satellite images. The east walls of the fortress were protected by the base of Barrow's Ridge. To the north and south, dense forests bordered the fortress and to the west, desert-like terrain and a scattering of large rocks blanketed the area between the canyon and the fortress entrance. The Winding River flowed underneath the fortress and supplied Ozone's chemical-producing facility with a constant supply of water. The north, south, and west walls of the fortress formed a semicircle with the eastern walls taking the shape of a wedge, conforming to the mountain base. There were two towers located on each side of the west entrance and three towers located at each point of the wedged section of the fortress wall. From the reports the GGB investigators filed, each of those towers were equipped with powerful chemical-emitting guns, similar to the guns on Ozone's aircraft.

Inside the walls, the fortress was comprised of four distinguishable areas. The first was an L-shaped building, located on the north side of the fortress and was identified as Ozone's chemical-producing facility. Just to the south of that was the second area, circular in shape and believed to be the courtyard. Further south of the courtyard was Ozone's mansion. The final building, located in the eastern portion of the fortress, contained housing for the ForLords. The remaining areas of the fortress consisted of the same desert terrain as found outside the western wall. Other than his beautiful courtyard, Ozone wasn't much into landscaping.

Willie pointed to the inner edge of the southern forest. "The forest is only guarded along the inside perimeter and there are several cameras on the outside wall. Hence, the last group of investigators didn't encounter any resistance until just before reaching the fortress."

"Why isn't it heavily guarded?" I asked.

"I guess because Ozone feels no one can successfully make it through the dense forest. In other words, he grossly underestimated our capabilities," Willie assured us.

"What kind of resistance did they encounter once they reached the fortress?" Pockets asked.

Willie pointed out the areas of resistance. "According to the reports, the top portion of the walls were lined with numerous ForLords, in addition to the guns in the southern tower. There also were a number of ForLords standing guard right at the perimeter of the forest."

"What about the northern forest?" I pointed to the area in question.

Willie rubbed his chin. "I'm not sure. We can only assume it is guarded the same way."

"That's a dangerous assumption, but I don't know what else we can assume at this point," I said as I folded my arms and furrowed my brow.

Willie stood up and put his hands on his hips. "It may be less guarded because the river acts as another deterrent for penetration."

"Or it could be more heavily guarded since they need the water supply," Pockets added.

"You could be right, Pockets, and we'll be better off making that assumption. In any case, I think we'll leave the northern forest alone for the moment." I put my hands on the desk and leaned over to get a closer look at the schematic. "There's something missing here," I said, pointing to the inside of the fortress.

"There shouldn't be." Willie scratched his head. "This was drawn from accurate satellite photos."

"No, that's not what I mean," I said, waving my finger over the area.

"Then what?" Willie and Pockets asked as they leaned over to get a closer look.

"Where's the airstrip?" I looked for other possible locations.

Willie paused for a moment and scanned over the schematic. He found nothing resembling an airstrip. "That's a good question," he replied, rubbing his fingers under his chin.

Pockets circled his finger around the outside of the fortress. "It has to be located out here somewhere, because the buildings take up too much room for anything to fly in and out of the fortress."

"Agreed, but where?" I asked.

"This schematic doesn't show any sign of an airstrip," Willie reconfirmed.

"Seeing those aircraft fly the other night, I don't think they use a conventional airstrip," I recalled, "but they still need room to take off and land."

"It has to be in this area between the canyon and the fortress," Pockets conjectured.

"My guess would be Ozone has them underground, under a camouflaged opening of some sort," I added.

"That's a lot of area to cover between the fortress and the canyon," Willie argued.

"Granted, but it can't be anywhere else. There's not enough room in the fortress, the forests are too dense, and the mountains are too rigid."

"Who gets to find out where it is?" Pockets wondered out loud.

"We'll get to our assignments in a minute," I replied. "OK, let's move on for now. Our objective is to destroy the fortress, but limit the number of ForLords killed."

"According to what, the Geneva Convention?" Willie asked sarcastically. "Let's go in and kick some–"

"Just listen, Rambo," I interrupted.

"All right." Willie sat down in the desk chair.

I pulled a piece of paper from a folder I had set on the floor earlier. "What I have here is a list of the different mascots, or Creatures, assisting us on this mission." I handed the list to Willie.

Willie glanced over the papers. "That's quite a list," he responded and then passed the list to Pockets.

"First, we need to get the Astronauts, or Astros as they're called, into orbit," I continued.

Willie leaned back in the chair. "What?   Are you nuts?" Willie was not at all amused by this part of my plan. "How do you propose we do that?"

"Isn't there a space station launch occurring tomorrow afternoon?" I asked.

"Yeah, but it may be canceled because of Ozone," Willie responded before realizing what I wanted to do. "Ohhhh noooo! You have me in enough trouble as it is."

Willie knew exactly what I was planning. We had to cut off Ozone's ability to intercept the GGB communications and eliminate his ability to view our movement as well.

I slapped my friend on his shoulder. "Willie, buddy ol' pal. We need them up there to dismantle Ozone's satellites. You know as well as I do, there's no other way to do it."

Willie leaned forward and buried his head in his hands. "Man, oh man, oh man. What have I gotten myself into?"

"You have to make sure that launch takes place tomorrow," I urged him.

"I will," Willie assured me.

"How do you propose we get the Astros to the launch pad without being noticed?" Pockets asked.

"Easy. Willie needs to use his GGB authority and expropriate a train to an area near the launch site."

Willie was not liking this plan. "Easy? You're not the one undermining the GGB."

"You really need to adjust your outlook," I said sternly. "I got news for you. Right now, we're all undermining the GGB."

Willie ran his hands over his face and looked up in the air. "You're right. I'll get a train for our Astro friends."

"What are the Astros going to do once they're up there?" Pockets asked.

Their responsibility will be to dismantle Ozone's satellites, but I'm sure Ozone has some sort of security system protecting them, so it won't be easy."

"No doubt. This guy seems to have every angle covered," Willie reminded us.

I took a moment to look over the list of mascots. "OK, once the satellites have been dismantled and we've moved into position, we will send the Pioneers, Tigers, Panthers, Wildcats, and Lions through the southern forest. I think they're more accustomed to that sort of terrain than any of the others. We'll also send the Hornets with that group." I crossed off the names on the list and then looked at Pockets. "The southern group is yours, Pockets."

A huge smile lit up Pockets' face. He had never really led anything before, and I could sense he was grateful I had confidence in his ability to do so.

"Why the Hornets?" Willie asked.

"Simple." I turned to Willie. "The Hornets will be responsible for making large nests to hold the captured ForLords. They will also attack the ForLords lining the top of the walls, as well as fly over the walls if we can't penetrate them.

"Got it." Willie was finally starting to get excited about our endeavor. "What about setting up nests in the northern forest?"

"It's too risky. We don't have enough information regarding the north side; besides, we have another group coming down the Winding River from the north. That group will consist of the Vikings, Indians, Warriors, and Gators and will be responsible for destroying the chemical-producing facility. We'll send the largest contingency, that is, the Spartans, Trojans, Raiders, Knights, Chargers, Huskies, Bulldogs, Dragons, and Cardinals in from the west. So, they'll not only be the most exposed but will have to find the hidden airstrip. Now here's the big question."

"Oh, I can hardly wait for this one," Willie said.

"I'm giving you a choice, Willie." I looked at him. "Which do you want, the western attack or the river attack?"

"That's like asking me if I'd rather be stung by a thousand scorpions or eaten by a school of piranha?"

"I don't need this, Willie."

"Sorry." Willie thought for a second and then responded, "I'll head the western attack."

"You sure?" I was surprised by his answer.

"Positive."

"Then the western attack is yours."

"That's the best thing you've ever given me," Willie joked.

I ignored his comment and proceeded with the plan. "The Dragons and Cardinals will help get your group across the canyon. The Dragons should also be able to assist with the air attack. You'll need the Huskies and Bulldogs to locate the underground strip. Use the remaining Creatures to destroy the airstrip and then penetrate the fortress. Let's hope, by the time you arrive, Pocket's group will have completed its part to allow your group entry into the fortress. Once there, the final group will provide the air assault."

"Final group? Who's in the final group?" Willie asked as he looked up at me.

I checked over the list of remaining mascots. "The final group will consist of the Hawks, Eagles, and Falcons. They will come from the backside of Barrow's Ridge and attack from the east. Silver, Gold, and Robohawk will lead that attack."

"Wait a second," Willie said as he shook his head, not believing what he was hearing. "You're going to put two Dropas and a painted Creature in charge of an attack?"

"Do you have anyone else in mind?" I asked, knowing he didn't.

"They'll do it," Pockets assured Willie.

"And who's this Robohawk?" Willie asked.

Pockets and I exchanged glances. "Ahhh, that's right, you haven't met Robohawk. I'll personally introduce you two when we meet the Creatures at the warehouse," Pockets assured Willie.

The three of us spent another couple of hours detailing the plan of attack. It was all the time we had. We were quite confident we would successfully end Ozone's reign of terror. I, however, was also concerned about rescuing Timm. I could only hope Timm was still alive, but even if he wasn't, the main objective was to stop Ozone. Willie continued to jot down notes about the mission as I wrote instructions on a small piece of paper for the Dropas to deliver to Timm. Meanwhile, Pockets appeared to be committing everything to memory.

Once the attack began, the Dropas and Timm were to meet my group and assist with the destruction of the chemical-producing facility and the capture of Ozone. I finished the note and rolled it into a small tube, which would be easy for the Dropas to carry. I checked the time and figured the Dropas should almost be finished assembling the Creatures.

"Do you have any questions about the plan?" I asked them before we concluded and rejoined the others upstairs.

"Not at the moment, Willie answered. "It's time to cancel the 'Ozone Alert'."

I slapped him on the back. "Now that's the Willie I know! Let's go upstairs and see how our needle painters are doing?"

"All right," Pockets and Willie agreed.

"You think Timm's all right, Scott?" Pockets asked.

"We can only hope he is."

"I really miss him," Pockets said sadly.

"We all do, Pockets." I put my arm on his shoulder. "We all do."

The three of us went upstairs where we discussed our plans with May, Lindsay, Silver, and Gold. The four of them had completed coating the needles and had all of the shipment packages ready to send. Lindsay received the plan better than May did – May actually broke out in tears. Although they were both unhappy about our decision to carry out the mission ourselves, especially behind the backs of the GGB, they both understood the possible consequences if nothing was done. Silver and Gold, however, were elated, more so because they would have the opportunity to ride atop Robohawk. It always amazed me how the Dropas viewed situations so differently from humans. They knew the importance and the danger associated with the mission as well as we did, but it didn't overtake their excitement of being able to ride Robohawk. As we waited for the other Dropas to return, we sat around the table. I held Lindsay at my side, and May clutched Willie's hand while we talked about what had happened over the last few days and what was about to take place.

We arose early the next morning. Willie had already acquired a train for the Astros and much easier than he anticipated. However, the passengers didn't understand why they had to take another train when the one leaving was empty. Willie convinced them the train needed repairs and, under the present circumstances, it was too risky for human travel. He also explained to them they should feel fortunate they were being allowed to travel to be with their loved ones, because those who were abroad were stranded until the situation improved.

The train wasn't entirely empty though, because the Astros formed themselves around the inside of the cars to conceal their true identity from the ForLords. The cars looked like they were painted in various colors, matching the colors Timm used to paint the Astros. They were completely unnoticeable. The train left on time, and Willie assured me that the launch was still on schedule. We couldn't afford any delays.

Once the Astros arrived near the launch pad, one of Willie's contacts, Newton, assisted them into the payload bay. It took quite a bit of explaining before Willie finally convinced Newton to help us. Newton was one of those guys who always did everything by the book and wasn't about to give in until Willie reminded Newton he owed him a favor from ten years back – too far for Newton to question. Newton, as expected, repaid his debt. I knew Willie would come through; he always did.

Lindsay and May took care of the shipments, coordinating them with the GGB, while Willie and I prepared the Dropas for their journey to Ozone's fortress. They were careful not to mention anything about what Willie and I were up to, but explained they were delivering the needles Willie had promised after he discovered they were used to destroy Ozone's bubbles.

Clearcoat reported they had successfully moved the Creatures without any problems, and it felt confident Ozone's ForLords were unaware of the activities. Once again, we all turned to wish the Dropas good luck on their journey and told them we'd see them soon. The Dropas then said their good-byes to Silver and Gold, mocking human good-bye gestures. They hugged each other, pretended to cry, and carried on like a bunch of goofballs. Based on what Clearcoat had told me, I thought it would be a serious ordeal for the little fellows, but as usual, they found humor in the situation. I think they knew they would be reunited shortly, and everything would return to normal. Silver and Gold ran up and sat on my shoulders while Willie took the rest of the Dropas with him to meet Jim. The three of us headed to the warehouse to meet the mural Creatures. Pockets was already there, and Willie would meet us a little later.

According to my plan, the Dropas would arrive at the fortress in the early afternoon. We would attack the fortress the following morning. It wasn't much time for Timm and the Dropas to carry out my instructions, but time was not our ally. It also had to be enough time for our friends in space to dismantle Ozone's satellites. We only hoped we were ahead of Ozone's schedule and everything was going to work as planned.

When I arrived at the warehouse, I was astonished by what was waiting for me. There was a group of thirty or more teenagers standing outside. They were all gathered around Pockets, asking questions about Timm and about the events happening the previous night. The assemblage of Creatures was no longer a secret. I could only hope the ForLords, as well as Ozone, were still unaware of what we were doing.

I parked the truck and stepped out, with Silver and Gold riding on my shoulders. As I walked toward Pockets, I could see the relief in his face as he noticed me approaching. Unfortunately, the kids did, too, and I knew I was in for a barrage of questions.

"They're all yours!" Pockets shouted as the kids came running toward me.

"Thanks!" I shouted back.

"Silver! Gold!" A few of the girls became sidetracked when they noticed the Dropas, who had willingly made themselves presentable.

However, the rest of the group was concerned about what happened the night before. "What's going on, Scott? How's Timm? Is he all right? Why won't Pockets let us in the warehouse?"

I couldn't tell who was asking what and I raised my hands in the air to try and quiet them enough to answer their questions. "Easy! Easy! One at a time." They quieted enough for me to continue. "Before I answer any questions, what are you all doing here?"

This time a barrage of answers came from their mouths. I could see Pockets laughing off in the distance. He was getting quite a kick out of the ordeal. Fortunately, I also noticed Lauren, who was now preoccupied with the Dropas.

"Lauren!"

"Yes!" She looked up at me, taking her eyes off the Dropas.

"I want you to be the spokesperson for this overly excited crowd."

"All right. What do you want to know?" she asked professionally.

The other kids finally quieted down, although some were still preoccupied with Silver and Gold.

"What are you all doing here?"

"Well, two nights ago Brad, Ti, Brian and I were out, well, uh, parking in one of the schools." Lauren blushed.

"Oooooooo!" The rest of the kids began to tease her.

"All right, all right. Let her finish," I said.

"Anyway, there we were, parking in the school lot, when we saw this beam of light break through the cloud cover and onto the roof of the gym. We were a little scared at first, but Brad and Ti wanted to get a closer look. Brian and I decided to wait in the car until they came back. So, they ran up to the school doors, which someone had left open, and walked inside. Once inside, they saw the light shining from underneath the gym doors, so they cracked opened the doors. Well, you remember that school, right? The one with the side view of the Tiger stepping onto the blocks."

"Yes," I replied.

"Well, the Tiger was now . . ."

* * * * *

Brad and Ti peered into the gym. The beam of light was almost blinding as it retreated from the twenty-foot Tiger and disappeared through the ceiling. They could feel their hearts pound harder as they watched the Tiger's head move from side to side, surveying the uncharted territory. Ti gasped, causing Brad to quickly cover her mouth so she wouldn't be heard. It was too late. The Tiger's sensitive ears heard her gasp and peered through the dimly lit gym in the direction of where they were standing. Brad and Ti could see the reflection of the light in the Creature's eyes. They both wanted to run back to the car, but knew if they moved, it could be the end for both of them.

"Don't move," Brad whispered into Ti's ear, "and don't make another sound, understand?"

Ti nodded her head ever so slightly as they continued to watch the Tiger watch them. They stared at the Tiger for several minutes, their muscles cramping as they waited, motionless, for an opportunity to make their escape.

Soon the Tiger became uninterested and continued surveying the floor below it. It's whiskers moved back and forth, and its nostrils flared as it tried to determine the unfamiliar scents in the air. Brad and Ti decided it was a good time to make a run for it, but their muscles wouldn't respond. Subconsciously, they also wanted to see what the Tiger was going to do next. The muscles in its rear legs tensed, and with one swift movement, the Tiger was airborne, leaping off the marble and floating blocks. It glided through the air with its front paws outstretched, ready to brace its impact with the gym floor. The front paws hit the floor with a loud thud, immediately followed by the back ones, buckling the wood strips in the process. Standing there at center court, the Tiger surveyed its new world before letting out a deafening roar that echoed throughout the empty gym.

Brad and Ti had hung around long enough. Brad, already clutching Ti, swung her around to face the exit doors of the building. Ti let go of the door allowing it to slam shut. The Tiger immediately responded to the sound of the door and headed for it. Brad and Ti could hear the Tiger's thundering footsteps as it crossed the gym floor. Out the exit doors they ran, not even looking back to see if it was following them. The Tiger burst through the gym doors, and into an empty hallway. It stopped in its tracks and scanned the area, attempting to pick up the scent of its illusive prey.

Outside, Brian and Lauren saw the two running toward the car. The motion-sensored lights had lit up the corridor from which Brad and Ti exited. Only then did Brian and Lauren see what Brad and Ti were running from – the Tiger peering out the door windows. Brian opened the door as Brad and Ti jumped into the car, gasping for air.

"What in the heck happened to you guys?" Lauren asked.

Brad and Ti couldn't answer them immediately as they struggled for air.

"Oh my God! Look!" Brian yelled as he pointed at several Tigers now peering out the windows.

"The other wall–" Ti gasped.

"What? What are you talking about?" Lauren asked.

"They must–be from the wall–outside the gym . . ."

* * * * *

". . . so we went back last night to see if they were still there," Lauren continued. "We didn't see them at first, but when we were about to leave, Brian noticed the Tigers were leaving the building. They were walking in a straight line as if they were being led away from the school by someone we couldn't see. We thought it was really bizarre, so we decided to follow, ending up in the underground tunnel where we saw a number of other mascots."

"It was amazing," Ti interrupted, "fifteen and twenty-foot jungle Cats and fifteen-foot Indians. We were amazed and curious so we continued to follow them to the warehouse–"

"How many other people know about the Creatures being led out of the schools besides everyone here?" I interrupted as I put my hands on my head.

The kids looked around at each other. "Nobody else we know of," they all responded.

"Are you absolutely sure you told no one else about this?"

"Positive," they all replied.

"Well, maybe one other person," Bob said meekly from the middle of the crowd. "Tony knows, but he's been acting strange the past couple of weeks and didn't want to come with us."

The kids turned toward Bob. My worst nightmare passed before my eyes. I braced myself, knowing I didn't want to hear what he was about to tell me.

"Strange in what way?" I asked, folding my arms as I looked at him.

"Well, we usually do everything together, sort of like brothers, but lately he's just been real negative and always wanting to start fights and stuff. He's never been like that before. He's the kind of guy who usually gets along with everybody."

"This is not good. He will soon join the ForLords, if he hasn't already. It's only a matter of time before Ozone discovers we're up to something."

"Did the bubbles do this to him?" a voice asked from the crowd.

"Yes, Ozone's bubbles did this to him. Ozone's been using them for some time now, but exclusively at night. Because of their discoloration, they are virtually undetectable in the dark." The anger rose in my voice. "The Bubble Festival was a perfect time for him to release his bubbles in masses knowing there would be a large number of people attending the celebrations."

I knew we had to get moving. If Ozone caught wind of our activities before we arrived, the element of surprise would be gone and we wouldn't stand a chance. My thoughts shifted to what had to be done.

I motioned for the kids to come closer to me. "All right. You all know a little about what's going on here. I can't change that, and

I'm not going to stand here and lecture you. Since you do know a little of what's happening, I'm going to give you two choices, but once you make a choice you have to stick to it until the end. Is that understood?"

"Yes," they said in unison.

"Tony is the only person who knows about this, correct?"

"Yes," the group reassured me.

I wasn't about to give them a fluffy story about what was presently happening, so I cut right to the chase and gave them the details. I could see the anger begin to boil in their eyes as well, which in a sense was good.

"OK. Now, here are your choices, and I want you to listen to them carefully. Choice number one: You can leave right now, but if you do, you must stay inside at night and not tell a soul about what you have seen or heard so far, not your friends, not even your family. Choice number two: You can help me bring down Ozone, but you must realize you may not live to tell anyone about it."

I knew what I had said was a heavy load to dump onto the kids, but they needed to know the truth, and we needed reinforcements quickly. Most people would have laughed at me for asking them to join me on my mission, but too many times kids aren't given enough responsibility because they are "too young to handle it". In many cases, experience is the best learning tool there is, regardless of age. I knew they could help us, and deep down inside, I hoped they would decide to join us.

They huddled together for a little while, discussing it however they needed to, but I knew they would reach a unanimous decision because they were all good friends. I also knew many of those kids remembered at least a small part of the War, the older ones more so than the younger ones. Many had friends and family killed in it, and the memories were still fresh in their minds, but I wasn't sure how willing they were to risk their lives for the cause at hand.   They discussed it for a good twenty minutes, and while they did, Pockets and I discussed our options regarding Tony.   We came to the conclusion we didn't have enough time or people to track him down. We just hoped Ozone would remain unaware.

"OK," Lauren interrupted us.

"OK, what?" I asked, turning toward her.

"Count us in," they replied, some raising their fists in the air.

"All of you?"

"All of us!" They all raised their fists in the air.

"You're sure? You realize you could lose your life."

"We could also die if we don't help," a voice answered from the middle of the group. "We would rather take the risk and try making something good happen rather than just sit around and hope for something good to happen."

"Besides," another voice added, "our parents fought in the War. They fought for their beliefs and a better place to live. The world we live in now is a great place to be. We want to keep it that way, don't we?"

"Yeah!" the group shouted.

"OK, then. Consider yourself part of the mission." Pockets helped me quiet them down again as they cheered and huddled around us.   "In order to carry out my plan and bring you all home safely, you must follow my instructions precisely, understood?"

"Yes, sir!" they all shouted as they stood at attention and saluted me.

"Follow me then, my anxious little soldiers."

The kids followed me to the warehouse entrance. They were ecstatic about being a part of my mission, but in the back of my mind, I wasn't sure if they really knew what they were getting involved in by joining us. Was I taking advantage of those kids' willingness to please? I thought about it for a moment as we approached the entrance, and decided they were the best people to have for our mission. I knew them quite well, and they were all positive, willing, and dependable. They were no different from Pockets, Willie, or myself except for their age. It didn't take much to convince myself I had the right group to help bring down Ozone and help rescue Timm, a group possessing a tremendous amount of energy and desire to accomplish the same goal.

As we neared the warehouse, Willie was approaching from the other direction, so we stopped and waited for him. Before we went inside, I assured the kids they would be safe with us. They believed me and, in turn, assured me they wouldn't let any of us down. But, above all, they expressed their concern for Timm. Unfortunately, I couldn't tell them anything they didn't already know; however, I made them promise that until we found out otherwise, we would maintain the hope that he was still alive, and we would free him and everyone else from Lord Ozone's grip. Willie was quick to figure out the kids were now a part of us, although I was surprised he didn't say much about it. I think his memories of the War accounted for his silence and he knew we needed whatever help we could find.

None of us expected to see what we saw as we entered the warehouse. Timm's painted mascots were, literally, larger than life. The warehouse was barely big enough to hold all of them as they stood motionless waiting for us to arrive. The most captivating sight was the look in their eyes, like hungry challengers waiting to take on the champion. They were with us for one reason, and one reason alone, to help bring down Ozone.

Silver and Gold stopped me at the first Creature, a twenty-foot black Panther. They motioned me to pet the Panther, so I did. Unexpectedly, my hand disappeared into the Panther's black fur, feeling like I had just dipped my hand into a gallon of paint. When I pulled my hand back, I was surprised to see it was as clean as it was before I touched it. The Dropas explained to me that, because of their size and presence in a different world, they use extreme amounts of energy and occasionally need to remain motionless to restore their strength. When they do, they are most vulnerable to Ozone's chemicals, to the point one strike could eliminate them. The Dropas went on to explain, when in motion, their clearcoat shells can withstand quite a bit of Ozone's chemicals; however, they will eventually wear down and be as vulnerable as when they are motionless. Their rests were infrequent but necessary, and could occur at anytime. Because of this time needed, the Dropas warned Willie, Pockets, and me to be aware of the Creatures in our respective groups at all times, so when they rested they could be protected by the other Creatures.

Pockets was standing next to me, translating the Dropas' instructions to Willie, while the kids ventured off on their own to get a firsthand view of the Creatures. They all searched for the one from their school, and they did so fearlessly. Once they found them, they treated them as if they were their own pets and like they belonged in our world. As the kids made their rounds to visit the Creatures, Silver and Gold informed Willie, Pocket, and me they had taught them our language the previous night. They now understood us as the

Dropas did. Although they couldn't talk back to us, understanding us was the single most important element we needed.

"Willie, I want to introduce you to a special friend," Pockets said as he pulled on Willie's elbow.

"Oh, yeah, you were going to introduce me to the one you call Rambohawk."

Pockets and I looked at each other and started laughing.

"Now there's a new one," Pockets said.

The three of us walked down to the end of the warehouse. A number of the kids joined us, for they hadn't seen Robohawk up close either. It happened to be keeping itself away from all the other Creatures as it waited for its assignment.

"I want to know what's so spec–" Willie said before stopping in his tracks, his mouth dropping to his chest as he gazed at the mighty Creature. "You needn't say any more."

"Whoa!" Brian exclaimed.

"Awesome!" called out another.

Robohawk stood motionless as the light reflected off its armor plates, its breast pushing high into the air and its head protruding forward with a laser stare. Suddenly, Robohawk spread its wings out and flapped them several times in the air, sending a whirlwind of dust from the warehouse floor into the air. The movement of air pushed us back a few feet before we regained our balance, and it sent Roberto's hat flying off his head. During its final flap, Robohawk let out one of its ear-piercing screeches. As it did, all of the other Creatures immediately awoke from their motionless state and turned to look at Robohawk. They knew Robohawk was their leader.

"I'm glad he's on our side," Willie whispered into my ear.

"I'm glad they're all on our side," I whispered back.

I signaled to Robohawk to bow his head down toward me. It responded, and I climbed aboard, situating myself as it raised it's head once again. It was time to explain to everyone our plan of action. Sitting atop Robohawk was the only way everyone could see and hear me. Only then did I realize why the Dropas were so excited to fly on top of the awesome Bird.

We spent a couple of hours at the warehouse, reviewing our strategy over and over again, knowing we didn't have much time left before traveling to the fortress. Once everyone felt confident in what we were supposed to do, we took the kids home to their families and explained to their parents about their children's involvement in this mission. All of them were saddened and some were understandably angry. No parent wanted their child to fight a war, knowing they may not return. But, in every instance, the children reminded their parents of the War they had fought in and that the children were now fighting for the same reasons – the most important one being, it could end humanity if they didn't. Their parents didn't like their children's decision, but respected and supported them. It was a tear-filled event and, expectedly, their parents feared the worst. I could only reassure them so many times that Willie, Pockets, and I would bring them home safely.

We all headed back to the warehouse and waited to hear from the Astros. According to the schedule Willie gave me, the Astros were now in orbit. Once we received the word they had dismantled Ozone's satellites, Willie's GGB officers would take us to our initial destinations. These particular officers were good friends of ours who could get us to a central location near Barrow's Ridge. More importantly, we could trust them not to inform the GGB of our activities.   From the central location, we would organize our groups, travel separately to our strike positions, and carry out the mission.

Doorstep Of Fate

Once Timm decided to paint for Ozone, his schedule consisted of rising early in the morning, painting all day, and then going to bed shortly after dark. What else was there for him to do? Besides, it was the only way he could keep his mind off us back home. Fortunately, the concentration needed to run Ozone's equipment kept him from thinking about Pockets and the Dropas, who were usually with him on a daily basis.

Ozone furnished Timm with his sophisticated hydraulic lift; the one he had invented himself, hoping to use if he ever painted again. It was guided by sight and thoughts received from a specially designed helmet. The lift would maneuver to the location the user focused on, but only if they thought about moving the lift to that position. Once Timm learned how to operate the helmet, he was able to cover a large area of the fortress wall during a very short time.

Timm was interrupted twice a day for meals. Shar typically brought his meals to him around noon and six each day. Although he asked for her company on several occasions, she replied saying Ozone would not approve. So, Timm ate alone and stared at the blue skies he was painting on the walls. His desire to see real blue skies was overwhelming at times as he yearned to feel the warmth of the sun again. Occasionally, his eyes welled up as he stared at the gray cover above, wondering if he would ever see the sky, clouds, moon, stars or even the sun again. But mostly he thought of Ozone's plan of human elimination. The thought typically upset his stomach, causing him to leave the uneaten portion of his food on the tray. He would then return to what made him happy, painting, even if it was for Ozone.

On this particular day, Timm's routine would not be the same. He was eating once again as he stared into the grayness above him when the horrible thoughts of Ozone's plan began turning his stomach. He had been thinking of Pockets, the Dropas, and me, wondering if we were still alive and if we were going to free him. He threw his sandwich down on the tray and climbed onto the lift's platform.

As he raised the platform to the area where he stopped painting prior to lunch, Timm was amazed at how much of the fortress wall he had covered. When the lift reached the desired height, he locked it into place. He walked over to his supply box and filled his spray gun can with paint. He then flipped the switch of the compressor's motor and pointed the gun at his box in order to check the pressure. The sound of the small motor, similar to a vacuum cleaner, resonated off the semi-enclosed section of the fortress wall. Noticing the gun was clogged, he turned the nozzle toward his face as he investigated the problem. He accidentally squeezed the trigger, only to get a face full of splattered paint.

"Geeezz!" he yelled.

While he wiped the paint off, he thought he heard a familiar giggling sound but concluded it was because he was thinking about the Dropas. He then figured it had to be one of the ForLords who occasionally came over to harass him, but when he turned around and looked up, there was no one to be seen.

With paint still dripping down his face, Timm heard the giggling noises again. This time he turned off the compressor so he could determine where the sound was coming from, but more importantly, what was making it. *It can't be the Dropas,* he thought.

The sound of the motor diminished, but the giggling grew louder. It was coming from inside the top drawer of his supply box. A huge smile came across Timm's face as he slowly opened the drawer, placing his eyes just over the top edge to peek inside. When he opened the drawer far enough, he was again splattered with paint.

"Darn you guys," he shouted as he wiped the paint from around his eyes with his fingers.

"Who you talkin' to, artist?" a voice bellowed from above him.

It was a ForLord, who was now standing above him with his chemical weapon pointed at Timm's back. Timm purposely slammed the drawer shut, sending the Dropas tumbling against the back of it. He then turned and looked up at the ForLord, squinting to avoid getting paint in his eyes.

"I'm not talking to anyone," he replied.

"I'm not an artist or anything," the ForLord smirked, "but aren't you supposed to be painting the wall instead of your face?"

"You're quite the comedian," Timm replied sarcastically.

The Dropas were giggling even louder as they made their way to the front of the drawer.

The ForLord raised his weapon. "You think it's funny?"

"You're right." Timm continued wiping his face with his hands. "I must look pretty funny with this paint dripping down my face."

"You look like an idiot if you ask me. Get back to work."

Knowing he still had paint on his hand, Timm saluted the ForLord, purposely sending spatters of paint flying through the air onto the ForLord's uniform. The ForLord raised his weapon at Timm.

"Watch it, painterboy, or I'll spray you with more than paint."

"Anything you say. You're the man," Timm replied, knowing full well that neither this guy nor any of the other ForLords would touch him without Ozone's order.

The ForLord returned to the watch tower where two other ForLords laughed at the paint on his uniform. The three of them started pushing and shoving each other before their commander finally put an end to their skirmish and ordered them back to their posts. Timm used a towel to finish wiping the paint from his face and hands, leaving faint streaks where he had wiped. He then opened the top drawer again where the Dropas were now standing in a straight line, side by side. Clearcoat stepped forward and handed Timm the instructions I had given it prior to their departure. Looking around to make sure no one was watching, he took the instructions and read them:

Timm -

I hope to God you're still alive. If all goes as planned, the surprise party will start at sunrise tomorrow morning. We need your help. You and the Dropas need to paint a blue sky, with a ledge, and cracks on the fortress wall near the main entrance. You need to paint faster than you've ever painted before. You'll understand later. Once you hear us attacking the fortress, head down to where the river runs under the fortress. I'll see you then.

- Scott

Timm laughed as he looked at the fortress wall. "You want a blue sky, then there it is," he said softly, pointing at the wall. A huge smile lit up Timm's face. *Once again, we're on the same page*, he thought. Deep down, he knew I'd find a way to get him out of there. When he finished reading the instructions, Clearcoat told him he needed to destroy it. Timm, being the movie lover he is, crumpled the note and swallowed it, choking as he did. The Dropas started laughing again.

"Couggggh! Shhhhh!" Timm whispered loudly as he finished gagging on the paper. "You guys need to stay quiet. I'm happy to see you, too, but we can't let anyone discover you."

Clearcoat settled the other Dropas as only it could. They were so excited to see Timm again and wanted to play with him so badly, but they knew there would be time for it later after their mission was completed. Timm could feel the adrenaline rush through his body after reading my note. He knew he had to hide his excitement to avoid raising any suspicion with Ozone.

"OK, guys. We're back. We need to paint a blue sky with clouds and cracks. Clearcoat?" Clearcoat stepped forward and saluted, playing along with Timm's charade. "Move 'em out."

The Dropas understood and waved to Timm as they positioned themselves on the wall. Timm restored the spray gun to its workable state, donned his helmet, and began painting the wall again, only this time with a purpose. Quicker than ever, Timm dispersed the paint from the spray gun, stopping only to refill the can and continue the ledge before moving the lift. The Dropas were painting only a short distance from the spray gun, making sure it looked like all the paint was coming from the gun. Together, they were transforming the fortress walls into a huge blue sky, with large floating clouds, and cracks. After a short time, Clearcoat ran up

Timm's arm and hid itself underneath the helmet. As Timm and the others continued painting, Clearcoat briefed him on my plan.

It was late afternoon before four of the five Astros made their way into space. They had to wait for one of the human astronauts to release a space marker out of one of the chutes. Already positioned inside, they were soon ejected with the marker into space. Fortunately, the human astronauts were preparing to deploy a weather satellite and were preoccupied with their duties, otherwise they might have detected the Astros floating outside their spacecraft. Willie purposely didn't tell the astronauts they had company for fear Ozone or the GGB might catch wind of it. It didn't take the Astros long, searching through several dozen satellites, before they identified one of Ozone's. They knew it was his because it was heavily armed with his distinct chemical-emitting weapons.

Ozone had three satellites to view the world from his fortress, one over Europe, one over Asia, and one over America. The satellite over America was by far the most important one. Besides feeding communications from the other two satellites, it was the air security system for his fortress. All three satellites were equipped with instruments capable of acquiring reconnaissance information through the pollution layer covering the globe. It was crucial for the Astros to dismantle the one over America first, because if they didn't, it would warn Ozone of a ground attack and destroy any airborne intruders, namely our Birds.

The Astros approached the America-hovering satellite as if it were a friendly dog. According to experts Willie had spoken with, destroying the first two satellites would be the easiest. The Astros used their only jamming device to disable the security systems of the America-hovering satellite.   Unfortunately, the satellites' defense systems were designed to ward off any attempt to do what the Astros were attempting to do, so they had to work quickly to reconfigure the defense systems.

Having rendered it momentarily defenseless, the Astros disconnected the satellite's communication switches and cameras, but not before it relayed an emergency, function-lost message to the Asia-hovering satellite, which immediately began moving toward the Astros. Knowing they had barely enough time before the replacement satellite would reach them, the Astros reprogrammed the defense systems so they could destroy the approaching satellite when it arrived. Their plan was to destroy that satellite while sustaining minimal damage to the reconfigured one, because when the Europe-hovering satellite approached, it would have already received information about the destruction of one of the satellites and would prepare itself for battle.   The Astros would then rely on the reconfigured satellite to distract the third satellite long enough for them to destroy it. As three of the Astros reprogrammed the defense systems to fire on one of its own, the fourth contacted us.

While moving toward the Astros, the Asia-hovering satellite relayed a message to Ozone, informing him the America-hovering satellite was malfunctioning, and it was repositioning itself to replace the damaged one. Based on Willie's intelligence information, we knew Ozone would be contacted and could only hope the Astros would finish the rest of their mission and Timm would finish his. Unless Ozone thought the malfunction was accidental, he was now right in step with us.

Immediately after hearing from the Astros, each group carefully loaded their Creatures, which had been put into special holding tanks and then into underground rail cars. The tanks were similar to a scuba diver's tank and could easily be strapped to our backs. Fortunately, we were able to load about three or four Creatures in each tank without worrying about having them combine forms. However, once inside those tanks, because they were compressed, they were completely helpless. Silver and Gold informed us that when the tanks were emptied, it would take the Creatures about four hours to restore themselves to their normal state.

After all the tanks were loaded into the cars, we headed for the GGB trains, where we then transferred the tanks and equipment to the trains, and traveled to the GGB regional office. The only thing I thought about during the ride was why we had not encountered any resistance from Ozone's ForLords. It seemed too easy.

Silver and Gold's fleet of Birds left the warehouse shortly after all the Creatures were loaded, heading for the eastern side of Barrow's Ridge. Once there, they would wait until just before sunrise to attack Ozone's aircraft. My group was dropped off at a remote site ten miles from Ozone's fortress where we then hiked through the forest until we were within about two or three miles. Willie's group continued on to the regional office where they would unload their Creatures before departing for the canyon. Pockets' group also rode to the regional office and was immediately transported to the edge of the southern forest. We only hoped Ozone's satellites had been destroyed, so we'd arrive at our destinations undetected and without resistance.

Timm stopped painting as he noticed an increased number of ForLords standing guard on top of the walls. He also observed, off in the distance, a number of Ozone's aircraft practicing maneuvers. Timm wondered what was happening but didn't have to wait too long to find out. Ozone was standing at the bottom of the lift, calling for Timm to come down off the wall.

"You're done for the night!" Ozone yelled.

Timm looked down at Ozone in amazement. "What are you talking about?" There are still a few hours of daylight left."

"Doesn't matter. You have sprayed your last ounce of paint, my fellow artist."

"What d'ya mean?" Timm demanded.

"You have your brother to blame."

"I wish you would tell me what's going on here."   Timm needed to stall for time.

The lift reached its final resting position, and Timm hopped off the platform so Ozone wouldn't notice the Dropas heading for the supply box.

"Your brother is more daring than I thought," Ozone said, looking right at Timm, "especially knowing you are my hostage."

"He doesn't care." Timm pretended ignorance. "He probably thinks I'm dead."

"We can arrange that. But, whether you're dead or alive, you two will never see each other again."

"We'll see." Timm looked at the wall toward the canyon. "So, is that why your aircraft are buzzing around out there, to protect you against my brother?"

"You're very perceptive, more than I give you credit for.   I'm getting ready to carry out my promise, but first, I will have to do away with your brother and whoever is helping him."

"Don't be messing with my brother," Timm warned.

"And I told you not to threaten me! Pack up your equipment, but leave it here when you're finished. My men will return it to my studio since you won't be needing it anymore."

"You have no right doing–"

"And then return to your room," Ozone interrupted him. "You will stay there until I decide what to do with you."

"Oh, am I being grounded?" Timm laughed mockingly.

"Silence!" Ozone wasn't at all amused by Timm's remark. He was obviously preoccupied with the loss of his satellite and abruptly left.

Timm turned to look at the wall. He and the Dropas had painted as much as they could in the time they were given; having painted a blue sky with a ledge about four feet above the ground, and yes, even the cracks were there. He stood back and admired how much he had painted. *I have to get one of those lifts*, he thought. He started cleaning up some of his supplies off the ground. *The Dropas.* He had almost forgotten them.

He hopped back up onto the platform and pulled out the top drawer, nearly scaring the daylights out of the Dropas, but not nearly as much as they scared him.

"What the heck are you guys doing?" he asked as he quickly turned to see if anyone was watching. "We don't have time for games." As disgusting as it looked, from a human perspective, the Dropas' new game was quite harmless to them. They were in the process of interchanging their heads, each one now having a different colored head from that of its body.

"All right you guys," Timm said as he pointed his finger at them, "get your heads on straight. I've got a job for you."

Timm chuckled at his pun. The Dropas began removing the heads from their bodies and tossing them to each other, like a juggling act. When they each found a match, they replaced them on their bodies and stood in a straight line, still giggling over the new game they had created.

"Listen closely," Timm whispered. "As soon as it gets dark and until the time Scott arrives, you guys need to paint more cracks in different locations of the wall, including the wall I haven't painted." Timm paused for a second. "Now why are you giggling?"

Clearcoat motioned for Timm to come closer to it and he did. It gibbered in Timm's ear, telling him they wouldn't need that much time to paint the cracks, rather they would finish the job that night.

"Sorry guys." Timm backed away and looked at the Dropas. "I thought, well, uh, never mind. Remember, wait until it gets dark."

The Dropas all saluted Timm before he turned around and finished cleaning up his supplies. He was quite concerned now, knowing Ozone knew I was on my way.

"What would Scott tell me in this situation?" he whispered to himself and then thought about it for a few seconds before forcing out a short laugh. "'Timm, you worry too much.' Yep, that's exactly what he'd say."

The second satellite arrived from Asia just as predicted. Fortunately, the Astros had just finished reconfiguring the defense system. As soon as the second satellite was in range, the first opened fire with three streams of chemicals. All three streams hit the oncoming satellite with pinpoint accuracy, completely disintegrating it; however, the second satellite was able to fire one shot, which destroyed the shield of the first satellite. Simultaneously, it sent a signal to the Europe-hovering satellite which received the message and immediately left its position and headed toward the Astros.   It utilized its thrusters and emergency fuel so it could reach the America-hovering satellite as quickly as possible. While in flight, it geared up its defense systems and shield for its anticipated conflict.

Waiting for the third satellite to appear, the Astros tried diligently to repair the damaged shield but were unsuccessful. With time running out, they could only improve the satellites maneuvering capabilities, which they thought might buy them enough time to destroy the third and final satellite.

It wasn't long before one of the Astros spotted the approaching satellite and motioned for the others to move away from the one they were repairing. The three Astros just barely dodged an oncoming stream of chemicals as they pushed themselves away from the satellite. Both satellites exchanged fire for several minutes, with the America-hovering satellite hitting its target and wearing down its enemy's shield, while the Europe-hovering satellite continuously missed as it tried to anticipate the other's movement. But each time it fired, it came closer to hitting its target as it continued to learn the other's maneuvering sequence. The four Astros watched anxiously, waiting for the shield of the Europe-hovering satellite to wear down before it pinpointed its shot. The barrage continued for several more minutes before time finally expired for the first satellite. The Europe-hovering satellite had found its mark and sent three streams of chemicals on a line, intercepting and destroying the America-hovering satellite.

Having destroyed its first enemy, the third satellite maneuvered to destroy the four defenseless Astros. Their only hope was to get out of its range, but none of them could assess the "safe" range. As the satellite maneuvered and realigned its weapons to fire at the fleeing Astros, a huge ball of fire erupted where the satellite had been located, but not before three streams of chemicals left its guns. The streams were on a direct course to hit three of the four Astros. Apparently only one of them would make it back to earth. The four Astros, unaware of what was happening behind them, continued to move through space as fast as they could. The light from the fireball reflected toward them off a nearby piece of metal debris. They immediately stopped and turned to see what happened, still unaware of the pursuing chemical streams. Now facing the explosion, they saw the streams were only a few feet away from disintegrating them. Having stopped, they could do nothing but wait to be vaporized. As the chemical streams neared them, the streams suddenly dispersed into space having reached their maximum range of fire, which had previously been set for the distance between it and the America-hovering satellite.

The Astros quickly directed their attention to where the attacking satellite was initially located. Floating in its place was the fifth Astro, and a gigantic one it was, measuring nearly thirty feet tall and eight feet wide. It was an awesome figure floating there before them. Because of its size, it wasn't able to exit out of the chute as the others did, even in liquid form. Instead it had to wait for the astronauts to open the payload bay before it could leave.

While the two remaining satellites were engaged in their chemical fire, the fifth Astro had somehow concealed itself behind a large weather satellite, hidden from not only the satellites but also the Astros. As soon as the Europe-hovering satellite destroyed the other, it released itself from the weather satellite, still undetected, and destroyed the satellite from behind, compressing it between its gigantic hands and causing it to explode into a fireball. Seeing the fifth Astro floating by itself, the others headed for it. Their mission was complete, and now they needed to return to the payload bay. It was their only way back to earth, and they knew they couldn't stay in "our" space because eventually, if they stopped to regenerate, their bodies would begin to disperse into small particles and drift away forever.

Greeted By Adversity

By the time we had finished setting up camp, the five of us were exhausted. I hadn't slept very much for the past few nights and Brad, Brian, Ti, and Lauren, who I assigned to my group, were still tired from being up late the previous night. Unfortunately, rest was not on the agenda just yet. We now had to release all of our Creatures from their tanks to allow them time to regenerate their much needed energy for the battle less than eight hours away.

We emptied the tanks, making sure the Creatures were released in locations near the camp but hidden from any ForLord scouts. It was quite incredible to see the Creatures reshape, growing from a small puddle to ten, fifteen, or twenty feet in height. I had to touch one of them again with my hand while it was in a motionless state. This time I chose one of the Gators, because I knew I'd never get that close to a real alligator. I was so enthralled by the idea of putting my hand inside an animal, even though I knew it wasn't real, well, real by normal standards. As I stood there in my own amazement, I was interrupted by a voice coming from the trees about fifty feet away.

"Oh, no!"

It was Brad. I saw the other kids running toward him but I wasn't sure what happened. My question was soon answered as I was witnessing the huge Viking boat returning to its normal size. We now had a major problem. It was the boat we were taking down the river to the fortress. The boat was seventy-five feet from the water, making it impossible for the five of us to move it down to the bank of the river.

"Way to go, Brad," Brian said, now standing next to the boat.

"Yeah, way to go, Brad," Ti added.

"Hey! We don't need any of that." The four of them jumped at the sound of my voice, unaware I was behind them. "You think Brad doesn't feel bad enough already?"

"I'm sorry, man. I'm really sorry," Brad said dejectedly, turning toward me and then pointing at the tank. "I didn't see a label on this tank."

"It's not your fault, Brad, there is no label on this one," I said as I picked up the empty tank and, unbeknownst to the others, carefully slipped the label into my pocket.

Brad was somewhat relieved at my discovery. I knew it was going to delay us significantly, but I didn't want Brad to have the burden of thinking it was his fault. After all, Brad, as well as the rest of the kids, had enough to think about on this mission.

As we continued to watch the boat reshape, the situation worsened. Because the tank was opened in the trees, the boat was now engulfing every tree in its path, making it nearly impossible to use if we did find a way to move it. Even if the trees were removed, gaping holes would remain in their place. Furthermore, we didn't have the proper tools to remove the trees, nor could we use them if we had them, for the noise would undoubtedly alarm the ForLords lurking in the forest.

"How are we going to move it down to the river?" Ti asked. "It's not even close to the water, and it has trees growing out of it."

"Well, instead of stating the obvious, let's focus our energy on trying to figure out a solution."

Ti hesitated before answering. I knew she felt bad, but she was tired and getting a little agitated. "Yeah, you're right. I'm sorry, Brad. I didn't mean to get on your case. I guess I just need some sleep."

Brian put his hand on Brad's shoulder. "Me, too, Brad."

"We're all tired," I added.

"Hey, can't we reload it into the tank and then empty it by the river?" Lauren inquired.

"That's a good idea, but we don't have any of the Dropas here to help us. Remember, Silver and Gold were with us when we loaded the Creatures back at the warehouse."

"Oh yeah." Lauren's look quickly turned from excitement to disappointment. "I forgot about that. What are we going to do?"

"For right now, let's get the last tanks emptied and then call it a night." I put my hands on the backs of Lauren and Brad as we walk toward the other tanks. "We'll have a couple of hours to figure something out after the Creatures are regenerated."

We finished unloading the tanks and laid out our sleeping bags. It was a chilly night by the mountains, and all of us couldn't wait to feel the warmth of the sleeping bags. Building a fire was out of the question for fear the ForLords would discover us. We situated ourselves into a comfortable position inside our sleeping bags, knowing it would be a short night's rest. I lay there for a while, listening to the night sounds of the forest – crickets singing, pine trees dancing in the wind, and the river rushing over the rocks. But, as exhausted as I was, I couldn't fall asleep as the thought of the mission cluttered my head.

"Scott?" Brian whispered. "You still up?"

"Yeah," I replied, somewhat surprised somebody else was also awake.

"Something's bothering me, and I need to talk to you about it." Brian rolled over to face me, put his elbow on his pillow, and rested his head on his hand.

I opened my eyes. "What's on your mind, Brian?"

"Well, um, I was–" He hesitated. "I was wondering. Have you ever killed another human being?"

I really didn't expect a question like that one, but under the circumstances, it was certainly appropriate.

"Yes, I have, Brian, but not because I wanted to."

"Why then?"

I turned my head and looked him in the eyes. "It was a matter of survival during the War. If I didn't kill them, they would have killed my family, my friends, or me."

"You killed more than one?"

I turned away. "Yes, I killed more than I can or would like to remember."

"How did it make you feel?"

"Awful."

"How come?"

I got up on my elbow and turned toward him again. "Because I had killed one of my own, Brian."

"But, didn't they deserve it?"

"Nobody deserves to be killed."

"What about murderers?"

"Not even murderers. What needs to be killed is the part of them that wants to kill."

"I'm not sure I understand."

I thought for a moment. "Take for instance, Bob's friend Tony."

"Don't you think he should be killed?" Brian argued. "He's one of Ozone's ForLords now."

I was now sitting up, trying to keep the sleeping bag wrapped around me. "Absolutely not. Tony is a wonderful person. Only now, he's acting as a ForLord because of what Ozone has done to him, similar to what drugs can do to people. Drugs can make people become something they're not and act in ways they don't normally act. In many cases, the drugs can even make them do wrong or horrible things. They change the way people think and act toward others, as well as toward themselves. The same has happened to Tony as a result of Ozone's bubbles. What needs to be killed is the element inside Tony which changed him. Do you understand that?"

Brian laid down and gazed at the sky as he put his thoughts together. "I think so. What you're saying is we all come into this world as good people, but things happen in our life that change us to something we're not or shouldn't be."

"That's pretty close. You have to remember though, those things making a person mean, greedy, inconsiderate, or even a criminal are negative events and influences. They can mold a person in a negative way, but we are also molded by the positive ones; however, both embody an individual's uniqueness.

Brian faced me again. "So, there are negative and positive events and influences?"

"Precisely. The tough thing about it is, we can't always control what influences or events affect us. Although it can happen during any time in our lives, it usually occurs when we're most vulnerable and most impressionable, during our childhood. The responsibility of molding us falls in the hands of the people closest to us, typically our friends and families, who are affected by their friends and families, and so on."

Brian folded his hands behind his head. "It's all interrelated, isn't it?"

"Yes, and very complicated if you really think about it. But the bottom line is, kids need to grow up with as many positive influences as possible and be taught to minimize their contact with negative influences, controlling the ones they can or turning the one's they can't into something positive, knowing those influences are almost always lurking out there."

"That makes sense."

"I hope so." I adjusted the position of my sleeping bag. "I didn't mean to get so philosophical on you, but that was one of the major problems that caused the War. People had so many negative influences around them they just couldn't deal with all of them. The provisions laid out in the Survival Treaty are trying to maximize people's positive influences while minimizing their negative ones, as well as giving everyone common goals, such as living with and for each other while also enriching their personal lives."

"I like the way things are changing, at least until Ozone interfered."

"I think a lot of people like the way things are changing," I added.

There was a long pause as Brian thought for awhile. "Scott?"

"Yes, Brian."

Brian turned his head toward me. "Am I going to have to kill someone when we face the ForLords?"

"I hope not Brian, but there is a strong possibility you will."

"I don't want to."

"I know you don't.   I don't either.   Just remember, our intentions are to capture the ForLords so we can try to restore them to the people they once were.   But prepare yourself, Brian, because when this thought enters your mind again during the battle, and it will, remember one thing. Ozone and his men want to kill you. And if you think about it too long, it will be your last thought.   Do you understand?"

"Yes."

"I'm not saying this with the intention of scaring you, but that's how it is."

Brad thought for a second. "Are you scared, Scott?"

"You're darn right I'm scared.   If we fail, none of us will survive. But I'd rather be in our position right here than back home waiting for the outcome."

"Me, too."   Brian put his arms back in his sleeping bag and shifted until he was comfortable. "Thanks, Scott."

I put my head back on my pillow. "Your welcome, Brian."

"Good night, Scott."

"Good night, Brian."

Willie and the GGB officers, who had accompanied us on the train, were busily emptying the tanks in a huge, underground storage facility. The facility was about fifteen miles west of the canyon. For the past twenty-four hours, a few more of Willie's closest associates had been scurrying to empty the storage facility in order to accommodate its new guests. During the next hour, the associates were amazed each and every time they emptied one of the tanks.

Willie was very proud of the army of Creatures he would lead. He walked from end to end of the facility, with his head high in the air, admiring each of them. As he neared the last Creatures, he noticed something peculiar about the Dragons. He knew, from what the Dropas had told him, that the Creatures remained motionless while in their state of regeneration, but he noticed the Dragons had small traces of smoke billowing from their noses.

Bob, one of Willie's teenage comrades, walked up and stood next to Willie. Bob looked up at the Dragons. "What's wrong, Willie?"

"I'm not quite sure," Willie replied as he rubbed his chin. "Tell me, Bob, does this seem strange to you?"

Bob looked at Willie. "Does what seem strange to me?"

Willie waved his index finger at the Dragons' heads. "The smoke coming from all of the Dragons' noses."

Bob looked at the Dragons and then at Willie. "I don't have a problem with it."

Now Bob was quite witty for a young man his age and he saw this as a perfect opportunity to freak out Willie's associates who had also gathered around to investigate the smoke billowing out of the Dragons' noses.

Bob walked over to the largest one, winking at his friends. "Well, everything seems to be all right. Let's have a check inside."

In one single motion, Bob took a deep breath and thrust his head into one of the Dragon's midsection, hoping his head would come out still attached as he had seen my hand do earlier. He only wished he could see the expressions on the faces of Willie's associates.

Noticing what Bob was up to, Willie decided to play along with Bob's little practical joke. "Oh my God, the Dragon has swallowed his head!" Willie yelled.

"We have to get him out!" one of the associates shouted.

The other students played along, as well, and began yelling and screaming frantically. Three of the associates ran over to Bob, who was now flailing his arms in the air, grabbed whatever limbs of his body they could and pulled Bob out of the Dragon's body.

"What – took you – so long?" he gasped trying to catch his breath.

The associates were amazed there were no traces of the Dragon's insides on him. Bob and the others burst into laughter, Willie included.

"You should have seen the looks on your sorry faces," Willie said, laughing so hard he could barely stand.

"Very funny. I don't think this is a very good time for a joke," Pete said.

Pete was the head of that particular GGB regional office and was obviously not at all amused. By this time, the other associates had joined in the laughter as well.

Pete turned to his immediate subordinates. "What are you laughing at? Get back to work."

They quickly stopped laughing and turned to walk away, taking about three steps before releasing another outburst.

"Sorry, Pete, but I couldn't resist the opportunity," Bob apologized, extending his hand to Pete.

Pete ignored it. "Don't let it happen again."

"Yes, sir." Bob turned to Willie. "By the way, Willie, I didn't see anything wrong inside the Dragon."

They all started laughing again. Even Pete smirked a little.

"Come on; we still have a lot of work to do," Willie called to the kids.

The kids followed Willie and Pete into one of the facility's conference rooms. Again and again, Willie went over their part of the mission, covering every detail. It was too important and too many people were counting on them to succeed. The plan had to be executed the way it was drawn out, and the kids knew it. They were more than willing to have it pounded into their heads until they could carry it out with their eyes closed, which many of them did during their short nap while the Creatures regenerated.

Pockets found himself in a very unusual position. He was not accustomed to having a leadership role, which he had now. It was a good thing he related well with the students at the schools, because he needed every bit of his charisma, having taken the majority of the kids with him. The large contingent was necessary since Pockets' main objective was to take the captured ForLords and detain them in the Hornets' nests. He needed all the help provided and then some. I had faith in Pockets' relationship with the kids, which is why I gave Pockets that assignment. It also was the least dangerous part of the overall mission, at least in theory.

The group had covered about two-thirds of the forest and everyone was quite tired from the long journey. Pockets decided their current location was a good spot to empty the tanks. They were well hidden by the dense forest and far enough from the fortress to stay undetected by the ForLords.

As the kids began emptying the tanks, Pockets laid out the sleeping bags for the abbreviated night's sleep. He was rolling out the last one on the ground when the kids walked up behind him.

"All finished, Pockets," Joshua said.

"Excellent," Pockets replied.

The kids stood around and waited for Pockets to finish. Joshua was the only one who noticed something strange about what Pockets was doing.

"Hey, wait a minute. Where did all of these sleeping bags come from?" Joshua asked.

"Yeah, none of us carried any, and come to think of it, you didn't carry anything on your back," another added.

Pockets looked up and smiled.

"No way!" Roberto said as he gave Pockets a most peculiar look. "There's no way you carried all that stuff in your pocket."

"That's awesome, dude!" another exclaimed.

"Finished," Pockets said, raising to his feet and purposely avoiding the interrogation about his pocket. "Let's go over our mission one more time and then get what sleep we can."

Pockets unrolled a map of the area onto a fallen log, and the kids gathered around him. The first thing they noticed was the seriousness in Pockets' eyes, a look they had never seen from him. They quickly became quiet, for they knew what he had to say was very important.

"I'm going to tell you right now I'm not good at making long speeches, so I will keep this short and sweet. Before I start, I want to commend you all for having the courage to be here."

"Any time," Roberto said before Pockets raised his hand to silence him.

"Now, I want to remind you why we're here." He pointed in the direction of the fortress. "Beyond those trees and beyond the walls past those trees, there is an evil man. A man who wants to eliminate each and every one of you, your family, your friends and their families, and their friends. A man who has so much hatred, greed, and self-pity he feels no human deserves to live. As part of his diabolical plan, he has also taken a very good friend from us. What you're going to see tomorrow morning is a close-up view of his hatred, the same hatred that also was evident before and during the War. Although many of you have heard, read, or even witnessed firsthand what went on during the War, you will now get the opportunity to be a part of it as well."

Pockets could barely see the scared looks on many of the kids' faces as he looked at them. His intentions were not to completely scare them but rather prepare them for what they were about to encounter. The realization of what was about to take place had begun.

"If this scenario I'm describing to you is too frightening, then speak up now." Pockets paused and waited for someone to speak or even walk away.

They all looked around at each other. Even if any of them were scared, they were more scared to walk away and leave their friends. All of them stayed and waited for Pockets to continue. Pocket held out his hand over the map. One by one, the kids extended their hands until all were gathered together.

"Good!" Pockets spoke softly, "then we're all in this together, and we're all in this until the end."

"Yeahhhh!!!!!" they all shouted in a loud whisper.

"OK. Everyone take a look at the map."

Pockets reached into his pocket and pulled out three flashlights. All the kids just shook their head in amazement. Pockets handed the flashlights to those standing closest to the map.

"As soon as the Creatures are able to move again, we will head toward the fortress. As we do this, the Hornets will separate from the group so they can build their nests." He pointed to the marked areas on the map. "Each nest should hold about a thousand ForLords."

"How will we get them into the nests, especially the ones farthest away from the fortress?" Kelly asked.

"Good question. The Hornets will transport the captured ForLords to those nests farthest away, while you and the Pioneers will fill up the closest ones. I will lead the Cats into the fortress for the actual fighting and capturing. The Pioneers will be located at the edge of the forest, closest to the fortress," Pockets pointed to the appropriate area on the map, "while you guys will be scattered throughout the forest waiting for the captured ForLords. Although I don't anticipate much resistance from them once we get them to, and inside the nests, I want you all to prepare for confrontations." He reached into his pocket, pulled out numerous immobilizers, and handed one to everyone in the group.

"What's this?" Kelly inquired, turning it in her hand as she examined it.

"It's called an immobilizer. Hold it in your hand like this, wrapping your fingers around it with your thumb on the black button." They did as Pockets instructed. "Now, if a ForLord should get free and approach you or run away from you, point the immobilizer at him or her and press the black button with your thumb. The immobilizer will send out a pulse beam at the target and immobilize or freeze the target in its tracks."

At that moment, Pockets pointed the immobilizer at a lightning bug and fired at it. The bug immediately dropped to the ground.

"Whoa, dude," Roberto exclaimed.

Pockets then pulled out a mobilizer and shot a beam at the paralyzed bug. Seconds later, the lightning bug was flying through the air again.

"Do we get one of those?" Joshua asked.

"No, only the Pioneers will have mobilizers. Anyway," Pockets continued his earlier train of thought, "once immobilized, you should then drag the ForLord into the nest. Any questions?"

"What if we accidentally hit someone in our group?" Roberto asked, somewhat jokingly.

"Don't! But if you do, get the nearest Pioneer to mobilize that person," Pockets replied with an unaccustomed glare at Roberto and then continued. "If, for some reason, you lose your immobilizer, don't be afraid to yell for help. The nests will be close enough for someone to hear you and the Hornets are capable of hearing you from anywhere inside the forest. Agreed?"

"Agreed," they all replied.

"This will become more clear tomorrow when the Creatures awaken and we actually start positioning ourselves. Now, Roberto, you are in charge of the capturing battalions. Can you handle it?"

At first Roberto was puzzled by Pockets' decision after the look he had received only moments before the request. However, deep inside, he knew he was the right one for the job. "Yes, sir, I can handle it," he replied.

"Good, I knew I could count on you. Now, before we call it a night, are there any more questions?" Pockets asked.

There was a long pause. They all seemed pretty clear as to what needed to be done.

"Good. Then good night everyone."

"Good night," they responded.

The kids turned and walked toward their sleeping bags, talking softly about the events about to take place. Pockets rolled up the map and stuffed it in its tube, not realizing Kelly was still standing there, waiting for him to finish. When he did, she spoke.

"Pockets?"

"Ahhhh!" Pockets jumped, tossing the tube in the air.

"I'm sorry," she replied as she knelt to pick up the tube. "I didn't mean to startle you."

"That's all right." Pockets leaned up against a tree. "What's on your mind?"

"Do you think this whole thing is going to work?" Kelly asked as she looked at Pockets.

"We have to believe it will, otherwise we have already put ourselves at a disadvantage."

"I know, but I've been thinking. I can't picture this world without any of us here."

"I can't either, Kelly." Pockets extended his hands and put them on Kelly's shoulders. "That's why we have to think positively."

"I mean no human beings at all," she continued, putting her head down.

Pockets took one of his hands and lifted up her chin. "It's hard to believe, but that's what Ozone is trying to do. He's trying to bring out the greed and hatred instilled upon us over the generations.

The same greed and hatred we have been trying to eliminate since the War. We're here to give our species another chance, almost as if we were the chosen ones. That is a great feeling to have bestowed upon us. I, myself, plan on fulfilling that. I will not let Ozone or anyone else capitalize on those negative attributes humans possess and keep within the walls they build around themselves. Those walls must be broken down and stay down, and we must realize it is more important for all of us to live, prosper, and enjoy the intangible elements of life. We are the only species possessing the intelligence and the ability, the ability to allow everyone of us to survive, not just the strongest, or the richest, or the smartest."

Kelly could hear anger, resentment, and yet sadness in Pockets' voice. She looked up at Pockets and extended her arms to him. They hugged without saying a word, knowing very well what was at hand. Their purpose was the same, as it should be. Pockets broke away first from their embrace.

"Come on. We need to get some sleep."

As they started walking toward Kelly's sleeping bag, Kelly reached out her right hand for Pockets' left one. Unknowingly, he grasped her hand as tight as he could without causing her any pain. He was as scared as everyone else, but knew he couldn't let any of the kids in his group know it.

"I'm looking forward to the Creatures waking up tomorrow," Kelly said, changing the subject.

"I am, too." Pockets looked around the campsite. "It must be a full moon tonight or close to it."

Kelly looked toward the sky. "How can you tell?"

"There is a faint light coming through the pollution cover. If you look closely, you can see the silhouettes of the Creatures."

Kelly looked around the campsite. "You're right. I can see them. They're magnificent, even in the dark." Kelly's mind wandered for a moment. "Do you think Timm is still alive?"

"None of us know for sure. But, we have to assume he is."

"I hope so. I really miss him."

"We all miss him, Kelly."

They stopped at Kelly's sleeping bag. Although most of the kids had taken Pockets' advice and gone right to sleep, Pockets could hear Roberto whispering to his friends. It was hard to make out what they were saying, but knowing Roberto, he was probably preparing them for the battle. Pockets unleashed his grip of Kelly's hand.

"Get some rest now," he said.

"Good night, Pockets," she replied as Pockets had already turned toward his sleeping bag.

"Good night, Kelly."

"Pockets?" Kelly whispered.

Pockets stopped and turned toward Kelly's silhouette. "Yes."

"I won't tell anyone."

Pockets looked at her quizzically for a second before realizing what she was talking about and then gave her a half smile, knowing she couldn't see it in the darkness. Pockets wanted to thank her, but she was already crawling into her sleeping bag. He turned and walked away, looking down at his left hand.

Wham! The chair crashed against the top of the door just missing the two head ForLords, Alpha and Bravo, as they entered Ozone's meeting room. Alpha was first in command of the ForLords and the chief strategist. Bravo was second in command and was the chief tactician.

"What the he–" Bravo exclaimed.

"Silence!!!!" Ozone yelled.

Ozone was furious about something, and they were about to find out what it was. Another chair went flying into the wall, this time as a result of Ozone's foot. He turned toward Alpha and Bravo.

"I want every man we have on double shift and every fortress gun checked and rechecked to make sure it is in top working order."

"Yes, sir!" the two shouted.

"I also want every aircraft we have checked and ready for battle by tomorrow morning. Is that understood?"

"Yes, sir!!" They turned and headed for the door.

"Alpha, you stay here."

Alpha stopped short of the door as Bravo exited. He turned toward Ozone. Ozone was staring out the window into the darkness of the night. Fortunately, the light in the room was bright enough to keep his infrared visor from activating. Had it done so, he would have noticed the Dropas still painting the walls which were only dimly lit by the lights on the towers. Fortunately, he was too preoccupied by the most recent chain of events.

Ozone turned and faced Alpha. "The time has arrived for the human race to be eliminated."

"That's earlier than we had planned, sir," Alpha contested.

Ozone turned away from the window. "Circumstances have altered our schedule."

"And what would those be, sir?"

"All three of my satellites have been destroyed."

"What?" Alpha was shocked as he approached Ozone.

"You heard me. Destroyed!"

"By whom?"

"I'm not sure exactly, but I have a good idea."

At that moment the door to the meeting room flew open again. Timm was being held on both sides by two other ForLords as he struggled to get loose.

"Don't you people ever knock?" Ozone asked angrily.

"Let go of me, you pieces of scum!" Timm yelled.

Ozone motioned to the men to let Timm go and leave the room.

Timm straightened out his shirt and stared at Ozone. "What's this all about? I was sound asleep!"

"I want some answers and I want them now." Ozone walked toward Timm. "What's your brother up to?"

"I don't know what you're talking about. And if I did, why would I tell you?"

Ozone raised his right index finger close to Timm's face. "Don't play coy with me, or I'll cut your throat right here."

"Why wait?"   Timm challenged.   "You're going to do it anyway."

Ozone turned away from Timm. "Tell me what your brother is up to!"

"Look!"   Timm took one step toward Ozone, before Alpha moved between Timm and Ozone. "I told you I don't know anything. How would I know anyway? First you kidnap me and bring me to this dump. Then you make me paint and sleep under twenty-four hour surveillance. And now you ask me how much I know."

Ozone faced Timm again and Alpha stepped back. Although Ozone didn't want to believe Timm, he could find no holes in Timm's story.

"How do you explain my satellites being destroyed then?"

Timm leaned forward putting his face in Ozone's. "I do have an answer for that. GOOD!"

Timm could feel the pain run through his face as the back of Ozone's hand struck it, but he wasn't about to give into Ozone. He could feel his hands clench as he leaned toward Ozone again.

"Save your anger for another day. Unfortunately, you're worth more alive than you are dead." Ozone waved his hand toward the door. "Take him to the bubble."

Alpha called for the men to come back inside and take Timm out of the room. As Timm turned to greet them with resistance, he could feel a warm rush go through his veins. Ozone had sedated him from behind with a needle concealed in his glove. Timm took one step forward and fell into the arms of the two ForLords. They each grabbed one of Timm's arms and carried him away, his feet dragging across the floor. They brought him down the stairs into the bowels of the fortress where they laid him in Ozone's bubble.

Alpha and Ozone walked to the meeting table to review their strategy. Ozone pulled his chair close to him and sat down. *Thud!* The chair crashed to the floor and took Ozone with it. A faint giggle could be heard in the room.

"Think it's funny?" Ozone asked furiously as he looked up toward Alpha who was standing over him.

Alpha pulled his hands into his chest. "I'm not laughing."

"Huh!" Ozone raised his right hand. "Help me up!"

Alpha helped Ozone to his feet. Ozone looked down at the chair and noticed it was missing all of the support braces connecting the legs.

"You must have broken the chair during your outrage," Alpha joked.

"I didn't touch this chair. Get me another one," Ozone demanded.

Ozone and Alpha began reviewing Ozone's well-thought out plan to eliminate the human race. With the satellites being destroyed and the strong possibility of being attacked, they spent the next several hours making adjustments. Underneath the table, Blue and Red were laying on two leaves of the Corinthian columns supporting the table, listening to every word spoken.

I awoke at one-thirty. I just couldn't sleep anymore as I lay there in my sleeping bag, staring up at the sky. Something had happened while I slept that night. I couldn't pinpoint it, but I could just feel it inside of me, like something had been torn from my body. I had lost something. Something very important to me. Something very dear to me. I checked my supplies several times and found nothing missing. All of the Creatures were still there, and the kids were sound asleep. I couldn't figure it out, but as I thought about it more, I felt very hollow inside. Very hollow. I walked down to the river, trying to rid myself of the emptiness inside me and the pain in my chest.

"Good morning."

A soft voice came from behind me, causing me to lose my balance and almost fall into the river. I didn't hear anyone come up behind me while I was thinking about my loss and throwing stones in the river. I turned and shined the flashlight on the person standing there. It was Lauren. Her long, blond hair was sticking out in all directions, her face was somewhat pale from lack of any makeup, and she had sleep lines on her cheeks. She sat down beside me, picked up a stick, and began stirring the water. I pointed the flashlight at the water's edge.

"Hi, Lauren. Did you sleep all right?" I asked.

"I could have slept longer," she replied, rubbing her eyes.

"Me, too."

Fortunately, Lauren was more interested in the Creatures than in our lack of sleep. I really didn't want to give her, or anyone, more to think about than what they already had.

She continued playing with the water. "Have you seen any of the Creatures moving around?"

"No, Brad and Brian are still sound asleep." We both laughed. "No, I haven't seen any of them move, yet."

"Any idea when it might be?"

"I would imagine pretty soon. The Dropas said about four hours, but I think it will be sooner since they really didn't expend too much energy before being put into the containers."

Just as I finished my last sentence, I saw a faint reflection of two horns in the water. I followed the horns with the flashlight as they moved toward the middle of the river. The rest of the mammoth reflection followed. Lauren and I looked at each other and smiled.

"Your wish is my command," I whispered.

We both turned to look and I shined the light at the Creature. There, standing behind us, was one of the Vikings. Again, we were in awe at the detail Timm had given those Creatures. The most notable of which were their eyes, showing the look of determination.

Lauren turned to the water again. "Ahhhhh!" she screamed, sending a piercing bullet through my right ear.

My back hit the ground as she knocked me over trying to get away. I struggled to get up to see why she was screaming. But I needed to calm her down first before she screamed again and alerted any ForLords that might be in the area.

"Ahhhggggh!" she screamed again, but this time her scream was muffled by the huge hand of the Viking which had covered her whole face. Noticing Lauren was somewhat detained, I turned to the river with my immobilizer drawn, pointed the flashlight at the water, and saw what she had seen. There it was, a twenty-foot Gator enjoying a late-night swim. Only its bulging eyes and large nostrils could be seen above the water.

It wasn't long before Brad, Brian, and Ti had risen to see what the commotion was. Lauren had finally calmed herself enough for the Viking to release its grip on her.

"What's all the noise? It's only a twenty-foot Alligator," Brian chirped.

Lauren ran over and clutched Brian. "Yeah, well that twenty-foot Gator almost took my head off."

"I highly doubt it," Brad added.

"I'm going back to sleep," Ti said.

"Nice try, Ti," I laughed. "Now that the Creatures are awakening, we can get started."

"Not without eating," Brad said.

"Eat while your cleaning up camp," I told him.

All of the Creatures were now awake. The first order of business was to get the boat down to the river. I conversed with the Vikings, Indians, and Warriors about what to do with the boat. They explained to me as best they could the boat could not be moved in its present state. They gave me two alternatives, both of which might delay our mission. The first was to put the boat back into the tank, which the Creatures could do; however, another three or four hours would have to go by before the boat would be ready. That was unacceptable. The second alternative was for the Creatures to take the boat apart, board by board, and rebuild it in the clearing by the river. They assured me it would take less time than putting the boat back in the tank, but they couldn't give me an exact time. Because they would be working at extremely high speeds to dismantle and rebuild the boat, they would need time to regenerate their energy as well. Although I didn't like either alternative, my hands were tied. I opted for the latter, and the Creatures immediately began dismantling the boat.

In the meantime, I walked over to explain the situation to the kids. "Relax for a bit. We're not leaving, yet."

"Why? Can't the Creatures get the boat down to the river?" Lauren asked.

"Yes, they can, but it's going to take some time."

I proceeded to explain to them how the Creatures were going to dismantle and rebuild the boat by the river. As I did, I could see Brad was starting to feel bad again.

"How long is it going to delay us?" Brad asked.

"It's too early to tell right now, but it shouldn't be too long. Brad, I need your help over here."

Brad walked over with me toward the boat. "This is my fault, Scott."

I put my arm around him. "Brad, I told you it wasn't your fault. The tank didn't have a label."

He turned toward me. "Thanks for defending me, but I found the label in your sleeping bag when we were cleaning up camp." He pulled it out of his pocket and showed it to me, crumpled it up, and threw it on the ground.

I put my hands on his shoulders. "Look at me."

Brad looked up at me, still dejected.

"Everything is going to work out. There's probably a good reason why this happened."

"Yeah, a good reason for Ozone. Maybe I should just head back home."

I shook his shoulders, catching him by surprise. "Look, this is exactly what Ozone wants from us, to work against each other. Did you not promise me back at the warehouse you would be in this until the end?"

"Yeah, but–"

"But, nothing! I need you as much as I need everyone else on this mission, but I don't need somebody whose going to whither when times get rough. There are a lot of people in this world who are counting on us to bring down Ozone. We'll overcome this, Brad, but only if we're working together. Now, are you with me? If you're not, you'd better be soon, because I'm not going to let you break your promise."

Brad looked up at me. I could sense a different feeling from him. I wasn't sure if what I said had anything to do with it, but it really didn't matter.

"Yeah, I'm with you. All of the way."

"Now that's the Brad I know. Come on, let's go see if we can help the Creatures."

Pockets' group arose just before two in the morning. The sleepy-eyed kids downed their breakfast meals as they swiftly cleaned up the campsite. Pockets was off discussing the plans with the Creatures. As with mine, Pockets' Creatures also arose before the full four hour period. Once the Creatures had been given their instructions, Pockets returned to camp and stored the equipment in his pocket.

A number of the kids were trying to get a little more sleep as they sat on the ground with their backs against one another. Pockets wanted to let them sleep a little longer, but he knew that was impossible. Roberto's "soldiers" were the only ones wide awake and ready to go. Pockets motioned to him to organize the rest of the group, and Roberto complied. The kids rose to their feet, many rubbing their eyes or displaying huge yawns and stretches as they huddled around Pockets. Without saying a word, Pockets signaled for the kids to follow him and the Creatures deeper into the dense forest.

Pockets led the way with his flashlight beam on dim and a rope tied around his waist. Each kid held onto a section of the rope and followed their guide. The Tigers, Panthers, and Wildcats were well in front of the rest of the group, scouting for any undesirable ForLords. The Lions and Pioneers stayed in the rear to protect the rest of the group, although a small number of the Pioneers were blazing a trail for everyone to follow. Every so often, on command from Pockets, a few of the Hornets would leave the group and begin building another nest to house the captured ForLords.

Occasionally, Pockets would shine the light on a Hornet. He was fascinated at the way they constructed those large, spherical shells. And because of their size, the nests they built were capable of holding several thousand ForLords, more than originally thought. The seemingly hollow shells were all but that, having layers and layers of interconnected cylinders. But the most amazing thing was the wind the Hornets' wings generated when they flew to gather their materials and build the nests. The wind they generated provided much needed relief in the dense forest where relatively no breeze existed.

Pockets couldn't help but imagine what kind of game the Dropas would have created using the nests. *A good game of hide-and-go-seek would probably have kept them occupied for hours*, he thought. He stopped for a moment and looked off in the distance, wondering if Clearcoat and the other Dropas had reached Timm and if Silver and Gold had successfully landed in the treacherous terrain of Barrow's Ridge. Pockets' wondering ceased when he felt a tap on his right shoulder. It was Kelly.

"Is everything all right, Pockets?"

"Yeah, sure. Everything's fine. C'mon, let's keep moving." Pockets motioned for everyone to move onward, otherwise he might have stood there all morning wondering what was happening to everyone else on the mission.

The time passed by rather quickly as the group made their way through the forest, stopping occasionally to listen for any ForLords. When the Cats had reached their final position, they scattered themselves out across the forest floor and amongst the tree limbs, keeping a watchful eye out for any ForLords. Pockets and the kids caught up to the Cats about ten minutes later. The last three Hornets had completed the final nest and rejoined the rest of the group. There, they immediately put themselves in a motionless state to regenerate their energy; however, they only needed a few minutes to do so. Afterwards, they flew to the closest nest and waited inside until it was time to attack. Some of the kids joined them to see what the inside of the nests looked like. Meanwhile, the Cats and the Pioneers stood watch around the perimeter.

Roberto soon gathered everyone together for one last review. Again, Pockets spared no details, making sure they were as ready as they could be for what lay ahead. The kids knew the importance of their mission and reassured Pockets they would handle their responsibilities. Pockets knew they would, smiled, and rolled up the area map. Everyone spread out to their positions.

Pockets was clearly bothered by something as he began to circle the camp. He couldn't understand why they hadn't encountered a single ForLord. Not one. Although he was relieved in a sense, realizing the kids had been momentarily spared from fighting the ForLords, he didn't feel good about the situation. He tried convincing himself it was because the Astros had been successful in destroying Ozone's satellites, but it was still hard to believe, as close as they were to the fortress walls, there were no ForLords patrolling the forest.

"Something's not right," he muttered to himself.

He paced back and forth before finally settling down. Looking at his watch, he saw they would begin in less than an hour.

Willie's group arrived at the canyon well ahead of schedule. Like the other ones, his Creatures also took less than four hours to regenerate. Willie's group had the easiest travel schedule, but at a price. They had the most dangerous part of the mission. Once they crossed the canyon, they would be completely exposed to the weapons, primarily the aircraft, of Ozone. That's why it was so crucial for Silver and Gold to get the Birds over the mountains before Willie's group crossed the canyon. Willie was confident the Huskies and Bulldogs would locate the underground airstrip although if you would have asked him, he would have much preferred some Hound Dogs. His group had also reviewed the plans one more time before making final preparations for the battle ahead of them.

After finishing, Willie decided to scope the area, not knowing exactly what he was looking for, if anything. Using his infrared binoculars, he peered toward the fortress to make sure all was quiet. As he scanned the fortress itself, something moved through his line of site. He pulled his head away from the binoculars and then looked through them again where he thought he saw the object, but saw nothing. He was about to put the binoculars down, thinking maybe it was a bug or a distant bat, when he saw it again. He pulled the binoculars away from his face, trying to identify the object. Then it hit him. He recognized the object as being one of Ozone's aircraft, similar to the one he witnessed in the field several nights before. He stood up and walked over to where the Creatures were gathered, telling them about what he had witnessed. Looking through the binoculars again, he saw two more aircraft, only they were landing in an area midway between the canyon and the fortress.

This is going to be a piece of cake, he thought to himself momentarily until his brain was finally jolted. *Why are they flying maneuvers in the middle of the night? Something's wrong. Something is very wrong.* He looked through the binoculars toward the aircraft. "He knows we're coming. Ozone knows we're coming," he mumbled to himself as he put the binoculars down. *I hope he doesn't know when,* he tried to assure himself, *but there's no way to let Scott or Pockets know. This is not good, not good at all.*

Willie raised the binoculars, peered through them one last time, and saw two more aircraft fly into view. He was totally helpless and knew he couldn't sneak over there because it would blow the whole mission. His mind was racing as he put the binoculars back in its case. He stood and stared in the direction of the fortress. *Well it won't be long until we know the outcome*, he thought as he checked the time. There was less than an hour before the fate of the world would be decided.

The Creatures had finished rebuilding the boat around three-thirty a.m. and, as expected, began to regenerate their energy. I didn't know how long they would remain dormant, but there really wasn't anything I could do about it. We couldn't leave without them, so all we could do was wait and wait some more. I checked the current of the river and it was moving at a good pace. Everything was in place at our end and we would head toward the fortress as soon as the Creatures were finished.

I rejoined the kids, finding a tree that provided a nice back support as I sat against it. I looked over at the kids. They were silent and deep in their own thoughts. I could sense they were more nervous than scared, knowing they were responsible not only for their future but for the future of the entire human population. It was a lot of pressure to put on kids their age – preserving the existence of mankind – it was a lot of pressure for all of us, but never had I seen a more courageous group of kids than what we had brought with us on our journey. As nervous and scared as they might have been, I also sensed a great amount of certainty of their decision to be a part of this mission. We were ready and, no matter the outcome, I was proud of all of them.

I closed my eyes for a moment and listened to the sound of the rushing river. Thoughts raced through my mind. Thoughts about tomorrow. Thoughts about growing up. The past. The present. And, of course, the future. I didn't know what the outcome was going to be. The thoughts continued as I drifted off to sleep.

* * * * *

By now, Apollo was barking furiously as the three men crashed through the door. In one swift motion, he leaped up toward the first intruder and bit into his arm, forcing him to release his weapon. Unsympathetically, the second intruder shot at Apollo, knowing if the bullet reached its target it would also take out the dog's victim. Apollo let out a high-pitched yelp as I had never heard. It was the last sound I heard from my furry friend, but if I survived, I would always remember and be grateful to him for saving my life. I reached for my weapon and fired a barrage of bullets upon the second intruder, sending several shells into his torso. His body flew backwards into the hallway before collapsing on the floor. I then sent another barrage into the hallway, hoping to scare off the third one. As I hurried to reload, I discovered my effort had been unsuccessful.

In walked a stocky, black man, with a rifle now pointed at my head. "Drop the weapon and get on your knees."

At that point of the War, I wasn't sure which would be better, dying or hoping it would finally end. I dropped my weapon, not knowing whether it would do any good. The man walked toward me and put the barrel of the gun right between my eyes. I could feel the beads of sweat roll down my face as I knelt on the floor, gun to my head, looking up at the man who was about to determine my fate. As I did, I noticed a confused look in his eyes, but I knew if I tried to get away, his eyes would be the last thing I would ever see. He put his thumb on the cock of the gun and slowly pulled it back. The sweat was now stinging my eyes as I continued to match the stare of the man who was about to blow out my brains. I was a proud man and I wasn't about to give in to him by looking away. The cock clicked into its final resting position, and his forefinger tensed on the trigger of the rifle. I stared at the man for one last time.

"What have we become?" I asked.

* * * * *

"WILLIEEEE!" I leaned forward from the tree, drenched in sweat.

I had that dream many times before, having awakened in similar fashion, but I hadn't dreamt it for some time. My loud call had startled everyone beside me and I sat motionless, staring and sweating.

Lauren was the first to arrive. "Scott, are you OK?" She put her hands on my face and looked at me.

For a moment, all I did was stare at her, unable to move any part of my body or hear anything she was saying.

"Scott, are you OK?" she asked again.

I finally blinked. "Yeah, I'm OK."

By now, the others were also around me.

"What happened?" Lauren asked.

"Just a recurring dream, that's all."

"That must be some dream," Brian added.

"It's a nightmare. A nightmare that keeps the memory of the War implanted in my head."

"Can you tell us about it?" Ti asked.

I wiped the sweat from my face with my sleeve. The kids sat down beside me and listened as I proceeded to describe my recurring nightmare.

"So what finally happened? How did you get out of it?" Brian asked.

"The man thought about my question, took his finger off the trigger, repositioned the cock, and lowered his weapon."

"Did you then kick his butt?" Brad asked.

"No, not at all." I paused and then looked at Brad. "He became my best friend."

"What?" they asked in shock.

"You mean you're telling us you became best friends with the man who was about to blow your brains out?" Brian asked.

"That's exactly what I'm telling you."

"That man's name wouldn't happen to be 'Willie', would it?" Ti asked.

"You are a perceptive one, Ti."

"No way!" the others exclaimed.

"What happened next?" Lauren asked.

"We talked." I wiped the remaining sweat from my face. "We talked for a very long time about what was happening and what we could do to try and stop the uncontrollable killing. We decided to take our followers and team up with the sole purpose of stopping the

War. Together, we then acquired more followers and still more until the fighting finally stopped."

"But, why do you keep having that nightmare?" Lauren wondered.

"Before, it was a constant reminder to me of what happened. But since I haven't had it for some time, I think its a reminder that Ozone is still alive, and as long as he is alive, we're not safe."

"It's up to us to stop him," Brian interjected.

"That's right," Lauren added.

"Yeah!" Brian bellowed.

"Your chance will be here soon enough," I said as I checked the time. "We have less than an hour before it all starts." I looked up and saw one of the Warriors approaching. "It's time to roll. The Creatures have completed their regeneration."

We quickly jump up from where we were seated and headed down to the river.

Ozone went downstairs to check on Timm's progress. The bubble he had Timm put in was different than the ones he had been unleashing on the public. It took longer than the other ones, but it was able to conform its victim to exactly the way Ozone wanted. It's only flaw was, if it was interrupted prematurely, the victim's mind would return to its original state. Ozone stepped up to the bubble and peered inside it. Although Timm had been in there for several hours, he was still fighting the bubble's effort to change him or, eventually, kill him. Ozone was quite surprised Timm was still fighting. Timm approached Ozone, refusing to give Ozone any indication of weakening, but was unsure as to how much longer he could actually fight the effects of the bubble.

"I'd really like to stay and watch this little show, but I have to get ready for your brother," Ozone said.

Timm put his hands on the inside of the bubble near Ozone. "What are you talking about?" Timm asked in a weakened voice, his eyes only half open.

Ozone backed away from Timm. "Let's just say my sources have told me they haven't seen your brother around for the last day or two. I believe he is coming to pay me a visit."

"You better hope he doesn't, because he'll kick your sorry–"

"Don't be so sure, my little friend," Ozone interrupted. I'm very close to being ready for whatever the little maggot has to offer. He won't last very long. Then once I'm rid of him, I can rid my eyes and my conscience of the remaining human race.

"You'll rot in Hell before we give in to you."

"That's very threatening coming from someone trapped in my bubble."

Timm knew Ozone was probably right as the pressure inside of his head continued to increase, but he had too much pride to let Ozone believe otherwise.

"Well, the next time we meet, you'll either join me or I'll have to toss your dead body into the river."

Timm could feel his knees begin to buckle. "I'd rather die than join you."

Ozone turned away from Timm. "Have it your way. As for me, I have more important things to do."

"Just remember, Ozone, things aren't always what they appear to be."

Ozone didn't think much of what Timm said as he walked away and headed up the stairs. Seeing Ozone had disappeared, Timm collapsed to the base of the bubble. He couldn't fight any longer. The effects of the bubble had taken over his mind. Rolling over on his back, he reached weakly for the inside of the bubble, his hand sliding down it. He had barely enough energy to breathe let alone attempt an escape. As he looked up toward the top of the bubble, his vision blurred and unconsciousness overtook him.

Silver and Gold's journey with the Birds was relatively uneventful until they were about halfway up the backside of Barrow's Ridge. There they were met by a severe, summer snow storm. The infamous Western Winds swirled in their faces at gusts of over seventy miles an hour. The Birds would not have enough energy to fly through the winds and then fight Ozone's aircraft when they arrived. In addition, the sub-freezing temperatures only complicated matters by hindering their flying abilities.

Silver spotted an area in the side of the mountains that looked like it would provide some shelter for them. Gold signaled for the Birds to follow it and Robohawk to that area. It was questionable whether the others could have seen Gold's signal because the visibility was almost zero, but Gold was counting on the Birds' excellent eyesight. Silver also had Robohawk utilize its piercing screech to call to them periodically, which helped guide them to the designated area.

Once they landed, Silver and Gold worked as fast as they could, painting a shelter big enough for all of them. They knew there was no time to waste for the cold temperatures were beginning to affect them as well. In about twenty minutes, they had successfully painted a large cavern and then led the Birds inside it. Silver then painted a door to protect them from the cold winds, and Gold painted some camp fires. As the cavern warmed up, the Birds began regenerating their energy. Side by side they stood motionless, gearing themselves up for the morning battle with Ozone's aircraft.

Silver and Gold decided they could do nothing more but wait out the storm. They had thought about painting a tunnel through the mountains, but realized it would take too long, even for them to complete. As the Birds remained motionless along the cavern walls, Silver and Gold decided to play another one of their favorite Dropa games. So, they painted a little race track, a car for each of them, and began racing around the cavern. They raced for hours, typically painting obstacles for the other to overcome. As the time passed, the storm began to subside and they hoped there was enough time to make it to the fortress. Their part of the mission was the most critical, and they knew it.

No Turning Back

Dawn was almost upon us. Had the Creatures taken any longer to regenerate, the delay might have put a dagger in the mission. The majority of the Creatures were already down by the shoreline, and the Gators were waiting in the water. The fatigue we were feeling earlier had been overtaken by the adrenaline flowing through our veins. Any events prior to our departure were insignificant. What mattered now were the events in front of us. One way or another, the fate of the human race was about to be determined. Would it exist and continue to evolve, or would it join the likes of the dinosaurs?

I raised my binoculars and scanned the sky above the fortress and out toward the canyon. The kids were now gathered around me as I turned toward Barrow's Ridge. Peering through the glasses a second time, my sense of concern grew stronger.

I handed the binoculars to Brad. "See anything?"

Brad dropped his gear on the ground to take a look. "No," he whispered, "not a thing." He handed the binoculars back to me.

"I don't see anything either. Where are the birds? Willie is about to cross the canyon, and there's no air support. He won't even come close to finding the airstrip before they discover him first. He doesn't stand a chance without any air support."

"Maybe they're so quiet we can't hear them," Brian said trying to give me a glimmer of hope.

I turned to him. "You think Robohawk would go into battle without letting everyone know whose in charge?"

"Sorry, I didn't mean– "

"All right," I interrupted. "Is everyone clear on what they're supposed to do once we get inside the fortress?"

"Yes," they replied.

"If not, this is the only chance you'll have to ask."

"We're sure," Brad responded for all of them. "Let's get going."

"Good." I stopped for a moment and looked at the kids. "I want you guys to know I'm extremely proud of you."

They looked at me and smiled.

"Now let's get this boat in the water," I commanded.

Lauren and Brad grabbed the ends of two ropes and formed a loop on each them. Then, they took the loops down to the river and gave them to the Gators. Still feeling the effects of her first encounter, Lauren threw her rope into the water about ten feet away from her targeted Gator. The Gators positioned their noses inside the loops and waited for the signal. Meanwhile, Brian and Ti had tied the other ends of the ropes onto the bow of the boat. The Indians and Warriors positioned themselves along the sides and rear of the boat so they could push, while the Vikings assisted the Gators, taking hold of the ropes and pulling from the front. Upon my signal, the Creatures began moving the vessel with relative ease: the Gators swiftly propelling their massive tails in the water while the Vikings pulled on the ropes, leaving large footprints in the dirt behind them. The Indians and Warriors could not be heard as they displayed their ease and silence of movement along the ground, and unlike the Vikings, they left no trace of where they had walked. Within minutes the boat had reached the water's edge, and the Indians were tying the looped ends to the trees along the shore. The five of us stood and watched the entire event in amazement.   As I marveled at their size and strength, I was beginning to feel more confident with every passing moment.

I informed the kids we had to keep silent until we reached our next destination and, if necessary, only talk in a soft whisper. We could not afford to reveal ourselves, especially since the tower guards were not yet distracted by Silver and Gold's group.

Having all climbed aboard, I signaled the Indians to untie and toss us the ropes. We began to move down the river to a point within a mile of the fortress. Once there, the five of us would leave the boat and travel the remainder of the river by Gator. I only hoped Lauren would overcome her phobia of our Gator friends. The Indians and Warriors spread themselves along the left and right banks, respectively, looking out for any ForLords who might be in the area, which I expected. The Gators swam on the sides and in front of the boat, while the Vikings stayed with us to navigate. The Gators in front provided some extra speed by pulling the boat along with the ropes we had provided them. They made sure we moved down the river as fast as possible, knowing we needed to arrive at the fortress by sunrise.

I kept a watch out for Silver and Gold's fleet of Birds, but saw nothing. My concern for Willie's group grew stronger, knowing if the Birds were even slightly delayed, it would threaten many lives and jeopardize the entire mission. I continued searching until we neared our destination. The Gators slowed the boat, and the Vikings steered it toward the shore. The cloud cover was beginning to brighten. It was almost sunrise, and I knew there wasn't much time left before the assault would commence.

Once on shore, I handed the ropes to the Vikings and immediately headed toward the Gators, but not before I pulled the kids together. They looked at me, seeking words of wisdom I could not provide. Instead I extended my hand to them and they followed, grabbing on to the hand below theirs.

"Just remember, I'm bringing you all home with me," I said.

Our hands gripped tightly around each others' before we finally released. We were ready. We had to be because there was no turning back.

We each crawled inside our assigned Gator's mouth, Lauren included. It was a tight fit and luckily no one was claustrophobic. The mouths of the Gators closed, but not completely, leaving enough space for fresh air to reach us. One by one, they crawled into the water. It was a strange feeling being inside an animal, so to speak. I felt like I was inside a torpedo bay waiting to be fired.

The powerful strokes from the Gators' tails and the aid of the river's current took us to the fortress in a short period of time. The Vikings were right behind us in their boat, armed and ready for their encounter with the ForLords. The Warriors and Indians were traveling along the shore, ready to overpower anyone who tried to stop them.

Many thoughts raced through my mind during that abbreviated trip inside the Gator. I thought about Lindsay, the many friendships I had made over the years, the War, and the progress we humans were making to better our world. And then I thought about Ozone and wondered how anyone could have the capacity for the amount of hate he had, so much hate he was willing to eliminate the entire human race. My thoughts were suddenly interrupted.

"FIRE!"

I heard several ForLords shouting from atop the fortress wall. They began firing on the Vikings as the Gators' mouths closed, engulfing us in complete darkness. We had submerged and were now traveling underneath the fortress walls. Once inside, we had no idea what would be awaiting us when the Gators' mouths reopened. We all readied our immobilizers for the "grand opening".

Swwwwish! Thump! The last ForLord outside the fortress fell quietly to the ground. The Lion's paw was like a large frying pan striking the ForLord's head. As soon as one hit the ground, a Pioneer stepped out from behind a nearby tree and carried the prisoner to the nearest Hornet's nest. In much the same manner, the other Cats had taken care of the numerous ForLords lining the edge of the forest and standing guard outside the fortress walls.

It was now time for Stripes (the Tiger Brad and Ti first encountered), Pockets, and the other Tigers to make their way into the fortress. Pockets leaned over and opened his pocket for Stripes' companions to enter. They did so with little difficulty, disappearing one by one into virtual nothingness until the last one was inside it. Pockets then climbed aboard Stripes, and they exited the safety of the forest's edge while avoiding the fortress cameras. Once Pockets and Stripes were inside the fortress, the Hornets would begin their assault on the fortress walls in hopes of drawing fire toward them and away from Pockets and Stripes.

Stripes, with its body low to the ground, began making its way toward the fortress walls with Pockets straddled on its back, gripping its short mane. With each stride covering a large amount of ground, the huge Tiger reached the fortress wall in very little time, but more importantly, unnoticed. It made its way around to the front entrance and upon reaching it, Pockets hopped off, staying close to the wall himself.

Pockets signaled to Stripes with his hand. Stripes immediately responded by walking into the huge fortress doors, its head slowly disappearing into the thick, wooden panels, followed by its paws.

Liquidating its body through the door, Stripes' head surfaced on the opposite side. As it did, it saw four ForLords standing with their backs to it. Their weapons were slung over their shoulders, and they were unaware of what was happening behind them, at least momentarily. Stripes continued to pull its body into the door, filling every crack possible until its body disappeared from the outside of the fortress.

"What the–" one of the ForLords said as he turned around in his tracks. He walked closer to the door.

Stripes pulled its head back from the surface of the door, concealing it in the pores of the wood.

The curious ForLord turned back to the others. "Did you guys see that?"

"See what?" one of the others inquired.

The ForLord pointed at the door. "I could have sworn I saw a tiger's head on that door."

"This double shift has you seeing things. There's nothing there," another ForLord assured his comrade as he gazed at the door.

"Yeah, you're probably right."

The ForLords turned around again while Stripes began to resurface. The one ForLord again saw something appear out of the corner of his eye and pulled his weapon off his shoulder. He turned quickly, again seeing Stripes' image on the door. Figuring his comrades wouldn't believe him, he investigated the image himself. He walked slowly toward Stripes, weapon raised in anticipation. Standing three feet from the wall, the ForLord leaned forward to get a closer look. Mesmerized by the Tiger's eyes, now glowing brightly on the door, the ForLord stared in amazement. As soon as he blinked, Stripes' massive paw emerged from the door and swatted the ForLord, sending him into the side of the wall, instantly knocking him unconscious.

The other ForLords turned and ran to aid their fallen comrade. As they neared the door, both of Stripes' paws emerged this time. Before the ForLords could react, the three of them were struck down by the force of the powerful paws smashing them together. Two more ForLords came to see what the commotion was as Stripes ran along Timm's painted ledge to greet them. It then leaped off the ledge and onto the approaching ForLords, sending them helplessly to the ground. Stripes was now inside the fortress and immediately opened the door, allowing Pockets to enter.

Seeing Pockets disappear into the fortress, the Hornets took flight toward the fortress walls. The rapid movement of their wings sounded like a squadron of single-engine planes taking flight. The ForLords along the walls peered into the forest, in the direction of the loud humming noises, but saw nothing. As they continued to search along the tree line, they raised their chemical weapons and directed the tower lights toward the forest. Without hesitation, the Hornets rose from the sides of the walls and snatched the curious ForLords from their positions. Chemical streams wildly filled the air, and the ForLords could be heard shouting and alerting everyone in the vicinity. Loud sirens echoed throughout, while additional lights from the towers illuminated the ground and the enormous tower guns began firing in the direction of the trees, but not before the other Cats had left the forest's edge. They entered the walls of the fortress through the sky Timm had provided them, much the same way Stripes entered through the doors.   Meanwhile, the assault of the devastating chemical streams emitted from the tower guns lasted only a moment before the Hornets captured the operators and sealed off the tower entrance.

Pockets saw several dozen ForLords running toward him. He knelt, leaned over, and opened his pocket flap, allowing the other Tigers to exit. The last Tiger had barely jumped out when Pockets found himself rolling on the ground to avoid one of the ForLord's chemical streams.   As he repositioned himself, he drew his immobilizer and began firing at the attackers.

Numerous ForLords had opened fire on the Tigers, but the protective coats, for the time being, were resisting the chemicals. The assault continued, but the Tigers remained unaffected. How long it would last, no one knew for sure, but Pockets remembered he had to stay alert when the Creatures stopped to regenerate. He only wished he had some idea of how long they could go between rests.

As the number of ForLords began to dramatically increase, Pockets felt a sense of doom. He knew there were, at a minimum, thousands of ForLords between those fortress walls, maybe even tens of thousands. *Would the Tigers alone be able to hold off the ForLords?* he wondered. As he ran for cover, firing his weapon along the way, he saw the Lions, Panthers, and Wildcats emerging from the walls. The number of ForLords was not so overwhelming now.

Pockets froze for a moment as he watched the huge Cats effortlessly paralyze the attacking ForLords. Over the tops of the walls, and now through the doors, came the Hornets. Each grabbed five, ten, sometimes fifteen ForLords at a time and carried them to the nests where the kids executed their duties with amazing efficiency. Pockets wanted to join in and help, but it was not his objective. He and Stripes were to find Timm.

Peering from behind some empty barrels, Pockets looked through the crowded battlefield, trying to locate Stripes. He saw numerous Cats fighting the ForLords, but where was his furry companion? Had they suffered their first casualty? And would there be more? Looking to his left, he saw a circle of Cats fighting off ForLords, but their heads were turned away from whatever they were surrounding. Only a few moments had passed before the Cats broke away from the circle. It became clear they were protecting Stripes, which was momentarily regenerating its energy. It was quite a sight to see the others sacrifice their life for the life of one of their own. *Humans can learn a lot from these Creatures, as well as the Dropas,* Pockets thought.

Suddenly, Stripes caught sight of Pockets and ran toward him. In fact, it kept running, faster and faster. Pockets held out his hands, signaling Stripes to slow down. What was happening? Had it been a victim of an Ozone bubble? Stripes was now within a few yards of Pockets who had ducked and closed his eyes, not knowing what the force of the giant beast was going to do to him. Stripes' powerful hind legs catapulted it up and over the top of Pockets and the barrels, hitting a half dozen ForLords who had been sneaking up behind him. With one blow from the gigantic Tiger, the ForLords lay motionless on the ground.

Pockets squinted one eye open, still bracing for the impact, which was not to be. Stripes was no longer in front of him.

"Stripes?!" he called out.

The huge Tiger let out a ferocious roar behind him, nearly causing Pockets to jump out of his pants. Pockets swung around to face the roar. As he did, he was greeted by Stripes' mammoth, sandpaper tongue licking his face.

Pockets stood there, not knowing how to react. "C'mon, Stripes, save the tongue bath for Timm."

Stripes jumped into Pockets' shirt pocket, nearly knocking him over in the process. Pockets then dragged one of the unconscious ForLords behind a barrier where they wouldn't be seen. He undressed the ForLord and put the uniform over his clothes, feeling very strange in the enemy's garb – it was the only way to go unnoticed and he didn't know how long it would take to locate Timm. Picking up the ForLord's weapon, he headed through the courtyard toward the L-shaped building, leaving the Cats and the Hornets to take care of the ForLords within the fortress walls.

The last of the Creatures had crossed the canyon and the Huskies and Bulldogs were already sniffing out the underground airstrip. Based on the GGB's previous effort to cross the canyon, Willie figured the aircraft would be approaching at any second.

"Let 'em. Our Birds will take care of them," Willie whispered.

Bob pointed toward the sky, in the direction of the fortress. "Look! Here come the Birds!"

It was still somewhat dark, so Willie pulled out his binoculars to take a closer look. Everyone was standing there, cheering the arrival of the Birds while Willie gazed at the approaching objects.

"No. No. Nooo! Take cover! Take cover now!!!!" he yelled.

It was Ozone's aircraft, and there were several large squadrons coming straight for them.

"Where's Robohawk?" shouted one of the kids.

"Take flight! Take flight!" Willie ordered the Dragons and Cardinals. "Oh, my God! Not now!"

The Dragons and Cardinals were all motionless, briefly regenerating their energy from carrying Willie, the kids, the Creatures, and all of the equipment over the canyon. Willie's group was completely defenseless. As the aircraft flew closer, Willie could see at least a dozen of them in front with several dozen more in the rear. The chemical streams began filling the air from their guns, first aimed at the Dogs locating the airstrip. Their streams were much more powerful than those of the ForLords' hand-held weapons, and the Creatures wouldn't be able to withstand but a few streams before disintegrating. And, worse yet, it would take only one stream to destroy the regenerating Creatures.

Stream after stream was fired upon the Dogs. They tried diligently to outmaneuver the chemical assault, but with little success. Because of their agility, the Huskies were more successful in avoiding the chemical streams than the Bulldogs. As a result, the Bulldogs began to quickly disappear, and unless the Birds arrived soon, everyone in Willie's battalion would follow their demise.

Knowing the rocks they were hiding behind would not protect them for long, Willie motioned to the kids and the Creatures. "Head for the canyon! Head for the canyon!"

"But we'll be shot!" Bob responded.

"It's our only chance." Willie waved at them to leave. "Do it! Now!!!"

Instantly, the Creatures and all the kids headed for the canyon. They quickly boarded the Dragons and Cardinals who had completed their regeneration cycle. The aircraft were still preoccupied with their attack on the Dogs which Willie hoped would buy everyone else enough time to cross the canyon. Fortunately, a number of the Dogs escaped into a small cavern, and for the time being, eluded the firing aircraft which had changed course and headed toward the rest of the group.

Willie saw the last set of kids being set down on the other side of the canyon. He now had to wait for either a Dragon or Cardinal to come back for him, so he figured he'd better get as close to the edge as possible to minimize the distance between him and the Creature retrieving him. He started running, continuously glancing over his shoulder as the aircraft approached within firing range.

"Run, Willie, Run!" the kids shouted at Willie from across the canyon.

Willie's leg muscles were tightening, and he couldn't get them to move any faster. Looking over his shoulder, he could see the aircraft closing in on him as he neared the edge. He again turned his head toward the canyon. Neither a Dragon nor a Cardinal had started heading back for him. The aircraft's guns powered up and aimed directly at Willie.

"Willie! Stop!!!!" the kids shouted as the edge of the canyon was now only a few feet away.

Willie glanced over his shoulder one last time, unaware of the approaching canyon and ignoring the kids' warning. The six lead aircraft fired on Willie, but their chemical streams were misdirected, and instead hit the far wall. Simultaneously, the ground had disappeared from beneath Willie's feet. He was now falling toward the bottom of the canyon.

"Willlliiieee!" the kids screamed.

A loud screech was heard ringing through the skies. Holding the steel neck feathers of Robohawk with one hand, and raising their brushes in the air with the other, were Silver and Gold. The chemical streams had missed Willie because Robohawk had plucked the firing aircraft out of the air with its mighty talons. There were three aircraft in each. And with its powerful grip, like a vice crushing an aluminum can, Robohawk crushed the steel aircraft and released them to fall helplessly to the ground. Robohawk then pulled its massive wings back and dove toward the plunging Willie. The speed of the Creature was awesome, piercing through the air like a guided missile. Into the mouth of the canyon it dove, its talons reaching forward to retrieve its prey, and its wings opening to redirect its flight. Unlike the defenseless aircraft, the talons gently grasped Willie ten feet above the chemical river. Robohawk redirected its flight pattern and flapped its steel wings to bring its catch to the top of the canyon.

Willie's head was spinning, and his legs wobbled as Robohawk set him on the ground. The kids cheered and gathered around Willie. Robohawk didn't stick around for the celebration, but rather joined its fellow birds in battle against Ozone's aircraft as Silver and Gold saluted their comrades below them. Once again, chemical streams filled the air, flying in all directions. The elusive Eagles, Hawks, and Falcons avoided most of the onslaught and, as time went on, were completely demolishing the ensuing aircraft.

The Dragons and Cardinals brought the rest of the group to where the Dogs were located, outside their protective cavern. They immediately continued their search for the underground airstrip, and

Willie motioned for the Spartans, Trojans, and Knights to proceed to the fortress. They complied, mounting their horses and chariots, and headed straight for Ozone's fortress, leaving nothing behind but a trail of dust.   The Cardinals joined the land attack and headed toward the fortress to assist the Hornets while the Dragons joined the air assault with the Birds.

The Dragons, in their onslaught of the aircraft, were just as impressive as their feathered companions.   The scorching flames shooting from their mouths melted the defenseless aircraft in mid-flight, transforming the chemicals into fireballs and sending metal rain falling to the ground. The Creatures seemingly had no problems with the aircraft, but there were so many of them, it would take some time before they were completely destroyed.

Meanwhile, the Raiders and Chargers stayed behind to assist Willie with any encounters they would meet in the underground airstrip, which had already opened as a result of the Birds destroying the first few squadrons. As Willie peered inside, his mouth dropped open as he saw thousands of Ozone's aircraft. Many of them were still capable of flying, but others had been disfigured in various, humorous ways. Some of the aircraft now had square tires, water guns instead of chemical guns, wings going in all directions and in the wrong positions, and some were shaped like bananas.

"The Dropas," Willie muttered.

"Look at that!" one of the kids yelled from behind Willie.

Willie and the kids looked up into the sky. Some of the aircraft still capable of flying were firing popcorn at the Eagles. Everyone was laughing at the fluffy kernels falling from the sky, but the laughter abruptly came to a halt. Several hundred ForLords, who weren't at all humored by the whole thing, emerged from the underground strip. The Raiders and Charges moved to the front of the group to intercept the enemy while Willie and the kids fired their immobilizers.

Several hours had passed before Ozone's entire fleet had been destroyed and the small ForLord battalion had been captured. And after having destroyed the last aircraft, the Birds and the Dragons landed on the ground to regenerate. They would rejoin the rest of the group at the fortress once their energy was restored.

Light entered the Gators' mouths as they resurfaced from under the water and took us to shore. We had reached the dimly lit bowels of Ozone's fortress.

"Is everyone all right?" I asked as the other four emerged from their Gators.

"Just fine," Ti replied.

"That was so cool!" Brad exclaimed.

"Glad you liked it," I said.

"How long before the Vikings get through the wall?" Lauren inquired.

"I'm not sure," I replied, looking around for ForLords. "It depends on how much resistance they had outside."

"Look out!" Brian shouted.

I ducked just in time as several chemical streams passed over my head. There was no more time for small talk as we were being assaulted by the ForLords standing guard. We all took cover by scattering behind whatever protection we could find and raised our immobilizers to return fire. In a relatively short amount of time, the kids had become quite proficient with their weapons. We managed to paralyze a large number of ForLords; however, we were forced to continuously change our position because their chemical streams were destroying the barriers temporarily protecting us. Meanwhile, the Gators had also joined in the effort and were sending ForLords airborne into the walls with their powerful tails, their protective coats still holding up against the enemy fire. We held our ground for some time, but our means of protection were disappearing, resulting in our hiding behind paralyzed ForLords piling up on the floor, but they also were quickly disintegrating from the chemical streams.

The ForLords seemed to have an infinite number of reinforcements fighting against us, but our assault improved immensely as the Vikings finally emerged from the fortress walls. Almost immediately, the ForLords' attention was redirected toward the massive Vikings who began attacking with shields raised and hand weapons drawn. With each massive blow, they were slaying several ForLords at a time or rendering them unconscious. The presence of the Vikings gave the rest of us a little time to catch our breath before we began assaulting the ForLords from the rear. Once we knew the Vikings and Gators were in complete control, the kids and I left in search of Ozone's chemical-producing equipment.

Back inside the fortress, the Cats were becoming weary, and it wouldn't be long before they would have to stop again to regenerate. If that had happened, the ForLords would have gained a major victory. The ForLords outnumbered the Cats by orders of magnitude, but the Cats, until that point, had no problems holding their own. However, the ForLords were able to force the Cats away from the fortress doors and barricade them shut, preventing the penetration of any large reinforcements. The guns on the far walls of the fortress were useless, having also been sabotaged by the Dropas. Instead of firing deadly chemical streams, they fired harmless gelatin cubes. That forced the gunners down from the wall, mostly from the west, to join the fight inside the fortress. The ForLords were feeling more and more confident with each assault on the Cats.

As they were about to apply the final wave, ultimately destroying the Cats, the walls of the fortress began crashing down to the ground. The sky, with the cracks Timm and the Dropas had painted on the walls, was now coming into play. The painted cracks had become real cracks on the walls and the Spartans, Trojans, and Knights came barreling through the walls with little effort. The fortress walls crumbled and the relief squad was full of tremendous amounts of energy. The Indians and Warriors, who had successfully scaled the north wall, took care of the ForLords lining the northern and eastern walls and then descended from the towers to assist their comrades. The ForLords abandoned their attack on the Cats and headed toward the new, more powerful intruders.

Streams of chemicals fired wildly, many missing their targets, while others hit their own men. The Cats used the brief amount of time they had to regenerate their energy and were soon attacking the ForLords from the rear. Moments later, the regenerated Birds and Dragons attacked from the air. It was now hopeless for the ForLords. Each of the Creatures took out ten or fifteen ForLords at a time, but the ForLords would not surrender.

The Birds veered off to assist the Hornets which were quickly filling the nests. Roberto's group, including the Pioneers, could hardly fill the nests fast enough to keep up with incoming prisoners. Over time, the ForLords realized their imminent defeat and began a mass exodus in every direction, only to be captured from the ground by the Cats or from the air by the Birds, Dragons, and Hornets. The ones heading for the canyon were intercepted by Willie's group who were approaching the fortress from the underground airstrip. There was no escape for the ForLords.

By nightfall, the majority of the ForLords had been captured, allowing the Birds, Dragons, and Hornets to once again regenerate their energy for the flight home. They stood motionless near the banks of the river by the southern part of the fortress.

Looking down on the darkened battlefield, Ozone could not believe his eyes. His desire for human elimination was strong, but his plan was literally crumbling right before his eyes. Even he realized defeat of his ForLords was inevitable. He knew we would soon come looking for him, and he couldn't let himself be captured. Allowing the GGB the opportunity to change his ways and accepting the new way of life were not options in his plan. Fighting until the death to realize his goal was.

He closed the blinds to his office and sat down at his desk, putting his elbows on top of it and holding his head in his hands. "I will not be defeated!" he shouted as he slammed his fist on the desk.

Ozone stared at the far wall for a few moments and then, from underneath the middle drawer, he pulled out a control console. He fumbled around underneath it until his hand found what he was looking for, the key to activate the fortress auto-destruct mechanism. It was time to execute his escape plan. He pulled the key off the bottom and inserted it into its slot.

"You haven't seen the last of me," he mumbled.

Ozone turned the key to the right and began punching in the code sequence. Just as he finished keying in the last number, Pockets and Stripes came crashing through the door. Still in search of Timm, they had traveled through the mazes of the fortress buildings and eluded hundreds of curious ForLords in the process. Although they were unsuccessful in locating him, they found the next best thing, Ozone.

"You're finished, Ozone!" Pockets shouted.

"No. You are." Ozone paused for a moment, looking at Pockets as if he knew him. He then redirected his thoughts back to executing his objective. "In less than fifteen minutes, this place is going to blow sky high and disintegrate everything around it, including your pathetic animal friends."

"Not if I can help it." Pockets pointed toward Ozone. "Stripes!"

The Tiger took one giant stride toward Ozone and leaped into the air. Simultaneously, Ozone pushed a blue button on the console and the floor below him opened up, swallowing him and the chair he was sitting on. By the time Stripes came down from its leap, the floor had closed again, and Ozone had vanished.

The chair hit the underground floor with a huge thud, a few feet away from where Timm was standing. Ozone rose from the broken chair, which had shattered to pieces. He was somewhat shaken but virtually unscathed.

Timm jumped back, wondering if any more people were dropping in on him. "Nice entrance, Ozone. Ever think about trying out for the circus?"

"We have to get out of here. This place is going to blow in less than fifteen minutes," Ozone said, ignoring Timm's comment. "Follow me."

Timm followed Ozone through a number of corridors, eventually leading to the south side of the fortress, where the river flowed to the outside of the walls. Ozone was met there by a couple dozen of his most loyal ForLords. Together, they all moved toward the submarine-looking vessels that would lead them to their escape.

Several ForLords reached over to unlock the hatches, only to be greeted by open mouths from the Gators who had left the Vikings to prevent Ozone's escape via the river. The ForLords lost their balance and splashed into the water, finding themselves swimming for their lives, unaware the Gators had no intention of eating them.

Having successfully destroyed Ozone's chemical-producing equipment, we had also made our way back to the river to join the Gators. Upon our arrival, we were amazed at what we saw. Timm was teamed with Ozone. He was standing there, with weapon drawn, ready to fire on his family and friends. I didn't want to believe it, but any hope I still had was soon shattered.

"Timm, I'm so glad you're alive," Lauren shouted as she started moving toward him from around the corner where we were hiding.

"Don't take another step, you spoiled, little brat! All of you, drop your weapons and move out here where we can see you!" Timm shouted.

It was obvious Lauren was hurt deeply by Timm's response. After all, she had regarded Timm as a very close friend, always visiting him wherever he painted. Tears filled her eyes as she walked toward the rest of us. I put my arm around her and pulled her close to my chest.

I was almost convinced Timm was with Ozone until I saw little, colored heads peek up over the top of Timm's pocket. I had been wondering for some time where our little friends had been hiding. Timm didn't notice Blue, Red, and Black taking a look at what was going on, and before he could, they quickly disappeared back into his pocket. Clearcoat had pulled them down to avoid being noticed.

I knew then Timm was playing along with Ozone, and for a very good reason. If he didn't, I'm sure we wouldn't have been standing there enjoying that delightful conversation. I decided the best thing to do was to be a part of the game until I thought of a way to get him out of Ozone's vice.

"He's not one of us anymore, Lauren. Ozone has transformed him," I said, trying to comfort her while at the same time playing along with Timm's charade. "C'mon, do as he says."

"Everyone move away except you!" Ozone shouted as he pointed to me. "I've been waiting to get my hands on you for some time."

"Why are you still doing this, Ozone?" I asked. "Things are different now, can't you see that?"

"Another philosopher. You're just like your brother, except your life is about to end right now."

"It doesn't need to end this way."

"Silence!" Ozone looked at Timm and then pointed at me. "Timm, he's all yours. Shoot him."

Timm gave Ozone a confusing look. He hesitated for a moment, then quickly thought of a different way he hoped would be more appealing to Ozone and would buy him some time to let me know he wasn't a ForLord.

"I'd like to do it with my bare hands, Lord Ozone."

"Ahhhh! You're more aggressive than I expected. So be it, but make it quick."

Timm laid his weapon on the ground. "I won't need much time."

"Time for what?" I inquired.

"Time before this place blows up!" Timm said before Ozone could hide what was going to happen.

"Blow up?"

"That's right. This place is going to blow in–" Ozone glanced down at his watch, "–less than ten minutes."

"Whoops," I said.

"What d'ya mean, whoops?" Lauren asked.

"Just a minor exclusion from my plan."

Before I could react, Timm came rushing toward me like a fullback on the one-yard line. I absorbed his initial blow, but couldn't prevent us both from falling to the ground. I tried to think of something to say to him, a code word of sort, to let him know I knew he wasn't on Ozone's side. Little did I know he was trying to do the same thing. I overlooked his first attempt, telling me Ozone was planning to blow the place, but until either one of us did or said anything else, we had to make this look like a real fight. As we rose to our feet, I let him have a right hook to the jaw, sending him to the ground. I only hoped I didn't hit him too hard to knock him unconscious.

As he hit the ground, the code word came out. "G-D-S-O-B."

I hadn't heard that since we were kids. It was typically used in a much more expanded version, but nonetheless, I understood the message. I reached into my right boot and pulled out a knife. Timm's eyes widened as he turned and faced me, still kneeling. He was certain that I understood his code word. I pulled the knife back. At the same time, several ForLords raised their weapons to stop me, but Ozone put out his arm to let me finish my deed.

"No, Scott, no!" Lauren shouted.

"I must Lauren. I must kill him, and I will do it with the knife of Red."

I thrust the knife into Timm's chest. He let out his most convincing grunt, but it was drowned out by Lauren and Ti screaming as they watched in disbelief. Instantly, the knife had transformed to paint as it came in contact with Timm's chest. Thank God he understood my message and realized the knife wasn't real, because if he hadn't, it would have been his blood instead of red paint covering his shirt. Timm rolled over on his side, facing away from Ozone and hiding the fact the knife wasn't sticking in his chest. As he lay there, he began thinking about how the Dropas saved him again from Ozone's bubble.

Several ForLords started to run toward me but tripped and fell. They ended up bringing the rest of the ForLords down to the ground with them. While Timm and I were fighting, the Dropas had painted shackles around all of the ForLords' ankles. The Vikings, who were hiding around the corner and patiently waiting for their opportunity to appear, ran toward the ForLords and collected their weapons. Meanwhile, Ozone had made his escape into one of the vessels. He had successfully eluded the Gators and was submerging into the water. I signaled for the Gators to go after him.

"Timm!" I looked down at him. "You can get up now."

Timm rolled over on his back, opened his eyes, and rubbed his jaw. I extended my hand to assist him from the ground. The kids were shocked when they saw him rise to his feet, especially Lauren and Ti. Lauren ran over and gave him a big hug.

"It's good to see you again, bro," I said.

"It's good to see you, too, but did you have to hit me so hard?"

"I had to make it look real," I replied.

"That was too close. I wasn't sure if you would understand my code."

We both started laughing as we embraced.

"How could I forget that line?" I stepped back from him. "It's embedded in my memory forever."

"I'm glad you guys came to get me."

"We're glad you're still alive," Lauren said.

Timm tried wiping the paint off his shirt. "By the way, what's going on above ground?"

"We don't have time to explain everything now, but you'll soon see for yourself," I replied.

"We have to get out of here," Brad reminded us, interrupting our little reunion.

"And quickly," I said, waving everyone to follow me.

We all hopped into one of the remaining vessels while the Vikings jumped into their boat and headed out through the wall. I was about to close the hatch when I heard a voice shouting from the corridor where Ozone and Timm emerged.

"Wait! Wait for us!"

It was Pockets. He and Stripes had made their way down the same escape hatch Ozone did. Because he was dressed in a ForLord uniform, Brian and Brad didn't recognize Pockets and were about to fire at him.

"Don't shoot, it's Pockets!" I shouted.

They took a closer look and realized it was indeed Pockets, and Stripes was following him rather than pursuing him.

"This place is going to blow!" Pockets yelled. "We have to get out of here!"

"We know!" I shouted. "Get those legs moving!"

Stripes leaped onto the Vikings' boat as they swiftly moved toward the wall. Once again, it would take them longer to get through the wall than it would take us to get under it. Pockets finally reached the vessel and climbed aboard. I slammed the hatch shut, sealed it, and we were on our way. Only a few minutes remained before the fortress, everything in it, and everything around it would be obliterated.

While submerged, one of the Gators had caught up with Ozone's vessel and pierced several holes in it with its large, sharp teeth. Water began filling the vessel, and Ozone knew he had to surface and escape by land. He reached an area of the river just past the fortress walls and surfaced, quickly opening the hatch and jumping onto the shore. The Gators were close behind but lost sight of him as he disappeared around the corner leading to the front of the fortress. The Gators continued their pursuit as our vessel reached the surface. Meanwhile, the Viking ship was now more than halfway through the wall. It didn't have much time left before the fortress would be engulfed in flames.

Fortunately, the Birds and Dragons had just finished regenerating in front of the fortress and were ready to evacuate everyone. I motioned for them to begin picking up as many kids and Creatures as they could possibly carry. Pockets sent some of the Hornets into the forest to do the same for Roberto's group, who were still tending the nests. Willie's group and the Creatures inside the fortress had now joined us and were boarding the remaining Birds and Dragons. I didn't know exactly how much time we had left, but I knew it was very little.

The Vikings' boat finally emerged from the wall. As Stripes jumped off, the Vikings signaled me to pick the Gators and them up downstream. I agreed, and like I'd never seen before, the Gators and the boat went cruising down the river to get as far away from the fortress as possible. We had to return for the captured ForLords at a later time anyway, but I figured the nests would withstand the effects of the chemical fallout.

Meanwhile, the remaining ForLords pleaded with us to take them, but there wasn't enough room for everyone. I didn't want to leave them behind, because I knew we could rid them of their evil ways, but my choice had been made for me. The Birds and Hornets were already in flight, and Timm and I boarded Robohawk once we were sure everyone was on their way to the canyon, knowing Robohawk didn't need much time to get us out of there. I looked around one last time. Everyone was accounted for, or so I thought.

"The Dropas? Where are the Dropas?" Timm yelled.

"I don't know. I haven't seen them since they tripped up the ForLords."

"We have to go back and find them!" Timm attempted to slide down Robohawk.

I grabbed his arm. "We don't have time!"

"I have to go back!" Timm shouted.

I signaled Robohawk to take flight. He responded, nearly knocking Timm and I off its back. Fortunately, I was able to grab hold of its armor as we left the ground. Timm continued to slide off until the grip of my hand was the only thing keeping him from plummeting several hundred feet.

"The Dropas, we have to save the Dropas!" he continued.

I wasn't sure if he was trying to get back on board or fighting me to let him go, but whatever he was doing, I held on as long as I could. "We can't, we just can't."

In a matter of moments, we had reached the canyon. Just after we landed, the fortress erupted in a massive explosion, producing an enormous fireball. Chemicals were emitted hundreds of feet into the air and in all directions, destroying everything in their path. As we stared at the blast, the night sky lit up like a football stadium. Time and time again, the explosions erupted, sending fire and chemicals everywhere. But the last, monumental explosion, was by far the most gratifying of them all. It hurled a tremendous fireball into the polluted clouds, igniting them and sending a fire blanket across the sky for as far as we could see. The fire burned away the cloud cover, like a section being ripped from the middle of a piece of paper. We could feel the heat of the fire as it ignited the clouds and passed over us, leaving behind only smoke and then the coolness of the night air. The pollution clouds had completely burned away and as the smoke cleared, the kids erupted with cheers. For the first time in weeks, we once again saw the moon and the stars and knew, in a very short time, we would see the blue sky, the billowy clouds, and the bright sun again. There was definitely another day beyond that turning page, a symbol so often found in Timm's murals.

"Look, there it is," Lauren said as she pointed toward the sky over the mountains.

We all turned and looked. There, streaking across the sky was the brightest shooting star I had ever seen. We all just gazed for a moment as it streaked across the night sky.

"Take hold of your dreams and never let go," I said as the shooting star faded into the darkness.

As Timm and I turned and walked away from the canyon, the excitement of our triumph had already diminished. I was just as sorrowed by the fact of leaving the Dropas behind as Timm was, but had we gone back to find them, Robohawk, Timm, and I would not have survived. I had a sense the Dropas knew what they were doing, whatever it was, but I couldn't convince myself even they could have survived the series of explosions we had witnessed.

Timm and I turned away and met up with Pockets' and Willie's groups. Everyone was joyous, for our mission had been successful, and we would all live to see another day. Many of the GGB staff from the nearest regional office were already there to greet us. They informed us they had proclaimed our victory around the world, but I was sure people already sensed it after witnessing the cloud cover burn away, allowing them to see the sun or the stars again.

Although Timm was happy for what we had accomplished, he didn't get too caught up in the excitement, for he had lost his dearest friends. The Dropas had played a major role in his life, influencing his artwork and making each day a wonderful time to live and to paint. He would miss them dearly. We would all miss them.

I wanted to console him at the time, but there was still much work to do. I knew he and I would sit down and talk some night about the entire series of events. But, for now, we had to load the land Creatures back into their tanks. The Birds, Dragons, and Hornets would not have enough energy to take all of us back immediately, so Willie took his group over to the river to meet up with the Vikings and Gators to bring them back.

Once everything was ready, Timm, Pockets, the remaining kids, and I began our journey back home, each of us exchanging stories from our part of the mission. Timm told us about his stay with Ozone – I kept referring to it as his vacation and telling him he should be fully rested now. But, as we shared our stories on the journey home, we all couldn't help but think of what happened to the Dropas. We tried convincing ourselves they may have survived and possibly went back home, knowing they helped save our world, but we couldn't figure out how, or why they didn't say "good-bye". Those sad feelings stayed with us for some time, but the immediate thoughts of going home made the trip a little more joyous.

Nature's Paradox

It was early morning when we finally arrived back home where thousands of people waited to greet us. What a wonderful feeling it was, sitting high atop Robohawk, seeing the blue sky, feeling the warmth of the sun again, and seeing all those people below us. We could have stayed up there for quite some time, but we were all anxious to see our loved ones.

As we landed, we were literally engulfed by the sea of people. There was Cherie, with open arms, making her way through the crowd to greet Timm. She somehow convinced the GGB to bring her home. It was hard to tell whether she was smiling or crying. I think she was doing both.

The kids' parents were also fighting their way through the crowd. I was so glad the kids survived this journey and all returned home safely with us. They played such a major role in the mission, and I was proud of every one of them. It was amazing to watch the energy of love flow around those families as they hugged and kissed each other.

As I stood waiting for Willie and his group to join us, I searched the crowd for Lindsay, stopping every so often to shake the hands of, or give a hug to people I didn't even know. I continued looking through the crowd for my wife, with no luck.

I soon spotted May, who was off in the distance looking toward the sky at the Creatures bringing home Willie and his group. May removed her hand she was using to shield her eyes from the glare and looked in my direction. We both caught each other's eyes and smiled at one another. But as I looked closer, her smile disappeared, and I could see tears running down her cheeks. I looked up in the sky for a moment, thinking something had happened to Willie, but saw nothing to prove my assumption correct.

Why is she crying? I wondered.

She came running over to me and tightly wrapped her arms around me.

"What is it, May? Tell me. What's wrong?"

"Liiinndssay was–" she sobbed.

I could barely make out what few words she said. I pulled her away from my shirt and held her shoulders in my hands, ignoring the people who were still congratulating me.

"Lindsay was what? Tell me May. Where is Lindsay?"

"We were with a group of kids when the bubbles started coming down from the sky. We destroyed all but the last one."

Suddenly, I felt the same empty feeling I awoke with the previous morning and my chest began to burn again.

May struggled to tell me the rest of the story. "As it came closer and closer to us, Lindsay reacted as it headed for Sonya, one of the children helping us. She pushed Sonya out of the way and was immediately engulfed by the bubble."

May continued to sob. I felt a huge lump in my throat and my eyes overflowed with tears. She didn't need to say another word for I knew what had happened. My entire body began to tremble.

"Did she fight it, May? Tell me she fought it."

"Yes. She fought it. She fought it until the very end. We tried, Scott. We tried everything we could to release her from the bubble, but we had used all of the needles. We were helpless and could only watch as she fought with every ounce of energy she had. Oh, God, Scott. I am so sorry."

"It's all right, May. It's not your fault."

Tears streamed down my cheeks as I pulled May close to my chest and hugged her. It was then I realized what the feeling was the other night, the empty feeling I awoke with, but couldn't determine what it was. The same feeling I was experiencing again. A very dear part of me had been taken away; ripped right out of my heart and soul. I could feel the rage build up inside of me again as I thought about the man who was responsible for taking my wife from me.

But as quickly as the rage started, it was replaced by a feeling of unexpected serenity. Then the noise around me disappeared and the sight of the thousands of people before me had vanished. It was replaced by the events of my life I had shared with Lindsay. I saw it playing before my eyes and the events felt like they happened the previous day. All of our experiences over the years played like a movie trailer. But, when the trailer finished playing, I already knew the ending. The emptiness and sadness overcame me once again.

"Scott? I'm so sorry," May cried again.

"It's not your fault, May," I replied as I wiped the tears from my face. "I'll be all right."

"You sure?"

The tears continued to flow again. "Yes, I'm sure, but don't worry about me because I think there's someone over there waiting to see you."

I turned May around in the direction of Willie, who was now on the ground with the rest of us. Without hesitation, May released her grip of my arms and ran toward Willie and embraced him emphatically.

I was still in a state of disarray. I couldn't believe Lindsay was no longer a part of my life after so many years. I walked away, I'm sure in a daze, not remembering what people had said to me as I passed by them. I eventually made my way through the crowd and just kept walking with no destination in mind, tears streaming down my face. A part of me wanted to celebrate with everyone else, but I needed to mend my wound, and mend it in my own way. Besides, celebrating really wasn't my style. I had accomplished what I had set out to do. Ozone was gone, and humanity had been preserved. We had finally broken through the last walls, those keeping our species separated. The same walls keeping love, unity, and peace outside, while holding hatred, dissension, and war inside, stood no longer. I knew deep down we would survive, and our lives would become serene and enjoyable again. But more importantly, we would learn to live with and love each other, each helping to create a wonderful world to live in for everyone, not just for one's own self.

The journey continues . . .

About the Creators of the Dropas

Scott Etters was born and raised in Cary, Illinois and now makes his home in the far west suburbs of Chicago. His childhood dream of becoming a professional baseball player came to an end as a freshman in college. It was time to move on to the next dream, one of owning his own business. After working for more than six years developing software, researching areas of Artificial Intelligence, and acquiring an M.B.A., he moved back to the Chicago suburbs where he would soon realize that next dream.

Timm Etters was born five and one-half years after Scott and also makes his home in the far west suburbs of Chicago. He is a gifted artist in multiple media and nationally recognized as a self-taught airbrush artist. His lifelong dream of becoming a successful artist also came true, but not without a slight detour. His redirection to his path came in two forms; an encounter with the law after openly celebrating his most recent graffiti mural and a triumphant battle with testicular cancer. Many months of soul searching during the latter resulted in Timm starting his own art company as a junior in high school. After many struggles with several business partners, Scott and Timm's paths converged.

In January of 1992, they co-founded Odyssey Creations, Inc. and since then, they have been providing the public with "high-quality art and creative ideas, impressing upon people the positive, yet intangible aspects of life". In 1993 they were inspired by a ceramic art piece sculpted by their friend Kris. From that inspiration and after many design iterations, Scott and Timm created the final concept of the Dropas; Timm's magical brush then created their physical appearance while Scott's imagination and magical pen brought them and their story to life.

Scott is currently working on the second book of the Dropa trilogy — about what lies beyond those walls, while Timm will paint the story's newest creations and characters.

Another Note From The Author

Thank you for experiencing THE DROPAS: Breaking Through The Walls. I hope you enjoyed your adventure with the Dropas. It is only their first but there are more to come. If you did enjoy it, please pass the word along to your family and friends. But, regardless of your opinion, I would like to hear your comments, either by e-mail or the traditional way.

Until the Dropas next adventure unfolds, please visit the Perikles Publishing website where you'll find Dropa products (T-shirts, music, etc.) and periodic updates on the Dropas' future adventures. You'll also find information on how to order additional books. Discounts are available for quantity orders.

Until next time, start realizing your dreams.

Scott R. Etters

Perikles Publishing, Inc.
P.O. Box 5367
Naperville, Illinois 60567-5367
(www.periklespublishing.com)